Praise for Detective Emilia Cruz

CLIFF DIVER

"From the moment I started the first one, I couldn't put it down. . . Her work touches on important issues affecting Mexico in a real, human way and is exciting, fast paced and utterly gripping." – *Mexico Retold*

HAT DANCE

[Emilia] is a force to be reckoned with." – *Mystery Sequels*

DIABLO NIGHTS

"Amato brings her characters to life with her vivid writing style and sets them on the streets of a Mexico steeped in Catholicism and corruption." – *OnlineBookClub.org*

KING PESO

"Danger and betrayal never more than a few pages away." – *Kirkus Reviews*

PACIFIC REAPER

"Carmen Amato . . . out does many of the best crime authors out there." – *Artisan Book Reviews*

43 MISSING

"A fast-paced procedural . . . a real page-turner . . . a very original plot." – *The BookLife Prize*

Also by Carmen Amato

DETECTIVE EMILIA CRUZ SERIES
CLIFF DIVER: Detective Emilia Cruz Book 1
HAT DANCE: Detective Emilia Cruz Book 2
DIABLO NIGHTS: Detective Emilia Cruz Book 3
KING PESO: Detective Emilia Cruz Book 4
PACIFIC REAPER: Detective Emilia Cruz Book 5
43 MISSING: Detective Emilia Cruz Book 6
RUSSIAN MOJITO: Detective Emilia Cruz Book 7
NARCO NOIR: Detective Emilia Cruz Book 8
MADE IN ACAPULCO: The Emilia Cruz Stories
THE ARTIST/EL ARTISTA: A Bilingual Short Story
FELIZ NAVIDAD FROM ACAPULCO: A Detective Emilia Cruz Novella
THE LISTMAKER OF ACAPULCO: A Detective Emilia Cruz Novella

GALLIANO CLUB SERIES
ROAD TO THE GALLIANO CLUB: Prequel
MURDER AT THE GALLIANO CLUB: Book 1
BLACKMAIL AT THE GALLIANO CLUB: Book 2
REVENGE AT THE GALLIANO CLUB: Book 3

THRILLERS
AWAKENING MACBETH
THE HIDDEN LIGHT OF MEXICO CITY

PACIFIC REAPER

A Detective Emilia Cruz Novel

Carmen Amato

Published 2023 by Laurel & Croton (second edition)
Trade Paperback Edition

Identifiers: ISBN: ISBN: 979-8-9885363-5-2 (print)
ISBN 978-0-9853256-8-8 (ebook)

Regarding names and monetary conversion

Regarding Mexican names: It is the custom in Mexico to use two surnames. The first is from the father's family and is always used. The second surname is the name of the mother's father. The second is sometimes dropped in conversation and/or to shorten the name in keeping with American and European naming conventions.

Conversion rate: For the purposes of this novel, $US1.00 = 10 Mexican pesos.

Spanish words: A glossary of Spanish words and terms commonly used in the Detective Emilia Cruz series is included.

A woman and glass are always in danger.

Mexican proverb

CHAPTER 1

"And this is our bedroom," Emilia Cruz Encinos said. She opened the door and led her mother Sophia Encinos into the cool and lofty room high above the Pacific Ocean.

Sophia tentatively walked a few steps over the threshold, followed by her husband, Ernesto Cruz. She stopped and the vague smile she normally wore faded from her face, to be replaced by an equally vague frown, as if she knew she should be worried but couldn't remember why. Ernesto stayed by his wife but his mouth dropped open; no doubt this was the most opulent home he'd ever seen.

"There's a bathroom, right through there." Emilia gestured to the ensuite door, wondering when her mother was finally going to say something.

Neither Sophia nor Ernesto moved.

"I put up my old crucifix, Mama," Emilia went on. She pointed to the small talavera pottery cross on the wall above the king-sized bed covered with a white matelassé spread. "Do you remember it?"

Sophia pressed a hand to her mouth. Not even 50 years old, she was still a beautiful woman, with the same long dark hair, high cheekbones, and smooth skin as her daughter. Her eyes slid past the huge bed to take in the built-in closets and large dressers, the seating area with plush upholstered furniture; and the gently rippling full-length linen draperies. Ernesto stared around open-mouthed.

Emilia felt her stomach tighten and she smoothed nervous palms down the front of the sleeveless teal linen dress she'd bought for the occasion. Although she had lived with Kurt for well over six months, this was Sophia and Ernesto's first visit to the penthouse apartment. Emilia had expected disapproval for being unmarried and living in sin with a gringo but so far, the reaction was stunned silence at the décor and architecture.

Kurt Rucker came to stand beside her, his blonde hair glinting silver as the late afternoon sun streamed through the floor-to-ceiling sliding glass doors. "You have a real future as a tour guide, you know," he murmured.

Emilia sighed and leaned her head against his shoulder in response. Sophia and Ernesto stopped talking as they'd walked into the lobby of the Palacio Réal, Acapulco's most luxurious hotel, which Kurt managed. Not a word in the elevator up to the penthouse or as they'd toured the living and dining rooms, and now finally, the master bedroom.

Sometimes it was easier to be a police detective investigating Acapulco's daily death toll than a dutiful daughter.

"Sophia, would you like to see the ocean from here?" Kurt asked.

Sophia turned to look at him, her mouth curved again into a vague smile.

"The sliding doors lead to the balcony, just like in the living room," Kurt said smoothly. "We can walk all the way around the apartment."

"It is very high up, no?" Ernesto found his voice at last.

"We'll be all right," Kurt said. He gave Emilia's hand a subtle squeeze then crossed the room to open the glass door, muscular and confident in khakis, loafers, and a white polo with the Palacio Réal crest.

Emilia ushered Sophia and Ernesto forward, feeling like an overdressed dog herding sheep. Once over the threshold both stopped, seemingly bewildered by the soaring sight of cobalt sky and aqua ocean.

"I think this side of the apartment has the best view," Kurt said. He gently took Sophia's elbow and guided her to the waist-high stucco wall encircling the wide balcony. Emilia watched as Ernesto followed his wife, gawking at the teak chaise lounges and cobalt glazed pots full of geraniums and trailing greenery.

As they leaned on the wall, Kurt pointed out the hotel attractions spread out below them: the huge two-level Pasodoble Bar, the secluded beach, the fleet of hotel boats anchored at the private marina, and the floating dock anchored out in the bay. A special Saturday afternoon buffet was being set up on the dock. They watched as staff wearing the hotel's trademark blue floral shirts and khaki shorts unloaded hampers and coolers from two motorboats, the distant figures rising and falling as the dock rode the ocean current.

Emilia glanced at her mother, wondering what was going on inside Sophia's head. Although Sophia had lived her entire life in Acapulco, Emilia knew she'd never been in a luxury hotel like the Palacio Réal, an architectural marvel hammered out of the cliffs above Puerto Marques, the famous bay-within-a-bay on the southeastern tip of Acapulco. The hotel guests they'd passed in the lobby on the way to the penthouse elevator were hardly the ordinary Mexicans that Sophia encountered in her central Acapulco neighborhood. For the most part, guests at the Palacio Réal were gringo diplomats, rock stars, filmmakers, and business executives enjoying one of the world's most exclusive getaway destinations.

As if noticing her daughter for the first time, Sophia turned to Emilia, her long dark hair and floral dress fluttering in the breeze. "Isn't this apartment very expensive?" Sophia asked.

"The apartment is part of my salary, Sophia," Kurt said.

"They pay you to live here, Carlos?" Sophia had called him Carlos ever since meeting Kurt months ago.

"In a way," Kurt said.

"It's far from school for Emilia." Sophia gave him one of her blank smiles and turned to look at the ocean again.

Emilia looked helplessly at Kurt.

"You have a very nice home," Ernesto said formally, as if to bridge the awkward moment. "I hope you and Señor Carlos are happy here."

"Thank you, Ernesto," Emilia said gratefully. Her mother's husband was a weathered man who often seemed as emotionally damaged as his wife, but now and then he surprised Emilia with his acuity.

"Shall we go inside for la comida?" Kurt asked. "I hope you two are hungry. Emilia spent all morning in the kitchen.

Sophia's smile widened into genuine amusement. "Emilia cooked?" she asked.

Emilia's hopes rose. The kitchen had always been a comfortable spot for Sophia. "Come on, Mama. I'll show you what I've made."

They walked around the balcony to the other side of the apartment. Kurt turned on a soccer game for himself and Ernesto while Emilia showed her mother into the gleaming kitchen with its stainless steel countertops, glossy Italian cabinetry, and commercial-grade range.

Sophia looked pleased and impressed. She opened cabinet doors and drawers and investigated the dishes and flatware. Emilia popped the main course into the oven, found the ingredients for her appetizer, and bumped the refrigerator closed with her hip.

"I made things ahead of time," Emilia said. "All I have to do is fry the flores de calabaza. I used a recipe Tía Lourdes gave me."

Earlier that morning Emilia had removed the woody stems and stamens from the sturdy yellow squash blossoms, then rinsed them in salt water. They were dry now, and ready to be fried. As Sophia watched, Emilia poured oil into a skillet and turned on the heat. Blue flame jetted around the burner ring under the pan.

"Lourdes?" Sophia sniffed. She sat at the table and watched Emilia stuff cheese cubes inside each flower, coat them in beaten egg white, and roll in breadcrumbs. "Why did you ask her? Lourdes knows nothing. Doesn't even know how to put salt on a jitomate."

At the stove, Emilia looked over her shoulder at her mother. "Tía Lourdes makes wonderful flor de calabaza guisada. Don't you remember?"

She flicked water off her fingertips to test the oil; a sizzle and pop assured her the pan was hot enough. Emilia carefully eased the breaded blossoms into the pan. The aroma of frying cheese and garlic filled the air.

"Lourdes was never nice to me, you know," Sophia muttered.

"How can you say that?" Emilia exclaimed. "Tía Lourdes is your sister-in-law. We lived with her and Tío Raul for years and they were the kindest people on earth."

When Emilia's father, the original Ernesto Cruz, died in a car accident with his wealthy employer, his 19-year-old widow Sophia had a nervous breakdown. Ernesto's brother Raul and his wife Lourdes took in the bereft woman and her child. Emilia grew up in a cramped apartment above Raul's car repair garage with her aunt and uncle, their sons Ramon and Alvaro, and a mother who lived in perpetual twilight.

When Emilia became a cop a dozen years ago, she rented a small house for herself and her mother. She'd woken one morning just over a year ago to find a strange man in the kitchen and her mother declaring that this Ernesto Cruz was the same husband she'd lost years ago. Sophia and Ernesto were married now, but Emilia knew her mother had merged the two men in her mind and nothing could convince her otherwise.

Her mother sniffed. "Raul was nice. But Lourdes never understood."

"Understood what, Mama?" Emilia asked. She looked away from the hot oil and crisping breadcrumbs, very curious about the implication of Sophia's words. "What didn't Tía Lourdes understand, Mama?"

Sophia drifted over to the bank of glossy cabinets. She opened a drawer and took out a handful of flatware. Two forks, three spoons. A steak knife.

"Did you and Tía Lourdes—." A spit of hot oil landed on Emilia's hand before she could finish the thought. She gave a start, wiped her hand on a kitchen towel, and flipped the blossoms. The tops were a perfect golden crust.

When she looked again at her mother, Sophia was at the table, pressing the sharp tip of the steak knife against the heel of her left hand. "Mama!" Emilia exclaimed. "What are you doing?"

Sophia thrust the knife away and it clattered on the table, now littered with the other flatware as well. "You're being rude, Emilia," Sophia scolded. "So rough."

"I'm sorry, Mama," Emilia said. "But you scared me. You shouldn't play with knives."

Sophia's unlined forehead creased in a frown. "Are they nice to you here, Emilia?"

"What? Nice?" Emilia wasn't ready for the abrupt shift in conversation.

"Are they nice to you?" Sophia seemed serious.

"Mama, this is my home." Emilia laid paper towels on a plate. "Do you remember Mercedes Sandoval? My friend the dancer? She loves it here."

Sophia nodded, eyes shining. Mercedes was still a local celebrity in the eyes of Sophia and other older women in the barrio.

When Emilia was small, her mother and Tía Lourdes had watched Mercedes and her late husband win ballroom dancing competitions on television, exclaiming over Mercedes's opulent costumes and her handsome husband's powerful moves. When he died, Mercedes moved back home, to the same neighborhood in Acapulco where Sophia and Ernesto lived, to eke out a living as a dance instructor. She was older than Emilia but tough, both mentally and physically. Outside of Kurt and detective Franco Silvio, there wasn't anybody Emilia would rather have behind her in a bar fight.

"Mercedes was here," Emilia went on, knowing that her friend's opinion would carry weight with Sophia. "We had dinner in the restaurant. Even met the head concierge, Christine. And Jacques, the head chef."

Sophia flounced out of the chair, her floral dress swirling around her bare legs, and came to the stove. She peered into the frying pan. "Did you turn them over?"

"Yes," Emilia said. "They're done."

"Very nice, Emilia." Sophia watched as Emilia lifted the fried flores de calabaza out of the skillet and onto the paper towels. "Just like I taught you."

Emilia bit her lip as she arranged the appetizer on small plates. Apparently, their conversation about Tía Lourdes had never happened.

Dinner was awkward.

Ernesto plowed through the squash blossoms and tackled Emilia's tuna steaks and tangy *tamarindo* sauce with gusto. Sophia barely ate, her attention on the dramatic view of the Pacific coast on the other side of the glass doors. Seated opposite Emilia, with the crystal chandelier turning his blonde hair to silver, Kurt tried to keep the conversation going. Emilia chimed in but it was hard to include the other two at the table and eventually they both stopped trying.

Kurt cleared his throat. "Perhaps we'd like some music," he said.

Anything to fill the silence. "Yes, please," Emilia said.

Kurt went into the living room to turn on the stereo. Emilia watched him. She never tired of his athletic grace or the confidence which he wore like a second skin.

The Acapulco Philharmonic Orchestra's rendition of *Rhapsody in Blue* soared around them. Kurt turned down the volume and came back to the table. The music was soft but the rhythm was energizing. Emilia smiled her thanks and Kurt winked back.

"Your tortillas are very fresh, Emilia," Ernesto said.

"Very good with the flavor of the *tamarindo*."

"Thank you." Emilia grinned and raised her glass to him.

He bobbed his head at her and took another tortilla from the serving basket. "Are you still working for the police?"

Emilia nodded. "Of course, Ernesto. Why do you ask?"

He gestured with his fork at the expensively appointed room; his hand scarred and weathered from years of sharpening knives and tools against a grinding wheel. "I thought maybe you didn't need to work anymore."

"Emilia's doing important things," Kurt said. "She was even asked to help select a new lieutenant."

"Yes?" Ernesto looked impressed.

"I just got to ask some questions," Emilia said. She didn't want to make her role seem more important than it was or reveal that she was part of the interview panel because of a deal she and Silvio had struck with Acapulco's crooked chief of police. "Lieutenant Baez is from Mexico City."

"Like me," Ernesto said.

"Yes," Sophia said, bringing her attention back to the table. "Where all the museums are. And the president."

Emilia felt herself relax a bit; they were finally having a conversation. "Actually, I have something from work for you," she said.

She went to the buffet, picked up two packs of playing cards, and spread out one set on the table.

Sophia fingered the cards. Each bore the likeness of a woman, with name and vital statistics underneath. The other side asked for help finding the woman and gave a phone number to call. "These are pretty, Emilia."

"They're cards to help find the missing, Mama," Emilia said. "I thought you could give them out when you go to the market. Ernesto, you could give them to customers who come to get their knives sharpened."

She'd kept a record of women missing from the Acapulco area for the last few years. *Las Perdidas*—the Lost Ones—had nothing in common except that no one else had the time to look for them. Emilia constantly combed police reports, news stories, and morgue records, but she was rarely able to close a case. The cards were the brainchild of the new operations coordinator for Acapulco's all-female patrol unit, a job Emilia once held, and the unit passed them out on every shift.

"I know this one." Sophia held up a card with the photograph of a stunning teen with short black hair and china doll features.

"That's Lila Jimenez Lata, Mama," Emilia said. "Berta's granddaughter. You know Berta from church. I've been looking for Lila ever since she ran away."

Kurt helped her clear the dishes as Sophia and Ernesto looked through the cards.

"You just have to get through dessert and the ride into the city," Kurt said as he put the plates in the kitchen sink.

"I feel as if I've run a marathon," Emilia confessed.

Kurt pulled her into a hug. "The next time they come it will be easier. Remember, this was a lot for her to take in all at once."

They brought out coffee and dessert. Sophia sat up straight when she saw the cake topped with whipped cream and dusted with cocoa.

Emilia grinned at her mother's reaction. "It's *pastel de tres leches*, mama. Chocolate *pastel de tres leches*. I wanted to surprise you."

"The only person I ever knew to make it chocolate was la señora." Sophia clapped her hands when Kurt set a slice in front of her. "Did you get the recipe from her?"

Emilia smiled. "Who is that, Mama?"

"La señora," Sophia said impatiently. "She was very good to us, you know."

Ernesto paused with his fork in mid-air and looked blankly at his wife.

Emilia took a deep breath. "Tell us about this señora, Mama."

"We lived with her and her husband when you were a baby," Sophia said, as if explaining to a child. "Ernesto, you drove the car for el señor. We lived in the little house and they lived in the big house on the hill."

It was a story Emilia had heard before. She gave Ernesto a reassuring nod and he began to eat again.

"You never told me very much about the family, Mama," Emilia said. "I don't even know their name."

"We had a wonderful life there, didn't we?" Sophia said to Ernesto. She didn't wait for a reply as her eyes grew unfocused, as if she saw something in the far distance. "Lots of parties at the big house. We went sometimes, just like we belonged there. But chauffeurs aren't supposed to do that. I didn't know until afterwards."

"After the accident, you mean?" Emilia asked.

"Yes. When the bad times started."

"Whatever happened to la señora, Mama?" Emilia never heard anything more about the widow of her father's employer, only that she'd forced Sophia and Emilia to leave immediately after the accident that took both husbands. No doubt the house was needed for a new chauffeur.

Tía Lourdes once said that la señora blamed the fatal accident on the close relationship between employer and chauffeur. Her husband had chosen to sit in front rather than in the back as was the norm. He might have survived the front-end collision if he had.

"There were swings in the yard where you played," Sophia said dreamily, as if Emilia hadn't asked a question. "Your hair was straight and his was curly. People laughed because you looked so different."

"Whose hair was curly, Mama?" Emilia asked.

"The little boy." Sophia sipped her coffee.

"The family had a little boy?" Emilia sampled her cake. "You never told me that. What was his name?"

Sophia set her cup back in the saucer with a jerk. "How would I know?"

"You just said I played with—."

"I told you not to be so rude," Sophia snapped. She shoved her chair away from the table and ran into the living room. Suddenly the Acapulco Philharmonic blasted at full volume.

Ernesto dropped his fork. Emilia blinked, totally taken by surprise.

Kurt held up a hand. "Em, let me."

He went into the living room. A moment later, the music quieted but even so it was impossible to hear a conversation taking place in the other room.

Ernesto finished his cake. Emilia served him another slice.

Kurt and Sophia came back to the table as if nothing had happened. They looked at the *Las Perdidas* cards and ate cake and finally it was time to take Sophia and Ernesto home.

Sophia was surprisingly animated in the backseat of Kurt's SUV as they drove along the coast road. While the scenic drive was a daily routine for Emilia, Sophia rarely left her own neighborhood in central Acapulco. Watching the ribbon of road unwind in the twilight between ocean and mountain was a rare treat.

Emilia didn't say much, but let Sophia and Ernesto enjoy the ride. Kurt drove skillfully as the sun sank ahead of them, painting the sky with swaths of orange and pink.

At the small house in central Acapulco, Emilia got out of the car.

"Have a good day at school tomorrow, *niña,*" Sophia said. She kissed her daughter and headed for the door.

Ernesto took Emilia's hand and gave her a clumsy peck on the cheek before jerking his head at Sophia, now out of earshot.

"I think she's getting better," he said.

Sleep wouldn't come. Emilia flopped onto her back and stared at the ceiling. The sliding glass doors were open and shadows from the softly billowing curtains danced across the ceiling. Moonlight gilded that side of the room, leaving the bed shrouded in darkness. The penthouse was quiet, save for the distant churn of the ocean and Kurt's even breathing.

The visit kept replaying in her mind. Sophia pressing the knife point against her hand. Sophia rushing out because she couldn't remember the name of some long-ago playmate. Anger at Tía Lourdes over nothing.

Emilia had seen both criminals and snitches deliberately misunderstand questions or attempt to redirect a conversation. But her mother was neither dishonest nor disingenuous. No, this was just how her mother was now and would forever be.

Sophia had once been clever and funny, as well as beautiful, according to Tía Lourdes. Emilia wished, not for the first time, that she'd known that girl, if only for a minute. A sigh escaped her lungs that went all the way up to the tall ceiling.

"What's the matter?" Kurt asked sleepily.

Emilia turned her head. "Did I wake you up? I'm sorry."

"Contrary to popular belief," he yawned. "I don't always

fall asleep immediately afterwards."

Emilia gave a soft chuckle and rolled onto her side to face him. "Good to know."

He grinned, teeth flashing white in the dark, and pulled her close. "What's going on?"

"Just thinking about my mother and Ernesto."

"They seem content with each other," Kurt said. "What was it that he said? She's getting better."

"Poor Ernesto." Emilia sighed again. Her bare feet found Kurt's under the covers. "He'll learn. Mama is always going to be the way she is."

"The important thing is that she's happy, Em," Kurt said quietly. "And she's happy that you're happy."

"It's not that." Emilia hesitated, loath to give voice to her thoughts.

"What's really bothering you, Em?"

"What if it happens to me?" Emilia whispered. "What if I lose my mind, too?"

"You're worried that it's genetic?"

"I guess."

"Your mother suffered a nervous breakdown because of a terrible trauma," Kurt pointed out. "When she lost your father. That's not a genetic event."

"But maybe I've inherited her weakness," Emilia said. "Something traumatic could happen to me. I'm a cop in the middle of a drug war. Work is one trauma after another. I could have a nervous breakdown, too."

"Your first partner died in the line of duty," Kurt said.

"You've been shot. You killed a man before he killed you. That's trauma, by anyone's definition. Yet you've worked your way through all of it."

"Still . . ."

"I think you've developed some impressive coping techniques," Kurt said. "You just need to recognize them."

"I cry a lot," Emilia said ruefully.

Kurt's arms tightened around her. "Didn't you once tell me that when you were little you wanted to buy your mother a new brain so she'd stop crying?"

"When I was really little." Emilia nodded. "But after awhile she stopped crying and she's been like this ever since."

"There you go," Kurt said. "As long as you can still cry, you'll be all right."

Emilia felt herself relax, warmed by his body and the common sense in his words. As a cop surrounded by danger and corruption, she often wept out of frustration, anger, or sheer fear. Each time she cried herself dry, picked up the pieces, and kept going.

"You're pretty smart," Emilia murmured into his shoulder.

"I have my moments," Kurt said.

"No." She pulled back to see his face. "These are our moments. *Our* moments."

Kurt smiled again. "I like the sound of that."

Emilia traced the line of his jaw. "You know, sometimes when we're together, I feel as if nothing really bad could ever happen. You make me so strong that I'm untouchable. Unbreakable."

He moved against her. It was a long time before they slept.

CHAPTER 2

Emilia regarded the young man sitting at the table. Rusty red hair braided into a beaded waterfall, baggy cargo shorts, ragged tee shirt, and the kind of suede and cork sandals that only poor *gringos* ever wore. His knee pumped furiously, as if electricity ran through his veins.

"Just calm down," she said in English and stayed standing. "Tell us exactly what you saw."

"Listen, dude. *Amigo*." The young man jiggled in the cheap plastic chair. "Like I told you. Grim reaper shit. The guy was covered in blood. We looked in, saw all the crazy shit, and didn't touch jack."

Emilia's partner Franco Silvio held up two Canadian passports from the couple's duffel bag on the table. Their meager belongings made an untidy heap on the blue checkered vinyl tablecloth.

"The passports look legit," Silvio said to Emilia. "They arrived in Mexico from Panama a week ago."

The young man jumped up. "Of course they're real passports," he said indignantly.

He was rawboned and thin and loops of braided string necklaces hung over the stretched-out ribbing of his tee. His teeth had the tell-tale rot of a heavy meth user.

Silvio swung his head. Menace radiated from his flat expression, accentuated by a crew cut and the muscle mass bulging against a khaki bomber jacket and dark jeans. The young man wilted back into his seat. Silvio tossed the passports onto the table.

Emilia folded her arms. "Where did you sleep last night?"

"On the beach, *amigo*."

"Did you hear anything?" she went on. "Shouts, a fight?"

"No, nothing." Again the ingratiating yet rotted smile. "Just the sound of the ocean, *amigo*. That's why we're here. For the waves."

Emilia resisted the urge to correct his grammar and tell him to use *amiga,* not *amigo,* when addressing a woman. Not that he should use either form of the word. They weren't friends.

"What made you go over to that tent?" she asked instead.

"This was supposed to be fun." His freckled blonde girlfriend wore a colorful hippie dress and the same scuffed sandals. "Surfing. Camping out. That's all."

"There's no surfing around here," Emilia said.

The girl burst into tears. The boyfriend put his arm around her as his leg pumped up and down like a jackhammer. "You can paddle surf in the lagoon," he said indignantly.

Emilia knew he needed another fix.

They were in the empty dining room of El Loro Rojo, a shabby beachside hostel and restaurant on Coyuca Lagoon, a few miles northwest of Acapulco. The young Canadians were like so many other junkies, vagrants, and penniless adventurers who often camped on the remote strip of beach which was no more than a thin barrier between the Pacific and the large inland lagoon.

Rural and remote, the perimeter of the Lagoon was dotted with small villages and hotels that mostly catered to ecotourists. The main draws were boating trips to see waterfowl and wildlife, as well as inlets and mud banks where a few Hollywood jungle escapades had been filmed. Every once in awhile the police were called to investigate a rape or robbery. Generally by the time they got there both victim and perpetrator were long gone.

But this time, it was murder.

Perched on the eastern end of the lagoon, El Loro Rojo was a collection of concrete shacks that managed to look squalid and cheerful at the same time. Herman and Itzel Schmidt, a couple in their late fifties, ran the place. Both were sitting at a nearby table watching the police detectives grill the young Canadian couple.

Herman was German, spoke heavily accented Spanish, and had phoned the police two hours ago. He had a mane of white hair that had once been blonde, a face leathered brown from the sun, and wore the loose white clothing traditionally favored by Mexico's *campesinos*. His outfit struck Emilia as an economic rather than a sartorial choice. If she had to guess, El Loro Rojo wasn't exactly a big moneymaker.

Without asking, Itzel Schmidt got up and lumbered to the kitchen, only to return with a tray of four mismatched mugs of black coffee. She wordlessly handed a cup to Silvio, then one to her husband.

Emilia wasn't served. She had to grab the last for herself.

Itzel Schmidt was Mexican. Emilia had seen a thousand

of her kind before. Heavyset and expressionless, in a shapeless dress with a threadbare apron, her hands gnarled by hard work. Long hours spent cooking and cleaning, with little to look forward to except more of the same. Itzel didn't look at the Canadian couple as she sat next to her husband again.

"Who else was around this morning?" Silvio asked, neither sitting nor drinking the coffee.

"No one else." Herman gestured at the Canadians. "Like I said on the phone, they rushed in, screaming about a dead man."

"What about people staying at the hotel?" Emilia asked, trying not to inhale. The coffee smelled like burnt cork. Dried green mucus clung to the rim of the mug.

"No one else here right now." As Itzel stared at the checkered tablecloth, Herman explained that the hostel rented out five rooms and booked the occasional tour group for a meal, but most of their business came from campers who used the outdoor facilities. Two pesos to use the toilet. Ten pesos for a shower. Twelve pesos if the shower included soap. No hot water.

"Any of your workers around?" Silvio asked.

"No, no one else works here." Herman spoke emphatically. Itzel's gaze shifted from the tabletop to her cup.

Emilia pretended to drink the evil-smelling coffee as Silvio asked the owners about the people who had passed through in the last few days. The dining room was open to the beach and covered by a thatch *palapa* roof. Six tables topped with blue and white vinyl tablecloths and ringed by four white plastic chairs. A motley assortment of colorful ceramics hung on the cement walls in no particular order, making for a mismatched farmyard of sun faces, chickens, frogs, and kitschy signs pointing to the beach.

A plywood bar ran the length of one wall, beyond which they could see into the kitchen. Papers overflowed a metal rack, which apparently served as their business accounting center, behind a tower of canned goods. Emilia watched a line of roaches skitter past a work table laden with dirty plates.

The stink of the coffee was getting worse as it cooled. Emilia excused herself and walked past the empty tables. The chalkboard menu above the bar featured cheeseburgers, fish tacos, and a *guisado de mariscos* likely made each day from whatever fish Itzel needed to throw out.

Silvio joined her as Emilia stood by the steps leading down to the beach. "Let's go see what's out there." He rolled his eyes toward the dining room. "The two Canucks can show us but there's no reason to keep them after that."

"He needs a fix," Emilia murmured.

"Far be it from us to keep him from it," Silvio said.

He gestured to the two uniformed cops who'd also responded to the call. With the Canadian couple in the lead, they all headed out of the hostel and onto the narrow beach. Emilia pulled on her sunglasses against the early morning glare as they walked parallel to the water, staying well above the tide line as the surf pulsed up to the seaweed-strewn shoreline again and again.

She cursed under her breath as the sand shifted and grains trickled into her loafers with every step. She could hear the two uniforms puffing as their boots left deep imprints. They were both burly young men with POLICIA stenciled across bulletproof vests. Bigger than either of them, Silvio nonetheless seemed impervious to the unstable footing as he pounded alongside Emilia.

This was not how she'd expected to spend Sunday morning, especially considering that she'd barely fallen asleep before the call came in from Dispatch. There were not enough detectives to cover all the calls plus let everyone have two days off in a row. Emilia and Silvio were up next on the rota and she had to go. Somehow, she'd managed to roll out of bed without waking Kurt, scribble him a note, and head out.

El Loro Rojo receded into the distance. No one else appeared besides the four sops and the nervous Canadian couple. Scrub pines and palms grew on the steep rises that surrounded the lagoon, providing shade and firewood for campers. The skinny beach looked hastily deserted, save for seagulls screeching in a competition for candy wrappers. Litter dotted the sand like abstract white droppings. Any early morning birdwatchers had been warned off by the sight of a marked police car parked by the hostel.

As the group trudged through the sand, they passed a burned-out campfire, rolled up sleeping bags, and two paddleboards stuck upright in the sand.

"This is our campsite," the Canadian girl said tearfully. Her boyfriend was sweating and his hands curled into nervous fists.

They kept going, the sand hummocked by wind and leftover footsteps. Emilia saw more than one used condom, as well as a discarded glass syringe winking in the sun next to a broken rubber cord used by junkies to make veins pop for an injection. Pelicans beat their wings as they rose from the sand to the water while seagulls poked at the debris and shrieked at each other.

"It's over there." The Canadian girl stopped and pointed to a small orange tent partly obscured by a patch of scrubby pine.

"Hardly a close neighbor," Emilia remarked.

The girl looked down. Her boyfriend looked sick.

"Stay with them," Silvio said to the two uniforms, with a jerk of his chin at the Canadians.

The nylon tent was big enough for two people and some gear. Otherwise there was nothing remarkable about the scene. It was just another hippie camp on the beach.

Before squatting to open the tent flap, Silvio pulled a pair of latex gloves out of a pocket and put them on. Emilia did the same.

Silvio's head and shoulders disappeared inside the tent. A second later his whole body recoiled.

"Shit," he exclaimed.

"What is it?" Emilia asked. Few things rattled Silvio.

"*Rayos.*" Silvio shot to his feet, drew a deep breath, then gave a gruff chuckle. "Don't see that every day."

"What is it?" Emilia repeated.

"See for yourself." Silvio was back in control. "Maybe some sort of ritual killing."

He opened the flap for Emilia even as he stripped off one glove and dug out his phone.

Emilia crawled halfway inside the tent and froze.

A man's body lay supine on top of an old sleeping bag, clad in faded jeans and a black tee shirt with some sort of logo on it. The feet were bare. A pair of cross trainers were placed neatly to one side.

The head was severed from the body. Blood had soaked into the sleeping bag and the nylon floor of the tent, forming a rusty stain under the shoulders. The eyes were open and stared blankly at dirty fabric.

Opposite the body, an image of Santa Muerte leered from a frayed poster-sized banner pinned to the tent wall. The Death Saint was depicted as a skeleton in a long hooded robe. The skull face was distorted by a mocking grin. One bony hand held a scythe like a Grim Reaper. The other held a globe to demonstrate the folk saint's command of the entire world.

Without thinking, Emilia made the Sign of the Cross.

She dimly heard Silvio outside the tent on the phone barking orders for the crime scene techs to hurry the hell out to El Loro Rojo and he didn't care that it was a fucking Sunday morning. She couldn't tear her eyes away from the

Santa Muerte image even as cold sweat drenched her hairline and trickled down her cheek.

Below the banner, several peso coins, a trio of white candles wrapped in black gauze, and a handful of shriveled brown marigolds had been placed on a charred piece of driftwood in a parody of a traditional Day of the Dead altar, known as an *ofrenda*. Cold candle wax spilled over the gauze and pooled on pieces of paper folded into triangles.

A small open bottle of tequila lay on the makeshift altar as well. Liquor darkened the tent floor. The sharp smell mixed with the cloying scent of congealed blood, both warmed and exaggerated by the October morning sun. Emilia pulled the neck of her tee shirt up to cover her nose and mouth.

She knew just enough about Santa Muerte to feel her heart race and adrenaline pulse down her spine as she realized what else the *ofrenda* held. Several *muerto* skeleton figurines, common items on altars, were nearly hidden under the wilted marigolds. At the end of the month, skeletons made of papier maché dressed in extravagant costumes would be displayed on Day of the Dead *ofrendas* all over Mexico.

On a traditional October *ofrenda*, the figurines might represent something related to the deceased, like their occupation, hobby, or pet. But these *muertos* were simple naked male figures, all painted black. Each was cut into pieces with clean and deliberate slashes through the thick papier maché.

Emilia used a gloved finger to move the bits out from under the marigolds. There were enough to form three full figurines. The resemblance between the broken skeletons and the beheaded body on the sleeping bag was unmistakable.

A gust of ocean breeze caused the side of the tent to billow, the Santa Muerte banner flapping against the fabric. Emilia nearly screamed as the lurid image blew forward and just as quickly receded, as if Santa Muerte had tried to touch her.

"*Madre de Dios*," Emilia muttered and gave herself a mental shake even as she felt the cold sweat soak her shirt. A Day of the Dead *ofrenda* was meant to attract and celebrate the spirits of the deceased. This *ofrenda* to Santa Muerte was meant to damage them.

Emilia swallowed hard, rifled the dead man's pockets, and came away empty-handed. She backed out of the tent.

Silvio pocketed his phone as Emilia stood up. "Techs are on their way," he said. "What do you make of it?"

"It's not the usual thing," Emilia said shakily. "He didn't put up a fight. No signs of a struggle. Like he just laid there and let someone cut his throat."

"He was asleep," Silvio said. "Drugged. Or passed out drunk."

"The autopsy will tell," Emilia said.

"Did you check for identification?"

"Nothing."

"Needle tracks?" Silvio asked.

"The light's not good enough to see." Emilia glanced toward the tent opening. "Did you notice there wasn't a wetsuit? Not even a pair of board shorts? Whatever else he was doing here, he wasn't on vacation."

Silvio stopped to peer inside the tent again. "You're right." He straightened. "What do you make of the Santa Muerte display?"

"I honestly don't know," Emilia said. "I guess the guy was some sort of worshipper."

They let the Canadian couple go and dispatched the two uniforms back to the El Loro Rojo hostel to wait for the crime scene techs.

Emilia sat down in the sand, her heart still beating uncomfortably fast. Silvio stayed standing, his back to her as he stared at the ocean churn against the shoreline. Emilia emptied the sand out of her shoes and focused on the water as well, letting her nerves ebb with the rhythm of the water.

Minutes went by. Silvio checked his watch. "Where the fuck are they?" he grumbled.

Emilia squinted at him. "Long drive out here," she said. "Took us at least 45 minutes."

Even closer to the center of Acapulco, the crime scene technicians often didn't come at all. They weren't lazy or incompetent. They were simply overloaded with work.

All the detectives had learned to carry latex gloves and plastic zip-lock bags in their pockets so they could handle any evidence they came across.

Silvio turned around. "How was your dinner thing

yesterday?"

"It was okay," Emilia said with a sigh. "My food didn't poison anyone. My mother got a little rattled at one point but Kurt calmed her down."

"Hollywood offer to buy everybody a hotel?" Silvio snorted with laughter.

It always set Emilia's teeth on edge when Silvio referred to Kurt as Hollywood. She knew her partner only did that to irritate her; the two men actually got along well.

"So what did you do yesterday?" Emilia countered. "Did you keep your counseling appointment?"

Silvio scratched his cheek. "Busy."

"That's the third time you've blown off an appointment," Emilia exclaimed. "What were you doing that kept you so busy?"

"I'll go when I'm ready to go," Silvio said.

"You need to do this, Franco." Emilia pointed at him. "Spending all day in the gym is not a substitute."

"Leave it alone, Cruz."

Silvio resumed looking at the ocean. Emilia closed her eyes. It was stupid to argue with the man; his wife Isabel had been killed in a home invasion not long ago and Silvio was still raw with grief. Emilia had helped him make an appointment with the counseling service free to all cops, but Silvio kept rescheduling. A former heavyweight champ, Emilia knew he was spending all his free time at his old gym, sparring with young boxing hopefuls and slapping the speed bag.

His phone rang, startling them both. Silvio answered with a terse *"Bueno?"* After a moment he broke the connection. "Crime scene techs are at the hostel."

It took another ten minutes before they saw the uniformed cops approach with a single crime scene tech.

What a shit job, Emilia thought as she watched the guy in a crime scene paper suit struggle across the sand, weighted down with a heavy case. The techs earned little more than an ordinary beat cop and had to handle dead bodies all day, much of the time in the hot sun. Yet they were subject to the same dangers as other cops in Mexico from drug cartels notorious for targeting cops as a means of intimidating law enforcement.

The uniforms and the tech finally made it to the tent. Emilia and Silvio both knew Bayardo, a young tech with a reputation for being both dependable and thorough.

"Dead male," Silvio informed him. "Youngish, probably in his 20's. Head severed from the body. No other wounds that we could tell."

Bayardo pulled on gloves, opened the tent flap and crawled in. A moment later, he backed out so rapidly the tent swayed from side to side.

"Madre de Dios," he exclaimed, his face working with fear. "I'm not touching this shit."

"Do you need help?" Silvio asked, pulling out another pair of latex gloves from his jacket pocket.

The tech's eyes bulged. "Do whatever the hell you want. I'm not touching any of it."

"Hey," Silvio started and grabbed the man's arm.

"Forget it." Bayardo shook off Silvio's restraining hand. "Report me, I don't care. I'm not touching any of this shit."

Before they could react, he picked up his case and loped off across the sand. Without a word, the two uniformed cops took off after him, leaving Emilia and Silvio alone again.

"But this is a crime scene," Emilia said in disbelief. She'd never seen a tech refuse to catalogue a crime scene before.

"What the fuck?" Silvio swore. He pulled out his phone and jabbed at the buttons. "He hauls all the fucking way out to Coyuca Lagoon and won't do his fucking job? You bet your ass I'm going to report him."

Five minutes later Silvio pocketed his phone. "Can you believe it?" he sputtered. "Lab says nothing they can do. Not going to send out anybody else. They'll pick up whatever we bring in tomorrow."

"Nice." Emilia stood up and dusted the sand off the seat of her jeans. "How to guarantee a cold case before we even start."

"You take some pictures," Silvio said. "We'll have to get him out and bag up all the shit."

Emilia took a deep breath of clean salt air, crawled back into the tent, and snapped pictures of the body and the altar. Santa Muerte's skeleton grin seemed even more malevolent as it glinted from her phone's screen.

With that done, she and Silvio each grabbed a corner of the sleeping bag and eased it out of the tent, sliding the body along as if on a stretcher.

The dead man looked even worse in the bright sunlight. The break between the lolling head and the supine body was as pronounced as the breaks between the pieces of broken *muertos*.

"Look," Emilia turned the left arm to reveal the outline of a dagger inked inside the forearm. "An El Machete tattoo."

The secretive gang was known to work in and around Acapulco for the violent Zetas cartel. Silvio stooped to take more pictures. "It's been a while since we've seen an El Machete member," he said.

Emilia bagged up the Santa Muerte altar. Handling the broken *muertos* gave her the shivers. The curiously folded papers stuck to the wax candles were covered in handwriting, but she didn't take the time to read them. Silvio helped her take down the tent and fold it up.

By the time they were done, the team from the morgue showed up. The morgue workers rolled the corpse into a black plastic body bag, tossed in the dead man's head, and retraced their steps across the sand.

Emilia glanced back. A small knot of *gringos* rounded the clump of scrub pine. They stopped by the edge of the water, seemingly nonplussed, as if they'd encountered a signpost with the wrong directions on it.

It was slow going across the ridges of sand, following the morgue workers and the body bag swinging between them. Emilia stopped to take off her loafers. When she looked back again, the people had disappeared, as if the ocean had swallowed them up.

CHAPTER 3

Back in the hostel dining room, Herman and Itzel Schmidt stared at the pictures on Emilia's phone display.

"Do you recognize him?" Silvio asked as Emilia flicked through the picture gallery to show them the face of the dead man and his El Machete tattoo. "Seen him around in the past couple of days?"

Itzel made a small sound. Herman looked at her. When Itzel gave her head a tiny shake, the German visibly relaxed. "No, we don't recognize him," Herman said.

"What about the tattoo?" Emilia pressed.

Once again, Herman looked at Itzel for a signal, then answered for both of them. "No, we've never seen anyone with that tattoo."

"We'll just take a last look around and be off," Silvio said. "Someone will probably be back tomorrow to follow up."

Emilia watched Itzel disappear into the kitchen. Herman stood up and said he'd show them the outdoor facilities the campers and beach-goers used.

There were two smaller square buildings outside the main guest house that served as toilet and shower facilities for men and women.

"Yours," Silvio said shortly. He jerked his thumb at the door to the women's outhouse and disappeared into the men's.

Emilia pushed open the outhouse door. The interior was

dark, with the only light coming from a small window high on the wall covered by a fine metal mesh. It was a cross between an outhouse and a locker room, with two toilet stalls, an open shower stall, three sinks, and a couple of cubbies ostensibly for storing clothes and towels. The place had that particular smell of sewage and salt that Emilia always associated with beach outhouses. She pushed open the doors to the stalls to make sure the place was empty.

A retching noise came from the last stall. The door was latched. Emilia peered under it to see a pair of stained canvas basketball sneakers. She tapped on the door. "Hello?"

The toilet flushed.

Emilia waited.

The stall door opened and a young man stumbled out. He looked around, clearly confused. Or drunk. Or high.

His eyes were bloodshot, as if he'd been crying. He had short dark hair, rough stubble on his chin, a tee shirt flecked with rust, and a knapsack slung over one shoulder. The knees of his jeans were stiff and bloodstained. She realized that his hands were spattered with dark stains as well.

Emilia barely had time to shout "Silvio!" before the kid swung at her. She managed to turn and his fist connected with her shoulder rather than her face. The force of the blow sent Emilia reeling backwards into a big metal trash can that clanged onto the cement floor, taking Emilia down with it. Foul-smelling garbage spilled over her jeans as she flailed for a handhold that wasn't there. Emilia ended up sprawled between the wall and the sink with the big metal can rocking crazily beside her,

Mouth open, the kid stared dumbly as Emilia scrambled to her feet, then he lunged for the outhouse door and got it open. As he shot out, his backpack caught on the edge of the door and he was yanked backwards.

Emilia got her hand on the backpack and pulled. The kid flailed wildly, catching her on the cheekbone with his fist and on her shins with his feet. Emilia hung on. He dragged her through the door as they tripped over each other, rolled down the concrete steps, and into the sandy seagrass between the two outhouses.

He fought like a man possessed but without skill. Emilia managed to wrestle him facedown with one arm twisted behind his back, his wrist nearly touching the opposite ear.

"Silvio!" she hollered breathlessly and suddenly the big detective was there. As he bent to slap on the cuffs, the kid reared up with astonishing strength and spilled Emilia off. She landed in a heap in time to see Silvio rear back, a hand to his nose.

The boy scuttled sideways like a crazed crab. Emilia threw herself after him and missed, landing on her stomach in the sand, but Silvio moved with his own brand of astonishing speed and caught the kid's ankle. As Emilia watched through a film of grit, Silvio managed to get a solid grip on the kid and swung him headfirst against the steps. Skull rapped against concrete and the kid went limp.

"Is he dead?" Emilia gasped. The entire episode took mere seconds.

Silvio felt the neck for a pulse. "No, he's just out for awhile." He pulled the knapsack off the guy and tossed it to Emilia. "Where did you find him?"

"He was throwing up in the women's toilets," Emilia said. "Check out his pants."

"*Rayos*," Silvio swore as he rolled the kid onto his back to cuff him and saw the blood-stained jeans. "I think you just caught yourself a killer, Cruz."

The kid moaned and blinked.

"Come on, you *pendejo*." Silvio hauled the kid to his feet. "We're the police and you're fucked."

The kid began to cry. Emilia carried the knapsack as they propelled the boy into the hostel. The fight had gone out of him and he swayed between them like a drunken sailor.

They hauled him into the dining room and plopped him into a chair. Herman and Itzel rushed out of the kitchen. Silvio kept a firm grasp on the kid. "Do you know who this is?" he asked.

"This is Marco," Herman said slowly.

"Just Marco?" Silvio asked.

Herman looked at his wife.

"None of these kids have other names," Itzel mumbled.

"How long has he been around here?" Emilia asked.

Herman cleared his throat.

"A day or two." Itzel eyed the boy. "He paid to use the showers and the toilet. That's all."

Silvio's hand on his shoulder kept the kid upright and in the chair.

"Marco, let's talk for a minute." Emilia pulled out another chair and sat facing him. "Is that your real name?"

"Leave me alone," he sniffled.

"What's your name?" Emilia asked.

"Leave me alone," Marco repeated.

Silvio slapped him. "She asked you a question, *cabrón.*"

Marco sobbed silently, cuffed hands behind his back.

Emilia stood up. The kid's teeth were beginning to chatter with shock and Silvio was on a hair trigger. The combination didn't need to be on display in some crap beach hostel. "Let's get him back to the station," she said.

Silvio looked at the Schmidts. "If anybody comes asking for him, call us. I gave you both our numbers."

"These kids got nobody," Herman lamented, spokesman for the older couple again. "They just drift. Some of them make a living with drugs to the tourists. Or steal."

Silvio hoisted Marco up. The kid sagged in Silvio's grip like a sack of onions.

Emilia helped him into the back of Silvio's unmarked police sedan. All of the evidence bags were already in the trunk. Silvio cranked the engine and swung out of the El Loro Rojo's rutted drive.

"Please don't arrest me," Marco mumbled. "I'll never get her back."

Emilia turned around to look at him as the sedan bounced onto the highway and headed east toward Acapulco. "Get who back?"

Marco curled onto the back seat, tears streaking through

the grime on his cheeks. "He made me."

"Who?" Emilia pressed. "Who made you do it?

But the kid was asleep, mouth slightly open and pressed against the car upholstery. His jeans smelled like blood and vomit.

"*Rayos*," Silvio swore in disgust.

"New boyfriend, Cruz?" Valdez, the uniformed holding cell guard who'd been unlucky enough to pull a Sunday shift, was a stocky beat cop who'd been shot and now walked a desk. In the past two years his attitude toward Emilia as the first and only female detective had gone from outright hostility to grudging acceptance. He unlocked a cell door as Emilia shoved Marco forward.

"Sure," Emilia said. She uncuffed Marco and made sure the bars locked behind him. The kid shuffled over to the wooden bench bolted to the wall and curled into a fetal position, arms wrapped around his knees.

He'd slept the entire hour it took them to drive in from Coyuca Lagoon through Sunday afternoon traffic jammed with tour buses, lost drivers, and beach-bound pedestrians. It was just enough time for a lump to rise on Emilia's cheekbone and her muscles to stiffen from the roll down those *maldita* concrete steps. All she wanted to do was go home and take a hot bath but hours of interrogation loomed ahead.

"You need anything?" she asked through the bars.

Marco ignored her.

Emilia turned to Valdez. "He's probably coming out of a meth high."

"Does he got a name?" Valdez asked.

"So far, all we have is Marco," Emilia said. "Won't give us anything else."

"What do I log him in for?"

"Murder of an El Machete gang member," Emilia said.

"No kidding," Valdez marveled. "Really got to be whacked out on meth or just fucking crazy to take them on."

"Probably both." Emilia shot him with her thumb and forefinger. "Get his prints and keep an eye on him until somebody comes and gets him for interrogation."

She headed down the hall to the detectives' squadroom, yet again surprised at how clean it looked. In just a few short weeks, the new lieutenant, Baez, had found funds to have the place painted and cleaned. All the furniture had been rearranged and a conference table installed. Next, he'd upgraded all the computers and brought in huge bulletin boards where photographs, drawings, maps, and other detritus from unsolvable cases were on display.

Some of Emilia's stiffness was erased by the scent of a fresh pot of coffee. The door to Lieutenant Baez's office was open but the room was dark.

Silvio wasn't at his desk, which was pushed nose-to-nose with Emilia's, but he'd dumped all of the evidence bags and Marco's knapsack on her desk and chair. Over by the copier,

Macias and Sandor were arranging photos on a board, both in rolled shirtsleeves and shoulder holsters. They were good cops and partners since before Emilia had shown up in the detectives squadroom. Neither was a friend, but they were less hostile to her as the lone female detective than some others.

"Anybody see Silvio?" Emilia asked.

Macias turned around. "He said something about El Machete and walked out."

Emilia took off her jacket, draped it over the back of her chair, and found her mug. "What are you two doing here on a Sunday?"

"Body hanging from a billboard this side of the Maxitunel," Sandor said as he pinned a picture to the wall above the copier.

Emilia walked over to see the day's latest murder. Two or three a day was the norm, a volume that far outstripped the police department's investigative capacity, but today Acapulco was getting a head start on violence.

Sandor's photograph was as unnerving as the beheaded body and *ofrenda* to Santa Muerte. Against a bright blue sky, a mutilated naked male body swung upside down below a billboard advertising real estate services. Clearly visible to drivers, the billboard stood on a thick metal pole and soared high above the buildings along the road. The pole was fitted with rungs and a wire ledge rimmed the bottom of the billboard so workers could climb up and stand on the ledge to change the advertisement. A rope was knotted over the ledge and the body dangled in the air, bound by the ankles. The arms hung down, partially obscuring a bloody face.

"Nose and penis cut off," Macias said.

"*Madre de Dios*." Emilia took a step back. "He had enemies. Was there a *narcomanta*?"

Display killings, like a body hanging from a billboard, were often accompanied by a *narcomanta*, a banner spelling out a threat or justification from one cartel to another. Other banners proclaimed that the dramatic display was the punishment a cartel meted out to those who helped rivals or law enforcement.

"Body was the *narcomanta*," Sandor said. "Check it out."

He pinned a close-up shot of the man's torso to the bulletin board. The number 9 was crudely cut into the flesh.

"Nine?" Emilia asked. "What's that supposed to mean?"

"Good question," Sandor said.

"Expect it to be all over tomorrow's front pages," Macias said. "Nothing attracts a crowd like a body swinging from a billboard."

Both Macias and Sandor were in their mid-30's and college graduates. Macias was the best looking detective in the squadroom, with wavy hair and deep set eyes while Sandor's straight eyebrows and full lips made him look younger than he was. Emilia didn't know if either of them had a personal life. The two were always together and a little apart from the rest of the squadroom.

Emilia stepped to the coffeemaker and poured herself a cup. "Did Lieutenant Baez come in, too?" she asked.

"Nice to know the guy will work on a Sunday." Sandor tapped the photograph, the stiff paper twanging against the wall. "Guess where he is."

"Chief Salazar's office," Emilia said.

Macias gave a short bark of a laugh. "You're slipping, Cruz," he said. "Guess again."

"No," Emilia groaned. "The mayor's office."

The drug cartel violence raging in Acapulco's poorer neighborhoods had pushed the city onto a *norteamericano* news channel's list of the Top 10 Most Dangerous Cities in the World, but Mayor Carlota Montoya Perez was still touting the city as a venue for the Olympics. Carlota had already hosted one Olympic exploratory committee visit and abhorred anything that made Acapulco look bad. High profile crime earned the police department a tongue-lashing as well as none-too-subtle attempts to downplay problems or ignore them.

Macias eyed the heap of evidence bags on Emilia's desk. "What have you got?"

"A kid killed an El Machete gang member out on Coyuca Lagoon," Emilia said. The hot coffee helped ease the soreness from the fight with Marco. "We've got him in the holding cell, covered in the victim's blood. I'm guessing he was on a meth high and looking for another score."

"Cruz and Silvio for the easy win," Macias said with mock jealousy. There was often a not-so-friendly rivalry between the teams of detectives over case closure rates. Emilia and Silvio consistently closed out the highest number of their cases; even so they barely made it to ten percent.

"When Silvio gets back we'll talk to the kid," Emilia said. "The crime scene was strange. A tent on the beach. Either the victim or the doer had set up an altar to Santa Muerte." She gestured to the pile of evidence bags. "Bayardo showed up for the crime scene techs but he wouldn't touch any of it. Silvio and I had to bag it all up and bring it back."

"Santa Muerte?" Macias frowned. "Patron saint of every drug cartel in Mexico. Just what we need around here."

Emilia finished the coffee and went back to her desk, which bumped up against Silvio's so they could speak face-to-face across a double desk wasteland of computer screens, paperwork, and fast foot wrappers. She shoved Marco's knapsack off her swivel chair and onto the floor, unlocked her desk drawer and dumped her purse on top of the thick binder containing the *Las Perdidas* records. Besides the playing cards she'd shown to Sophia and Ernesto yesterday, she hadn't made a dent in the hunt for Acapulco's missing women in weeks.

Emilia sank into her swivel chair, kicking aside the knapsack under the desk in the process, and balefully eyed the heap of evidence bags.

Again, the black and broken *muertos* made her shiver but the scraps of paper stuck to the black-wrapped candles intrigued her. She pulled on a pair of latex gloves, opened the bag with the candles, and peeled away three small scraps of paper folded into triangles.

The paper was flimsy and lined, like schoolchildren used,

with spidery letters printed in blue ink. Emilia unfolded the first.

Sainted Santa Muerte. Cast Your divine protection over your believers. Bring anguish and destruction to Your enemies and to all they hold dear. Destroy those who seek to destroy Your will. In the complete destruction of Our enemies Your disciples will find mercy and redemption.

Emilia felt an icy touch slide up her spine, as if by simply reading the prayer its evil intention had rubbed off on her. The second was a similar plea for the folk saint to destroy enemies and nonbelievers. She unfolded the last note.

A paper bag sailed through the air and landed on her desk with a thump. Emilia flinched, gave a small shriek and dropped the paper.

Silvio guffawed as he settled into his desk chair.

"*Madre de Dios*!" Emilia exclaimed. "You are such a *pendejo*, Franco."

"You can thank me later," Silvio said. He opened a paper bag of his own and pulled out a double order of fish tacos.

The smell was tantalizing and Emilia realized that neither of them had eaten anything all day. She shoved the notes aside, stripped off her latex gloves, and opened the greasy bag.

Silvio rolled a bottle of sparkling water across their desks to Emilia. "I think the El Machete victim was probably selling meth to campers like the Canadian couple."

Emilia twisted the cap off the bottle. The seal broke with a sigh of escaping carbonation. She washed down crisp fish and warm tortilla. "You think the kid killed him because he couldn't pay?" she asked after she'd swallowed.

Silvio drank down half a cola. "Probably."

"Okay." Emilia wiped her hands on a wrinkled paper napkin from the bottom of the tacos bag. "But if our victim was dealing, why scare away customers with a strange *ofrenda* to Santa Muerte in the middle of Coyuca Lagoon?"

"Santa Muerte is a folk saint," Silvio said. "Everybody knows that it's become a cartel talisman. Maybe the victim was a disciple. Or maybe the kid who killed him set it up. A way to atone."

"Well, whoever did it, they had to haul all this crap out across the beach." Emilia waved at the evidence bags on her desk. "That took real dedication."

"Done?" Silvio wiped his mouth with the back of his hand, wadded up the paper bag, and neatly flicked it into the trash can by the copier. "Let's get a few answers out of Marco with the no last name."

"Hey, uh, Detective Cruz." It was Valdez, the holding cell guard. He was a rare visitor to the detectives squadroom.

"Valdez." Silvio stood up. "How's it going?"

The tubby uniformed cop looked sick. "The kid you brought in."

"Did you get his prints?" Emilia asked.

Valdez shook his head. "He's dead."

CHAPTER 4

Throughout the selection process for the position of chief of detectives, neither Emilia nor Silvio needed to remind either Chief Salazar or Obregon of the deal they'd struck weeks before. The two detectives would choose the new lieutenant and in return did not make public the details of a money laundering operation Salazar and Obregon had been running through the El Pharaoh casino.

Emilia and Silvio had both liked Lieutenant Juan Luis Baez's impeccable record and professional approach to investigations. He'd been the head of a Financial Crimes unit in Mexico City before applying for the Acapulco position through a national police program that sought to reduce corruption by encouraging senior officers to take rotational assignments. Plus, the man had done his homework when it came to the types of cases the detectives squadroom handled and wasn't surprised when two potential subordinates ran his interview panel.

Chief of Police Salazar questioned if Baez's financial background and lack of recent street work was the right fit, but approved the selection, as did Victor Obregon Sosa, head of the police union for the state of Guerrero.

On Monday morning, Emilia grabbed the coffee cup and notebook from her desk and slid into a seat next to Silvio just as Lieutenant Baez came out of his office with a messy sheaf of papers. A handsome man with thick wavy hair, deep-set eyes, and a slightly thickening waistline, he sat at the head of the table on the stroke of 9:00 am, wearing another perfectly tailored suit.

"Good morning, everyone," Lieutenant Baez said. "Monday. The start of a fresh new week."

As they went through current cases, Emilia felt tension circle the table. Macias and Sandor were friendly enough with her and Silvio, but Castro and Gomez had caused enough problems for them to be wary of a boss who wasn't an Acapulco insider.

Ortega and Nuñez, two new detectives that Lieutenant Baez had recruited from Financial Affairs, were quiet. They were older than Emilia and wore suits and ties, as if they hadn't quite made the adjustment to the street work that came along with a job in the more free-wheeling detectives squadroom where homicide was the crime of choice.

"All right." Lieutenant Baez shuffled some of the papers in front of him. "Last, we all know that a murder suspect identified only as Marco died in the holding cells yesterday. Post mortem fingerprints came back negative. There will be an inquiry, but seeing as how there was an overwhelming amount of circumstantial evidence that he had just committed murder, I doubt it will amount to much. That's just my personal opinion. The autopsy will be helpful in letting us know how he died and if the police department is culpable."

They all knew that the police station had erupted in chaos after Valdez's discovery last night. Internal Affairs came in, everybody in the place was questioned, and things didn't quiet down until Marco's body was finally hauled off to the morgue. By the time Emilia got home, she was too tired to do more than give Kurt a brief description of her day and fall into bed.

As Lieutenant Baez continued talking about what they could expect in the next few days, Emilia resisted the urge to look at Silvio. The big detective seemed relaxed as he flipped through his notebook, as if Marco's death had nothing to do with him. As if he hadn't subdued the kid by knocking his head against those concrete steps.

"This brings us to the billboard murder," Lieutenant Baez went on. "Cartel profile and lots of negative press. What's the plan?"

"A good one, *teniente*." Gomez smirked. "Macias and Sandor are looking for somebody with a carving knife who knows how to count."

"Thanks, Gomez," Macias said with barely controlled disgust.

"You need any help, you know where we are," Gomez laughed. He had a ponytail and a feeble goatee underscored by a metal rock band tee shirt, low riding jeans, and a shoulder holster. His partner, Castro, was a shade younger but otherwise a close copy.

"Thanks for volunteering," Lieutenant Baez said evenly. "Macias, Sandor, you use Castro and Gomez any way you want. I told the mayor we'd put more manpower on it, get that neighborhood scoured in the next 48 hours. There's a witness somewhere."

Gomez slammed a hand on the table. "We've got open cases, *teniente*. Give it to Cruz and Silvio. They got one less now that their perp croaked himself."

"Your current cases will be listed as Pending." Lieutenant Baez replied.

"Pending?" Gomez sputtered. "What the fuck is Pending?"

"The department is instituting a new tracking system for cases," Lieutenant Baez said, his gaze sweeping around the table. "Every case with a file number will be logged into a new database and assigned a status."

"There's already a system," Emilia said.

"This is a new system," Lieutenant Baez said, his voice perfectly neutral. "All of our 325 open cases have to be entered and assigned a status this week." Again, he circled the table with a glance. "Gomez, you and Castro will report to Macias and Sandor to help on the billboard case. Silvio and Cruz will follow up with the autopsy results for both the Coyuca Lagoon victim and suspect. Find out what the medical examiner has for the billboard murder as well. Ortega and Nuñez, you'll manage the rota. Here's the morning take from Dispatch. Looks like a string of robberies last night." He slid the Dispatch slips across the table to Ortega. "Any questions?"

No one spoke.

Lt Baez stood. "Meeting adjourned."

As the detectives pushed out their chairs and got to their

feet, Lieutenant Baez lifted his chin at Emilia. "Detective Cruz, can I see you for a moment?"

Emilia tucked her notebook under her arm and reached for her empty coffee cup. She was the only female in the squadroom. No doubt *el teniente* was going to ask her to enter the cases into the new database, as if she was a secretary.

She followed him into his office, mentally searching for a polite but firm refusal. Lieutenant Baez gestured for her to take a seat. Emilia perched stiffly on the edge. To her surprise, he settled into the other chair fronting the desk, as if they were two colleagues having a chat.

"I wanted to speak to you." Lieutenant Baez stopped. "Are you comfortable, Detective?"

"Yes, I'm fine." Emilia clasped both hands around the notebook.

"All right." The corner of his mouth quirked up. "I wanted to talk to you because I heard a rumor that Detective Silvio recently lost his wife. A murder. Is that true?"

"Yes, it is," Emilia said. "A home invasion."

"Ah." Lieutenant Baez nodded sadly. "They were married a long time, I take it."

"Twenty years," Emilia said. "They got married as teenagers when Silvio was a boxer."

Lt Baez smoothed his tie. It was not a gesture of nervousness but of wanting to stay unwrinkled. "How's he doing? Do you think he's ready to be back at work?"

Emilia swallowed hard. "What do you mean?"

"Let me be more specific," Lieutenant Baez said. "Someone who has gone through that sort of trauma can have some real emotional issues. Unresolved anger. Grief."

Emilia picked at the edge of the notebook.

"Do you think any of that could have led to the death of the suspect you and Detective Silvio brought in yesterday?"

Madre de Dios, I hope not. "The kid was on a meth high," Emilia said. "It took both of us to subdue him."

"Detective Silvio looks like he can handle just about anything that comes his way," Lieutenant Baez said leadingly.

"Franco's a good cop." Emilia kept her voice neutral, wondering just how much Lieutenant Baez knew about her partner.

Silvio had a long history of walking the edge of career oblivion, starting long ago when his partner Manuel Garcia was killed and trumped-up charges were brought against Silvio. While suspended, Silvio started a side business as a bookie and kept it going even when reinstated. The bookie side job had kicked off a bizarre chain of events related to the money laundering case against the El Pharaoh casino and created the uneasy ceasefire that currently existed with Chief of Police Salazar and union strongman Victor Obregon Sosa, brother of Silvio's late wife Isabel.

"We'll see how it goes," Lieutenant Baez said.

Emilia half rose, still clutching the notebook with both hands. "If that's all then, *teniente*."

Lieutenant Baez circled his desk, sat, and opened a folder.

"One last thing. Your training record."

"Training?" Emilia lowered herself into the chair again.

"I see you have never been to the Senior Investigative Conference," he said. "I'd like to put your name forward. With your permission, of course."

Emilia blinked in surprise. The Senior Investigative Conference was an annual event in Mexico City. For a week, promising law enforcement officers from all over the country trained on all the latest technologies and techniques, attended lectures from experts, examined case studies, and networked with each other. No one made it to a significant leadership position in any police department without attending the Senior Investigative Conference at least once.

"I'm still pretty junior," Emilia pointed out.

"You're ready." Lieutenant Baez smiled, showing perfect white teeth. "Can I put your name forward?"

"Yes, thank you," Emilia said. She owed him now. "*Teniente*, would you like me to input the case files into the new database?"

Lieutenant Baez pushed her training folder away. "Sorry, but I can't spare my best detective for data entry work. I'll get someone from the central administration building's office pool to do it."

"Thank you, *teniente*." Emilia said.

"Thank you, Detective." Lieutenant Baez smiled again as he turned to his computer screen, signaling that the discussion was over.

Emilia closed the office door behind her, almost giddy.

My best detective.

☼

Silvio fell into lockstep with Emilia as she left the squadroom. "What did Baez want?" he asked.

"He asked if I wanted to go to the Senior Investigative Conference this year."

Silvio gave a low whistle. "Nice," he said.

"Look," Emilia said, forcing herself into work mode again. "After the morgue, I think we should go back out to El Loro Rojo. Something about the Schmidts didn't feel right."

"You noticed that too?" Silvio passed a hand over his bristly crew cut. "Their whole dynamic changed when they saw the picture of the El Machete tattoo. She was in charge all of a sudden."

"You think there's a connection to El Machete?"

"Might be paying protection money to them," Silvio said.

"What if the Schmidts are dealing for them?" Emilia asked.

Silvio checked his watch. "The traffic out there is going to fuck up the day if we wait until after Prade does all the autopsies," he said.

Of course he doesn't want to go to the morgue. "Let's go out there first," Emilia said and grabbed her bag and jacket. "Prade won't be done until this afternoon."

They passed the holding cells. Valdez was off. Puente

was behind the desk and gave them a mock salute. Emilia shot him with her thumb and forefinger as Silvio pushed open the door to the parking lot.

They walked out into the sunshine. Silvio grabbed Emilia's arm and hauled her to a stop. "Did he think I killed that kid?"

Emilia yanked her arm away. "What are you talking about?"

"Baez," Silvio said. "Did he say anything about the dead kid?"

The sun glared remorselessly on the rows of parked cars. Most of the unmarked vehicles were impounds seized by the police and unlikely ever to be claimed by their owners. Emilia drove a white Suburban once owned by a couple of money launderers named Hudson from the *El Norte* state of Arizona.

"I told him the kid was probably on a drug high and fighting hard." Emilia pulled on her cropped linen jacket. It was just long enough to hide her shoulder holster.

"I saved you from an ass-kicking," Silvio said.

"Did I say you didn't?" Emilia demanded. "Prade's probably going to find enough drugs in his body to kill an elephant. You heard Lieutenant Baez. There's not going to be a big inquiry over some no-name kid who killed an El Machete meth dealer."

"Maybe," Silvio said. "Maybe not. I'm just checking to make sure you aren't going to throw me under the bus here."

"Maybe I should go back inside," Emilia said tartly. "Tell

Lieutenant Baez how many times you've skipped out on counseling. You and I both know a supervisor can make it mandatory."

Silvio's beefy finger poked the air in front of Emilia's face. "You're not my mother, Cruz. Or my babysitter." His tone was low and controlled, yet full of anger. "I'll decide when the fuck I need to talk to a counselor. You don't get to decide shit."

"Well, hurry up and decide," Emilia snapped. "Because if you killed that kid, we're done. I'm not going down with you."

"Just like a woman," Silvio sneered. "Run out when things get tough. You still don't know what it takes to do this job."

"*Madre de Dios*, Franco," Emilia swore. "You wore that one out long ago."

"Fuck off, Cruz." Silvio abruptly turned and walked away.

Emilia counted to ten before she followed.

Emilia dreamed up a dozen cutting retorts as Silvio drove west. She wished she'd been frank with Lieutenant Baez and said that Silvio had turned into a giant *pendejo* with anger management issues. The loss of his wife had made him unstable and unpredictable and he was making her crazy.

But partners didn't do that to each other.

Silvio turned on the radio to fill the silence as they cruised the winding coastal road toward the beaches at Playa Pie de la Cuesta. Emilia texted Mercedes, whom she hadn't seen in a few weeks. *Shopping soon? I need new work clothes.*

They passed the turnoff for the airport, veered north and finally trundled onto a narrow road that circled the top of the lagoon.

"Why are we going this way?" Emilia demanded. "The El Loro Rojo is closer to the beach."

"Shut up, Cruz. Doing a little recon here."

He swung the car off the pavement and onto a dirt road. They ended up in a clearing that served as a picnic area and launch site for kayakers, as well as local fishermen.

"If I'm not mistaken," Silvio said as he unfastened his seat belt. "The place is on the other side of those trees."

They tramped through a grove of palms, guided by a glimpse of a thatched *palapa* roof. The ground was spongy and Emilia was glad she had on cross trainers instead of loafers or sandals. Mosquitos sang past, speedier here than their cousins in the city. Emilia continually swatted at her ears.

As they neared El Loro Rojo, Emilia saw that they were on a rise. Below them, the hostel huddled in faded glory. The *palapa* was stained with rot near the eaves. The thatch had to be the roof of the big dining room with its sticky vinyl tablecloths, ceramic nonsense on the wall, and the line of well-fed roaches.

The rear door by the kitchen was open, either for

ventilation or as an invitation to scorpions to come feast on the roaches. The two outhouses were as dingy as before, with their scratched signs for *Hombres* and *Mujeres*.

The road leading to the place was quiet except for the screech of seagulls circling overhead. Two minivans were parked in the small lot. If they walked around the side of the building, Emilia knew they would see the skinny strip of sand where they'd found the tent.

She kicked aside a fallen coconut and leaned against the smooth trunk of a palm. They were well concealed on the rise behind the trees.

"You think the German and his wife know more about the dead guy than they let on?" Silvio asked, staring at the hostel.

"Maybe," Emilia said. Silvio never apologized, just picked up the conversation at a point before the argument started. "They switched roles when we showed them his picture."

"He wanted to know if she recognized him." Silvio stared at the hostel. Seagulls fluttered down and pecked at the ground near the rear door. "Why would some dowdy housewife know an El Machete gang member?"

A couple of tanned *gringos* came out of the hostel and crossed to the men's outhouse. Both looked like the Canadian kid they'd interviewed; latter-day hippies paying two pesos to use the toilet when they should have shelled out 12 for the premium shower with soap. They came out a few seconds later and disappeared towards the beach.

Five minutes later, a couple of Mexican teenaged boys emerged from the scrub on the far side of the hostel and stole into the men's outhouse.

"Honor system?" Emilia asked softly.

Silvio snorted. "A deal just went down."

The teens left the outhouse and scrambled back up the rise without sparking a reaction from anyone inside the hostel. As they headed for the safety of the tree line, they took the same overgrown path that Emilia and Silvio had followed.

Silvio moved out of the shadows and blocked the path.

Both teens stopped. "Dude," one of them said nervously.

Silvio opened his jacket to reveal his gun. He held out his hand.

The kid handed over a small plastic bag. After a moment Silvio handed it back. The teens ran off.

"Couple of joints," Silvio said dismissively in response to Emilia's questioning look.

A few older *gringos* in expensive shorts and Panama hats trekked to the outhouses, joking with each other and nervously looking backwards as they returned to the hostel.

"Tour group just discovered the local plumbing," Emilia observed, waving at mosquitos again.

"Wonder what's on the menu down there." Silvio unwrapped a piece of gum.

"Ptomaine," Emilia said. She checked her watch.

"With a side of E.coli." Silvio grinned at his own wit.

"I don't think watching *turistas* is a good use of our time," Emilia said. "We should go back to town. Prade should have the autopsy reports by now."

"Another couple of minutes," Silvio said and snapped his gum.

The stream of tourists using the facilities petered out. A woman in an apron, carrying a plastic bucket of cleaning supplies, stood in the open doorway and spoke to someone over her shoulder. It was a brief conversation. She shuffled over to the men's outhouse and banged on the door.

"That's not Itzel," Emilia said. "Too thin."

"Didn't they say no one else worked here?"

Emilia slapped a mosquito on her hand and flicked away the tiny corpse. "Indeed they did."

"You think they'd be happy if we asked why they lied?"

"Ecstatic," Emilia said.

Itzel appeared carrying a mop. She yelled something indistinct and got an answer from inside the outhouse. She left the mop propped against the wall by the sign reading *Hombres* and went back into the hostel.

The first woman lumbered into the women's outhouse with the mop. Two minutes later she took her cleaning supplies back to the hostel.

"Bet that place sparkles," Emilia said.

They drove out of the clearing and circled back to the road that would take them past the hostel. By the time they could see the front, a local *colectiva* bus was parked in front. The thin woman came out of the hostel with a worn Corona beer tote on her shoulder, and got in.

"Our lucky day," Silvio said, slowing the car to a crawl.

The bus rattled out of the drive and headed west. Silvio tucked in behind, just another vehicle on the road trekking around the lagoon.

The local bus stopped at every collection of cinderblocks and thatch along the roadside. People got on and off carrying chickens, jugs of water, plastic baskets and sweaty toddlers. Every time it slowed, Silvio braked and Emilia stuck her head out the window to see if the Corona tote got off.

The woman finally got off at Barra de Coyuca, a tiny hamlet perched on the west end of Coyuca Lagoon that served tourists lured by the site of the freshwater lake on one side and the ocean on the other. Emilia knew that the lack of potable water was a longstanding problem, no doubt the reason why the residential area was nothing more than a cluster of cement block houses festooned with hammocks and stray goats. The tourist zone was a trio of restaurants and a dock for lagoon rides, with a couple of canopied longboats pulled up on the shore as free advertising.

The Corona tote shuffled off the bus, her flip flops scuffing dust with every step, and headed for a small market building. Silvio parked and they followed her.

The entrance to the market was crowded with displays of knotted twine hammocks of every color, as well as Day of the Dead sugar skulls. Inside, all the stalls looked the same; a jumbled and colorful mass of carved soapstone animals, traditional *muerto* figurines, capiz shell wind chimes, black *barro* pottery vases and ashtrays, paintings of girls and donkeys or girls with earthen water jugs.

The lagoon's cinematic fame lived on, too, in every counter's obligatory selection of bootleg postcards of Rambo looking hungry and invincible and Humphrey Bogart towing the African Queen through leech-filled water.

They found the woman behind the counter of a stall at the back. The same tired merchandise was brightened with the addition of silkscreened tote bags. Shoppers could choose from the seal of Mexico, Corona beer, the likeness of Che Guevara, or a shaggy-haired Sylvester Stallone clutching a knife.

"There you go." Silvio jerked his chin at Rambo as they strolled in, just another couple of tourists. "Eye candy when Hollywood can't get it up."

"Shut up," Emilia muttered. She walked to the counter. "Hello. Do you have any postcards with pictures of birds?"

It was the right question. The woman spread out an assortment of dusty cards with photos of herons and pelicans. Emilia took her time and finally selected two. Silvio looked over her shoulder. "Come, on," he said. "You know you want a bag."

Emilia picked a bag with the iconic Che sketch. "He looks like that guy," she said leadingly.

"Herman Schmidt," Silvio supplied.

The woman smiled uncertainly.

"Do you know him?" Emilia asked. "He runs the El Loro Rojo on the other side of the lagoon."

"Yes, I work there sometimes," the woman said. "On the other side of the lagoon."

Silvio showed her his badge and made introductions. After they all agreed that she wouldn't have to tell Herman and Itzel she'd spoken with them, the woman relaxed. Her name was Ana and it was clear she didn't like her part-time employers.

"I work there three days a week," Ana said. 'The rest of the time I work here."

"Have you worked there long?" Emilia asked.

Ana rolled her eyes. "Too long for what they pay me."

"Docs anyone else work there?" Silvio leaned against the counter.

"Not now but sometimes there is a waitress." Ana blushed a little. "Herman always hires the pretty ones, you know. They work good for a couple of weeks. Then they meet a boy and *pffft*. They don't want to work no more and they disappear."

Emilia tried to look sympathetic at the increased workload this must mean for Ana. "Are they looking for a replacement?"

"After the last one, Itzel said enough," Ana said. "She was mad at Herman but her boy always came around more when there was a waitress."

"Her boy?" Silvio straightened.

"Pablito is a grown man from a different father."

"What does he do?"

"The circus maybe?" Ana grimaced. "I don't ask. He's a strange one. Travels all over, she says. He's not a good son."

Emilia showed Ana the picture of the beheading victim.

"Is this Pablito?"

"No." Ana pushed a knuckle to her mouth. "*Por Dios.*"

Emilia scrolled to a picture of the tattoo. "Have you ever seen anyone around here with that tattoo?"

"No, never."

"Anyone with that tattoo ever come to talk to Herman?" Silvio stuck a Rambo tee shirt on top of the Che tote bag and laid down 200 pesos.

"No."

Ana didn't know anything else. She slowly wrapped their purchases with waxy paper, darting smiles at Silvio as she painstakingly sealed the packages with cellophane tape. Emilia bit the inside of her cheek to keep from laughing at his discomfort.

"*Rayos.*" Silvio took a deep breath as they left the market to amble along the sandy waterfront. "Okay. The Schmidts lied to us about their help."

Emilia ripped open the package, extracted the Rambo tee, and thrust it at Silvio. "She only works part-time. Maybe they forgot."

"Still doesn't explain why they acted strange about the tattoo."

"I know. They recognized it."

Silvio beeped open the car and tossed the tee into the back. "I think the Schmidts are probably paying protection money so El Machete doesn't burn the place down."

"El Machete is using their beach to sell meth and the Schmidts know it?"

"Probably part of the deal." Silvio shrugged, the heavy shoulders moving like fluid machinery. "They've got a vested interest in turning a blind eye to whatever El Machete is doing outside their front door. The El Loro Rojo stays open and they stay alive."

Gangs threatened small business owners every day. Those that paid up stayed in business. Those that didn't were burned out or the owners mysteriously disappeared.

The dismal cycle was helped along by cops who colluded with the gangs and got a slice of the protection pie.

"Same old story," Emilia said.

CHAPTER 5

"Here for three, Detective Cruz." Doctor Antonio Prade looked over the top of his tortoise shell reading glasses. "You must have won the *lotéria*."

"You're having a slow day, despite my three," Emilia said. She coughed, tasting the morgue's cloying smell of dead flesh and eye-watering antiseptic in the back of her throat.

Silvio had gone back to El Loro Rojo to ask about El Machete gang members using the hostel and Emilia was stuck on morgue duty. She liked the medical examiner, but trips to the gruesome place never got any easier.

The last time Emilia was at the morgue, body bags on trolleys lined the hallways courtesy of a prison uprising. Most of the dead were victims of gang rivalries. Usually affiliated with one of the powerful drug cartels, the gangs fought for a share of Acapulco territory to use as a lucrative transit point for drugs headed for *El Norte*.

She and Prade were in the main examining room next to a body table covered with a white sheet. Prade usually wrote up his reports sitting at his worktable and Emilia was gratified to see progress in the form of a laptop computer and small printer. For as long as she'd been a detective Prade had written out reports longhand on an antiquated form interleaved with carbon paper. Detectives were sent the yellow copy from the middle unless they wanted to wait as long as a week for Prade's secretary to type up the report and email it. Every detective had taken to frequenting the morgue for the more important cases in order to get the quick and dirty results while they were still fresh in Prade's mind.

"It won't last." Prade fished a paper surgical mask out of a box on his worktable and handed it to her. "The slow days never do. So which would you like to see first?"

The medical examiner was in his mid-50's, with cropped brown hair and tortoiseshell reading glasses perched on the end of his nose. He wore a plaid shirt under his white lab coat, which today was misbuttoned, the hem and collar higher on one side than the other.

Emilia respected him, not only for his obvious medical skill and dedication to a difficult job, but because he treated her as respectfully as he treated the male detectives. Moreover, he knew about the *Las Perdidas* list and always let her know when an unidentified woman passed through the morgue.

"The billboard victim," Emilia replied.

Prade adjusted his glasses, consulted a clipboard, then crossed the room to the bank of body drawers set into the wall. "Steady now," he cautioned. "It's not a pretty sight."

Emilia pressed the surgical mask over her nose and mouth as Prade hauled open the drawer to reveal a flaccid body. An involuntary shudder rolled down her spine at the sight of what had once been a face. Shredded gray skin surrounded a gaping hole. The head was hollow and she could see through it to the bottom of the drawer.

The torso was laced with knife wounds and the crudely carved number she'd seen in the photograph in the squadroom. The genitals were missing as though bitten off by a wild animal.

"The cause of death was an execution-style gunshot to the back of the head," Prade said. "Ligature marks on the neck and wrists suggest the victim was bound while alive. The ligature marks around the ankles were made with a different diameter material. Those were created after the victim was deceased."

"And the mutilation?" Emilia gestured vaguely at the torso and groin.

"Done while the victim was still alive."

Emilia felt nausea rise and fought it down. "Time of death?"

Prade raised his eyebrows in a silent question if she'd seen enough. Emilia nodded and he rolled the mutilated body back into the drawer before answering. "At least 24 hours before the body was found."

"So tortured, killed, and strung up," Emilia said.

"In that order."

"Unidentified?"

"His fingerprints weren't in the system."

Few bodies in Acapulco's morgue were ever identified. Unless relatives could be notified to come and collect the body, unidentified bodies expired after ten days. Any unclaimed were then cremated.

Prade closed the drawer and opened the one next to it.

"The beheading victim is here."

Emilia felt queasy. Prade's world was quiet, yet full of the voices of the dead. He was showing her bodies as casually as if he was showing her shoes in a store but she felt all their unspoken stories tugging at her.

"Cause of death was blood loss from rupture of the carotid artery," Prade said. "The assailant used two implements. A very sharp knife for an initial left to right slash and a tool such as an axe to break the neck and sever the head completely."

Over the top edge of her surgical mask, Emilia gazed down at another mutilated body. Another wave of nausea, smaller this time, rose up. Again, she fought it down, grateful that she had a mostly empty stomach.

The body was intact except for the head, which was posed as if it still was attached. At least the eyes were closed.

The man had been fit and muscular. Even in death, his body was contoured like that of an athlete. No telltale needle marks to identify him as a junkie. His hands were not hardened with the scars and callouses of manual labor. The El Machete dagger tattoo etched down the inside of his forearm but otherwise his skin was unblemished.

"There's not a scratch on him, is there?" Emilia asked.

"If you are thinking he just laid there and let the assailant do whatever, you're right." Prade nodded. "Toxicology showed that his system was full of Rohypnol."

"The date rape drug?"

Prade pulled the drawer out to its fullest extent and

pinched the flaccid left thigh muscle. "There's a small puncture wound. The Rohypnol was injected. Within a matter of minutes the victim was immobilized with a very high dose."

Reinas, as Rohypnol was called on the street, was hard to get now. When Emilia was in high school it was so common that girls at parties knew to never drink from an open container. She and her friends always broke the seal on a bottle or can themselves, never drank a shared beverage, and of course, no one ever, ever gave their drink to a boy to hold.

"Time of death between 3:00 and 4:00 am yesterday morning," Prade went on.

Emilia stepped back. Her stomach was roiling.

"Are you ready for the last one on your list?"

Emilia held her thumb and first finger together in the universal Mexican *wait a moment* sign, then fled down the hallway to the exit. She shoved open the door and sucked in clean air. The stench of the morgue clung to her clothes. Her skin crawled as if her clothes had turned into cockroaches.

A few deep breaths and she went back. Prade didn't say anything but rolled out a third drawer to show her Marco, too young to be dead. Much too young to be a murderer. Too young to be sliced open for a full autopsy and laced back together with twine.

"Our young heart attack victim," Prade said.

"Heart attack?" Emilia had not expected to hear that.

"He had myocarditis, an inflammation of the heart muscle," Prade said. "The condition, coupled with overexertion, methamphetamine use, and severe dehydration, produced cardiac arrest."

"Are you sure? It wasn't a brain hemorrhage? Nothing like that?"

"I have my notes right here." Prade went to his worktable and scooped up some papers. "He had bruising on the right temple along with residue consistent with sand and cement. Is that significant?"

Prade had been a friend for too long to lie. Emilia nodded. "He was wild. Attacked me, nearly broke Silvio's nose. It took the two of us to subdue him and get him cuffed."

Prade peered at Emilia's cheek. "Is your bruise from that altercation?"

Emilia self-consciously fingered her swollen cheekbone. It wasn't as bad as last night but was starting to discolor. "Yes."

"And you were worried," Prade asserted. "Detective Silvio would be blamed for manhandling a suspect and leading to his death. Yet another black mark on your partner's record. You shouldn't be protecting him, Emilia."

Emilia didn't reply, uncomfortable with how easily Prade had seen through her. Yes, she wanted to protect Silvio, at least until he got over the loss of his wife. Not that helping him was an easy thing to do.

Prade left the papers on the desk, went back to the drawer, and rolled Marco's body back into its slot. Emilia dropped her mask into the step-on trash can by the worktable. "Did the bloodstains on his clothes and hands match that of the beheading victim?" she asked.

"It's all in the report," Prade said and nodded over his shoulder at the worktable.

Emilia picked up the paperwork Prade had left. "I thought you were using a computer now," she said.

Prade gave a sardonic laugh. "Dinosaurs still roam the earth."

The report on Marco was on top. Emilia skimmed it until she saw what she was looking for. Blood taken from the fibers of Marco's clothing and on the skin of his forearms matched that of the beheaded man found in the tent. In addition to the victim's blood, the medical examiner had also found sand and wood fibers under Marco's fingernails, tequila on the right knee of his pants, and minute amounts of black paint in the creases of his right palm.

Emilia put down the report, a new scenario unfolding in her head. Marco had handled the broken and blackened *muerto* figures in the tent and poured out the tequila as an offering to Santa Muerte. But if Marco had created the altar, he would have had to carry supplies for the *ofrenda* with him, get them from another camper or someone at the El Loro Rojo.

"Are all three victims connected?"

"What?" Emilia jumped, so lost in her thoughts she didn't realize Prade was standing next to her.

"Are the three victims connected?" Prade asked again as he took off his lab coat. He draped it on a hook.

"No," Emilia said. "Only Marco and his murder victim."

"Not the other victim?"

"They were found miles apart," Emilia pointed out. "One in a tent on the beach at Coyuca Lagoon and the other swinging from a billboard along the highway this side of the Maxitunel. Why do you ask?"

Prade opened the door for Emilia. "Both carried very imaginative messages, don't you think? Santa Muerte. The number nine."

"Simple murder isn't good enough these days," she said.

By the time Emilia dragged herself back to the squadroom, most of the other detectives had left for the day. Silvio had not returned, which didn't surprise her given the distance to Coyuca Lagoon and the gridlock traffic he'd encounter at the end of the workday.

The lab hadn't picked up the evidence bags and they were still on her desk. The Santa Muerte banner was folded and sealed in a plastic evidence bag but somehow Emilia still felt its malevolence. The broken black *muertos* stared at her through the clear plastic. She was drawn to the paper triangles. Almost against her will, Emilia took out one, unfolded and read.

Sainted Santa Muerte. Cast Your divine protection over your believers. Bring anguish and destruction to Your enemies and to all they hold dear. Destroy those who do not understand Your will. In the complete destruction of Our enemies Your disciples seek mercy and redemption.

The prayer, if that's what it could be called, was almost identical to the other she'd read. Not some crude cartel screech but an invocation written by someone with education, good handwriting, and a deeply held belief in Santa Muerte's power.

Emilia stuffed the note back into the evidence bag, made a pot of coffee and logged onto the police intranet, hunting for information about the secretive El Machete gang. She'd run into the gang before but from a safe distance. It was thought that the gang was aligned with the violent Zetas cartel but there was precious little in the online files and no indication that the gang was devoted to Santa Muerte.

Her phone chimed with a text. She was surprised to see it was 8:00 pm. Kurt was checking to see that she was okay. Emilia swiftly texted back pounded out her report on the medical examiner's findings, and logged off.

She grabbed her shoulder bag from its resting place atop the *Las Perdidas* binder, knowing she was stretched too thin both physically and emotionally. Sore from the fracas yesterday and rattled by the Santa Muerte connection. Mental pictures of the bodies at the morgue were stuck in her head. Neither could she shake off the argument with Silvio or the dread of knowing that it wasn't finished.

The last one out of the squadroom was supposed to turn out the lights. Emilia hesitated, her hand on the switch, oddly loath to turn her back on Santa Muerte in the dark.

She dropped her hand and walked out. The fluorescent ceiling lights hummed softly.

CHAPTER 6

Only crazy people swim this early. Still half asleep, Emilia clawed her way through the water. The waves continually pushed her backwards, but she kicked hard and reached deep. The floating dock rose and fell ahead of her like a tantalizing target. Kurt and Jacques Anatole, the Palacio Réal's head chef and Kurt's best friend, reached it before she did. Both were on their feet, rivulets of water running off their bodies, as she grabbed the ladder. Kurt helped her climb up.

"You are both *loco*," Emilia gasped as she bent double and tried to catch her breath. She'd always thought of herself as a strong swimmer, but these men were triathletes. They swam nearly every day, constantly competing against each other.

"Nice job, Em." Kurt gave her a wet hug.

"I can't believe you talked me into this." Emilia straightened and adjusted the straps on her red two-piece suit.

Kurt turned her to face east. "Just watch."

The three of them stood on the gently bobbing dock as the sun came over the horizon. Gold streaks flared over the ocean and light gradually etched across the sky. The whole world looked clean and new. Emilia felt as if they were the only souls awake to see it.

"*Magnifique*," Jacques murmured. "This is why I stay."

"I thought you stayed," Kurt said, his arm around Emilia's bare waist. "Because you like working for me."

Jacques grinned. Lean and angular, with a sharp, pointed chin, the Frenchman had also worked for Kurt in Las Vegas. "No, I stay because I hope to steal Emilia one day."

"You stay to keep me from starving." Emilia bumped her head against the chef's shoulder. Originally wary of the hotel staff, Emilia had gradually come to know and like most of them, but Jacques was the only one she considered a friend.

"Tonight, I will make the risotto especially for you, Emilia," Jacques said.

Kurt kissed her cheek. "It means you have to come home at a decent hour."

"Well, if it means Jacques will make me risotto," she said. "I guess I can make an effort."

"Your strategy is working," Kurt said to Jacques and Emilia laughed.

She watched as the two men dove off the side of the dock and struck out for the buoy marking the entrance to the hotel's boat marina. Kurt swam a two-mile circuit when he came out this early.

Emilia stepped off the dock and plunged feet first into the water. She bobbed to the surface, unable to keep a grin from her face. It didn't matter that she had a murder to investigate or a partner who needed counseling. Jumping in feet first was always just plain fun.

She struck out for shore, feeling intensely alive. The ocean was calm, yet the current gently helped her toward the sand. When Emilia felt her foot drag against the bottom she stood and walked out of the foamy water to the teak lounge chair where she'd left her towel.

Christine Boudreau, the Palacio Réal's head concierge, dropped her own towel on a nearby chair, revealing a pink bikini and white skin stretched over a bony frame. "Good morning, Emilia."

"Hello, Christine." Emilia managed a smile as she found her sunglasses on the seat of the chaise and put them on. "Early morning workout?"

"Whenever I can." Christine flashed the pained smile she gave to difficult guests and headed for the water. She was so thin that Emilia could count the vertebrae inching down her spine between the bits of pink nylon. Her elbows could probably cut paper.

Emilia knew that Christine was there to watch Kurt. The concierge no doubt thought she hid it well, but Christine's crush on her boss was clear as day to Emilia. Kurt wasn't interested, but it had taken Emilia months before she believed him. After all, Christine spoke English with Kurt and was in the same business. Plus, she had that milky *gringo* skin.

Christine hit the water with an ungainly splash and dog paddled towards the swimming dock. Emilia swallowed a laugh, tied the towel around her waist and walked toward the hotel, swinging her arms as she went.

She felt strong.

Unbreakable.

☼

The body hung from a billboard for the famous Las Brisas resort. The picture of a pool shaded by palms, with a pink jeep parked in the distance, was marred by bloody feet thumping against the bottom half.

The man hung head down, the head hidden by the foliage lining the side of the Carretera Escénica highway. The groin and torso were hacked and bloody. The upside down number 9 carved into the abdomen appeared as 6.

Emilia heard herself scream as she braked the Suburban, nearly standing on the pedal as the heavy vehicle fishtailed all over the road. Coffee sprayed out of her Palacio Réal mug and into her lap as the Suburban ground to a stop just beyond the billboard. Gulping air, Emilia cut the engine.

Maná bellowed from the stereo. Emilia jammed her hand against the knob to turn it off.

A car shot by, horn blasting in annoyance, the driver obviously paying no attention to the body swinging above.

Emilia found her phone and got out of the Suburban. Her jeans were soaked with cappuccino. Her throat was raw from the involuntary scream.

The Carretera Escénica was an extension of the main artery that ran all around the lip of Acapulco Bay before straightening into a scenic drive between mountain and ocean. It was the oceanside route between Acapulco and the upscale resorts along Puerta Marques like the Palacio Réal,

Las Brisas and the newer hotels further east along the Costa Grande.

It continued into downtown Acapulco and went around the lip of the bay, lined with shops, skyscrapers, and signage as its name changed to Costera Miguel Aléman, better known as la Costera. This was the most heavily travelled piece of real estate in all of Acapulco. Probably in the entire state of Guerrero.

In another hour, when the traffic got heavy in both directions, a mutilated body swinging above the highway was going to attract a lot of the wrong attention.

It wasn't just a body. A white cloth flapped below the billboard, tied into place with more of the same rope wrapped around the corpse's feet. It was a *narcomanta*, a banner often left with cartel victims to send a specific message. This one was no exception.

As the cloth billowed in the breeze, the words painted in block letters were easy to read.

COMUNICADO! Do not follow a worthless priest and traitor. He will be destroyed and you as well. ATTN, El Commandante.

The irony of signing the message with *ATTN*, the abbreviation for *sincerely*, wasn't lost on Emilia.

She snapped some pictures of the *narcomanta and* the dangling body. The area between the road and the pedestal supporting the billboard was full of scrubby pines. Whoever had put the body up there, with the big sheet billowing next to it, had worked hard.

Back in the Suburban, Emilia drew in a couple of shaky breaths before she called Silvio.

"Pretty early, Cruz," he said without preamble.

"I'm on the Carretera Escénica," Emilia said in a rush. "There's a body strung up on a billboard. Cut up just like the one on Sunday. This time there's a *narcomanta*, too."

"*Rayos*," Silvio swore. "Okay, on my way. I'll let Macias and Sandor know. You call Dispatch and Baez."

Emilia told him where to find the Suburban, broke the connection, and called Dispatch.

The morning traffic grew increasingly heavy as she waited for the crime scene techs and tried not to look at the bloody husk of a man whose feet thumped into the billboard with every gust off the ocean. Two patrol cars showed up and blocked traffic in both directions to the accompaniment of angry horns.

Emilia talked briefly to the uniformed cops but they soon had their hands full. People got out of their cars and came to look and complain, only to be stunned into silence or sobs and be chivvied back into their vehicles by the uniforms. Eventually the honking subsided.

Ten minutes later, Macias, Sandor, and Silvio arrived, followed by the morgue wagon and the crime scene van. Both vehicles drove up on the shoulder to get by the stopped traffic.

Emilia climbed out of the Suburban and met the other

detectives as they approached. Bayardo got out of the driver's seat of the crime scene van. The passenger was Rodriguez, a senior tech.

Rodriguez shook hands all around, then peered at the bloody body still swinging from the billboard. "Same thing as the Maxitunel on Sunday," he said.

"With a *narcomanta* signed by somebody calling themselves El Commandante," Emilia replied.

"Just what Acapulco needs," Rodriguez said. "More people in charge."

Sandor cut his eyes to the banner still flapping overhead. "Let's find some prints on this thing."

"Can you touch this shit?" Silvio asked Bayardo.

Rodriguez glared at Silvio.

"Sure," Bayardo said without looking at either man.

Rodriguez gave the group a curt nod. He and Bayardo took their cases from the van and headed to the base of the billboard pedestal.

Silvio pulled Emilia to the Suburban as Macias and Sandor plunged into the scrubby pines around the base of the billboard pedestal along with the techs. "What did you find out at the morgue yesterday?" he asked quietly.

"Marco was full of meth and his victim's blood was under his fingernails as well as all over his clothes," Emilia said. "He was definitely the killer."

"And." Silvio looked at her as if he couldn't believe she'd missed the point of the conversation.

"And he died of a heart attack. Had some sort of heart

condition. My-o-something. I don't remember. Prade said it kills student athletes. The combination of the disease, meth, and dehydration killed him."

"Prade was sure?"

"He had a bruise on his head, but it wasn't a factor."

"Okay, then." Silvio sagged against the Suburban as if all the air had gone out of him.

Emilia folded her arms and watched Bayardo play out the rope from his perch on the billboard. She shielded her eyes with her right hand. The body was heavy and the breeze made it twirl and bounce against the pedestal of the billboard.

Silvio pushed himself off the fender to better see Bayardo lower the body to the morgue team waiting below the billboard. "Shit, that guy's got guts to get up there and do that. Wonder what was wrong with him on Sunday?"

"Santa Muerte," she reminded Silvio.

"I'd be a lot more worried about being three stories up on a tiny ledge," Silvio said, staring at the unfolding drama. "Instead of stuffing some crackpot saint shit into a plastic bag."

"*Madre de Dios*, he's going to fall," Emilia gasped. Bayardo dropped the rope and nearly missed his footing on the catwalk rimming the bottom of the billboard.

Rodriguez called up to him and was rewarded with a thumbs-up signal.

Emilia held her breath as Bayardo gingerly made his way back along the catwalk and untied the *narcomanta*. The cloth flapped in the breeze and it was a miracle that the tech kept his balance. Finally, Bayardo dropped the banner to the ground and levered himself down the rungs of the pedestal. Emilia huffed out air and drew in a clean lungful.

The morgue workers came out of the scrub pine below the billboard with the body bag, followed by Rodriguez and Bayardo weighed down with cases and evidence bags.

"Do we have any fallout from the Coyuca Lagoon case to clean up?" Emilia asked. "See if El Machete sends somebody else out to sell meth on the beach? Ask the Schmidts if they are paying protection to the gang?"

Silvio snorted. "Coyuca Lagoon was a murder case. We caught the killer. Not our problem he had heart trouble. Case closed."

Bayardo stowed the crime scene gear in the van while Rodriguez spoke to Macias and Sandor. The young tech worked conscientiously and never once looked at the two detectives standing by the Suburban.

But somehow, Emilia knew that he wanted to.

The billboard murders were the new priority. The Coyuca Lagoon case was done and dusted, the murder of a meth addict looking to score who killed the dealer, both of whom would probably remain unidentified. Emilia figured that she and Silvio could keep an eye on things out there, but it was off the beaten path and unless Herman or Itzel Schmidt made a statement, there was no reason to investigate anything else.

People like Herman and Itzel never went to the police. The few that did never survived.

After the morning meeting, Emilia tossed her shoulder bag into the drawer on top of the *Las Perdidas* binder. All the evidence bags from the Coyuca Lagoon murder were still on her desk.

"Call the lab and tell them to pick this shit up," she said as Silvio lowered himself into his desk chair.

Silvio snorted as he pecked at his keyboard. "It's a closed case. They won't want it now. Call them yourself."

"I already did and it's still here."

"Not my problem." Silvio slid his mug across the two desktops to her. "Here, *chica*. Make yourself useful."

"*Pendejo*. Get your own coffee." Emilia grabbed her mug, filled it from the coffeemaker by the copier, and came back to the pile of Santa Muerte paraphernalia on her desk.

Silvio leaned back in his swivel chair and regarded her. "You know, you don't look so good."

"Like you'd know what 'good' looks like." Emilia inhaled some caffeine then sent his mug skittering back to his desk.

Silvio caught the mug before it smashed against the back of his computer monitor. "Maybe you should go home. Get one of Hollywood's minions to rub your feet or something."

"I just need to stop seeing that guy's guts in my head." Emilia slumped into her desk chair, stretched out her legs, and smacked her foot into something lumpy and unyielding.

"What the hell?"

There was a knapsack under the desk.

Emilia hauled it out. "*Madre de Dios*. It's the knapsack Marco had with him at El Loro Rojo."

Silvio opened his desk drawer and grabbed some latex gloves. "Let's hope we don't find some medicine for whatever crap heart disease the kid had."

"That's all you can say?" Emilia found a pair of gloves of her own.

Silvio unzipped the main compartment, took out a wadded-up nylon bag, and handed it to Emilia. Inside were more plastic zip top bags each containing several dozen pills. Next came a small aluminum box, the kind that expensive mints came in.

Emilia opened it to see three small blue pills.

"Blue *reinas*," she said. "Date rape drugs. The same stuff that was injected into our Santa Muerte victim."

"Evidence against little Marco is piling up." Silvio unrolled a stained tee shirt to reveal an old fashioned straight razor and a small hatchet. The razor was closed but dark with the same dried blood crusting the hatchet's blade."

"He had wood under his nails." Emilia knew that a sample of wood from the scratched axe handle would match.

"Nice." Silvio pulled out more incriminating items: a large canvas print of Santa Muerte, a wad of papers and photos held together with a wooden clothespin, a wrinkled paper bag, a small bottle of tequila, three black gauze-wrapped candles, a notebook with a school crest on the cover, a cheap pay-as-you-go cell phone, candy wrappers, peso coins. The last thing he pulled out was a skinny paperback book entitled *El Libro de la Santa Muerte.*

"What the hell kind of kid was he?" Emilia quickly scrolled through the cell phone log. "One outgoing call. That's it."

Silvio tossed his gloves and sat in front of his computer. "What's the number?"

Emilia read off both the cell phone number and the one from the call log.

A moment later Silvio worked his swivel chair around the side of their joined desks. "Unlisted, both of them. Burner phones. Call it."

Emilia hit redial. The logged number rang five times and disconnected. "Out of service."

He snorted. "No surprise."

She tossed the phone aside and unclipped the bundle of papers and photos. More handwritten prayers plus three index cards, each with an address in the same handwriting. There were also three photographs, each showing a group of people. In each photograph a man's face was circled.

"Was this our victim in the tent?" Emilia showed one of the photos to Silvio.

He studied it. "Yeah, maybe."

She spread out the index cards. One simply said *tent, El Loro Rojo, Coyuca Lagoon.*

Silvio looked over her shoulder. "Addresses and pictures of his victims. Little Marco was a hitman. A *sicario.*"

The paper bag held more broken black *muerto* figurines. Emilia closed it up again without touching any of the fragile Santa Muerte symbols. "All this stuff. Marco hauled all this out to the beach to make the altar, didn't he?"

"Wrong question, Cruz." Silvio looked grim. "Three pictures and enough shit for more altars. Who's supposed to be next?"

Emilia slumped into her desk chair. "Three pictures but only one Santa Muerte banner."

Silvio scowled at her. "So?"

"Three pictures. Three intended victims. We know he already made one altar, and this is enough crap for another. Does that mean there's another altar somewhere?" She tapped the pictures. "With another victim?"

Silvio nodded. "Okay. Kid was a *sicario*. Walking around with information about his targets, including addresses and pictures. Kills them and leaves a scary *ofrenda* to Santa Muerte next to each body. Why?"

"These pills have to be worth some big money."

"Killing's a cheap game these days." Silvio grabbed his coffee mug and stalked away.

Emilia picked up the school notebook. The maroon cardboard cover was embossed with a shield backed by crossed swords and the words "Colegio San Bruno" centered in the design. The first page was a form completed with the owner's name and personal information. She flipped through the pages. Algebra equations. Math problems. Worksheets.

"Marco Sandino Varela," she read out loud as Silvio

came back with a steaming mug. Emilia turned the notebook and held it up so her partner could see.

"What's that?"

"Looks like he was a student at a school called Colegio San Bruno."

Silvio sank into his chair with the mug. "I'll check to see if he's got a record."

Emilia stripped off her latex gloves, punched her password into her computer and entered the name in the national *cédula* identity database. She got a hit for Marco Sandino Varela and pulled up his *cédula*.

The smiling young man in the grainy ID photo was less gaunt than the wasted kid she and Silvio had arrested. There was an address in Chilpancingo, the capital of the state of Guerrero. Emilia plugged in a reverse search and found the *cédulas* for Vicente Sandino Hoya and Paulina Varela Lopez. From the dates of birth, she was certain that they were Marco's parents.

Emilia was also certain that she recognized the name of Vicente Sandino Hoya.

"No record," Silvio reported over the top of their computer monitors. "What have you got?"

"I'm not sure." Emilia went over to the single computer in the squadroom that had an open internet connection. Two minutes later she was staring at a screen full of links with the name of Marco's father, Vicente Sandino Hoya, emblazoned across each one.

She clicked the first link and was taken to a recent story

from the online edition of *Reforma*, the leading newspaper in Mexico City.

Vicente Sandino Hoya, chairman of the PRI political party for the state of Guerrero, and his wife, a noted physician, issued an impassioned plea today for the safe return of their son, missing since early September. Marco Sandino Varela aged 17 was an honor student at the exclusive Colegio San Bruno boarding school in Acapulco when he went missing. The family has not received a ransom request.

"Franco," Emilia called. "Look him up in the Missing Persons database.

"Already on it," Silvio growled.

Emilia printed the *Reforma* story.

"*Rayos*," Silvio swore loudly.

Emilia came back to his desk, printout in hand. The report on his screen made her stomach cramp.

The Missing Persons report on Marco Sandino Varela was dated a few days before the news story in *Reforma*. The case number revealed that it had been generated in Mexico City, not Chilpancingo or Acapulco.

Administrators at the Colegio San Bruno, an exclusive preparatory boarding school in Acapulco, reported Marco Sandino Varela missing to his parents a month after the beginning of the term in August. Kidnapping was suspected but the school did not report any suspicious persons on campus. Detectives from Mexico City travelled to Acapulco to interview friends, teachers, and administrators, all of whom described a well-adjusted student who enjoyed water sports and planned to go to medical school. No one had claimed responsibility for his kidnapping nor had a ransom been demanded.

Silvio's finger jabbed at the screen. "Why the fuck were cops from Mexico City investigating a Missing Persons case in Acapulco and no one told us?"

Emilia pressed a hand to her forehead. This was not how she had wanted her day to end. There was risotto waiting for her. "We are so screwed."

"We just identified the kid," Silvio pointed out and printed the Missing Persons report. "That's a good thing."

"No, it's not." Emilia perched on the corner of his desk and read the rest of the article out loud, making sure he paid attention to the last two sentences.

Vicente Sandino Hoya is the PRI party chairman for the state of Guerrero. He is a close political ally of Carlota Montoya Perez, the up and coming political powerhouse who is the mayor of Acapulco.

There was a long silence as Silvio regarded the ceiling.

"You're right," he said at length. "We're screwed.

Emilia collected all the printouts and the school notebook and went to Lieutenant Baez's office. His door was closed. Their new *teniente* probably had no idea about the uneasy relationship between Carlota Montoya Perez and the Acapulco police department.

She hesitated. It was never easy to be the bearer of bad tidings.

Silvio's fist reached around her shoulder and thumped on the door.

CHAPTER 7

The next morning when Emilia drove into the parking lot behind the police station, four big black SUVs idled parallel to the rear entrance. Two carried discreet flags with the seal of the city of Acapulco.

Carlota's security detail.

Emilia dug out her phone. Her querying text to Silvio was answered with a succinct warning: *Carlota in office*.

Puentes was behind the holding cell desk. The young man's eyes were as big as *jitomates*. Emilia raised her eyebrows in a silent question.

"Your lieutenant's got company," Puentes said. He leaned over the desk, looked from side to side before confiding, "They called Valdez to come in early. It's about the kid that died the other day, isn't it?"

"Don't worry," Emilia said with more conviction than she felt. "Meth and a bad heart killed him, not any of us."

She shot him with her thumb and forefinger and went down the hall.

Half a dozen burly men in dark suits and earpieces leaned against the wall outside the squadroom. She recognized two of them, not from Carlota's security detail, but from that of Chief of Police Rodrigo Salazar.

Inside the squadroom, every desk was empty as if the other detectives had fled before an impending storm. Lieutenant Baez and Silvio were both seated at the conference table, along with the visitors.

Even if she hadn't seen his elaborate uniform, she would have recognized Chief Salazar's bald head, high domed forehead, and long aristocratic nose. His eyebrows were thick, nearly coming together over his nose, and balanced the lack of hair on the top of his head.

Victor Obregon Sosa, head of the police union for the state of Guerrero, sat across from Chief Salazar, wearing a black suit. His eyes flickered over Emilia.

At their last meeting, she'd seen him broken and afraid for his life. In every encounter before that he'd looked at her as easy prey. Sex was always on offer. But since she and Silvio busted the money laundering ring at the El Pharaoh casino, things were different. Emilia wasn't quite sure what to expect from him today.

Carlota sat next to Obregon, impatiently jabbing at the screen of her cellphone with a red lacquered fingernail. Her jet black hair brushed her shoulders and framed the well-known face. Carlota's makeup was so perfect as to be nearly invisible, but Emilia knew no woman was that gorgeous without some help. Her age was a well-kept secret; the woman could have been anything from 25 to 50 years old.

The mayor's face adorned posters all over the city, exhorting citizens to recycle and telling tourists that the city was the safest party they'd never want to leave. Today she wore a pale blue knit suit with a ruffled blouse in the same shade.

In her jeans, skinny black tee shirt, and beige linen jean

jacket, Emilia felt at a distinct disadvantage.

"Please join us, Detective Cruz," Lieutenant Baez said formally.

There was no where to hide. Emilia took a seat at the table.

"Detective Cruz," Carlota said. Her voice was like steel. "How nice to see you again."

"Good morning, señora," Emilia said. "Chief Salazar."

Lieutenant Baez introduced Vicente Sandino Hoya, a handsome, bespectacled man in a finely tailored suit and silk tie. Emilia guessed him to be in his early forties, youthful good looks enhanced by regular facials, massages, and expensive food supplements.

His wife, Doctora Varela, was a thin woman wearing a severe black sleeveless dress. Her hair was pulled into a sleek bun. Unlike her husband, she looked exhausted and her eyes were red-rimmed from weeping.

"Detectives Cruz and Silvio were the arresting officers," Lieutenant Baez said. "I'd like to ask them to add any relevant information as we discuss your son's situation."

Emilia realized that there was a folder in front of each of the four visitors. Lieutenant Baez walked them through the discovery of the murder victim at Coyuca Lagoon, Marco's arrest, and his death and the internal inquiry. Sandino intently examined the various reports as *el teniente* referred to each one, as if the political boss was not accustomed to reading swiftly.

"No." Doctora Varela slammed her hands on the folder

after five minutes of dry police reports. "I cannot believe that my son took drugs and killed a complete stranger. You have no proof. No proof of anything."

"Doctora," Lieutenant Baez said calmly. "You have our deepest sympathies. But the autopsy and toxicology results for both the victim and Marco are not open to a different interpretation."

"This says he died of heart failure," Sandino protested. "That's a clean and tidy way to absolve your police department of guilt, Carlota."

"If he had myocarditis, I would have known." Doctora Varela's voice rose an octave as she spoke over her husband. "I would have known if my own son was dying."

Carlota reached across the table and put her hand over that of Doctora Varela. The mayor's dark nails set off a ring with a raw aquamarine stone in a gold setting.

Emilia had never wanted such jewelry before, but she did now.

"Paulina," Carlota murmured. "There's been a mistake, I'm sure of it."

Chief Salazar didn't react. Lieutenant Baez stiffened, as did Silvio. Ignoring the others, Obregon smiled lazily at Emilia.

"Detective Cruz," Lieutenant Baez said. "Do you still have the evidence taken from the crime scene and the knapsack belonging to Marco Sandino Varela?"

"Yes, *teniente*."

"Bring it here, please."

"Rodrigo," Carlota said to Chief Salazar, her tone laced with warning.

"I don't think the bereaved family needs to see this, Baez," the chief said sharply.

"If it has to do with my son," Sandino snapped. "I want to see whatever trick you're going to pull."

"If you please, Detective," Lieutenant Baez said forcefully.

Emilia felt every sullen stare like a bullet in her back as she went to her desk and got the knapsack and the evidence bags full of Santa Muerte paraphernalia. She put them on the table in front of Lieutenant Baez.

Carlota drew back in distaste. Obregon looked amused.

"That's Marco's pack." Doctora Varela blinked rapidly. "He carried his laptop computer in it when he went to school."

"Could you please describe what you found, Detective." Lieutenant Baez's tone was even.

Emilia admired his composure. Even Silvio looked composed, the *pendejo*, while she felt like a flea on a hot skillet. A trickle of sweat ran down the side of her neck and into the cotton of her tee shirt.

"Yes, *teniente*." Still standing, Emilia took a deep breath. "As Lieutenant Baez said, on Sunday morning, Detective Silvio and I responded to a report of a dead body on the beach at Coyuca Lagoon. Upon arrival, we found a body with a severed head next to a shrine to Santa Muerte. We have pictures as well as the items from the altar." She unfurled the Santa Muerte banner and set out the evidence bag full of broken *muertos*.

Sandino and his wife both recoiled.

"We found duplicates of the Santa Muerte altar items in Marco's knapsack," Emilia went on. "Along with the address of the hostel near the beach and a picture of the victim with his face circled. In addition, the murder weapons were in his pack, rolled up in a bloody tee shirt. A razor and a small hatchet, the kind gardeners use. Wood fragments from the hatchet were found under the fingernails of Marco's right hand."

Carlota looked furious, as did Chief Salazar. Lieutenant Baez acted as if his boss's eyes weren't boring into him.

Doctora Varela wept silently.

Sandino looked as if he was having breathing problems. "You're telling me that our son, our son who was going to become a doctor, who was my pride and joy for his entire life, was a Santa Muerte-worshipping killer?" Sandino jumped to his feet, the swivel chair zooming away. "He was a good boy, an athlete who brought honor to the name of Sandino! And you try to tell me he was a crazed killer?! He died because of you. Died in your jail and this is your explanation why?"

Carlota turned toward him. "Please, Vicente. You must calm down. This isn't helping."

"Why?" Doctora Varela raised her hands as if beseeching heaven for an answer. "Why would Marco do such a thing? He's a good Catholic boy."

"I tell you he didn't!" Sandino pounded a fist on the table. "This is all lies. Lies to protect the cops who killed him."

"Your son was found only meters away from the crime scene." Silvio spoke up for the first time. "He was covered in his victim's blood and very obviously under the influence of illegal substances. He did not deny the murder."

Sandino took a step back, blinking rapidly behind his spectacles.

"The kindest thing we can do for your family," Silvio said bluntly to Sandino, "is to find out his motivation for the murder he committed. Obviously, it was out of character. That speaks to pressure. I suspect that the answer lies in what he was doing between the time he disappeared from his school in September, and Sunday, when he was arrested."

"Carlota." Sandino swallowed hard and adjusted his glasses. "Your detective here may have a point, but I don't trust your people to find a drop of water in the ocean."

"Is that why the initial Missing Persons report was filed in Mexico City?" Silvio asked.

"Detective," Chief Salazar snapped. "I'm sure el señor had his reasons."

"I'd like to hear them, *mi jefe*," Silvio said.

Silvio spoke deferentially, but the dynamic between him and Chief Salazar was that of peers. Emilia knew that Lieutenant Baez knew it, too.

Sandino sat down heavily and removed his spectacles, holding them in one hand and pinching the bridge of his nose with the other. "When the school reported Marco missing we thought it was a kidnapping. After all, both my wife and I are quite well known. We hired a private company. Pinkerton. After weeks with no ransom and no information, Pinkerton went to its law enforcement contacts in Mexico City."

"Unfortunately, there was no coordination with police here in Acapulco," Lieutenant Baez said. "We could have helped. At least we would have been looking for your son and able to identify him as soon as he was arrested."

"I want to see where he died," Doctora Varela announced.

"Paulina, please." Carlota reached across the table again, her voice trembling with sincerity.

"Carlota, don't." Doctora Varela brushed aside the mayor's hand and got to her feet. "Will someone show me or do I just have to walk around this horrible place asking who saw my son die?"

"Detective Cruz will show us," Carlota announced.

Emilia led Carlota and Doctora Varela out of the squadroom. The mayor's security detail closed ranks behind them. Emilia felt as if she was leading a small parade as they went down the hall and around the corner to the holding cells. Carlota was recognized by everyone she passed and she smiled and nodded like the perpetual candidate that she was. Emilia reflected that the mayor was almost certainly the best dressed person who'd ever been at the station.

Puentes and Valdez were both behind the holding cell desk radiating nervousness at the sight of Acapulco's famous mayor.

"We're here to examine the cell where Marco Sandino Varela was held," Emilia said.

"Of course, Detective." Valdez was ready. He unlocked the cell, pushed open the door, and stepped aside.

The holding cell looked the same to Emilia; steel toilet, concrete floors, hard shelf that served as a bunk. No evidence of death or loss.

Doctora Varela walked into the cell. She ran her fingers over the bed-sized shelf and the seams in the concrete block walls.

"Was he on the floor or here when he died?" She touched the bunk again.

"On the bunk, señora," Valdez said.

Doctora Varela looked at Valdez. "Did you find him?"

"Yes, señora." Valdez said.

"Did he die in pain?"

Valdez looked uncomfortably at Emilia.

"Officer Valdez," Emilia said. "This is the young man's mother, Doctora Varela."

Valdez looked down the hallway, as if looking for a more senior official to tell him what to do."

"He'd been in the cell about an hour, señora," Emilia said. "Asleep the entire time. He didn't wake up when Officer Valdez came to get him for questioning."

Doctora Varela continued to look around dazedly. Carlota

made a point of walking into the cell and examining the bunk as if she'd find evidence of a poison dart or toxic gas. At last, evidently satisfied, she clicked her way out, a slight frown turning down the corners of her lightly glossed lips. "Who was in the cell with him?" she asked.

Emilia looked pointedly at Valdez.

"No one, señora," he said. "He was alone."

"Did he ask for food or water?" Carlota pressed.

"No," Valdez said. "He didn't speak at all while he was in custody."

"Surely he cried out," Doctora Varela said, tears streaming down her face. "Or asked for help?"

"Señora," Emilia said. "The, uh, prisoners in the holding cells are in full view of the officers at the desk. There are also cameras. Marco appeared to be asleep for the entire time he was in the cell."

"Ignored?" Carlota asked crisply.

Emilia felt the emotion spiral like a gathering storm. "Señora, I think we should leave these officers to get on with their work."

Doctora Varela gave a little sob. Carlota snapped her fingers at a man with an earpiece whom Emilia supposed was the head of her security detail. "Tell Señor Sandino that his wife wishes to leave," Carlota commanded. "Then escort Doctora Varela to the car."

"Don't tell me what to do, Carlota," Doctora Varela snapped, making no attempt to hide her sudden anger in front of Emilia or Valdez. "My husband got you elected but that doesn't mean you're my friend."

Carlota stiffened. Doctora Varela stormed out of the cell and down the hall to the squadroom. After a moment Carlota followed her, as if the exchange had not happened. The security team closed ranks around the two women. Emilia brought up the rear.

Sandino met them halfway down the hall. He and Carlota exchanged a few words before Sandino took his wife's elbow and marched her to the exit. Half of Carlota's detail ushered them out. The others stayed with the mayor as she made her way to the squadroom. Again, Emilia trailed behind.

Still around the table, Chief Salazar, Obregon, Lieutenant Baez, and Silvio stood as Carlota approached. Emilia hung back by the door but could see that the index cards and photographs they'd found in Marco's pack were on the table.

"This is exactly the sort of bad press this city doesn't need," Carlota said. Her ageless face was tight and her words were clipped. "Every time I turn around, this police department is stumbling over itself again. Destroying our tourism industry." She snapped her fingers; *pop, pop, pop,* like an exploding heartbeat. "Not only do we have Santa Muerte on our beaches and bodies hanging from billboards, but now we have lost school boys dying in our jails. I want this cleaned up *now*."

"Of course," Chief Salazar said. "But as the autopsy showed, the burden of proof has been established. The boy took drugs, committed a murder, and worshipped Santa

Muerte, all while suffering a chronic heart condition."

"I don't care what your autopsy says," Carlota said with heat. "The fact is that a boy died in your jail and everyone is going to know it was the son of the leader of my political party in Guerrero. That will be the story, not that the boy tangled with a drug dealer or fancied himself part of a cult. Fix it, Rodrigo."

"Señor Sandino is very concerned about what led his son to commit murder, señora," Lieutenant Baez interjected. "We'll be opening a new investigation."

"Open a new investigation," Carlota echoed with mock incredulity. "If that's the best you can do, things have come to a very sorry state."

Obregon stepped to her side. "You have another appointment, Carlota," he murmured.

As Obregon put his hand under her elbow, leaning close enough to whisper in the mayor's ear, Emilia was struck again by the mystery of their relationship. Once upon a time, she'd thought they were dating. But Obregon had gotten one of Carlota's flunkies pregnant. The mayor had to know. Yet nothing appeared to have changed between them.

"You'll be part of the new investigation, I assume, Detective Cruz," Carlota said with a withering glance that suggested Emilia's jeans and tee had been a bad choice. "Try not to make this situation any worse."

"I will do my best, señora," Emilia said.

Obregon smiled at her in his old way; a hawk assessing the potential speed of its prey.

"Too bad you're still just a detective," Carlota said cuttingly. "You had potential."

CHAPTER 8

"As good a place as any to start," Silvio said and tossed all the index cards and photos from Marco Sandino Varela's knapsack into Emilia's lap.

"Sure." Emilia fastened her seatbelt and stuffed the card with the address for the El Loro Rojo into her bag. She studied the other two cards and picked the one with an address in Colonia Quebradora, a hardscrabble neighborhood tucked between the Maxitunel, the main artery into Acapulco, and the mountain that rose to the north of the city. Quebradora was one of Acapulco's unknown *barrios*, the neighborhoods that were hidden away from tourists, ocean, and the luxury skyscrapers, hotels, and restaurants that ringed the bay.

The traffic changed as they wove their way northeast and left downtown Acapulco behind. Fewer tour buses, more small cars and motorcycles. The height of the buildings lowered and the architecture became simpler until all the buildings they passed were one or two stories of cement and corrugated metal. Most were fronted by either painted stucco walls or fences made of thick iron bars.

The sidewalks narrowed. There was no room for the palm trees that lined downtown boulevards. Houses huddled together in the face of poverty and vandalism. Safety in numbers. Many had big mercury lights over the front; illumination to deter the thieves that thrived in darkness.

Layers of unreadable graffiti decorated walls and kiosks and sidewalks. Posters advertising everything from protest marches to movies obscured the graffiti and turned telephone poles into layers of peeling paper. Electrical wires crisscrossed the sky. Rusting water tanks topped every structure.

"El Machete territory," Silvio growled.

"Slow down," Emilia said, looking at her phone's GPS app. "I think the address is this store."

Silvio pulled into a tiny vacant lot paved with dirt and gravel. Ragged weeds grew against chain link fencing on two sides. "Thirsty?"

"Sure," Emilia replied. She unfastened her seat belt when he killed the engine. "Try not to look like a cop."

Next to the car lot, the Mini Super Mickey was one of the hundreds of small convenience stores, or mini supers, scattered across Mexico. Little more than a gray concrete box, the store was generously spray painted with profane graffiti which spattered over the front sidewalk as well as the barred windows. The only surface spared was the sign of a grinning mouse, a rip-off of the famous cartoon character. Rippled roof tiles formed a small porch over the open front door.

"Señor!" A ragged boy ran towards them, waving a red rag to signal his self-appointed role as a parking attendant. "Five pesos to watch your car, señor. Ten to wash."

"Five when we come out," Silvio countered.

"Si, señor." The kid grinned. "I'll take good care of your

car."

Emilia's jeans and cross trainers might not be the right outfit to wear for a meeting with the mayor, but were perfect for the Mini Super Mickey. The gravel lot was rutted and littered with food wrappers and old newspapers. A metal barrel made aromatic by time and heat overflowed with trash. Carlota's decorative recycling containers had yet to make it to this part of the city.

Inside, three aisles held typical *tiendita* goods; candy, snacks, soda, canned food, detergent, diapers, cheap makeup, car air fresheners, gallons of cooking oil. A rack held *telenovela* magazines and well-thumbed newspapers. A freezer full of ice cream bars hummed loudly.

The painted-over windows created irregular bands of light across the shelves. The floor was tacky and Emilia's cross trainers made a slight popping sound as she walked around. Silvio's footsteps were even louder.

As her eyes grew accustomed to the haze, Emilia realized that there was a booth like a bank teller's station at the end of the center aisle, complete with a bulletproof glass shield and a cutout for passing money.

Behind the glass, a hard-faced woman watched television and counted packs of cigarettes. Her hair was coiled around fat pink curlers and her eyebrows were two elaborately drawn arches, as if she was prepped to star in a 1950's melodrama.

"*Hola*, señora," Emilia called. She got a nod in return, delivered without any sign of friendliness.

They'd been marked as outsiders.

Bottles of water, soda, and sports drinks cooled in a plastic bin of mostly melted ice. Emilia fished out two bottles and was rewarded with a river of water down her forearm. Silvio grabbed some snacks at random and slid payment through the hole in the glass. The woman made change without speaking. As they turned to go, Emilia saw the woman pick up a cell phone.

Back outside, the kid with the red rag reappeared, looking for his five pesos. "See, señor," he said proudly. "Your car is fine. No scratches. No one touched it."

"Good, good." Silvio made a show of examining the car from all angles. The kid followed him. Silvio stopped at a point when the car screened them from the street. He dug in his pocket for change. "You're good at your job."

"Si, señor." The kid stood straighter, obviously impressed with the big man with the crew cut and heavy shoulders. "I'm very good."

Emilia watched the street over the top of the car and wondered how much time they had before someone responded to the cashier's call.

"So maybe you can help me with something," Silvio said.

The kid spread his arms as if to say he could accommodate anything Silvio wanted. "Does señor need his car washed now?"

"No, I'm looking for my friend," Silvio said. "I thought he would be here. Maybe you've seen him lately."

The big detective fanned out Marco's three pictures like

a deck of cards, making sure the kid could see the circled faces.

The boy glanced at the pictures, looked at Silvio, and grinned. "You are friends with Gogo or Renzo, señor?"

"Both," Silvio said, his voice perfectly neutral. "Have you seen them around lately?"

"Sure." Skinny shoulders went up and down in a shrug. "Gogo always wears his Réal Madrid shirt."

Emilia snatched a glance around Silvio's arm. Sure enough, one of the photos was of a man in a white shirt with FLY EMIRATES emblazoned across the front.

Silvio grinned encouragingly at the kid. "Have you seen Gogo around lately?"

"Gogo worked in the *tiendita* yesterday." The kid grinned and cocked his head toward the store. "He had a big argument with his mama, too."

Silvio laughed as if he knew Gogo argued with his mama a lot. "About her hair curlers?"

"No. About Renzo." The boy tapped on the photo of the man who'd been found dead at Coyuca Lagoon and laughed. "She says Renzo is lazy and runs around with girls too much. That's why he didn't come to work. Gogo said to leave his brother alone, he works harder than she does because she's a fat *mamacita*."

A blue truck turned down the street and cruised by the Mini Super Mickey too slowly for Emilia's taste. "Time to go," she said.

Silvio handed the boy 20 pesos. "Next time, you can wash

the car," he said.

Silvio drove erratically through the Quebradora neighborhood, both he and Emilia checking the mirrors. It took 10 minutes and four stop lights before they shook off the blue truck.

Emilia let out her breath.

"You think we should go back and tell the woman that one son is dead and the other is a marked man?" Silvio turned onto the wide Adolfo Cortines highway that rambled through the hilly neighborhoods above the western side of the bay.

"We could probably buy some blue *reinas* there while we're at it." Emilia said.

"I'll bet Mini Super Mickey is a central distribution point for El Machete," Silvio said. The sedan sped along easily but his eyes continually flashed to the rearview mirror. "Renzo was expanding their sales out at Coyuca Lagoon."

"If that's the case," Emilia went on. "Whoever hired Marco as a *sicario* knows all about El Machete's network."

"Yep."

"With help from Santa Muerte." Every time Emilia thought of the folk saint she got the shivers. Billboards for Tía Rosa snacks and Osborne brandy flashed by and she found herself looking for a dangling body. "Did you see any Santa Muerte stuff in the store?"

"No," Silvio said. "I gotta tell you, Cruz, I don't know what the hell to think of that. Who was supposed to find the altars? Read those messages?"

"Prayers," Emilia corrected.

"Answer the question."

Emilia said the first thing that came to mind. "His enemies."

"He was a kid from a swanky Catholic prep school," Silvio argued. "How is it that his enemies are a couple of El Machete gang drug dealers? How did he know where the one in the tent was going to be? This Renzo character didn't exactly live in the tent, did he?"

"Okay." Emilia closed her eyes and tried to concentrate. "Marco was a student from Chilpancingo, studying here in Acapulco. Good student. Swimmer. Surfer. Paddleboarder." Her eyes popped open. "Maybe he hung out at Coyuca Lagoon. Bought some bad shit off of Renzo out there."

"Marco decided to get even?"

"Santa Muerte was the most evil thing he could think of to get his message across."

Silvio nodded. "Being outlawed by the Church and all."

"But Marco decided to get even with three people," Emilia said slowly. The pieces didn't exactly fit. "Why these three people?"

"Renzo and Gogo are brothers," Silvio said. "They took turns selling on the beach?"

"But Marco didn't write those prayers."

"What?"

Emilia grabbed her phone and flicked through the picture gallery. "The handwriting is different than Marco's writing in his algebra notebook."

"You think Marco had help?"

"I'm just saying that he didn't write out those prayers himself."

"You're having a good day, Cruz," Silvio said grudgingly.

It was the first nice thing he'd said to her in weeks. Emilia let herself enjoy a moment of smug satisfaction.

Her cell phone's GPS app chimed with directions to the last address from Marco's knapsack. As instructed, Silvio turned right onto Calle Escudero and climbed into the Colonia Solidaridad neighborhood. There the streets dissolved into a maze that wound around long thin canyons called *arroyos*. Like the previous neighborhood, the houses were low and jammed against narrow sidewalks that were in turned jammed against narrow streets. Electrical wires hummed overhead and poles were plastered with advertising posters.

Emilia's GPS led them through the labyrinth to a small house on a corner lot. It was surrounded by an iron fence that looked as heavy as the bars on the holding cells. The whitewash on both fence and house was cracked and peeling. The gate was latched with a big lockbox soldered onto the fence bars. More metal bars formed an arch above, waiting for a climbing rose that was now a mass of dead thorns.

They both got out of the car and peered through the bars.

The house had a blank look of emptiness. Weeds grew between the cement blocks of a front patio that stretched from the front door to the fence. Rose bushes along the side of the house were nothing but leggy stalks with big barbs and no blooms. The bulb inside the lamppost by the front door was broken.

The house's front windows contained not glass but perforated concrete blocks. The whitewash around the blocks was stained dark.

"Smoke damage?" Emilia asked, pointing to the discoloration.

"Probably." Silvio rattled the locked gate, then pressed his forefinger against the buzzer. Emilia heard a grinding ring from inside the house. No one answered.

"So welcoming," Emilia observed.

"Maybe they're all cooked to a crisp." Silvio produced a small tool from his back pocket. A moment later, the gate swung open.

No one jumped out of the house or shot at them. No cars stopped on the street.

Up close, the house looked even worse. Rusty water dripped from an air conditioning condenser on the flat roof. Electrical wiring protruded from a wall-mounted junction box and coiled on the weeds.

As Silvio picked the front door lock, they heard the scrabbling of small animals.

"Rats," Emilia whispered.

"We should be so lucky," Silvio said. Something clicked.

He pocketed his tool and eased open the front door.

A thick stench of death and decay boiled out.

"*Madre de Dios.*" The smell was so strong Emilia had the sensation of chewing it. With one hand she yanked up the neck of her tee shirt to cover her nose and mouth. She drew her handgun with the other.

"*Policia,*" Silvio called, his own automatic in hand.

They stepped into the house.

The room was partially burned and completely destroyed. The walls around the front windows were black with the tar of a recent fire. Shreds of what had probably once been curtain fabric hung from iron rods.

A big recliner was on its side, the busted frame poking through burned upholstery. A sofa was upside down, its wooden feet pointing to the ceiling. Two small wooden tables were likewise on their sides as if tossed by a giant hand. An ancient television, the kind with a heavy rear projection, lay on its side, the screen smashed. Besides the glass shards, the floor was littered with broken lamps, cracked picture frames, and bits of crockery. Irregular shafts of light from the perforated cement blocks formed random patterns across the damage.

"Somebody put up a fight," Silvio said.

Emilia's gaze moved around the room as if pulled by a magnet and stopped at the image of Santa Muerte.

It was the same banner of the folk saint as at Coyuca Lagoon. The skeleton face leered from under a black hood. She held the scythe with one bony hand and the globe in the other. Emilia's heart skipped a beat as she realized the manner in which the banner had burned. All four corners had clearly been alight and were now crumbly and brown. But the flames had only rimmed the image itself, as if even fire was afraid of the power of the saint of death.

Below Santa Muerte, a pine shelf served as an altar. Melted stubs, bent wicks, and twisted fabric clustered together, the remnants of three candles wrapped in black gauze. A small tequila bottle lay on its side, peso coins were scattered about, blackened twigs had once been a bunch of marigolds. Slashed pieces of three *muerto* figurines duplicated those at Coyuca Lagoon.

Emilia followed Silvio through the rest of the house. Kitchen, two bedrooms, and a bathroom were all empty but for evidence of small rodents. The electricity was off. The few things in the refrigerator had spoiled long ago.

They came back to the main room and the leering image of Santa Muerte.

A rat nosed around the pile of broken furniture beside the altar. Silvio threw a scorched chunk of plaster and the creature skittered away.

"What was it eating?" Emilia asked shakily.

Silvio blew out his breath. "Look."

A stain, the rusty color of death, trailed from under the pile of furniture. Emilia and Silvio pulled the sofa to one side, exposing more of the stain, then he righted the recliner to reveal a naked and headless male body. It was disfigured and blackened by fire; the muscles stringy and the fingers and toes curled into claws. The stain's trail began and ended under the neck where the cement floor was dark and matte with a thick layer of blood. Flies boiled up from the neck, revealing a roiling mass of white maggots.

Rats had evidently been feeding on the corpse, exposing white bone that contrasted with the fire-burned flesh. Even so, the El Machete tattoo on one forearm was clearly visible.

The rat skittered across the room and over the corpse's chest, bumping into a dark round object by the shoulder. A cloud of flies rose into the air, revealing more writhing maggots.

It took a long moment before the round object registered as the dead man's head.

"*Madre de Dios*," Emilia gasped and fled for the front door.

She made it to the fence before throwing up lunch, breakfast, and everything else she'd ever eaten. Shaking with chills in the sunshine, she clung to the fence to keep from sinking to her knees. Waves of nausea wracked her again and again as involuntary tears ran down her face.

Somewhere near her, Silvio was retching, too.

Fresh air gradually helped her regain control. Emilia blundered through the gate to Silvio's car and did a runner's stretch against the fender. She'd never thrown up before at a crime scene. Despite encountering dismembered bodies, pools of blood, damaged children, and too many gunshot victims to count, she'd always been able to handle it.

So had Silvio.

But this place was different. Emilia had never been this close to evil.

CHAPTER 9

Emilia was glad to see that Rodriguez led the tech team again, this time accompanied by Suarez instead of Bayardo.

Wearing gloves and surgical masks, Emilia and Silvio followed the techs into the house, leaving half a dozen uniformed cops to unwind PROHIBIDO EL PASO crime scene tape around the fence. The curious came out of nearby shops and houses.

More uniforms busily collected names and statements. The exercise would please Carlota, and in turn Obregon and Chief Salazar, but they all knew no one would have seen anything, heard anything, or know anything.

An El Machete gang member had been brutally murdered in the house on the corner. Who would put their life at risk by talking to the police about it?

The rats were scared off by the parade of techs and uniformed officers. But when Emilia saw the distorted body and the altar again, she found it hard to stay calm.

Rodriguez slowly revolved as he took pictures from all angles. Suarez began measuring.

"Any problem if I open the back door?" Silvio asked.

"Don't think we need to worry about crime scene contamination," Rodriguez replied dryly.

Conversation was sparse and terse as they took more pictures and bagged up evidence. They dusted for prints where they could. Emilia wondered if they would find those of Marco Sandino Varela.

She picked her way across the debris to the altar, drawn by the image of Santa Muerte. Suarez came over with evidence bags. "I've worked a few fire scenes before," he said. "This one is interesting. I'll let the medical examiner make the final determination but it looks to me as if someone killed the guy, chopped off the head, and set the body on fire. Burned the corpse and the curtains then put out the fire."

"So they didn't want to burn down the house" Emilia asked. "Just the body?"

Suarez pointed to the pile, his paper crime scene suit crackling with the gesture. "Tried to make a bonfire with the furniture but it smothered the fire rather than burned."

"I hate fire," Emilia heard herself say.

"I worked the El Tigre restaurant scene after the fire there," Suarez said. "I heard what you did, getting those people out."

Emilia gave a shiver. "Seems like a long time ago."

Suarez peeled the Santa Muerte banner off the wall. As he rolled it, the edges crumbled. Emilia stared at the ashes as they floated to the ground.

"Don't move," she said to Suarez.

The tech froze. "What's the matter?"

Emilia brushed aside ash near the tech's bootie-covered foot and picked a folded paper triangle off the floor. "We found these at another crime scene with an altar," she said. "They're prayers."

"For the police?" Suarez asked.

"I'm not sure who they are for." Emilia opened the triangle, careful to keep the dry paper from crumbling into confetti. "'Sainted Santa Muerte,'" she read aloud. "'Bring anguish and destruction to Your enemies and all they cherish. Death to El Commandante who seeks to destroy Your will. Cast Your divine protection over your believers.'"

Silvio clumped across the debris to her. "Read that again," he barked, eyes burning above the mask.

Emilia complied, then raised her eyebrows in a question.

"You remember that *narcomanta* with the body on the Las Brisas billboard?" Silvio asked.

"Signed by El Commandante," Emilia recalled. She held up the prayer. "Maybe he's the leader of the El Machete gang."

"That's what I'm thinking." Silvio looked around the scene of destruction. "You seen enough?"

Emilia refolded the message and followed him out. Mask off, she blinked in the sudden sunlight. On the other side of the fence, people chatted animatedly as they clustered near the police cars parked on the curb. The van from the morgue pulled up. The uniformed cops shooed people away to let the vehicle pull in near the gate. Two morgue workers got out with their black body bag and went inside without a glance at either Emilia or Silvio.

Squinting against the glare, Silvio untied his surgical mask. "We've got a range war on our hands," he said. "Santa Muerte versus El Machete. Altars versus billboards."

"They're each trying to scare the shit out of each other."

Emilia tamped down a hysterical laugh. Neither law enforcement nor the Mexican military had any degree of success when rival cartels clashed. All they could do was hope that attrition eventually whittled down the number of combatants to the point where public displays of violence petered out.

Two news vans blocked the side street. Reporters and photographers spilled out.

"*Madre de Dios*," Emilia said. "Carlota isn't going to like this."

Silvio crumpled his mask in a fist. "I didn't vote for her."

CHAPTER 10

Once a week there was a novena to San Judas Tadeo in the church of San Pedro de los Pinos in Emilia's old *barrio* in central Acapulco. It wasn't a Mass, although Padre Ricardo Suarez Solis offered Communion, but a prayer service dedicated to the patron saint of impossible causes.

Surely surviving a gang war endorsed by Santa Muerte qualified as an impossible cause.

Emilia showered in the station gym and changed into the workout clothes she always kept in the Suburban, getting to the small church a few minutes before the service began. She paused and scanned the pews. Most of the older women in the neighborhood came as a matter of course, not just the nine times required by a novena for a saintly intercession.

One of those older women was her Tía Lourdes. Emilia slipped into the pew beside her aunt.

"Emilia, what a treat to see you," Lourdes whispered. She gave Emilia a swift kiss and hug just as Padre Ricardo walked onto the altar and intoned the opening prayer.

Emilia followed along from memory, letting the familiar ritual replace the gruesome memories of the past few days. Padre Ricardo's voice and the repetitive invocations soothed her. Emilia's gun in the shoulder holster under her cotton jacket felt heavy and out of place.

She hadn't been in church for several weeks. Missing Sunday Mass at San Pedro de los Pinos was the one thing she regretted about moving into the hotel with Kurt. Sunday was often the only day neither she nor Kurt worked and thus the one day they had to spend together.

Unless, of course, an El Machete gangbanger was murdered out at Coyuca Lagoon.

When the time for Communion came, Lourdes gave Emilia a sideways glance. Emilia managed a smile and moved her knees to one side so Lourdes could leave the pew to receive the host. As a woman living in sin, Emilia was not entitled to receive.

She watched as Lourdes joined the line, still trim and energetic in a blue skirt, floral knit shirt, and a white cotton *rebozo* shawl over her hair. One-by-one, each woman murmured "Amen" as Padre Ricardo softly pronounced the host "the body of Christ" and put it on her tongue.

While her mother Sophia accepted the situation, Emilia knew that Lourdes strongly disapproved of living with a man without the benefit of marriage. Lourdes had met Kurt at the wedding of Sophia and Ernesto and the fact that he was a *gringo* compounded the sin. *Gringos* came and went; any relationship was therefore temporary and foolhardy.

But Emilia also knew that for Lourdes, family came before sin. Lourdes was her second mother and Emilia had often talked to her aunt about things that were too complex or upsetting to discuss with Sophia. Her aunt's love would outlast any fly-by-night *gringo* whose temptations Emilia couldn't resist.

When the service was over Padre Ricardo always lingered

in the aisle to chat with his parishioners. When he came by Emilia put a hand on his sleeve. "Can I come by the rectory in a few minutes, Padre?" she asked.

"Of course." The priest smiled and patted her hand. "It's been quite some time. I'll make us some tea."

When he moved on, Lourdes tugged Emilia back into the pew. "Do we have marriage bans to announce, Emilia?"

"What?" Emilia blinked and realized what her aunt meant. "No, no. I need to ask Padre Ricardo about something at work."

"Oh." Her aunt's mouth turned down in a slight frown. Her thin face was heavily creased around the eyes and mouth. She lifted the *rebozo* from her head and resettled it on her shoulders. The hair scraped back into a tight bun was shot with gray.

"But I'm glad I saw you," Emilia said. "I'm a little worried about Mama. Kurt and I . . . uh, we . . . uh . . . had *la comida* with her and Ernesto on Saturday. I made your *flor de calabaza guisada*."

"With the cheese?" Lourdes asked. "Did you rinse them in salt water first?"

"Yes, it was delicious," Emilia confessed. "But that's not what I wanted to talk to you about."

Lourdes frowned. "What happened, *niña?*"

"Nothing exactly happened," Emilia said. "But Mama acted like you and she had an argument. She seemed angry that I was using your recipe. Said you didn't understand her. Got upset when she was telling a story about where we lived before my father died. Something about a little boy."

Lourdes startled Emilia by gripping her wrist hard enough to hurt. "When was this? Saturday, you said?"

"Yes."

"Ah." Lourdes relaxed her grip. "Saturday was the anniversary, Emilia."

"Anniversary?" Emilia echoed. "Mama and Ernesto haven't been married that long."

"The anniversary of your father's accident," Lourdes said.

Emilia felt as if Lourdes had just socked her with a bag of wet sand. "I didn't know," she said slowly. "I've never known the date. Never even occurred to me to ask."

"Who would expect you to?" Lourdes patted Emilia's hand as if to make up for the red mark from squeezing her wrist. "You were too little to remember your father, let alone the day he was killed."

"Why didn't Mama say something to me?" Emilia heard the resentment in her voice. "I would have understood if she didn't want to be with us that day. We could have planned it for another time."

"You don't remember, do you?" Lourdes wrapped the white *rebozo* more tightly around her shoulders. "For years Sophia would be depressed the entire month of October. I'd tell her to get up, get a job, take care of her daughter. But she'd just sit and cry and cry."

"My first memories are of her crying," Emilia admitted.

"Your mother is a beautiful flower," Lourdes said. "One

rain shower and the petals fall away. Not a worker. You got that from your father."

Emilia had a sudden flash of insight into how hard it must have been for Lourdes to live with her vague and dependent sister-in-law for so many years. Lourdes had always been busy; cooking, cleaning, mending clothes, stretching Tío Raul's paltry income from the garage to feed six people, including three growing and rambunctious children. The small apartment over the garage was always a sanctuary while Emilia was growing up, but it was also hot, crowded and often filled with tension as Lourdes and Raul struggled to make ends meet.

Sophia was immune to the problems everyone else had, such as putting food on the table and surviving the street gangs and the pushers and pimps. She never worked, never brought in any income, but simply existed beautifully while the rest of the household swirled around her. She sewed and cooked and went to church and watched the children when Lourdes went out, but her main role was as a guest in her brother-in-law's home.

"I wish I knew her when she was young," Emilia said impulsively. "Before the accident. Maybe I wouldn't get so upset with her."

"You're a good daughter, Emilia," Lourdes said. "But there's no point in getting upset. Sophia doesn't understand."

Emilia sagged against the hard wooden back of the pew. "I was convinced you and Mama had a terrible argument."

Lourdes patted Emilia's hand. "Why would I argue with

your mother? It would be like arguing with a child."

Emilia knocked on the rectory door and Padre Ricardo ushered her in. "Emilia!" he exclaimed. "This is a lovely surprise."

Dressed in a faded denim *guayabera* shirt and dark cotton pants, Padre Ricardo gave her a warm embrace. The wiry gray-haired priest's days were packed with children's religious instructions, adult craft sessions, clothing and food drives, and one-on-one counseling sessions, yet Padre Ricardo exuded both energy and calm.

"I don't want to keep you long," Emilia said. "But I need to talk to you about a case."

"We can talk and work." Padre Ricardo led the way to the kitchen where a pile of painted *talavera* pottery filled the small table. "Then I'll make you a cup of tea."

Emilia took a seat. "I need you to tell me a little bit about Santa Muerte."

Padre Ricardo hastily made the Sign of the Cross as he sat. "Why should you need to know anything about Santa Muerte?"

"We have a case," Emilia said. "A teenager from a good family killed two gang members. He was going to kill a third but we caught him."

Padre Ricardo handed Emilia a cloth and a piece of blue and white painted pottery.

"It's the strangest thing," Emilia went on. "He went to a good school. Was going to be a doctor. But he went missing for two months before hitting the radar screen as a murderer who worshipped Santa Muerte. Built an altar to Santa Muerte next to both of his victims. Like an *ofrenda*."

"You're speaking in the past tense?"

"He died in custody. A heart problem."

Padre Ricardo picked up a piece of *talavera* and began to wipe it. Emilia saw that all the pieces of pottery were the small holy water fonts usually mounted by the doors of the church. The white glaze was decorated with blue crosses on the backsplash while and pine trees curved around the oval bowls that held the blessed water, appropriate for a church named after San Pedro de los Pinos. It had never occurred to her that the fonts were removable or that they needed to be washed now and then.

"And you want to know about Santa Muerte," the priest said at length.

"I've heard it referred to as The Bony Lady. The Skeleton Saint." Emilia felt a chill etch up her spine.

Padre Ricardo polished the oval bowl of a font. "First, you know the Catholic Church does not condone the worship of Santa Muerte, no matter what it is called."

Emilia wiped down another font. "It seems like a good place to start."

"Santa Muerte adherents have a whole protocol associated with worship and none of it is healthy." Padre Ricardo got up from the table and went over to a cupboard.

Emilia half expected him to pull out garlic and a crucifix but he merely came back to the table with a plastic jug of water that he'd marked with a cross. "Come," he said. "Let's put these back."

Emilia collected up the four *talavera* pieces and followed him into the empty church. It was dim, the pews silent and dark. They remounted the fonts on its hook by each door and Padre Ricardo filled them with holy water.

Back in the rectory kitchen, Padre Ricardo stowed the water back in the cupboard. "Have you eaten?" he asked.

"You don't need to feed me, Padre," Emilia said.

"We can't talk about serious things on empty stomachs." The priest puttered about the small cooking space.

Emilia set out plates and flatware. She'd been there so often she knew where everything was kept. The church had been their social center when she was a child. As an adult Emilia counted Padre Ricardo as both friend and mentor.

From the table she could see down a short hallway to a sitting room. Several bedroom doors opened along the way, the rooms available as needed for families in trouble or visiting priests.

The rectory was small, but like the church was kept immaculately clean by the women of the parish who also did the priest's laundry, mended and pressed his vestments, and polished the church so that it shone every Sunday. Sophia was a member of the neighborhood army that supported the church; there was little money to donate to the upkeep of the church, but it was a point of pride that the priest never go hungry nor the brass candlesticks on the altar ever tarnish.

"Now." Padre Ricardo set down two steaming mugs of tea, then scooped *arroz con pollo* from a hot skillet onto their plates. "We'll be better able to discuss serious things."

The *arroz con pollo* was delicious. The tea, however, was the priest's signature recipe of hot water and hope. Padre Ricardo was infinitely generous but he re-used tea bags until there was more goodwill in the cup than flavor.

As they ate, Emilia described the week's disconcerting haul of murders. Two hanging from billboards. Two beheadings decorated with Santa Muerte altars, which she described in detail.

She also told him about Marco Sandino Varela, the schoolboy turned murderer and Santa Muerte cult follower. Last, she recounted the meeting with the boy's parents and the mayor, Marco's distraught mother and the mystery of what had led him to take up with a cult forbidden by the Catholic Church.

She wound down and scrolled through her phone's image gallery to the scenes of Coyuca Lagoon. "This is what I'm talking about, Padre."

Padre Ricardo stopped with his mug halfway to his lips, brows coming together in a frown as he stared at the little screen. "You say there were prayers?"

"Three on each altar. To Santa Muerte."

"Did you bring them?"

"Yes." Emilia plucked the evidence bag out of her shoulder bag and passed it across the table to the priest. He fished a pair of reading glasses from his shirt pocket and settled them on his nose.

He unfolded a prayer and read it aloud.

Sainted Santa Muerte. Cast Your divine protection over your believers. Bring anguish and destruction to Your enemies and to all they hold dear. Destroy those who seek to destroy Your will. In the complete destruction of Our enemies Your disciples will find mercy and redemption.

The priest's voice trailed off.

"They're kind of creepy," Emilia conceded.

He silently unfolded and read all of them before looking up at Emilia. "This young boy didn't write them, did he?"

"No," Emilia said. "How could you tell?"

"They are probably the work of a Santa Muerte priest." Padre Ricardo looked ashen in the light shining down from the fixture over the table. "The tone. The references to disciples. There was intention behind these prayers and the altars."

"Anguish and destruction to Your enemies and to all they hold dear," Emilia repeated. The phrases had stuck in her head. "We think the prayers are meant to scare a rival gang."

"No, no." Padre Ricardo agitatedly drank some tea. "What you have here is much more than that. You said three candles, three messages, and three broken *muertos* on each altar."

"Yes."

"Which add up to nine, the number associated with evil." Padre Ricardo clasped his hands around his mug.

"Nine." Emilia felt that cold finger trace its way up her back again. This time it dug into her spine, as if searching for a way inside past her vertebrae, all the way into her head to access images of a man mutilated with the number 9 cut into his body.

"The color black is significant, too," Padre Ricardo said. "Black is for rituals against enemies. For Santa Muerte adherents, black is the color of complete protection, particularly against hostile spirits."

"Or enemies?"

"Or evil," the priest said. He massaged his left shoulder with his right hand. "White Santa Muerte candles or statues are for spiritual cleansing, peace in the home, purity. A red Santa Muerte will be used to call forth love and passion. Gold represents economic power, success, and money. Devotees maintain that this color is suited for businessmen. Yellow is for healing diseases. Quite a bit of yellow in rituals intended to break addictions."

"What about the tequila and the money?"

"Customary offerings on an altar. Meant to be collected by the priest later to ensure passage of the intercession."

Emilia scooped the prayers back into the evidence bag and stuffed it into her shoulder bag at the foot of her chair. "More tea?" she asked. Reading the prayers again made her uneasy.

She didn't wait for Padre Ricardo to respond but collected

their empty mugs, relit the stove and waited for the water in the kettle to boil again. Padre Ricardo leaned back in his chair, one hand still massaging his shoulder.

"Emilia," the priest said quietly. "Santa Muerte has no power here."

"Of course not." Emilia knew he felt her restlessness. She cleared the table and brought their plates to the sink.

Padre Ricardo sighed. "Santa Muerte is not a saint like the Virgin or even San Juan Diego. The church believes that it is a superstition gone to an extreme."

Emilia glanced over her shoulder at him as she rinsed the dishes in the sink. "But the Church hasn't been able to discredit belief in it."

Padre Ricardo's face tightened. "The Mexico City Archdiocese has condemned Santa Muerte as a phenomenon against Christianity and not just because it is the favored cult of gangs and cartels. Santa Muerte is popular with organized crime because it can be distorted into some desperate concept of divine protection like you see in those notes. Others believe the false promises of Santa Muerte because they are exhausted from poverty and willing to believe that sacrifice and prayers to Santa Muerte will get them what they want."

Emilia stared at the wet dishes without seeing them. Somewhere, a Santa Muerte priest wrote prayers, plotted to kill, and generated evil. Whoever it was, his arm was long enough to reach her.

The kettle whistled, breaking into her thoughts. Emilia

whisked it off the gas and refilled their mugs. The only tea bag was the soggy one on a plate by the stove and she dutifully reused it.

"This was supposed to be a murder case," she said as she set the mugs on the table and sat down. "I've handled plenty of those. But this turned into a gang war. On one side it's the El Machete gang. On the other side it's some new group." She paused. "Using evil to kill and intimidate."

"Yes." The priest's voice was breathy. "I want you to be very careful, Emilia. If a Santa Muerte priest is recruiting killers, it means he holds great power over his followers. His disciples."

"Wouldn't someone like that be known to the Church?"

Padre Ricardo grasped at his left forearm and his face turned vermillion. He half rose from his chair, his breath coming in guttural gasps. Emilia ran around the table and caught the priest as he pitched forward. He was heavier than he looked. Emilia barely managed to break his fall and ease him onto the floor next to the kitchen table.

Pressing an ear to Padre Ricardo's chest, Emilia heard only silence. Fighting panic, she felt for the heartbeat in his neck. There was no responding pressure against her fingers.

"No," Emilia heard herself yell and then she was pumping and blowing like an automaton, resuscitation training coming to the fore as if she'd taken the final examination yesterday.

She didn't know how long she went through the routine but the priest finally opened his eyes. His mouth moved in a weak cough.

"Padre," Emilia gasped.

"Not my time yet," Padre Ricardo wheezed.

Emilia found an aspirin in her shoulder bag and placed it under his tongue. "You're going to be fine, just fine, really," she babbled.

After a few minutes they staggered together to the Suburban. Face creased with pain, the priest slumped in the passenger seat. One hand on the wheel and her cell phone in the other, Emilia barked out her badge number and the priest's condition to the hospital emergency staff as she drove. Padre Ricardo was silent, his chest barely moving for the entire ten minutes it took Emilia to blast her way through traffic to the hospital.

She honked and swung the big vehicle into the emergency drive. Two nurses ran out with a wheelchair. An orderly in a starched white uniform opened the passenger door as the Suburban rolled to a stop. Before Emilia was even out of the vehicle, Padre Ricardo was in the wheelchair with an oxygen mask over his face. The big glass doors to the emergency room slid open. The nurses and their patient disappeared inside.

Emilia threw her keys at the valet and ran after them.

She left three hours later, her vision blurry with fatigue. Padre Ricardo was still alive.

But just barely.

CHAPTER 11

Clad in one of his oversized tees, Emilia was drinking coffee on the balcony outside their bedroom when Kurt came back from his morning swim. She watched through the glass doors as he stripped off his tee shirt and came outside in just swim shorts. His body was ripped from the work of plowing through the early surf and his blonde hair was damp.

Emilia's mood lifted just at the sight of him. "Good swim?"

Kurt kissed her cheek. "Jacques is all right, but it's more fun with you."

Emilia leaned into his bare shoulder as he tugged her close. His skin was cool and smelled like salt. "Thanks for letting me sleep," she said. "I promise I'll come with you tomorrow."

Kurt lifted his chin at her phone on the top of the balcony wall. "Any news about Padre Ricardo?"

"No, it's too early. But thanks for asking." Emilia put her mug down on the stone next to the phone and slid her arms around his waist. "I want to talk to you about Jacques."

"Jacques?"

"Is he seeing anybody right now?

Kurt laughed. "Jacques is always seeing somebody," he said. "He's a Frenchman living in a city full of barely clothed women. Why?"

"I thought it would be nice to introduce him to

Mercedes," Emilia said. "He's single, she's single. They met before and she thought he was interesting." The actual term Mercedes had used was *different* but it amounted to the same thing.

"No, we are not fixing up the two of them. Jacques goes through women like water and you want to keep Mercedes as a friend." Kurt gave her a mock frown, blonde eyebrows coming together. "Why this sudden interest in playing matchmaker?"

"Last night," Emilia said. "Padre Ricardo and I talked about what's going on with this Santa Muerte case. It made me think. About life. Being short. Too short to be alone. So I thought maybe Mercedes and Jacques. They could . . . you know."

"Ah," Kurt said knowingly.

"I'm happy and I want everybody else to be happy, too."

"What about me?" Kurt said.

Emilia rose up on her toes to kiss his chin. "You're already dating Jacques."

One thing led to another. Emilia barely got to the police station in time for the 9:00 am meeting.

"Gather round, folks," Lieutenant Baez said and led the way from the conference table to the other side of the squadroom where a double murder board filled the wall. The billboard and Santa Muerte slayings were posted side by side. The left side displayed photos of the two beheading victims and altars to the Death Saint. Marco Sandino Varela's *cédula* picture was posted above them.

"Fingerprint report just came in from the house in Colonia Solidaridad," Silvio said. "Marco's thumbprint was found on the Santa Muerte banner and a doorknob. They found different prints on the furniture stacked on top of the body, but no matches for those."

Lieutenant Baez smoothed his tie. Emilia recalled that he'd been to the house in Colonia Solidaridad, just as the morgue workers prepared to take out the charred body but hadn't stayed long.

"First things first," he said. "Who are the players?"

"Santa Muerte versus El Commandante," Silvio said. "Two proxies fighting for control of the Acapulco meth trade."

"We got a tip might be related to the billboards," Sandor said. As always, Macias stood right next to him. "Macias and I shook some trees last night. "There's a rumor going around of a new gang trying to crack the Acapulco plaza. Los Nueves."

Los Nueves. The Nines.

Silvio grabbed a marker and scribbled on a whiteboard next to the pictures. "You think they left their signature on the guy with the number on his chest?"

"Could be."

"Are they local?" Silvio asked.

"Nobody knows," Macias said. "One snitch repeating a

rumor. But he seemed pretty scared of them."

"Nine is the number associated with evil," Emilia said.

Lieutenant Baez glanced at her. "Where does Marco Sandino Varela fit in here?"

"Recruited," Silvio said simply.

"Recruited by a Santa Muerte cult," Emilia corrected him. "That's what Los Nueves is. I've got a contact at Pinkerton. Marco's parents said they initially worked with Pinkerton when they thought he'd been kidnapped. Maybe there's something that didn't get included in the Missing Persons report."

Lieutenant Baez nodded. "All right."

"If Los Nueves is recruiting, somebody on the street will know," Macias said.

"*Jesu Cristo*," Sandor muttered. "What a way to lose your kid."

"Yeah," Castro said around a wad of gum in his mouth.

Gomez laughed loudly. "Shoulda growed up and become a cop."

Both Castro and Gomez were perched on the latter's desk facing the murder board. Castro sported an orange baseball cap, the bill jutting backwards and the plastic sizing tab running across his forehead like a bandage. The two kept up a sidebar conversation, punctuated with snickering, gum chewing, and Gomez's attempt at card tricks with a grubby deck.

Ortega and Nuñez stood by Lieutenant Baez. Both wore button down shirts and ties but had left their suit jackets at their desks. Ortega was the older of the two, with prematurely iron-gray hair and a habit of looking past the person with whom he was speaking. Nuñez was in his 30's, seven or eight years older than Emilia, and gave off the perpetual gleam of the golden boy who thought he was just passing through on his way up.

"What do we have on Marco so far?" Lieutenant Baez asked.

"Marco killed two El Machete members within the last ten days, leaving Santa Muerte altars at both murder scenes." Silvio folded his arms as Gomez lapsed into snickers. "From the state of the place, Colonia Solidaridad was Marco's first kill. Whoever was supposed to find the altar to Santa Muerte did and tried to burn down the place to hide it. The extra set of prints on the stacked furniture confirm it."

"Another El Machete member?" This from Macias.

"Likely, but hard to know," Silvio said. "Whoever it was, Marco was certainly long gone and on to his next target before the house was set on fire. First victim still unidentified but the second was Renzo Garcia Figueroa." He tapped the photo of the tent victim. "I found the commercial license for the Mini Super Mickey. The owner is Graciela Figueroa Campos. Renzo was her son, just like we thought. Her other son is Gregorio Garcia Figueroa, known around town as Gogo. From the materials we found in Marco's pack, he was the third target."

Lieutenant Baez looked at the *cédula* picture of Gregorio Garcia Figueroa. "Do we know if this Gogo is still alive?"

"Probably," Silvio said. "Kid hanging around the parking lot at the Super Mini Mickey said he was in there day before yesterday. If he's running the store as a meth *tiendita* distribution point for El Machete he's probably in and out. It's a long shot, but if he finds out he's a target and that his brother is dead, he might open up about his enemies."

"Bring him in," Lieutenant Baez said.

"Excuse me, *teniente*," Emilia interjected, her notebook open. "What if there are others out there like Marco?"

"What do you mean?"

"Recruits whoa re committing crimes and leaving a Santa Muerte altar."

Ortega gave a funny cough. Nuñez looked past Emilia.

"Cruz has a point," Macias said, Sandor nodding next to him. "If Los Nueves is the gang behind the Santa Muerte killings, maybe they've left a trail."

Emilia was silently grateful for the support. "There could be related crimes with Santa Muerte signatures in other neighborhoods. Even in other cities."

Lieutenant Baez regarded one of the Coyuca Lagoon pictures. "All right, Cruz and Silvio keep working the Santa Muerte angle. If there are more kids like Marco out there walking around with Santa Muerte altar parts and a target list, we need to find them before this goes any further. Good instincts, Detective Cruz. I can give you some contacts in Mexico City who could be helpful as you look for similar crimes."

He walked to the right side of the murder board where the

disturbing images of mutilated men swinging from the billboards were pinned. "This is the mess that has the mayor wound up. What have we got?" He raised his eyebrows at Macias and Sandor."

"No prints, no witnesses," Sandor admitted. "The only thing we have to go on is the *narcomanta* found with the second body that was signed by El Commandante."

"The billboard killings are retaliation for the Santa Muerte murders." Silvio pointed to the other side of the murder board. "Which brings us right back to where we were."

"Is that it?" Lieutenant Baez asked the room in general.

"The *narcomanta* on the second billboard also referred to a worthless priest," Emilia said. She folded her arms to forestall that cold feeling but it didn't work. "I've been doing a little research. Given the format of the prayers we found on the altars and Santa Muerte cult rituals, the priest referred to in the *narcomanta* is probably a Santa Muerte priest."

"Creepy shit, Cruz." Gomez winked at Emilia. "Let me know if it keeps you up tonight."

"We know that El Machete has moved into the meth market," Macias said. "Maybe they're expanding under new leadership."

"El Commandante?" Silvio theorized.

"Range wars always come down to money and territory," Macias said. "This Marco kid was just some foot soldier."

"He's not the key issue," Silvio said. "But the best link to who is running the war we've got so far. If we can't stop the range war, we're going to lose the city."

Lieutenant Baez took a step back, as if struck by the reality all of the detectives in the squadroom lived with every day.

Gomez laughed again as he shuffled his deck, the laminated cards snapping together like the rip of a machine gun. "You don't have a hope in hell of doing that, Franco."

A ham-sized fist slammed against the metal desktop, causing the deck of cards to shiver and slide out of Gomez's skinny hands. "We stop crime in this shithole," Silvio growled. "Unless you've forgotten."

The tension in the room was palpable. Gomez gave a nervous laugh. Castro grinned at his partner's discomfiture.

Lieutenant Baez clapped his hands, breaking the tension. "All right, folks. We're working on a theory but it's a good one and in the absence of something better, that's what we'll go with. Cruz and Silvio, I want you to keep on the Santa Muerte angle. Widen the net but get some answers to the Marco Sandino Varela situation. Figure out what he was doing for the last two months. Follow up with your Pinkerton contact, the school, whatever."

"Got it, *teniente*," Silvio said.

"Macias and Sandor, you dig into the gangs," Lieutenant Baez went on. "Pick up the Coyuca Lagoon victim's brother. Figure out who is selling what and where. Talk to your snitches, whatever it takes. Map out whatever you find. Let's get some actionable information."

Macias and Sandor both whipped out notebooks.

Lieutenant Baez looked at everybody. "Our priority is to prevent another public display of mutilation and murder. Is that understood?"

Everybody nodded. Gomez shuffled his cards again.

"All right then." Lieutenant Baez swung his head to make eye contact with Ortega and Nuñez. "You two will own the rota until further notice. Any questions? No? Then get to it."

As the detectives went back to their desks, Lieutenant Baez raised his chin at Emilia. "Can I see you in my office, Detective?"

"Yes, *teniente*."

Lieutenant Baez shut his office door and went behind his desk. Emilia took the same seat as the last time she'd been called in alone.

"I'd like to ask you a few questions about Castro and Gomez," he said.

"I don't know anything about the cases they are working on," Emilia said, instantly wary.

Lieutenant Baez leaned back and picked up a pen, a move that projected ease. He was a confident man, like Kurt, but it didn't come naturally. *El teniente's* manner was more deliberate, as if he'd taken a course.

"I'm told that you've had run-ins with both Gomez and Castro," he said. "Specifically in the detectives' restroom, which they tried to prevent you from using. You didn't report either assault, although I gather you came out ahead both times."

Emilia's grip on her notebook tightened; she couldn't tell

where this conversation was leading. Was he going to claim that no matter how good she was, a woman detective caused too much trouble?

Lt Baez raised his eyebrows at her silence. "Is this information correct?"

Emilia squared her shoulders. "We've had our differences in the past. There's no reason to bring it up now."

"I need to know if I have a rapist in my squadroom, Detective," Lieutenant Baez said quietly.

On the one hand, the thought of getting Castro and Gomez kicked out of the squadroom was delicious. But on the other hand, Emilia knew they'd exact a brutal revenge. She stared down at her notebook, unsure what to say.

"Detective?"

"It never came to that, *teniente.*" Emilia's voice sounded hoarse in her ears.

"Even with Gomez?"

Emilia wondered who Baez had been talking to.

"You think your guy from Pinkerton might have something?" Silvio asked.

"Alan Denton," Emilia supplied. "If he ever responds to the three voicemails I've left him."

"Might have to go knock on his door."

Emilia almost laughed. "He'd be furious. He's got some sort of phobia about dealing with cops."

"Why he's still alive." Silvio stopped for a red light and rolled up the sleeves of the black cotton shirt he wore over jeans and a white tee to hide his shoulder holster.

Despite the air conditioning, the inside of the car was warm. Emilia fanned herself with her phone. "If Pinkerton found something besides what's in the Missing Persons report, Denton is just the sort of *pendejo* who would know."

"What really gets me," Silvio said. The light changed to green and he accelerated. The air conditioner spewed out a fresh batch of cool air. "If we put two and two together, then Marco Sandino was kidnapped by a Santa Muerte priest who didn't bother with a ransom note."

Emilia blinked. "You're right. It sounds totally ridiculous. A Catholic honor student from a well-known family."

"You said your parish priest gave you the idea. I'd like to talk to him after we get this school shit out of the way."

"He's in the hospital," Emilia said. "We were sitting in the rectory kitchen and he'd read the prayers and we were talking and wham, he had a heart attack. Still in Intensive Care. I want to go over to the hospital after we're done here."

"*Rayos,*" Silvio said but the word came out more in wonderment than a curse. "Talking about Santa Muerte and has a heart attack. That's a fucking coincidence, don't you think?"

Bring anguish and destruction to Your enemies and to all they hold dear.

Emilia didn't reply. They'd arrived.

The Colegio San Bruno in upscale Colonia Loma Hermosa was an imposing collection of whitewashed buildings in the old Spanish style, spread out on a gently rolling campus behind a wall topped with iron spikes. The gate was manned by an equally imposing guard, whose uniform was decorated with loops of gold braid. Emilia saw the corner of Silvio's mouth twitch as he showed their identification. The guard studied their identification and compared their names to a list on a clipboard. He finally handed Silvio a parking permit and directed them up a gentle hill.

Emilia got out of the car and looked around. The school's administration was housed in a two-story hacienda-style building, with tall narrow windows stretching in an orderly row on either side of the wide front door. Black shutters framed each window, as well as the door. The effect was stark and not especially welcoming.

The building was on a gentle rise and Emilia could see much of the huge campus. The whitewashed buildings were linked by wide and curving stone paths. The landscaping was lush yet perfectly manicured, with fat pink hibiscus blooms nodding in the breeze.

Despite the heat of the day, the students walking across the campus were in full prep school turnout: dark pants or pleated skirts, white button down shirts, striped ties, and maroon blazers.

"Did you go to a school that made you wear a jacket all the time?" Emilia asked Silvio. Both public and private schools required uniforms but in the poorer sections of the city the only requirements were dark pants and a white polo. Maybe that was why she felt most comfortable in casual clothes, like the khaki ankle pants, black tee, and denim jacket she was wearing today.

"You know where I grew up, Cruz," Silvio said. "In El Roble, the only thing you had to bring to school was a fist and the ability to get up again."

Emilia would have laughed if she didn't know he was telling the truth.

The dean of Colegio San Bruno was named Enrique Calvo Santana. His secretary made them wait on the other side of a long counter as school business swirled around them. The setup reminded Emilia of the Records department in the police station. Self important women who looked seriously at computers but in reality watched cat videos or *telenovelas* all day.

Students came by the counter to ask questions about the school newspaper or sending transcripts to colleges. They all had that easy arrogance that came with money and privilege.

Calvo came out of his office, bustled his way around the counter, and said how pleased he was to meet Detectives Silvio and Cruz. So sorry, of course, under the circumstances but happy to assist in any way he could. Without mentioning Marco's name, he insisted that he was only too glad to put the school at their disposal. He gestured for them to proceed him into his office.

Emilia walked in and slowed, hit by the plethora of

framed diplomas, photographs, and certificates that covered the walls like paper. The only visual relief in the entire office was a window coated in maroon draperies that reached to the maroon carpet. The effect was of a tasteless funeral home.

Calvo sat behind his desk and indicated the maroon brocade wingback chairs that fronted it. Emilia sat and felt the narrow chair pinch her hips. Silvio fit into his chair so snugly he looked like he was going to explode out of it.

Obviously, Dean Calvo had spent so much of the school's money on framing his certificates that he couldn't afford bigger chairs.

"We know you've talked to the Pinkerton Agency about Marco Sandino Varela's disappearance," Emilia began. They'd decided ahead of time she'd take the lead in the interview. "And detectives from Mexico City. But we need to follow up with some additional questions."

"His kidnapping," Calvo corrected. He clasped his hands on the leather desktop and regarded her earnestly. He was short and stout, with pasty pockmarked skin that spilled over the collar of his shirt to rub against the knot of his maroon tie. "A horrible, horrible thing."

"Of course," Emilia echoed.

"I can't imagine there is anything new that I can tell you," Calvo said. "As you say, we talked to the private security company and the family and even our insurance company. Those other police detectives were from Mexico City and certainly knew what they were doing." He gave her a knowing smile, as if Acapulco police should understand that they were outclassed by those from the nation's capital.

Emilia got out her notebook, enjoying the sound of Silvio grinding his teeth as he shifted to get comfortable. "Tell us a little about Marco," she said to Calvo. "I understand he was an honor student."

"Absolutely. A popular boy. A rule follower. On the right path."

The dean sang the praises of the boy, whom he declared was destined for great things. From a fine family, too.

Emilia walked him through the timeline of Marco's disappearance. The semester began in August. Marco was in his last year and beginning the college application process. He planned to attend the Universidad Nacional Autónoma de México, known as UNAM, for a medical degree.

"We were all pleased by his choice." Calvo smiled, his jowls dancing. "Graduates who go on to UNAM traditionally are generous alumni donors."

Silvio shifted sideways in his chair and gave a small cough.

"Yes." Emilia was nonplussed by Calvo's random comment. "Can you tell me about the day Marco was discovered missing?"

"It was a Thursday, I believe." Calvo flipped pages of a spiral-bound desk calendar. "Yes, yes. A Thursday."

"Any significance about Thursday?"

He looked at Emilia as if she was a child. "Thursday is steak night."

"What's Wednesday night?" Silvio asked.

"Wednesday." Calvo's hand fluttered calendar pages again. "That Wednesday was a movie night. Every two weeks the school organizes a cinema outing into the city. Of course, in the wake of Marco's kidnapping we have stopped the outings."

"So Marco went to the movie?"

"We believe so." Calvo spread his hands. "We don't take attendance at evening events unless they are academic in nature."

"Does a teacher go on these trips?"

"The Head Boy chaperones these outings."

"We'll need to speak to him."

"We require permission from his parents and the school board before exposing any of our students to your questions," Calvo said stiffly. "They have not yet been told of Marco's death. The school board will send a statement to parents first."

Silvio leaned forward, his shoulders actually bursting out of the chair. "Did Pinkerton or the detectives from Mexico City talk to the kids who were with Marco when he was kidnapped?"

"The school board is still reviewing the request." Calvo tried to sound apologetic and failed. "Many parents are opposed to their children becoming involved. We have a duty and a privilege to protect and nurture our young charges."

Silvio made a noise like a bull pulling a hoof out of the mud.

Emilia tapped her notebook to divert attention from her partner's ire. "Señor Calvo, what about the security staff that was on duty that week? Can we speak to them?"

"Once again," Calvo said. "Your request must be made to the school board."

"What fucking kind of school are you running here?" Silvio leaned so far out of his chair that Calvo shrank back despite a meter of shiny wood desk between them. "People pay through the nose to send their kids here and you can't keep track of them."

Calvo's jowls quivered with indignation and discomfort. "We are sickened by Marco's kidnapping and the loss of this fine young boy. That's why the school board is in the process of changing all our security protocols and we have augmented our security staff."

Emilia stood up, furious with Silvio. "Señor Calvo, I think we're done here. It would be best if we could walk around. See Marco's dormitory room. Speak to his counselor and teachers."

"Unless you have to ask the school board about that, too," Silvio cracked.

Calvo got to his feet and gestured toward the door. "We can arrange that now."

He turned them over to Señora Fortunada, who reluctantly tore herself away from her computer screen, gave them a frosted lipstick smile, and said she'd escort them to the counselor's office. Calvo didn't offer to shake hands but simply bobbed his head at Emilia and said she could call him at any time, any time at all. He gave them half a nervous smile and scampered back to his office like an overfed puppy.

Señora Fortunada led them up a flight of stairs to the Counseling Center. A bell rang as they took the steps and the hallways filled with noisy, jostling students. Emilia caught snatches of conversations. *Test scores. Study groups. Essays due.*

Nothing about dates or clothes. The students were all business as they rushed to their next class. No cell phones. No flirting.

Colegio San Bruno was a serious place.

Marco's counselor was Gustavo Cortez Mendoza, a solemn young man wearing a bow tie and a gray tweed jacket that looked ridiculously out of place. His outfit was no doubt the reason for the high octane air conditioning. Silvio acted as if he didn't notice the sub-zero temperature in the man's office, but the cold sliced through Emilia's lightweight denim jacket like a knife.

Cortez Mendoza had Marco's school record for them to look at. Emilia skimmed through it, resisting the urge to rub her fingers together for warmth. Marco had enrolled as a freshman and was an excellent student.

"Quite the academic star," Cortez Mendoza said.

"We hear he was planning to become a doctor," Emilia said. "Were you encouraging him in that direction?"

"Marco had a lot of talent," Cortez Mendoza said. "I know his parents expected him to become a doctor."

There was just enough hesitation in his phrasing to give Emilia pause.

Cortez Mendoza glanced at his closed door. There was a window at the top. Through the glass they could see his secretary chatting with Señora Fortunada.

"Did he talk to you about his plans?" Emilia asked softly.

"Marco seemed rather, well, distracted when I spoke to him at the beginning of the semester," Cortez Mendoza said quietly. "He didn't actually say that he wasn't interested in pursuing the UNAM plan, but he wasn't excited by it either."

"Did he say there was something else he wanted to do?"

"No." Much more than Calvo, Cortez Mendoza looked distraught. "He wondered if he was really cut out to be a doctor and I suggested he could do an internship with a practice in Acapulco before he made that decision. We have quite a few partnerships in the city for our students to do shadowing opportunities or internships."

"Of course," Emilia said. Rich people always had those types of opportunities tossed in their laps. "Did he want to do that?"

"He said he'd think about it but there was no enthusiasm in his face," Cortez Mendoza said. "We talked about surfing for a few minutes and he left to go to class."

"Did you see him again before he disappeared?"

"No. That was our last conversation."

"He didn't want to go to UNAM?" Silvio asked. "Or he didn't want to be a doctor?"

"Both," Cortez Mendoza said. "He said Mexico City was

too far away. He wanted to stay in Acapulco after graduation." He frowned, lips thinning in disapproval. "I don't think he wanted to give up surfing and paddleboarding."

Señora Fortunada gave them a tour of the school, pointing out the various buildings where Marco had attended classes. Emilia was again struck by the soberness that hung over the school. The students all walked fast and carried piles of books. Every conversation was about homework or extra credit assignments or cram sessions. Nobody laughed, checked a smartphone, or wore anything that wasn't regulation.

They ended the tour in the dormitory for junior and senior boys. Like the rest of the school, the building enjoyed a certain Spanish flair; whitewashed stucco, clay tile roof, narrow arched windows with iron trim. Pots of geraniums flanked the heavy wooden door.

Marco's room was on the second floor. "Room 210," Señora Fortunada puffed as they climbed the stairs. She was a stout woman with jowls to match Calvo's wattles.

"Señora Fortunada!" A teen in the requisite school uniform of dark pants and maroon blazer stopped on the steps, blocking the secretary's way. "The schedule for the leadership club has changed and it needs to be corrected in the newsletter.

"Fernando," the woman said crossly. "I told you the deadline was today."

"It's still today." The boy checked an expensive watch.

"It's only 3:00 o'clock."

Silvio continued to the second floor.

Señora Fortunada pursed her lips as she saw him go up. "I'll only be a minute," she said to Emilia.

"Take your time," Emilia replied.

Señora Fortunada clumped her way back to the first floor, the teen on her heels.

Emilia trotted the rest of the way to the second floor. Like the outside of the building, the walls were whitewashed and pristine. No artwork, only notices telling the boys to conserve water and turn lights out at 11:00 pm. No girls were allowed after 9:00 pm and then only in the community lounge. The floors were terracotta tile. Nothing softened the hard surfaces of either wall or floor.

She made her way down the hallway. A communal bathroom smelled strongly of chlorine bleach. Dorm room doors were open. Boys at their desks turned to look as Emilia went by, her loafers rapping on the tile.

Silvio was in the room. There wasn't much to see. A bed, desk, dresser. Other than that the room was empty. Nothing on the walls, nothing on the dresser.

"They must have sent everything home to his parents," Emilia said.

She walked to the desk and stared out the window. Whitewashed buildings ringed a central green. There was a statue in the middle surrounded by benches and spreading jacaranda trees. Students rarely stopped to sit on the benches and chat. Everyone at Colegio San Bruno was so purposeful.

"The exercise yard," Silvio said.

He was right; the place felt like a prison. "Marco must have sat here, doing homework," Emilia said.

"Who are you?"

Emilia and Silvio both turned. A young student stood in the doorway, jacket gone, tie loosened, shirtsleeves rolled to his elbows.

"What are you doing here?" he asked.

"We're police," Silvio said. "From Acapulco."

"Here about Marco?"

"Were you a friend?"

"Yes. We were on the debate team together." The corners of the boy's mouth drooped. "Are you helping to look for him?"

"He's dead," Silvio said, with no effort to soften the blow.

The boy took a step back. His face worked with the effort not to cry.

Emilia stepped in front of Silvio, promising herself that she would crucify him later. "Can you help us? When was the last time you saw him?"

"It was a Wednesday," the boy said. "I asked if he was going to the movie. He said no, he had to study. I wasn't surprised. I mean, the movies are usually for couples."

"He wasn't seeing anyone?"

"He had a girlfriend. But she wasn't a student here."

"What was her name?"

"Liliana," the boy said. "I don't know her surnames."

"Liliana?" Emilia verified and the boy nodded, his hands

jammed into his trouser pockets. "Do you know where we can find her?"

"No. They kept it real secret." The boy looked down and kicked at nothing before staring out the window past Emilia. "She didn't go to school. Was a waitress someplace. Marco knew his parents would be totally opposed to her. You know. Not his family's type."

Emilia knew it would never occur to the boy to have to say it aloud. Whoever this girl was, she was a social inferior. Marco had had no hope of introducing her to the Sandino family.

Silvio moved into Emilia's line of sight.

"Did you ever meet her?" Emilia asked.

"No, but I saw a picture once." The boy turned away from the window and gave Emilia a watery smile. "No wonder he was crazy for her."

"What happened to the picture?

The kid sniffed, struggling not to break down in front of them. "I guess Marco took it with him when he went."

Emilia and Silvio exchanged glances.

"When he went?" Silvio asked leadingly.

"Marco took his stuff with him." The kid made a vague gesture as if to say *isn't it obvious?* "Clothes, his guitar, even some books. Except for his school uniforms. Left those."

Footsteps rang against the tile in the hallway. The kid turned, face twitching like a frightened rabbit.

"No, no, no." Señora Fortunada's voice reverberated against the stucco walls. She bustled into the room and spun the boy by the shoulder. "We have to get parental permission for you to speak to any of our students," she said to the two detectives.

The boy darted into the room across the corridor and shut the door.

"We were just leaving," Silvio said.

CHAPTER 12

Thursday wasn't a training day for Jacques, which meant that Emilia had Kurt to herself.

The sun was already awake by the time they made it down to the beach. The morning air was warm and calm. It was good to slough off the images of gruesome murders, settle her swim goggles, and stroke alongside Kurt. His length and reach far outstripped hers, however, and by the time they were a half mile past the swimming dock all of her muscles burned with the effort to keep up.

Her phone chirped as soon as they got back to the penthouse. It was the hospital, notifying Emilia that Padre Ricardo had been transferred to the cardiac care unit and was asking for her. She promised to come by that morning.

"That's a good sign," Kurt said. "They're letting him have visitors."

"I wonder if he remembered something important." The conversation with Padre Ricardo about Santa Muerte rushed back at Emilia, sucking the energy out of her.

"About what?"

"The Santa Muerte case. That's what we were talking about when he collapsed.

Kurt led the way into the bedroom. "You act as if you don't want to hear."

"I'm not sure I do."

☼

"I just wanted to thank you, Emilia." Padre Ricardo reached out a hand as Emilia sat on a chair near the bed. "The doctor said that aspirin saved my life."

"I don't even remember giving it to you," Emilia confessed. "I was on auto-pilot."

His grip was still firm, although his color was ashy. Plastic tubing carried oxygen into his nostrils and various wires snaked from the neckline of his blue hospital gown to an array of electrical equipment with blinking green charts.

"So did you solve your mystery of the young man?"

"Not really, although we visited his school yesterday."

"And his family?"

"There's really nothing more to tell them."

"You must find this Santa Muerte priest, Emilia," the priest said seriously. "It's the only way his family will know the whole truth."

Emilia tried to smile. "Don't worry, Padre. I will."

"It's the family that matters," Padre Ricardo said. "The way you've always been good to your mother. Because you understand family."

"Family is important," Emilia said soothingly. The priest was obviously exhausted and rambling. "You're part of ours, you know."

"Family." His grip tightened. "It saves us all in the end."

It was a relief when the nurse came in and said her patient had to rest. Emilia promised to come back tomorrow.

As she walked to the car, unsettled by the priest's condition, Emilia glanced at her watch. If she hustled, she'd make it in time for the morning meeting. Or she could take an hour and check in on her mother and Ernesto, let them know that Padre Ricardo was able to have visitors. They could spread the word; no doubt the entire *barrio* was anxious for news about the priest.

She texted Silvio, letting him know she'd be in late but was still working on contacting Alan Denton, the Pinkerton agent. Later she'd draft a letter to Colegio San Bruno requesting access to the security staff.

Emilia didn't wait for his reply before tossing the phone back into her shoulder bag. A moment later, she grabbed the phone again and muted it.

That *pendejo*. She didn't care if he never texted her back.

Emilia was pleased to see not only Sophia and Ernesto in her mother's kitchen, but also Tía Lourdes and Tío Raul. The four were seated around the kitchen table eating a breakfast of *chilaquiles*. Sophia kissed her daughter then busied herself at the stove. By the time Emilia had gone around the table giving everyone a kiss hello, there was another plate on the table brimming with the fried tortilla pieces bathed in thick sauce and topped with *queso fresco*. Sophia also set out slices of fresh mango and pineapple.

"This is great, Mama," Emilia exclaimed. The *salsa verde*

was perfect; enough zing from the tomatillos to wake her up but not so much she'd have heartburn later.

Sophia put a cup of coffee in front of Emilia and sat next to her. "A good breakfast then off to school."

Across the table, Lourdes exchanged a knowing smile with Emilia. Like Sophia, Lourdes wore a cotton floral housedress and plastic flip-flop sandals. "You look hungry, Emilia," Lourdes said. "They don't feed you in that fancy hotel?"

"I forgot to eat," Emilia confessed. "I went to see Padre Ricardo. He's finally out of intensive care and can have visitors. But that doesn't mean everybody from the church should rush down to see him. He's still very weak."

"We'll have to bring him some food," Sophia said. "I can roast a chicken."

"Fry some tilapia," Lourdes suggested. "Fish is good for the heart. Maybe a *guisada de mariscos.*"

Emilia held up a hand. In two minutes they'd be organizing a parade of women carrying pots of fish stew and whole chickens into the hospital. "It's not allowed yet," she said. "All he can have is broth and gelatin from the hospital."

Both women deflated a bit.

Raul held up his empty mug.

"Will he be back in time for Mass on Sunday?" Lourdes asked as she fetched the coffee pot. She topped up her husband's cup first. Sophia patted her sister-in-law's arm as Lourdes poured. Obviously, like Lourdes said after the novena, everything was fine between the two women.

"I doubt it." Emilia thought of Padre Ricardo's ashen face against the white pillow. "He's still quite ill."

"The bishop will send a temporary replacement." Tío Raul wore clean blue garage coveralls and his curly hair was cut short. He wasn't tall but had a broad chest and muscular arms that made him seem bigger than he was.

Lourdes turned to Sophia. "We'll have to make sure there are clean sheets in the bedrooms. And fresh food in the refrigerator."

Raul pushed his empty plate away. "You don't even know another priest is coming."

"Don't be disrespectful. Of course a priest is coming," Lourdes said indignantly. "There's always a priest in the church on Sundays even if one has to come from across the city."

"If they can't get another priest to stay longer than Sunday," Emilia observed. "The church might have to cancel the Day of the Dead service and the All Saints Day pageant for the children."

Lourdes stiffened. "Impossible. Alvaro's children are in the pageant."

Emilia grinned. Her cousin Alvaro and his wife Daysi had two children. No grandparents were prouder or more possessive than her aunt and uncle. "Was Padre Ricardo planning a Halloween party, too?" she asked.

"These *norteamericano* crazy ideas," Tío Raul said.

"Once when Padre Ricardo had influenza, we had a priest from Chilpancingo," Sophia interrupted, her happily vague smile in place. "I remember we got to church and everyone was so surprised."

"Are you sure it was Chilpancingo?" Lourdes asked. She stirred sugar into her coffee. "I thought he was from Iguala. He was tall."

"Iguala," Raul scoffed. "No priest would come all the way from Iguala to say Mass in Acapulco."

"No," Sophia said firmly. "It was Chilpancingo."

It had happened before. Every time Emilia found it amazing that her mother could remember the details of other people's lives—what they did a year ago, last week, yesterday—but was caught in her own personal time warp in which she was a teenager and Emilia still went to school.

The friendly bickering went on as Emilia finished her food. Padre Ricardo was right. Family was the most important thing.

It was just when she was a kid, except that her noisy cousins weren't there.

Her mother's husband rarely spoke and this morning was no exception. Ernesto silently finished his food, dressed in his usual work clothes of nearly threadbare brown pants, long sleeved dark shirt and leather apron, the uniform of a knife-grinder. The brown leather apron was worn white on the sides, evidence of sharpened blades wiped across to remove steel filings thrown up by the grinding wheel.

"Lots to do today, Ernesto?" Emilia queried as she scraped up the last bit of salsa and cheese with the edge of her fork.

"Yes." Ernesto slurped his coffee.

"Ernesto has a big order to finish." Sophia beamed with pride. "The sewing factory brought him a dozen scissors to be sharpened."

Raul pushed himself away from the table. "I'll help you set up before we go."

Ernesto and Raul left the kitchen.

Lourdes took their plates off the table. "Are you working today, Emilia?"

"Yes, but I wanted to stop by first. Let you know about Padre Ricardo. Check in on Mama."

Sophia gave Emilia a frown. "I'm fine, Emilia. But I worry that you're missing school. I don't want you to get in trouble."

Emilia stood, kissed her mother on the head, and brought her plate to the sink. "I'm fine, Mama."

"Good, because there is something we need to discuss." Sophia's voice was unusually stern. "You can hear this, too, Lourdes."

"What's going on, Mama?"

"You've been spending a lot of time with this Carlos fellow," Sophia said.

"Yes," Emilia said slowly.

"It's time I met his parents. You're there every day, it seems. They must be wondering why a nice girl like you is there so much."

Emilia sighed. "Mama—."

A sudden scream pierced the front wall of the house. It

was the cry of a trapped animal, the gut-tearing sound of pain and terror.

Raul's voice was unnaturally high as he shouted for his wife.

The three women charged through the tiny living room to the open front door, Emilia in the lead. She skidded to a halt in the courtyard.

The grinding wheel was big, about 12 inches in diameter and two inches thick. It was still whirling, the pedals still spinning merrily, winding down slowly as the momentum slackened.

Ernesto was seated at the grinding wheel with half of a large sewing shears protruding from his cheek.

The scissors had split lengthwise. The other half was under the wheel.

Raul held one hand to Ernesto's face below the steel and held the scissors with the other to keep it from slicing down any further. At least two inches of sharpened steel was in Ernesto's mouth. Blood flooded down his cheek below the steel and cascaded out of his open mouth. His eyes were wide and his entire body shook.

"*Madre de Dios*," Emilia exclaimed. She heard a gasp behind her.

"Ernesto!" Sophia screamed as she pushed by, a hand out to stop the wheel.

"Mama, stop!" Emilia tackled her mother just before the spinning metal tore off Sophia's hand. They fell heavily on the dusty concrete.

"Ernesto! Ernesto!" Sophia screamed.

Lourdes grabbed Sophia around the shoulders and hauled her screaming sister-in-law across the courtyard. Emilia scrabbled across the concrete to the grinding wheel.

Both Raul and Ernesto were splattered with blood. Ernesto's normally swarthy complexion was pale. Raul looked grim. Emilia hoped neither man passed out.

"Ernesto, Tío Raul" Emilia panted. "You both stay there. Don't move. We need some ice, then we'll get the scissors out. You'll be all right."

Sophia continued to scream. She shoved at Lourdes with both hands, nearly knocking down the smaller woman, and launched herself at Ernesto.

"Mama, stop!" Emilia wrestled Sophia into the house as if her mother was a violent criminal, one arm jacked up behind her back, the other in an iron grip. Sophia yowled like a wild animal. Lourdes helped to propel Sophia all the way to the kitchen. Emilia grabbed a dishcloth and raided the freezer for a handful of ice cubes.

Back in the courtyard, the two men were still locked in place. Ernesto's eyes were closed and tears mixed with the blood on his face. His leather apron was streaked with red. Emilia didn't know if he was crying from the pain or his wife's anguished screams.

"You're going to be all right," Emilia said, hardly knowing what she was saying. She tucked the towel under the hands clenched around his jaw. "I'm going to touch your face, Ernesto. Press this against your jaw."

While Raul held ice to Ernesto's jaw, Emilia gingerly probed around his fingers, trying to see how bad of a gash the scissors had made. From what she could tell, at least two inches of steel were in his mouth. What she didn't know was how badly the scissors had chopped up his tongue and teeth. "Can you open your mouth any wider, Ernesto?"

He blinked in terror. *No.*

"Okay." Emilia took a deep breath. "We're going to count to three and then I'm going to pull it out. When you feel me start to pull you press on your jaw as hard as you can. Raul will numb it with the ice."

Blood and tears made his face slippery.

"Look at me, Ernesto," Emilia said. "Focus."

She locked eyes with the knife grinder and pressed her fingers over his. "One." She put the fingers of her right hand on the steel closest to his cheek. "Two." She probed gently to find the angle of the steel inside his mouth.

"Three," she shouted and pulled.

The scissors scraped against bone and teeth but came away clean in her hand. Blood gushed from his mouth.

Emilia dropped the scissors. Raul caught Ernesto as he slipped off the grinding stool.

She used the ice and towel to staunch the blood coming out of Ernesto's mouth. His tongue was cut but still intact. A molar had broken. Emilia managed to collect up bits of tooth before he choked on them.

With Ernesto pressing the handful of ice to his face, Emilia and Raul hauled him into the house as far as the living room sofa. Sophia's screams still pummeled the air.

Emilia ran into the kitchen to find more ice. Sophia broke free of her sister-in-law's restraining hands.

"He's dead!" Sophia's screams turned to wild sobbing as she clawed at Emilia. "He's dead, isn't he? Just like before."

"No, Mama, please." Emilia evaded her mother's hands. "Stop it."

Lourdes pulled Sophia off her daughter. "He's not dead, Sophia," she shouted. "He's not dead."

It took 15 excruciating minutes to get Ernesto to the emergency room in the same hospital Emilia had left an hour earlier. Raul came with them, keeping a cold towel on Ernesto's face to staunch the blood.

The nurse recognized Emilia.

"You're that police woman," the nurse said. "You must like hospitals."

"A streak of bad luck," Emilia said.

The doctor who came in was about Ernesto's age. "What happened here?"

Emilia briefly explained.

Within a few minutes Ernesto's face and gums were numb. The doctor pulled out the remaining bits of molar, filled the bloody hole with gauze and expertly stitched up the gash in his cheek. An X-ray revealed no other damage. Raul was given a bottle of painkillers and told to come back in a week to have the stitches taken out.

When they got home, Sophia fell on her husband, crying and screaming again.

Emilia and Lourdes peeled her off. Raul helped Ernesto upstairs to lie down.

Feeling hugely guilty, Emilia gave her mother one of the painkillers. "Here, Mama." As she held out a glass of water and the pill, her cell phone vibrated in the back pocket of her jeans. She ignored it.

"I want you to take this," Emilia said to Sophia.

Her mother slumped into a chair and continued to weep. "He's going to die, isn't he?"

"Sophia," Lourdes said sternly. "He won't die if you take this pill. It's a magic pill."

Sophia took a shuddery breath. "If he dies, I won't do it again. I promise."

"What are you talking about, Mama?" Emilia

"She's stupid with fear," Lourdes said dismissively. She took the water and pill from Emilia and made her sister-in-law take them. "Nobody is dying. Ernesto is going to be fine. Now take this and we can all forget what happened."

Emilia's phone vibrated again. She pulled it out and checked the display. Three missed calls and two texts from Silvio including the one causing the phone to buzz now.

"I've got to go," Emilia said. She never should have muted the phone. Three missed calls. Silvio would be apoplectic.

"Go to work, Emilia," Lourdes said. "Raul and I will stay. We'll take care of your mother and Ernesto."

"I'll call later," Emilia said. "Let me know if you need anything."

She kissed Lourdes, squeezing her aunt's thin shoulder. Sophia didn't react when Emilia kissed her goodbye.

Emilia had passed through the doorway between the kitchen and the living room when she heard Sophia give a plaintive sob.

"I promise, Lourdes," Sophia said. "If he's dead, I won't let her do it again."

Emilia stopped and strained to hear her aunt's response.

"Ah, Sophia," Lourdes replied sadly. "What's done is done. No one could ever to do that twice."

CHAPTER 13

Emilia's adrenaline level was still high as she walked into the police station. Puentes was behind the holding cell desk. Emilia shot him with her thumb and forefinger, like she always did, and was surprised when he leaned over the desk, checked to see that no other cop was around, and crooked a finger at her.

Emilia went to the desk. "What's new, Puentes?"

"Your pal, Detective Gomez." Puentes raised his eyebrows meaningfully.

Not my pal. Emilia bit back the words. "What about Gomez?" she asked instead.

"He's been assigned to check up on us, that's what." The young cop's face tensed with outrage. "Starting tonight he's working the graveyard shift at the desk here."

"Why? To check on the holding cells?" Emilia asked. She'd never heard of a plainclothes detective working the holding cells.

Puentes leaned even closer. "Because of the kid who died while Valdez was on duty. Now we gotta have a babysitter."

Emilia opened her mouth to reply but a voice shouting down the hallway made her look around.

"Cruz!" Silvio snapped. "Let's go."

"Hang in there, Puentes," Emilia said.

She caught up with Silvio as he turned the corner and headed for the new interrogation rooms.

"We picked up Gogo Garcia Figueroa while you were on the beach with Hollywood," Silvio said.

"Family emergency," Emilia said, resisting the temptation of an angry retort. "Get anything interesting out of him yet?"

"We let him cool down by himself for awhile. I sent Sandor in to ask if he wanted coffee or a cigarette."

"Of course you did," Emilia said. "But he hasn't gotten either." It was a simple and effective trick that always worked; leave the suspect alone waiting for some sign of kindness long enough for their anxiety level to ratchet up.

"Cops," Silvio said mockingly. "So fucking incompetent they can't even find a fucking cup of coffee."

Emilia watched her partner as they walked down the hall. He was wound up by the first glimmer of progress in the case, snapping his fingers and almost bouncing on the balls of his feet.

Lieutenant Baez, as well as Macias and Sandor, stood in the narrow anteroom outside the new interrogation rooms. From that vantage point, they could all hear the audio and observe the interrogations while remaining hidden behind the one-way mirror.

Gogo Garcia Figueroa sat slumped behind the table in the first room. His cuffed hands were clasped and a chain ran from the handcuffs to an iron loop embedded in the tabletop. The table itself was bolted to the floor. He wasn't a big person and his lean physique was exaggerated by loose jeans, canvas sneakers, a Réal Madrid jersey, and dark hair worn slicked back from a narrow, square-edged forehead. Emilia saw the distinctive El Machete tattoo on the inside of his wiry left forearm.

"I thought he'd be older," she said. She didn't remember Gogo's age from the birthdate on his *cédula* but the young man looked to be no more than 17 or 18 years old.

Silvio gave a hard laugh. "There's no such thing as an old El Machete gangbanger."

Lieutenant Baez had brought his mug. The coffee gave off a warm aroma. "I want Macias and Sandor to go in first," he said. "Ask him about the billboard murders. Show him the pictures. Play it like you have inside information and he's expected to corroborate a story. He'll deny it, but it'll make him nervous. Then Silvio and Cruz will show him pictures of his brother and the Santa Muerte altars, see what he'll give up to avoid being linked to the billboard killings."

"Hey! Hey!" Gogo shouted at the empty interrogation room. He rattled the chain keeping him tethered to the heavy table.

Emilia saw sweat bead on the young man's forehead.

They talked through strategy for a few minutes more. Silvio was impatient to get things started. Emilia wondered how her partner would act when it was their turn; she knew that after the morning's drama, she didn't have many reserves left to deal with a bad situation.

Ten minutes later, as Macias and Sandor sat in the room and talked to him, Emilia watched Gogo's body language as he repeatedly denied knowing anything about bodies hung from billboards. He worked in the family store for his *mami*. How would he know anything about this shit? As for the tattoo, it don't mean nothing. Just cool shit. Not a crime to have a tattoo. And where the fuck was his coffee?

His voice was defiant, but the tight muscles in his jaw and tiny squints of his left eye gave him away. Gogo kept yanking on the handcuffs and shuffled his feet restlessly.

"He's lying," Emilia said.

Silvio stepped closer to the glass. "I can smell his sweat from here."

"Do you think he's El Commandante?" Lieutenant Baez asked.

"He hasn't been around that long," Silvio said. "Too inexperienced. Too nervous. If El Commandante has the balls to carve up his enemies, string them up for the world to see and sign a *narcomanta*, he's tougher than this."

Lieutenant Baez gestured with his now-empty mug. "You think you can break him?"

Emilia didn't like the smile that lit her partner's face.

"He's a pup," Silvio said. "He'll talk."

Lieutenant Baez hit the button by the one-way mirror. Inside the room, a small light in the ceiling flashed on. Macias and Sandor gathered up their pictures and walked out. Gogo partially stood, leaning as far away from the table as the manacles allowed and yelled something about his fucking coffee.

Both detectives ignored him. The door clicked shut. The chain rattled against the table as Gogo threw himself back in his chair.

"Detective Cruz," Lieutenant Baez said, staring at the solitary figure on the other side of the glass. "Our guest probably hasn't eaten in quite some time. Please find a large cup of very sweet coffee. Extremely sweet."

By the time Silvio finished laying out all the big photos of the interior of the tent on the beach at Coyuca Lagoon and the headless Renzo Garcia Figueroa, Gogo was twitching with sugar and caffeine.

The last photo was a close-up of Renzo's head. The eyes were open but dulled by death, staring at nothing. Emilia remembered taking it and had to suppress a shudder.

Gogo was unable to do the same. An uncontrollable tremor went through his body, making the chain attached to the handcuffs rattle.

"Do you recognize the man in these pictures?" Silvio asked.

"No." Gogo looked away, his mouth trembling.

This was obviously the first news of his brother's violent end but he wasn't going to break the El Machete code of silence and admit anything.

Emilia leaned against the wall and folded her arms, trying to look nonchalant as she waited for her turn. Silvio's bad cop act always came first; she hoped he'd remember that Lieutenant Baez was watching and not take it too far.

"Drugged with blue *reinas*," Silvio said mockingly. "Like a girl in a bar. Got his throat slashed and his neck chopped"—he made a slashing motion by Gogo's face—"and his fucking head just rolled away. What do you think of that?"

Head down, Gogo shrugged.

"You're sure you don't recognize him?" Silvio demanded.

"No," Gogo said under his breath.

"Here." Silvio rearranged the pictures to showcase a shot of Renzo's tattoo. "He had the same ink as you."

Gogo shrugged again.

Silvio tapped on a photo of the Santa Muerte altar. "That mean anything to you? Santa Muerte? You some kind of cult worshipper?"

Gogo shook his head, his upper lip quivering again.

"Let me help your memory." Silvio grabbed Gogo's shirt and hoisted him out of the chair to the full extent of the chain, letting the young man's wrists strain against the handcuffs and eliciting a gasp of pain as metal cut into flesh. "The dead man is your older brother Renzo Garcia Figueroa. He was selling meth out at Coyuca Lagoon just like you're selling out of the Mini Super Mickey to keep your *mami* in hair curlers and cheap tequila. Somebody killed old Renzo in retaliation for the billboard murders. You're next on the list and just like Renzo, Santa Muerte is going to take your soul to hell."

He dropped Gogo back in the seat. The young gang

member stared at his reddened wrists, indented by the strain against the handcuffs.

My turn.

"Aww, can't you see he doesn't understand?" Emilia asked, larding her voice with sympathy. She sat down facing Gogo and took out the folded prayers she'd read with Padre Ricardo just a few hours ago. Her stomach lurched and cold sweat dampened the back of her neck but Emilia picked through the papers until she found the one she wanted.

"You see." She forced a smile. "Someone built this nice *ofrenda* right next to your brother. Probably so you'd know that his death was treated with respect. Prayed for Renzo, too. What do you think of that?"

She shoved the prayer under his nose. Gogo turned his head.

"No matter. I can read it to you. Ready?" She paused but Gogo didn't react. "Right. Well here it is. 'Sainted Santa Muerte. Bring anguish and destruction to unbelievers.' Wait. Was Renzo an unbeliever?"

"I don't know nothing about no Santa Muerte shit," Gogo said as his upper lip twitched uncontrollably.

"They're coming for you, Gogo," Emilia said softly. "Just like Renzo, they're going to cut your throat, chop off your head, and build a black altar to Santa Muerte next to your body unless you let me help you. Help protect your *mami*, too. But you need to help me, too."

"He's got nothing." Silvio smashed a fist down on the table, making both Emilia and Gogo flinch. "Just like his brother. Laid there like a drugged up whore while somebody gave him a new smile.”

Emilia bolted to her feet. “Have some respect for the dead!”

“This is a waste of time.” Silvio backhanded Gogo’s shoulder. “He’s probably sucking Santa Muerte’s tit every chance he gets.”

“*Por Dios*,” Emilia exclaimed theatrically and made the Sign of the Cross.

Gogo started to cry.

Emilia glanced at Silvio. He lifted his chin at Gogo and took a step backwards.

“I’m sorry about your brother Renzo,” Emilia said. She sat down again.

“I told Renzo not to go.” Gogo’s face was wet with tears and snot. “It was too far away. But he had to.”

“Who sent Renzo to Coyuca Lagoon?” Emilia asked.

“I can’t,” Gogo mumbled.

“You can’t protect your mother if you’re dead, Gogo,” Emilia said.

Gogo exhaled as if in pain. “Adonis.”

“Adonis sent Renzo out to Coyuca Lagoon?”

Gogo nodded. “Adonis supplied the shit. We sell and pay Adonis a percentage.”

“Is Adonis also El Commandante?” Emilia asked quietly.

Gogo hung his head. “I don’t know any El Commandante.”

“This guy is El Commandante,” Silvio announced loudly

with a jerk of his thumb at Gogo. "Killed both of those stiffs and hung them from billboards in retaliation for the Santa Muerte killings. Put his name on the *narcomanta* to get back at somebody for killing his brother. The Sinaloa cartel?"

Gogo's head snapped up. "No!" he shouted. "But I wish I had."

"You think the Sinaloa cartel killed your brother?" Emilia asked. The brutal cartel might not be involved but the name might shake out a bit of information.

"No," Gogo protested. "I don't know."

"The Santa Muerte altar next to his body," Emilia pushed on "It was a message. To you? Or to Adonis? Is he a worshipper?"

Gogo's eyes widened.

"Look at that face," Silvio jeered. "Won't last long in the bull pen. Especially if it gets out he killed two Sinaloa *sicarios* and strung them up for the world to see."

The bull pen was the nickname for a temporary holding prison for men on the north side of Acapulco. Everyone knew the squat cinderblock facility was perpetually full to bursting with gang members, thieves, and other criminals who lived in pens of 40 to 60 men each. Silvio had been there once on trumped up charges and had fought hard for a week to survive. Young and scrawny, Gogo stood no chance of lasting half that long.

Gogo jutted out his chin in defiance but Emilia saw tears well in his eyes.

"I know you didn't kill them," Emilia whispered, leaning

over the table as if to speak in confidence. "You didn't even want to join El Machete. Renzo made you, didn't he? And look what happened to him. Adonis let it happen to him."

"I don't know anything," Gogo gulped.

The ceiling light flashed. Emilia left the photos on the table in front of Gogo. Silvio opened the door and she followed him out.

They rejoined Lieutenant Baez, Macias, and Sandor in the viewing corridor. Through the glass they could see Gogo slumped in his chair, his manacled hands clasped together on the table. Every once in awhile he took a shaky breath.

"So what do we have?" Lieutenant Baez asked.

"I think he just gave up El Machete's El Commandante," Silvio said.

Lt Baez made a come-on motion.

Silvio glanced at Emilia and she gave him a *go-ahead* nod.

"The crime scene at Coyuca Lagoon was on a strip of beach served by the El Loro Rojo guest house," he said. "Owned by a couple. She's Mexican, he's German. We heard she has a son by another father who's into some bad shit. He could be this Adonis."

"How does this help us find out who recruited Marco Sandino Varela?" Lieutenant Baez asked.

"Whoever hates Adonis the most," Silvio offered.

"All right." Lieutenant Baez took a last look at Gogo through the window. "Cruz and Silvio, keep on the recruitment angle. Find this so-called Santa Muerte priest.

Macias and Sandor, you sniff around, see what you can turn up on this Adonis and his friends and enemies. In the meantime, we have no cause to retain Señor Garcia Figueroa. Give him taxi fare and send him on his way."

"*Teniente*," Macias said uncomfortably. "That's not really how we do things in Acapulco. If we put him back on the street, he'll be dead in a day."

Lieutenant Baez frowned. "There's no legal reason to detain him."

"Either the next Marco Sandino Varela will get him," Emilia said. "Or Adonis will kill him for talking to us."

"What do you usually do in such a case?"

"Use him as bait," Silvio said.

Lieutenant Baez looked through the glass again. Emilia saw the morality of the situation play out in the stiffness in his mouth and the flare of his nostrils. In *el teniente's* eyes Gogo was a kid caught up in something he didn't understand and shouldn't be punished for being young and stupid.

"This time," Lieutenant Baez said. "We'll err on the side of straight investigative work. Send the boy home."

CHAPTER 14

Emilia called Tía Lourdes and heard that Sophia and Ernesto were now at the apartment over the garage and resting. Lourdes didn't think Sophia could care for her injured husband. Her aunt waved off Emilia's offer of help.

Feeling relieved and a little guilty, Emilia left the squadroom early and stopped by the hospital. Padre Ricardo was still weak, but every nurse on the cardiac care ward said he was their favorite patient and was coming along nicely. Emilia left considerably cheered.

The central police administration building was next on her list. She made her way to the Archive offices and put in a requisition for a data run of crimes committed in Mexico that had some connection to Santa Muerte. The clerk nearly threw her out.

After a test of wills with the head minion, Emilia was able to extract a vague commitment to email her any case file citations from the collection of notoriously inaccurate national databases. She left her contact information and headed for the gym. A good workout beckoned like cool water.

The gym was ostensibly available to the entire department but in practice was only used by the police hierarchy with offices in the building. As a beat cop, Emilia hadn't even known she was entitled to use the gym.

The facility was large and modern. There was a decent

women's dressing room with lockers and clean shower stalls. It was open all the time.

During the day the gym was usually crowded but only a handful of hard-core exercisers would be there in the early evening. That was Emilia's preferred time to go, when she could throw on her crappiest shorts and her lightweight boxing gloves and take out all her frustrations on the 100-lb heavy bag. Once in a while someone else would be there, tacking and weaving and pounding on the leather beast, and she'd have to take out her frustrations on the speed bag. And while the speed bag was great for concentration and working her upper body, it didn't have the same satisfaction that socking the heavy bag did.

The heavy bag was built more like Silvio.

Tonight the gym was nearly empty. A few men were on the machines in the far end and no one was using any of the boxing equipment. Emilia tied her hair back, pulled on her gloves, did some warm up stretches, and finally focused on the leather log dangling from the ceiling by a web of steel chain.

Emilia hit the bag 10 times, 20 times, weaving around it, hitting and kicking it hard enough to make it bounce on the chain and start a rush of sweat sliding down her neck. Her body warmed easily, her muscles glad for the release and she alternated kicks with punches, focusing on the bag as if on an opponent in the ring.

She lost track of time, the world narrowing to the bag and her fists and feet. A volley of punches slammed the bag backwards. Emilia chased it with a roundhouse kick that she knew would bring a strong man to his knees. Two jabs and a backward skip and another kick, the chain jinking.

The bag jolted to a stop, its momentum arrested. Emilia paused, wiped sweat off her face with her forearm, and saw Victor Obregon holding the bag steady on the other side.

He wore black basketball shorts and cross trainers. His chest was bare and while his body was good, he had the typical Mexican male padding, not Kurt's toned athletic power.

"Nice work, Cruz," he observed. He gave her a predatory look.

Maybe it was the slight squint or the curve of his lips, but it always reminded her of a hawk assessing how fast a mouse could run when everyone knew the little creature would never be fast enough to avoid being scooped up by his talons.

"I'm not done," Emilia said shortly. She waved a glove at him to let go of the bag.

He stayed where he was, his hands keeping the bag stationary. "How is the Sandino case going?"

"We've got some leads," Emilia said. She wiped her face again, feeling the sweat trickle through the hair plastered onto her forehead. "The big question is how did the kid get involved with these gangs."

"That's your main line of investigation?"

"That and why the hell his parents called on both private security and the cops in Mexico City instead of here."

"Leave the parents out of it." Obregon relaxed his hands

on the bag.

"Did you see the kid's school?" Emilia punched the bag again and was gratified to see Obregon rock back on his heels. She followed up with a second jab, then a kick.

Obregon grabbed the bag again and it stopped rocking. "What are you talking about?"

"The school was like an expensive prison."

"What does that have to do with the parents?"

"Lots of bad choices." Emilia bounced on her toes and feinted at the bag.

"Leave them alone," Obregon warned. "They're up in Chilpancingo. Out of your orbit. You get my meaning?"

Emilia dropped her fighter stance. "What's your interest here?" she asked.

"Protecting good people. You and Silvio have a reputation for being overzealous."

"Overzealous?" Emilia echoed. "Look, if you've got something to say, just say it."

"I shouldn't have to," Obregon said, his tone one of implied threat.

Overzealous. He was being nasty for the sake of being nasty because she and Silvio had uncovered the money laundering scheme he'd been running with Chief of Police Salazar.

"How's Claudia?" Emilia asked icily, referring to the pregnant girlfriend. "Asked Carlota to be the godmother yet?"

"You take care now, Detective." Obregon shoved the bag

toward Emilia and left the gym.

She had to hop backwards to avoid being knocked down as the bag rattled and jerked on its chain.

CHAPTER 15

To Emilia's surprise, she had three emails from the Archive section the next day. Each was a case file citation from different states in Mexico that included "Santa Muerte" as a database keyword. The citations gave the date, type of crime, location, file number, and a point of contact.

"You coming?" Silvio loomed over her desk. Macias and Sandor had their heads together behind him.

"What?" It took a moment for her to mentally switch gears. They'd all agreed to watch the Mini Super Mickey in case a Marco Sandino Varela copycat came for Gogo. "Look at this."

She pulled up the emails and Silvio ran a hand through his crewcut as he read.

"Los Nueves?" he asked skeptically.

"I don't know."

They agreed she would stay to dig more deeply and the squadroom emptied out.

Emilia stared at her screen. The citations weren't very descriptive.

Nine months ago: A murder in Colima, the small state further north along Mexico's Pacific coast.

Seven months ago: The theft of Santa Muerte merchandise in Puebla, near the border with Guerrero.

Six months ago: A street fight in Oaxaca, in the eponymous state capital. One of the combatants sported a

Santa Muerte tattoo.

She called the contact for the murder in Colima. Lieutenant Diego Villalobos seemed surprised to hear from a female colleague claiming to be handling a similar murder investigation.

"We didn't take it very far," he admitted frankly. "It was a bad crime scene. The body was found several days later in a known gang neighborhood."

"Was your victim beheaded?" Emilia asked.

"No. Unidentified victim shot in the head, execution style. The chest cavity was opened and the heart removed. The Santa Muerte altar was set up on the body, with the heart in the center."

"Any symbols for the number nine?" The description of the murder made Emilia queasy. "Nine things found with the body? The number nine used in crimes around the same time?"

"We didn't count."

Emilia thanked him and rang off, then left messages for the contacts in Puebla and Oaxaca. The latter called her back quickly. The fight in Oaxaca was connected to a prostitution ring. The man with the tattoo was an enforcer type, kept the girls in line. Family paid his bail. Case closed.

Emilia tried a few searches of her own on the single open internet machine in the squadroom and was quickly swamped with lurid blog posts as well as some academic articles about Santa Muerte. Interesting, but not what she was looking for.

Two more citations rolled into her inbox at midday. A robbery of Santa Muerte merchandise from a street vendor in Michoacán a few weeks after the Colima murder. A murder in Iguala, just a short drive from the border with Morelos.

Emilia called and left messages with both investigating officers.

At 4:00 pm, two more murder citations hit her inbox. Both were from Tlaxcala two years ago. Again she called and left messages.

There was a pattern, she just needed to find it. Emilia looked around for a map to plot out the crimes, checking the supply cabinet and the filing cabinets. Nothing.

The only other detective in the squadroom was Ortega, tapping determinedly on his keyboard. "Do you have a map of the country?" she asked.

Ortega looked past her. "Are you talking to me?"

Emilia peered around, the edge of her hand shielding her eyes like an explorer in the sun. She was getting damn tired of both Ortega and Nuñez pretending she didn't exist. "Yes, I'm asking you. Got a map?"

"No," Ortega said shortly and glued his eyes to his computer screen again.

Emilia's phone rang. She trotted back to her desk and picked up.

"Detective Jose Avila Menendez calling for Detective Emilia Cruz."

"Speaking." Emilia sat and hurriedly rifled through the

case file citations. Avila was the officer who'd handled both murders in Tlaxcala.

"I got a message. You're in Acapulco." Avila sounded tired and distracted. "What can I do for you, Detective?"

"I have two murders here in Acapulco that might be similar to yours." Emilia read off the case file numbers. "Santa Muerte signatures."

"*Rayos*," Avila swore like Silvio.

"I take it they ring a bell?"

"I don't remember the case file numbers," he said, voice sharper now. "But I'd never seen anything like it before. The first was never identified. All cut up next to an altar. Candles, prayers, a statue, broken black *muertos*. We never got an ID or a suspect."

"And the other victim?"

"Yeah, I'm still thinking about that one," Avila said. "We decided to see if we could find out where the black *muertos* came from. Hit the local markets, craftsmen who make their living on Day of the Dead sales. Couple of folks mention that Jorge Peralta over there in stall 49 boasted about making dozens of black *muertos* for a very important customer. A priest. Not a Church priest, but a priest. But when we ask Jorge, he says no, no, that was just talk. Two days later, he's dead. Beheaded. Nobody saw anything. Case closed."

CHAPTER 16

"If you don't eat that," Kurt said. "Jacques is going to quit."

"I'm sorry," Emilia sighed. "I'm terrible company tonight. My mind is all over the place."

"You don't have to say a word," Kurt said. "But Jacques made that risotto for you three times this week and this is the first evening you've actually shown up to eat it."

"I know." Emilia dug her fork into the artistic bowl of broth-infused rice and mushrooms.

They ate in silence for a few minutes as twilight spread across the water beyond the restaurant. The leading edges of the small rippling waves shimmered as they strove for the shore. Candles flickered on the table, protected by glass chimneys.

They didn't often eat in the Palacio Réal's famous restaurant. The outrageous prices and formal dress code made the place more of an event than dinner for Emilia. But tonight Kurt said they owed it to Jacques so here she was, cleaned up after her rollercoaster week, wearing a skinny black dress and high heels while drinking wine and eating food she could never afford on her own.

The restaurant was open on all sides. Long and narrow like a ship, it overhung the water and appeared to be sailing through Puerto Marques. The roof was cleverly constructed of soaring canvas sails and the teak floor was planked like a ship's deck. Emilia noticed that an antique diving suit, complete with bulbous brass helmet, now occupied a corner near the expansive bar. It complimented the heavy antique silverware at each place setting, the thick white linen tablecloths and napkins, and the mahogany and brass chairs.

"Jacques wants to get a pirate cannon, too," Kurt said.

Emilia blinked. "What?" Her mind had wandered again.

"Nothing." Kurt topped up their glasses with the bottle of pinot grigio from the cooler by the table. He had on a navy blazer, white shirt open at the collar, and gray slacks. "I was just checking if you were still with me."

Emilia put down her fork. "I'm sorry," she said. "It's been a strange week."

Kurt stretched a hand across the table. "Do you want to talk about it?"

Emilia laced her fingers with his. "I think there's a pattern to the Santa Muerte killings."

Kurt raised his eyebrows.

"There are some similar murders in other states," Emilia went on. "But I've only been able to talk to two of the detectives. It's just that . . . well, I have a hunch."

Kurt squeezed her hand. "Your hunches are usually pretty good."

"We brought in this kid," Emilia heard herself say. "A teenager who got mixed up in a gang because of his brother. You know, the one found dead at the beach on Sunday."

"Did he know his brother was dead?"

"No," Emilia said simply. "Silvio broke the news to him

like a sledgehammer. The kid tried not to cry, but we all know he's not going to survive this range war."

Gogo Garcia Figueroa was bait now, whether Lieutenant Baez wanted it that way or not. So far, nothing bad had happened at the Mini Super Mickey but it was just a matter of time.

"Did he give you anything?" Kurt asked.

"Yes, sort of." The air cooled as the sun sank below the horizon and Emilia pulled her hand out of Kurt's in order to slip her embroidered *rebozo* shawl over her shoulders. "He gave us a name. Another thread to pull."

"So what's the matter?" Kurt asked. "Are you getting pressure from the mayor's office?"

Emilia sank deeper into the comforting wool. "Apparently Carlota calls Lieutenant Baez every day to ask if there's going to be someone hanging off a billboard or if he has properly whitewashed what happened to Marco Sandino Varela."

"Is Baez unloading that on you?"

"No," Emilia said. "He's a decent guy."

She looked out over the ocean again. The restaurant was full of well-dressed diners, yet the tables and chairs were spaced far enough apart to give each table maximum privacy. She was sure that no one else was discussing gang wars or street violence.

Or Santa Muerte.

Waiters unfurled two sails to block the breeze coming off the water and lit more candles to replace the setting sun.

Little flames flickered across the water. The wavering reflections stayed in place. Underneath the ocean rushed and retreated.

"Are you done?" Kurt asked, startling Emilia.

She stared at her empty risotto bowl, unable to remember finishing the meal.

"What's really the matter, Em?" Kurt asked. "Talk to me."

"I'm worried about Santa Muerte," she said softly.

The waiter came by and removed the plates. Kurt ordered coffee and chocolate-dipped cannoli for dessert, another of Emilia's favorites.

"I thought Catholics didn't believe in Santa Muerte," Kurt said when the waiter left.

"I know, I shouldn't." An involuntary shudder went through Emilia and she pulled the *rebozo* more tightly around herself. "But we found these prayers to Santa Muerte to bring anguish and destruction to enemies and everything the enemies love. The person who wrote them probably recruited that young boy to become a killer."

"Okay."

Emilia leaned forward. "I'm that enemy," she whispered across the table.

"Em," Kurt said sternly. "You're talking about the supernatural."

"We were discussing Santa Muerte when Padre Ricardo had his heart attack," she pointed out, keeping her voice low. "Ernesto's accident was awful. My mother fell into a million pieces and started talking nonsense. Worse than when she was here. Thankfully, Tía Lourdes was there to take care of her."

The waiter came by with coffee and dessert. The crisp cannoli, rolled and fried like a *taquito* then dipped in bittersweet chocolate, was filled with custard and chocolate chips. Like the risotto, it was Italian and yet another thing Emilia would never have experienced but for Kurt.

"Padre Ricardo's not a young man, Em," Kurt said. "I'll bet he never sees a doctor. Ernesto handles sharp things for a living. It's not surprising that he had an accident. Or that it would upset your mother."

"I know," Emilia said. "But being a cop has taught me not to believe in coincidences."

"Maybe." Kurt stirred his coffee. "Maybe this once you should look elsewhere for an explanation."

"Just the same, you're not going anywhere in the near future, are you?" Emilia asked. Kurt travelled frequently; hospitality industry conferences, purchasing trips, meetings at the headquarters of the hotel chain in London, marathons and triathlons he competed in. "I have visions of a giant Santa Muerte swatting your airplane out of the sky."

"I promise," Kurt said. "I have no trips planned. I'll just stick to my dull, boring routine for awhile and avoid any encounters with the supernatural."

"Thank you." Emilia hadn't really expected him to say that her fears were justified. In truth, she'd raised the issue with Kurt just to hear it refuted.

She bit into the cannoli, savoring the crunch of the shell and the cool smoothness of the filling, both punctuated by chocolate. "How did I live without this for so long?" she murmured.

Kurt grinned. "I keep telling you, a good meal puts everything into perspective."

Emilia felt herself relax as they lingered. The waiter brought small glasses of port. Kurt was pleased with the new assistant manager he'd hired a few months ago. Reservations were holding steady but he was considering advertising in a British magazine. As always, when Kurt talked about running a luxury hotel and his business contacts, Emilia was whisked light years away from crime scenes and murder victims and interrogation rooms that smelled like fear.

As they stood to leave and walk back to the penthouse, the wind sang through the sails and extinguished a dozen candles. Nervous laughter rippled around the restaurant. The candles were quickly relit and another sail unfurled against the unruly elements.

Emilia held Kurt's hand very tightly as they strolled back to the penthouse.

CHAPTER 17

"I tried to explain it to Kurt last night," Emilia said. "But he says he doesn't believe in the supernatural."

"Hollywood's not Mexican," Silvio said, as if that explained everything.

As they started down the hallway toward the holdings cell and the rear exit just beyond, Emilia saw Puentes at the desk. The young officer looked glum and didn't do more than lift his chin when Emilia shot him with her thumb and forefinger.

"What's wrong with him?" Emilia asked Silvio as they walked out into the bright sunshine.

"I hear Gomez is making life hell for everybody on the desk," he said.

"Why is Gomez even on the desk?" Emilia wondered. "It's not like Holding needs a babysitter. And even if they did, he'd be the last person I'd pick."

"*Rayos*, Cruz." Silvio shook his head in disgust even as he unlocked his car. "Baez has had it in for Gomez for weeks. When the kid died in the cell it gave him the perfect opportunity to shove him out."

"You think?" Emilia buttoned her denim jacket over her shoulder holster. "I mean, Gomez is an idiot, but—."

"Nothing to do with how good or bad a cop Gomez is," Silvio interrupted. "Everything to do with you."

"I didn't tell *el teniente* to stick Gomez back in uniform,"

Emilia countered as she reached for the seat belt.

Silvio started the engine. "I'm saying Baez likes what he sees and didn't like what he heard."

Emilia laughed. "You think Lieutenant Baez has a crush on me?"

"Don't make me have to tell Hollywood," Silvio said.

"Feeling left out?" Emilia cooed. "There's always Ana in Barra de Coyuca and her market stall full of Rambo shit."

Silvio turned on the radio and pumped the volume. "Can't hear you, Cruz."

"You are such a *pendejo*," Emilia said.

Emilia went to the Mercado Municipal now and then. The city's main open air market sold everything from food to furniture to pets. For many in Acapulco it was where they shopped for food, bought gifts, and found the odds and ends that decorated their homes.

The Mercado Oriente was different.

It was a high crime area and tourists were recommended to stay away but the whiff of voodoo and witchcraft that hung about the market made it an irresistible tourist attraction. Foreigners and Mexicans alike were always calling the central police number to report being pickpocketed or having bags stolen but as far as Emilia knew no one ever followed up on any of those calls.

Half tourist trap and half spiritual center, the Mercado

Oriente was a rabbit warren of stalls hawking costumes, party decorations, and statues of the Holy Family. Vendors sold candles by the truckload, most decorated with the Virgin of Guadalupe, San Judas Tadeo, San Miguel slaying the dragon or San Juan Diego receiving the image of the Virgin on his white *tilma* poncho.

Silvio paid two pesos to park in the lot. They waded into the market and were greeted by a stink of blood and flesh reminiscent of the house in Colonia Solidaridad. The butcher section offered chicken feet and entrails for potions. Feathers for pillows and talismans and dreamcatchers. Bones for fortune-telling. Meat for dinner.

Emilia stifled a retch as she followed Silvio, both often turning sideways to pass through the narrow aisles full of dawdling shoppers and aggressive vendors in blood-striped aprons.

Two old ladies argued over a piñata of an orange and black striped cat. Silvio boomed *"Permiso!"* and they stepped to the side, ready to scold but left standing open-mouthed as the big detective plowed through.

Day of the Dead candy was everywhere and the smell of chicken blood gave way to the perfume of chocolate and sugar. They passed masses of marigolds in tin buckets, picture frames for photos of the departed, and pillars of wax decorated with pictures of Our Lady of Guadalupe, San Juan Diego, and San Miguel el Arcángel. Aisles on either side were packed with stalls touting everything needed to celebrate the upcoming Day of the Dead; sugar skull candies, skeleton candies, Halloween decorations, stacks of *papel picado* banners, *muertos* of every size in every outfit. Hundreds of *muertos* in every stall as far as the eye could see.

Also hundreds of tourists.

Lured by the fanciful Day of the Dead displays as well as Halloween candies and decorations, the aisles were jammed by loud shoppers in shorts and flip-flops carrying plastic bags and speaking a babble of foreign languages. English predominated but Emilia caught snatches of German and Russian.

"We'll go faster if we split up," Silvio said. "I'll take the next aisle over. Text if you find anything."

"Sure."

Silvio plunged into the crowd. People stepped aside as he shouldered his way to the front of the first stall.

Emilia meandered down the aisle. All of the stalls had some *muertos* and sugar skull candies but most of the shelf space was devoted to candles. Plain wax candles, religious candles plastered with pictures of saints, candles that smelled like apples or melon, candles that had strings and plastic coins wrapped around them to bring luck and wealth.

She stopped halfway down the aisle. A tiny stall offered candles wrapped in different colored gauze. Red for love and passion. Yellow for healing. Gold for wealth.

None wrapped in black.

As she continued down the aisle, booths had candles and Day of the Dead sugar skull candy, but more real estate was devoted to *muertos*. The small skeleton statues were dressed to entice tourists. There were mermaid *muertos*, bride and groom *muertos*, doctor *muertos*, solider muertos, and female *catrina muertos* dressed in old fashioned gowns and picture hats.

No black *muertos*.

As Emilia passed each vendor she asked if they ever made black muertos. They all laughed, said no one wanted black *muertos. Look, chica*, see the best prices here. She should buy from them. Emilia smiled and kept going.

The path between vendors was barely wide enough to pass through. Candles, statues, bundles of wood, wreaths, and paper garlands were piled higher than Emilia on both sides. Burning incense thickened the air. Her head began to pound.

Emilia got to the end of the aisle and found that it looped back on itself. She turned around, trying not to inhale the smoky fug, and went back the way she came. The displays looked different and she realized she wasn't in the same aisle any more after all. She looked up to get her bearings and realized with shock that dozens of papier maché statues of Santa Muerte were strung overhead. They were tall and short, narrow and wide, dark and light and every hue of the rainbow, all suspended from wires and packed together like piñatas at a party stand. Skeleton faces leered down at her, a jumble of malevolence and color.

Cold traced up Emilia's back. She hesitated, went towards the other aisle, and saw the black *muertos*.

The stall was hardly bigger than a telephone booth and lined with makeshift wooden shelves on both sides. A red curtain covered the back.

Dozens of *muertos* crowded each shelf, skeleton figures of every size and occupation. A display of three black *muertos* stood out. Each figure wore a white shirt and short pants, a parody of traditional Mexican *campesino* work clothes.

Emilia quickly texted Silvio.

A pudgy woman in a tight tee shirt, jeans, and a threadbare cotton apron hunched over a small table in front of the curtain, playing checkers with a little boy who looked about five or six. She had a tangle of hair caught up in a twist, a broad flat face, and startling blue shadow caked in the creases around her eyes.

"How much?" Emilia asked, pointing to the *campesinos*.

The woman came around the side of the table, the heavily made up eyes darting over Emilia as if memorizing her. "Not for sale."

"Why not?"

"Special order," the woman said simply.

"Someone wanted black *muertos*?"

"I have many better than those." The woman steered Emilia to the other side of the stall as her son watched. "Beautiful *catrinas*. See?" She took down a mermaid *muerto*. The tail was a dazzling shade of blue and decorated with beads and sequins.

"It's beautiful," Emilia admitted. No doubt a well-heeled

tourist would buy it soon. "But black *muertos* are more interesting."

Obviously chagrined, the woman replaced the mermaid on the shelf.

Emilia went back to the black *muertos* and picked one up. Except for the white tunic and trousers, the figure was the same size and style as the broken papier maché figurines found on the altar at Coyuca Lagoon. "Who ordered them?" she asked. "I'll pay double what they promised."

The woman grimaced. "A man with a big knife tattoo. The kind of man pretty girls like you don't need to know."

El Machete buying black muertos? It didn't make sense.

"Are you sure it was a knife tattoo?" Emilia couldn't help asking. "Like a big long one on his arm?" She gestured to her forearm.

"Yes, like that," the woman said dismissively. "Crazy men and their tattoos. They spend good money to decorate themselves when they should spend it on food and medicine for their babies."

There was no doubt a story of abandonment behind the words, with the little boy playing checkers as proof, but Emilia didn't have time for that. "Why did he want black *muertos*?" she pressed.

"No, no," the woman said. She plucked the *campesino* figure out of Emilia's hand and replaced it on the display shelf. "You don't want to buy black *muertos*. They are bad luck."

"How can that be?" Emilia said. "Black is the color of

protection from evil spirits, isn't it?"

"Sometimes," the woman said.

"And other times?"

"They are a curse."

"I've had bad luck," Emilia said. She scanned the aisle for Silvio. Her view was blocked by a gaggle of elderly *norteamericano* tourists wielding plastic tote bags and talking loudly.

"You are worried," the woman said. The woman stepped close enough for Emilia to smell onions and cheese on her breath. It made for a rancid combination. "You need to pray to Santa Muerte?"

"For healing," Emilia said. The words came out before she had time to think. "For my mother. To make her like she was before."

"Ah. That is the real reason you are here." The cadence of the woman's speech had the same flow and pace as if she was reciting the Hail Mary or the Our Father in a church.

"Yes," Emilia heard herself whisper.

Hope that Santa Muerte could cure Sophia's vagueness overwhelmed her like a breaking wave. Emilia knew it was simply the incense or the dozens of staring *muertos*.

The woman told the child to watch for shoplifters. She held open the thick curtain to reveal a small workroom. Emilia slipped inside. The woman let it fall closed and they were abruptly enveloped in red-tinted darkness.

Emilia blinked, trying to refocus. She heard the sizzle of a match and followed the pinpoint of flame as the woman lit a candle.

The small space held a tiny table laden with unpainted *muerto* figures and plastic boxes full of paints, glue, and scraps of wood. Sheets of newspaper, cut into small squares, overflowed a plastic tub. Half finished Santa Muerte statues, some as tall as Emilia's arm, hung from a rope stretched across the ceiling. They were close enough for her to reach up and touch.

The woman held the dying match to a stick of incense and the smoky scent of sandalwood spiraled into the air. The cement floor and walls radiated damp but the room felt stuffy and tight. The noisy market faded away.

The woman sat on a small stool. Emilia found another. A tabby cat appeared and rubbed against Emilia's legs. When Emilia went to rub its ears, it hissed and clawed at her hand. She jerked back just in time.

"For healing." The woman's singsong voice was soothing. Another match flared and she pressed it to the wick of a candle wrapped in yellow gauze, with charms pressed into the wax. The flame caught, then abruptly went out. The woman struck another match and this time the flame caught and held. The two candles lit the table, sending the walls and half-finished Santa Muerte statues into the shadows.

The space was tight enough to smell the woman's fetid breath. Emilia felt the cat press against her legs. The woman took Emilia's hand. "Is your mother's illness very bad?"

"Yes," Emilia said. "She has been sick for a very long time. Her mind is broken."

"You wish Santa Muerte to intercede?"

"To make her mind sharp again," Emilia said.

"Do you believe in the power of Santa Muerte?"

"I . . . I think so."

The candle flame wavered, bouncing mysterious shapes across the red curtain. "Santa Muerte can grant great healing," the woman said. "But you must pay for the prayers to Santa Muerte. Five hundred pesos and we will say the prayers together. This will heal your mother."

She looked at Emilia's shoulder bag.

Five hundred pesos. This was nothing but a scam the woman had worked a hundred times before on unwitting tourists.

Emilia pulled her hand away, feeling like a fool. She'd let herself forget why she was in the market hunting for Day of the Dead decorations. Silvio was probably looking for her and cursing right now.

"How many black *muertos* have you made?" she asked.

The woman frowned. "I told you," she said. "The black *muertos* are not for you. Five hundred pesos and we'll say the prayers together."

Emilia opened her bag and took out a card with her cell phone number printed on it. She held it out. "When the man with the tattoo comes to get the black *muertos*, call me. I need to speak with him."

The woman got to her feet, blew out the candles, flung back the red curtain, grabbed Emilia's arm and shouldered her out of the space. The little boy looked up curiously from his checkerboard.

"Get out," the woman said angrily.

"If you are afraid," Emilia said softly. "I can protect you."

The woman darted into the aisle and pointed at Emilia. "Thief," the woman bawled. "Thief!"

A clamor instantly rose up from the stalls on either side. Shoppers in the aisle jostled each other to see.

"I didn't steal—."

Something bludgeoned Emilia's shoulder blade and she crashed to one knee. She looked up dizzily to see an unkempt security guard raise his nightstick again. Emilia managed to twist and the blow handed on her elbow. Her arm went numb, she toppled sideways, and her vision turned into fireworks.

"I'm not a thief," she gasped but her voice was lost in the uproar as the market erupted in a commotion of frightened tourists and excited vendors.

A stranger hauled Emilia to her feet only to yell accusations in her face. The woman continued to scream that she'd been robbed. Tourists backed away in panic as the aisle filled with angry men. As her vision cleared, Emilia saw Silvio in a wrestler's crouch, his arms outstretched. Another man, wearing the trademark bloody apron of a chicken butcher, circled the big detective, a heavy cleaver in his hand. Spectators pressed into the stalls on either side, shouting and hollering and panting for a fight.

The butcher waved the cleaver, his hands streaked with animal blood. Sneering and taunting, he rushed at the big detective. Silvio spun to the side and punched the other man in the kidney as momentum carried him past. The butcher gasped and flailed out with the cleaver.

The spectators shouted and swirled around the two fighters. Emilia shoved past the stranger still admonishing her. The security guard and his nightstick was nowhere to be seen. She found her phone and called Dispatch, barely able to make herself heard above the noise of the crowd.

The butcher rushed at Silvio again, and again Silvio sidestepped and dealt a hard blow. The butcher struck out clumsily and the cleaver sliced into Silvio's khaki cotton jacket, splitting the fabric from armpit to waist. Under the tear, bright red bloomed across his white tee shirt.

The next thing Emilia knew, Silvio had the man in a chokehold. The cleaver clattered to the cement and she wriggled in between restless feet to scoop it up. The butcher's eyes rolled back in his head. Silvio let the man fall, his body thudding to the floor like dead weight.

"Franco!" Emilia brandished the bloody cleaver to open a path to Silvio. "Show's over," she shouted at the crowd.

No one moved. The silence was as tenuous as the anticipation between lightning and thunder.

"Get us out of here, Cruz," Silvio said out of the corner of his mouth.

The entire side of his jacket was soaked with blood.

Like a gift, a *taqueria* appeared. Market patrons sat on tall stools to wolf tacos and colas between shopping forays to the stalls. Still clutching the cleaver, Emilia shepherded Silvio through the little taco restaurant and out a side exit. He kept up a good pace as they backtracked to the parking lot, but by the time they got to his car the color had washed out of his face and the stain had spread from the side of his jacket to the back.

"You drive," he said and handed her the keys.

She knew the way to the emergency room by heart now. For the third time in a week, she greeted the same nurse, showed her badge, and followed a wheelchair through the sliding glass doors of the emergency room.

Two hours later, Emilia was shown into a treatment room where she found a shirtless Silvio sitting on an examination table. Closed with angry black stitches, a slice ran diagonally across the right side of his ribcage and disappeared into the waistband of his jeans.

"Seventeen stitches," he said by way of greeting, studying the remains of his jacket.

"You should have just shot him," Emilia said. She plunked down the gym bag she'd found in the trunk of his sedan on the table next to him.

"I would have if I didn't think the crowd would rush us." Silvio unzipped the bag, all of his abdominal muscles flexing as he moved. Emilia had known he was working out instead of going to counseling but hadn't thought much about it. Now she realized grief had honed him into a Mexican

Schwarzenegger. Even with the row of stitches marching around his torso, Silvio looked able to twist horseshoes.

He pulled a clean white tee out of the gym bag.

"Need some help?" Emilia asked.

He gave her a *don't be stupid* look, stuck his right arm into the tee, wrangled it over his head, and shoved his left arm into the other sleeve. As he yanked the shirt over his stomach, Emilia looked away, surprised at herself for thinking that Silvio was rather attractive in a wounded rodeo bull sort of way.

He eased himself off the exam table and washed his hands in the sink. "Did you find out anything before you decided to steal crap out of the market?"

"The woman running that stall had some black *muertos* dressed like *campesinos*. They were a special set for a buyer."

"She tell you anything about the buyer?" Silvio took a paper towel from the dispenser, his right arm staying close to his side.

"Yes." Emilia paused. "He had a big knife tattoo on his arm."

"El Machete?"

"Sounds like it."

Silvio passed the damp paper towel over his face. "That doesn't make sense," he said and threw the paper towel into the trash can, making the lid swing. "Los Nueves is using the black *muertos* and making the altars. El Machete is going for the billboard concession."

"It could be that El Machete is planning some sort of retaliation," Emilia said.

"Another word for escalation," Silvio said grimly.

Emilia's phone rang.

It was Mercedes. "Emilia, are you busy right now?

"I'm at the hospital," Emilia said.

"With Padre Ricardo?"

"No, something else," Emilia said. "What's the matter?"

Silvio raised his eyebrows at her as he pulled a warmup jacket out of his gym bag. Emilia gave him the just-a-minute signal with her thumb and forefinger.

Mercedes gave a little sob. "My place was robbed. I got roughed up a little.'

"*Madre de Dios*," Emilia exclaimed. "Are you all right?"

"They stole my computer." Mercedes gulped audibly. "The stereo."

"Oh, no."

"I'd forgotten my cell phone in the bathroom." The dancer's voice rose and Emilia knew she was close to hysteria. "If I hadn't, they would have found that, too."

"Go next door," Emilia said. "I'll be over as soon as I can."

"I can't," Mercedes sniffed. "Somebody else will steal what's left."

Silvio fought his way into the warmup jacket. He put his gun, still in the shoulder holster, in the gym bag.

"Sit tight," Emilia said. "I'll be there as soon as I can."

"What's going on?" Silvio asked.

"My friend Mercedes Sandoval." Emilia stowed her phone back in her shoulder bag. "She was robbed. Beat up. I need to go over there."

"Mercedes Sandoval the dancer? She's a friend of yours?" He hefted the gym bag with his left hand and walked to the door. "Let's go."

"Look, I'll take you home," Emilia said. "That shot is going to wear off and those stitches are going to hurt like hell.

"I got some steam left, Cruz." Silvio held out his hand.

Emilia dropped his car keys onto his palm.

Mercedes Sandoval's dance studio was in a strip mall in Emilia's old neighborhood. A metal grille that protected the heavy brown front door was still in place. The sign by the door was still hung straight. The windows were unbroken, the interior of the studio still hidden by heavy white draperies. Emilia pressed her finger on the buzzer. A metallic voice asked who was there.

Emilia bent down and answered into the speaker fitted into a gouge in the green concrete wall. "Emilia and Silvio."

The door swung open immediately, as if Mercedes had been waiting for them.

Before Emilia could stop herself, she gasped at the sight of her friend. One eye was swollen and purple and her chin was scratched and raw. As Mercedes unlocked the metal grille to let them in, Emilia saw that her hands were scraped and bruised as well.

Emilia immediately pulled Mercedes into a gentle embrace, leaving Silvio to close and lock the door behind them. "You're okay," she said quietly.

Mercedes took a shaky breath. "You think that it happens to other people but never to you. What am I going to do? I can't afford to buy a new stereo. Or a laptop."

"We'll figure it out," Emilia said.

Mercedes sniffed, stepped back, and saw Silvio. "Hello," she said before Emilia could introduce them. "I'm Mercedes Sandoval. Welcome to my robbery."

"Franco Silvio. What happened?"

"They pried open the back door while I was shopping," Mercedes said. "I came in the front door and there they were."

"How many?"

"Two."

Silvio led Mercedes through the usual questions asked of a robbery victim. She'd come in the front door and they'd jumped her. They fought and Mercedes was battered to the ground. The thieves grabbed her electronics and ran out the same way they'd come in.

"Show me," Silvio said.

Mercedes led them across the pale wood plank floor, worn white in many places. She wore loose linen trousers and a matching cream knit tank which showed off muscular bare arms. Her clothes were streaked with dirt, she was barefoot, and her hair threatened to escape the single loose braid that snaked down her back.

Emilia knew that Mercedes had been left nearly penniless when her husband and ballroom dance partner died years ago. The dance studio gave her independence but not enough money to rent an apartment so she lived there as well.

They passed the single room that served as the dancer's office, bedroom, kitchen, and entertainment area. Just beyond, a short hallway led to the rear door.

The two bottom hinges had been pried apart. The door swung drunkenly on the single top hinge. Silvio pulled on a pair of latex gloves from his back pocket, pushed it open and stepped down.

Emilia watched from the hallway. The narrow strip of asphalt behind the strip mall was bordered by a wall taller than her partner and topped with coils of razor wire. The wire was cut and pulled aside, leaving a narrow slot wide enough for a ladder and a man carrying a good quality stereo.

"What's on the other side of the wall?" Silvio asked.

"A parking lot for the grocery store."

Which meant it would have been easy for the thieves to access a getaway car.

"What's left in your refrigerator?" Silvio asked abruptly, looking down at the barefoot dancer.

"Some mineral water, some soup from yesterday," Mercedes floundered.

"Ice?"

"There's some in the freezer."

"Go make her put it on her face, Cruz," Silvio said. "Call Dispatch, get some techs out here to take prints. I'll get some supplies and be back in an hour."

"Are you sure you're up to it?" Emilia asked.

"I'll be back in an hour," he repeated.

It was a miracle but a tech team came quickly, dusted for prints, and left. True to his word, Silvio was back in an hour with his cousin Antonio, a tool box, and a soldering iron. Emilia watched, flabbergasted as Silvio and Antonio repaired the door. She had no idea her partner had any talents besides boxing, terrifying suspects, and making her crazy.

They worked through a jazz class. Mercedes put on makeup and taught her students a new step, counting the beat by thumping a stick on the floor. Emilia waited in the office-cum-bedroom.

When she heard Mercedes dismiss the girls, she went back into the studio. Silvio was there, sitting on the floor with his back against the wall, watching Mercedes demonstrate the step to two of the girls who wanted to polish their routine.

His tee shirt was sweat-stained around the neckline and armpits. A thin trickle of blood from his stitches had seeped into the clean cotton.

Emilia settled onto the floor next to him. "Did Antonio go?"

"We got the door bolted shut," Silvio said. "Added a new padlock."

Emilia rested her arms on her knees and her chin on her

fists. "I didn't know you were so handy."

Silvio snorted.

"Or interested in dance," Emilia said.

"Isabel used to watch her on television," he said, staring at Mercedes.

Emilia watched him out of the corner of her eye as she waited for the extra dance tutorial to end. Silvio hadn't mentioned his late wife Isabel in a long time. She didn't know if that was a healthy thing or not.

The beat of the stick as Mercedes instructed her students reminded Emilia of the woman in the market and her singsong cadence. It had all been an act. Emilia mentally berated herself for being taken in so easily, as if she was some unsuspecting tourist.

Her mother Sophia was always going to be what she was.

CHAPTER 18

Kurt hauled Emilia out of bed at 6:00 am. She groused about the hour as she climbed into her red two-piece but his energy and good humor were infectious. By the time she braved the first wave she was glad she'd kept her promise.

Not surprisingly, Kurt and Jacques beat her to the floating dock. Kurt plucked her out of the water and onto the gently tilting platform. The sunrise was achingly beautiful, painting the sky with shifting bands of rose and apricot. The three stood on the dock, swaying a little as it rode the waves, and watched the glimmering light spread over the water.

"This never gets old," Jacques said.

"I know." No matter how violent Acapulco became or hard her job was, moments like this reminded Emilia why she would never be happy anywhere else.

Kurt had tugged off his swim goggles to watch the sunrise and now he stretched the band above his ears and settled the slanted blue lenses over his eyes. "Time for the training swim. Have a good day if you head out before we're back."

Emilia gave him a salty kiss. "See you tonight."

His own goggles in place, Jacques gave her two Gallic kisses, one on each cheek. Kurt and Jacques dove off the dock and struck out toward the mouth of Puerto Marques. Emilia watched muscular arms cleave the water with long, powerful strokes. As a native of Acapulco, she'd always been cautioned not to swim too far from shore. The open ocean was for fishing boats, not swimmers.

But *gringos* had different ideas.

Emilia floated on her back, letting the waves gently splash her back to shore. For once she wasn't going to rush. The rest of the day would be hectic, not least because she hoped to follow up on those other Santa Muerte case citations.

The rising sun dried her as Emilia sat on her towel by the water's edge and checked text messages. Mercedes was up early, too.

How are you feeling?

Sore but okay ☺

A couple of hotel employees in their signature hotel print shirts started raking the sand and opening umbrellas. They recognized her and smiled. Although she hadn't ordered it, a waiter appeared with a cappuccino on a tray.

It was the start of another perfect Palacio Réal day.

Holding the cappuccino made it impossible to text. Emilia hit the talk button and Mercedes answered right away.

"Guess what I'm doing right now?" Emilia asked.

"Sitting on the beach," Mercedes said. Even the dancer's voice was graceful.

"Yes." Emilia took a sip. "I'm on the beach drinking cappuccino."

Kurt and Jacques came back in sight. Two heads bobbed in the distance, one fair and the other dark.

"I swear, *chica*," Mercedes marveled. "You are living the

high life."

"I know." Emilia watched the swimmers. The two men were evenly matched, but Kurt slowly pulled ahead as they approached the floating dock. "Half the time I feel guilty and the other half of the time I feel guilty about feeling guilty."

"On another topic," Mercedes said. "Your buddy Franco was quite the surprise."

"He surprised me, too," Emilia said. "Did you know he got 17 stitches about two hours before he fixed your door?"

"Can I get his number?" Mercedes asked. "I want to thank him. I don't know if I said anything coherent yesterday."

Emilia pulled the phone away from her ear as the air filled with the raucous buzz of a motor. A jet ski sped across the water, the front of the craft slamming up and down like a cigarette boat. A bikini-clad woman clasped a man around the waist and squealed at him to go faster. The man turned his head to talk to her as the jet ski shot across the water, churning the water into foam on a trajectory that would intersect with the two swimmers.

Kurt and Jacques kept stroking, apparently oblivious.

Emilia scrambled to her feet, shouting and waving her arms. The hotel employees readying the beach did the same. Their voices were lost in the rev of the engine and the heave of the waves slapping against the swimming dock.

Buffeted by the chop, both Kurt and Jacques swiveled in the water, looking for the source of turbulence.

The jet ski slammed over them and kept going.

The water heaved in its wake. Emilia saw a cobalt sky,

turquoise ocean, white foam. No swimmers.

"Kurt!" Emilia screamed. "Kurt!"

Jacques popped up, shouting.

Kurt didn't resurface.

"Call the front! Call the front!" One of the young men, who a minute before had been arranging chairs, pounded past Emilia, shouting as he went, his feet thudding on the packed sand. As he ran, he carried a floatation device attached to his wrist by a cord. A moment later, another young man flew by in a whirl of sand and blue print, another floatation device carried under his arm.

Emilia cut the call with Mercedes, called the hotel front desk, and reported the emergency. It was almost as if she was two people, one calmly but urgently telling Luis what had happened. Her other self was desperately scanning the water, heart beating wildly, wanting to scream with the tension.

One of the speedboats backed out of its berth in the hotel marina, the engine gunned and it aimed directly for the floating dock. At the same time, the two rescue swimmers reached Jacques, who was spinning in the water, shouting for Kurt.

One of the rescue swimmers dove under the surface, his flotation device bobbing on the waves but still tethered to him. Jacques dove under as well.

After a minute of agony both resurfaced, Kurt lolling between them, obviously unconscious. The speedboat glided to a stop between the dock and the swimmers. Kurt was handed aboard, the others climbed up the ladder, and the boat headed back.

Emilia couldn't breathe. Phone in hand, she raced across the beach and through the series of open air corridors that connected the main hotel to the marina. The hotel's in-house doctor and nurse were already there, the doctor in shorts and a tee shirt as he bent over the prone figure of Kurt in the bottom of the boat.

Luis from the front desk was there, too, as was Christine. The head concierge looked hastily dressed in a knit dress and uncombed hair. At least a dozen other hotel employees were there, including several from the ever-present security staff.

Jacques huddled under a blanket in the bottom of the boat, answering the doctor's questions as his teeth chattered. Emilia slipped through the knot of people to the boat.

Still unconscious, Kurt was barely recognizable as the man who'd woken Emilia with a laugh an hour ago. His face, arms, and torso looked like ground meat. The doctor fixed an oxygen mask over Kurt's face and inserted an IV needle. With half a dozen helping hands and the doctor barking orders, Kurt was eased onto a stretcher and carefully lifted over the side of the boat. His bearers sprinted toward the small clinic on the first floor of the hotel, the doctor and nurse running alongside.

Jacques dropped over the side of the boat, shaking from exertion and adrenaline. The remaining hotel employees clustered around him. The chef said something in French, which from the vehemence and the word *jet-ski* suggested his intent to kill the person who had plowed into them.

Emilia had never felt so helpless in her entire life.

An ambulance took Kurt to Hospital Santa Lucia, the new private hospital downtown. Promising Jacques she'd call as soon as she knew anything, Emilia threw on jeans, sandals, and a tee shirt and got there half an hour later. As she wasn't family, the hospital staff loftily told her, Señor Rucker's condition could not be discussed with her. Emilia's police badge broke down that barrier and she was shown to a private family waiting room on the trauma services floor.

Christine Boudreau walked in an hour later, interrupting Emilia's agitated pacing from one end of the room to the other. The hotel concierge had taken more time than Emilia in getting dressed. She wore a fitted pink cotton sheath, high heel sandals, and pink quartz earrings that dangled to her shoulders. Her blonde hair was artfully tousled and her makeup was fresh and subtle.

"What are you doing here?" Emilia asked bluntly, her nerves stretched too thin to be diplomatic.

"I could hardly stay at the hotel while Kurt fights for his life."

"He's not fighting for his life," Emilia snapped.

"No?" Christine sank into a chair. "He's going to be fine? What did they say?"

"They haven't said anything yet," Emilia admitted. "He's still in surgery."

Her phone rang.

"Where are you?" Silvio demanded as soon as Emilia answered.

"At the Hospital Santa Lucia," Emilia said. She turned her back on Christine as she spoke. "Kurt's had an accident."

"How bad?"

Emilia recounted the event. "He's still in surgery."

"You need anything?"

"Just some good news," Emilia said.

"Stay in touch," Silvio said brusquely, as if he'd sensed her thoughts, and hung up.

The doctor came to the waiting room three hours later. The lacerations to Kurt's chest, shoulder, arm, and face required multiple stitches. They'd found no damage to internal organs. A CAT scan revealed a slight concussion. Considering the nature of the incident, he'd come out of it remarkably well, no doubt due to his overall excellent physical condition.

"When may I see him?" Emilia asked.

Christine gave a slight cough. The doctor looked from one woman to the other. "As soon as he's awake. An hour or so."

"Thank you," Emilia said.

Christine followed the doctor out of the room, cell phone in hand.

Emilia sat down again and dialed Mercedes. "*Por Dios*, Emilia!" the dancer exclaimed. "What happened?"

An hour later, as Emilia paced and Christine looked at her

phone, Mercedes swept in, wearing beet red capri leggings and a matching sleeveless silk tunic that swayed with every movement. Her wavy hair streamed down her back as she hugged Emilia.

"We're still waiting for him to wake up after surgery," Emilia said chokingly.

"He will be fine," Mercedes said, her hands framing Emilia's face. "It might just take a little time."

Emilia introduced Mercedes to Christine and watched the two women exchange the perfunctory ladies' greeting of a kiss, as well as a glance of mutual assessment and mistrust. In other circumstances, this would be funny.

"Christine is the head concierge at the Palacio Réal," Emilia said and couldn't resist adding, "Kurt is her boss."

Staff from the hotel came and went. Christine stayed. Morning turned into afternoon. The concierge was on her phone half the time, irritating Emilia for no good reason as they waited for the doctors to say that Kurt was awake.

To her surprise, Silvio showed up.

"Made an arrest," he said. "I called the head of security for the Palacio Réal to let him know.

Emilia had lost track of time. "Already?"

"Wasn't that hard." Silvio looked out of place in the hospital waiting room. It was a surprisingly nice space, with cool pale blue walls, photos of Acapulco sunsets, and comfortable chairs. "Rich honeymooners from Spain. Staying in a rental on the other side of Punta Diamante."

"Emilia hasn't seen fit to introduce us." Christine came

forward with her hand outstretched. "I'm Christine Boudreau, the head concierge at the Palacio Réal. Thank you so much."

Silvio chose that moment to take off his jacket. Without it, the big detective's cropped head, shoulder holster, heavy gun, and white tee stretched tight over heavy muscles made him more menacing than ever.

Christine dropped her hand but not her professional hospitality smile.

"Detective Silvio," Mercedes murmured.

"Señora Sandoval," Silvio said, his gaze swinging to the dancer.

"I was just going to get coffee," Mercedes said. "Would you like some?"

"Let me help you." Silvio said.

He pulled the jacket on again to hide the gun and they walked out. Emilia slumped into a chair. Christine sat across from her and pulled out a magazine. After two minutes Emilia turned on the television and stared at a morning talk show that assumed the viewer had the attention span of a Coyuca Lagoon mosquito.

Silvio and Mercedes returned with four cups of institutional coffee. Emilia held the proffered cup, knowing that if she drank her stomach would not cooperate.

Silvio leaned forward, elbows on his thighs, and stared at Christine as he drank his coffee. The blonde woman carefully avoided looking at him. Mercedes looked everywhere but at either of them.

"How long has it been?" Emilia fretted. "The doctor said he'd be awake in an hour."

"Maybe he's groggy," Mercedes said.

"You said you work at the Palacio Réal, *chica*?" Silvio abruptly asked Christine.

Her eyes darted to him and her hotel smile made a reappearance. "Yes."

"You drive along the Carretera Escénica a lot?"

"Yes, of course." Christine sipped coffee. "Now and then."

"Did you see the body hanging from the billboard last week?"

"I'm sorry?" Christine's eyes opened wide.

"Never mind." Silvio drank more coffee. "You don't look like the type."

Mercedes made a strangling sound. Christine looked at her. Mercedes buried her nose in a magazine.

The four of them sat without speaking for a while. Silvio continued to stare at Christine. The concierge jabbed at the screen of her cell phone. Outside the reception room a voice murmured over the hospital intercom for Doctor Covalin to go to Pediatrics. Someone pushed a metal trolley past the doorway. Two nurses talked in hushed voices as they passed.

Silvio stood up. "I gotta get back, Cruz," he said.

"Sure." Emilia stood up, glad for a distraction no matter how small. She walked with him down the corridor to the bank of elevators.

"Hollywood should cut out that swimming shit," Silvio

said. "Bad for the health."

Emilia smiled in spite of herself. "I'll tell him you said so."

"So the blonde," Silvio said as he punched the button for the elevator. "You said she works with Hollywood?"

"Yes. For him. Head concierge."

Two nurses passed them in the wide corridor.

"She the rival?" Silvio asked.

Emilia shrugged. "She thinks so."

"She's cardboard," Silvio snorted. "Not Hollywood's type."

"You were deliberately trying to make her nervous," Emilia said. "Thanks."

"Shoulda shown her my stitches," Silvio said.

Emilia laughed. The elevator doors slid open and he stepped inside. The other people in the elevator jostled to give him room.

Not Hollywood's type. It was good to hear someone else say it. Emilia felt marginally better as she went back to the waiting room and settled down next to Mercedes.

"About Franco," the dancer said. "He's not what I expected."

"I know what to do when he's *a pendejo*," Emilia replied. "But now and then he's decent and I'm lost."

A different doctor came to the waiting room. Mercedes still beside her, Emilia jumped to her feet when she saw the grim expression on his face. Christine rose slowly, gripping her phone so tightly that her knuckles were paper white.

"Señor Rucker has not yet woken," the doctor said. "We've done an MRI and while we cannot detect any abnormalities, apparently the trauma to his head was more severe than we first assessed."

Trauma. "What does that mean?" Emilia heard herself ask.

"Señor Rucker has lapsed into a coma."

CHAPTER 19

It was 4:00 am. Emilia was wide awake. Without Kurt, the penthouse was cavernous and unwelcoming. She made coffee and draped herself over the dark balcony. Sunrise was still an hour and a half away.

So much had changed in less than 24 hours.

Knowing she could either break down and sob or do something constructive, she threw on jeans and a tee. The valet was startled when she asked for the Suburban but in less than a minute, she was urging the big vehicle up the winding road from the hotel to the highway.

Without any traffic, she made it to the Colegio San Bruno in 20 minutes and parked along the quiet private street leading to the school.

The night guard would no doubt be ending his shift soon. There would be no other cars. Unless the guard lived on campus, he'd have to pass her on their way home. She didn't know when the night shift ended.

It didn't matter. She could wait.

It was just past 5:00 am when an older black sedan puttered past. Emilia counted to five then started up the Suburban and followed. She kept her distance as the sedan got on a four-lane road. The traffic picked up, but Emilia stayed with the sedan, turning off the big road and into the maze of streets of Colonia Loma Hermosa.

The sedan turned into a privada gate and stopped at the

barrier. Emilia hauled the Suburban to a stop right behind, pinning the sedan between the barrier and the Suburban. A security guard came out of the guard shack, blinking sleepily. Emilia lowered her window and held out her badge. "*Policía*," she called.

The sedan driver got out of the car and came to the Suburban. In his mid-50's and still in good shape, he wore the gaudy maroon uniform of the Colegio San Bruno's security force. The gold braid on his uniform made him look like a banana republic dictator.

Emilia continued to hold out her badge. "I'd like to speak with you," she said.

He studied her badge. "Is this about Marco?"

"Yes," Emilia said. "Were you on duty the night he disappeared?"

His shoulders tensed. "Yes," he said.

"Five minutes," Emilia said. "Routine questions. Here or at the station."

"All right," he said. "I live here. Follow me and we'll talk."

He went back to his car and the barrier lifted.

The *privada* was a horse-shaped neighborhood of large stucco houses. Architectural planning was evident. The houses weren't identical, but all were yellow stucco with red tile roofs, fancy elements like an arched entrance, and blue and white *azulejo* tiles inset into the stair risers.

At the center of the horseshoe, a child's play area rose out of the darkness, haloed by the first morning light. The sedan pulled into a driveway just beyond the swing set. Emilia parked in front of the house.

The guard got out of his car and extended a hand. "Carlos Rizo."

Emilia introduced herself and he offered her a seat in a heavy wooden armchair on the porch. It wasn't a finely milled teak chair like the ones at the Palacio Réal, but Emilia knew it was expensive.

"You were the guard on duty the night Marco disappeared," Emilia guessed.

"Yes, that's right." Rizo sat in a matching chair to Emilia's right and carefully placed his hands on his knees. "It was a Wednesday night."

"The school says he disappeared while on a school trip to the movies," Emilia went on, trying to sound relaxed as if she had conversations with strangers before dawn every day. "None of the students who were with him have been questioned. The movie theater didn't report any violence, anything that would lead us to expect a kidnapping had taken place."

"I wouldn't know about that," Rizo said.

"No, I guess not," Emilia said agreeably. "It's just that my partner has a theory and he wants to take it to the school board."

"What's that?" Rizo asked warily.

"We think Marco packed a suitcase and left," Emilia said. "Walked out the gate while everybody else was at the movies."

"Not Marco," Rizo said. "Everybody knows he wouldn't do that. He's a real good kid."

"He was a good kid," Emilia said. She stiffened her spine and channeled Silvio. "Marco's dead."

"*Oye.*" Rizo passed a hand over his face. "When?"

"Two weeks ago. I don't know when Calvo will notify the school."

"How?"

"Meth and an undiagnosed heart condition," she said simply.

Rizo leaned back and regarded the play area across the street, the monkey bars and swings coming into focus in the early morning light.

Emilia waited.

"I've worked at Colegio San Bruno almost 20 years," Rizo said at length. "Before that I was in the Navy. Working at the Colegio is good. Good discipline. Like in the Navy."

"Sure," Emilia said.

Rizo took a deep breath, "But the kids, well, not all the kids can handle the discipline. First it was candy and snacks. Now it's cell phones. Drugs sometimes."

"What about Santa Muerte?" Emilia asked. "Are the kids looking for that?"

"Santa Muerte?" Rizo frowned, eyebrows coming together into a crease above his beaked nose. "*Dios mio.* No, never. Mostly these kids want freedom."

"Sure," Emilia said again.

"I took night duty because that shift paid the best," Rizo

continued. "Now and then the kids would pay me for a favor. Open the gate, close the gate, get them cell phones, weed, pills."

"So when Marco asked you to open the gate," Emilia said. "It wasn't a surprise."

"That's right." Rizo's voice was an embarrassed whisper.

"So tell me about that night," Emilia pressed. "When did you open the gate?"

"I come on duty at 10:00 pm," Rizo said. "Six nights a week. The bus had already left to take the kids to the cinema. They usually got back at midnight. Marco called down around 11:30, asked me to be ready to open the gate in five minutes. He showed up when he said he would. Had a suitcase and a guitar. Said he wouldn't be coming back."

"You opened the gate and he walked out." Emilia said. "Did you watch where he went? The school isn't near anything else. He would have had to walk quite a way to catch a bus."

"There was a car waiting for him," Rizo said. "A flashy car. Bright blue with stripes on the hood."

"You're sure?" Emilia pressed. "You saw it in the dark?"

"It was parked close. Under the school lights." Rizo clasped his hands together and rested his elbows on his knees, the heavy gold braid on his uniform shirt dragging the shoulder seams forward. The dictator distraught over the failure of this year's banana crop. "Marco recognized it. Even loaded down as he was, he ran like lightning. A girl got out of the car, Marco tossed his gear in the back, jumped into the driver's seat and they drove off."

Emilia was nearly speechless. "And you didn't tell anyone? Let his family believe he'd been kidnapped?"

Rizo didn't reply.

The sun had crept up without Emilia noticing the spreading daylight. Now she looked around and the costly neighborhood came into sharper focus. The curved street was newly paved. Tall and slender royal palms, planted at precise intervals, shaded the sidewalks. The grass in front of every house, including Rizo's, was lush and well tended. A maid swept the front porch of the house next door.

Emilia could never afford a house in a *privada* like this. Yet a police detective earned much more than a school security guard.

She stood up. "You have a very nice house, señor."

The implication twisted in the thin morning light.

"Colegio San Bruno is a hard school." Rizo didn't rise. "The kids, well, they are miserable. Homesick. Bored. I help them get a cell phone or open the gate. A little money in my pocket and no harm to anyone."

"Except Marco," Emilia said.

Emilia got to the hospital in time to be Kurt's first visitor. Before going in, the nursing staff made her put on a long green cotton hospital gown and hide her hair in a paper bonnet.

She sat down in the chair by Kurt's bedside. He was partially propped up in the hospital bed, giving her a good look at his purpled and swollen face. Lacerations crisscrossed his shoulders and arms, many closed by dark stitches. His left hand was wrapped in gauze.

Oxygen tubes in both nostrils connected to a clear thin hose. A dozen wires and tubes led from his body to an array of equipment that pumped air or dripped liquid or beeped green signals.

Everything in the room made noise. Except Kurt.

"Only a crazy *gringo* would get hit by a jet-ski and live to tell about it," Emilia said out loud. "You really gave everybody a scare yesterday."

The air pump continued its *swish puff, swish puff* rhythm. Kurt's chest rose and fell with his breathing.

"I've got some things to do," Emilia went on. "Work stuff. That kid wasn't kidnapped. He ran away with his girlfriend. Can you believe it?"

She stared at his closed eyes, at the thick blonde lashes resting on bruised cheekbones. There was no eye movement under the lids. "We still don't know who recruited him. Turned him into a killer." Emilia paused and slid her hand into his. "I'm scared, Kurt. I feel like Santa Muerte is out to get me. Everybody . . . and now you."

Emilia stared at the ceiling as she fought for control.

"Now would be a good time for you to wake up," she said when she was sure she wasn't going to cry. "Tell me I'm being crazy. You could do that now, you know. Just open your eyes. Say 'Hey, Em,' the way you do."

The heart monitor bleated at regular intervals. Emilia squeezed Kurt's hand as hard as she could, hoping for a reaction. His hand was cool but unresisting.

"Wake up, Kurt," Emilia urged. She searched his face, praying for a flicker, a twitch, anything.

The machines continued to puff and beep. They were signs of life, but not of awareness.

Emilia curled his right hand into a fist and covered it with her own. She leaned down so that her mouth was close to Kurt's ear. "Remember when I said that you made me so strong that nothing could hurt me? Now it's my turn. I'm going to be strong enough for both of us. So strong it will make you wake up."

The nurse tapped on the window in the door to say that Emilia's time was up.

Emilia kissed the top of Kurt's head "I'll be back," she whispered.

CHAPTER 20

Emilia was too late for the 9:00 am morning meeting. Silvio gave her a questioning look.

"He's in a coma," Emilia said shortly as she sat at her desk.

"Brain damage?" Silvio asked.

Emilia's computer screen blurred for a moment. "They're doing tests," she said.

"You sure you want to be here?" Silvio asked.

"No," Emilia said frankly. "But I can't sit in that damned waiting room for a whole day again. Besides, I've got something."

She told him about the daybreak encounter with Rizo. "Marco wasn't kidnapped. A girl picked up Marco in a blue car with stripes on the hood."

"Paid the guard to let him out on a night he knew nobody was watching," Silvio said.

"A premeditated getaway," Emilia offered.

Silvio leaned back in his chair and put his feet on his desk. He unconsciously rubbed his side. "So now we're looking for a girl. All we know is that she's probably a waitress and she's got a blue car."

"With white stripes." Emilia logged on and found two more case file citations from the Archive researcher with a Santa Muerte angle.

A street fight in Morelos a year ago. A murder in Puebla

more than two years ago.

The spreadsheet now had more than 20 citations but they needed to be mapped out if any sort of pattern was going to emerge. Emilia shut down the computer, grabbed her shoulder bag. "I'm going to go find a map," she announced.

"Will you be at the hospital later?" Silvio asked.

"Yes."

"Let me know if anything changes," Silvio said.

Don't be decent to me, Emilia wanted to say. Tears were too close to the surface.

She spent the afternoon in the central police administration building, first picking up a map in the Research unit and then stopping by the Archives to thank the librarian who'd been forwarding the case file citations. There was one more database they could check for her and would send her the final results in a day or so.

Emilia wound up in the basement, working out in the gym to generate some energy before heading to the police evidence locker run by her cousin Alvaro.

Along with his older brother Raul, they'd grown up together in that crammed apartment over Tío Raul's garage with the boys' parents and Sophia. Both boys had attended a private security academy and joined the police department. Emilia had followed their example. Raul was still in uniform, Emilia had gone the detective route, but Alvaro was the one who'd made good.

The head of the evidence locker had the power to adjust cases, right wrongs, and grant favors. Lose or replace questionable items and make sure official records were adjusted as needed. Any rewards received for a job well done were handled with discretion, of course.

The locker was a huge gray vault in the basement. Both staff and evidence were shielded by a combination of bulletproof glass and a metal-fronted counter. Beyond the desk area, an enormous wire cage held a shopping mall's worth of electronics, jewelry, automatic weapons, and anything else that once belonged to Acapulco's criminal class. Everything was packaged in plastic bags or steel bins and shelved according to a bible written and maintained by the overlord of the locker, her cousin Sergeant Alvaro Cruz Ochoa.

Alvaro raised a hand in greeting as Emilia walked in. No one else was there except Alvaro and the two uniformed officers who worked for him.

"Detective Cruz," he greeted her through the speaker in the bulletproof glass. "This is a nice surprise."

"Can I come through?" Emilia asked.

"Of course." Alvaro hit a button on his side of the glass, a solenoid sounded, and the door by the counter popped open.

Emilia gave her cousin a quick hug. He wore a stiffly starched short-sleeved uniform and Emilia knew it was a particular point of pride with his wife Daysi that Alvaro look polished. After all, he was a good provider with two children. They also had a new maid to iron his uniforms. Emilia had a good idea how Alvaro could afford a maid, as well as the nice house, modern appliances, and the private preschool for the oldest child.

Alvaro adjusted the chair near his desk to give her a view of the new framed pictures of the children when she sat.

Emilia oohed and aahed, which wasn't hard. Her niece and nephew were adorable, healthy children whom she didn't see nearly enough now that she lived all the way out at Puerta Marques. They chatted a few minutes about the children, Emilia restless and starting the feel the effects of the sleepless night.

"Is this visit business or pleasure?" Alvaro asked at length.

"Both." Emilia swallowed hard.

Alvaro abruptly stood. "There's something I'd like to show you," he said.

Emilia trailed after him as Alvaro walked into the holding area stacked floor to ceiling with industrial gray shelves laden with metal bins marked with numbers. He stopped in the middle of an aisle. "What's the matter?"

She didn't cry, but Emilia felt tears on her cheeks. She wiped them away. "Kurt's had an accident. He's in a coma at Hospital Santa Lucia."

"*Por Dios*," Alvaro exclaimed softly.

Emilia gulped to staunch the tears. "Did you hear about Ernesto's accident?"

"Yes, my mother told us," Alvaro said. "But she said he's going to be fine."

"Mama went crazy when it happened," Emilia said.

"Simply crazy."

"She'll be all right," Alvaro said.

"There's more.' Emilia pressed a hand to her forehead. Fans whirred overhead, keeping the evidence locker cool and dry. "I'm working on a case. The Santa Muerte murders."

"I heard the killer died in custody," Alvaro said.

"He did," Emilia said. "But ever since I started looking into the murders, bad things have happened. To everybody important to me."

"Ah shit," Alvaro breathed.

"Padre Ricardo had a heart attack as we were talking," she said. "Ernesto got stabbed by a scissors and Mama went crazy. Mercedes Sandoval got her place broken into. Everything was stolen. My partner got knifed in the market. Kurt is in the hospital."

"Are you all right?" Alvaro asked.

"I'm all right," Emilia said. "But bad things are happening to everybody and it's all my fault."

"*Prima*," Alvaro chastised her. "I don't think you should talk like that."

"You take care," Emilia said. All she could do was give him a warning. "Take care of those kids."

"I will," Alvaro promised.

Emilia took a deep breath. Could she call herself an honest cop after this? Had she ever?

"And I need a favor," she said.

Mercedes was speechless when she saw the stereo. And the laptop.

"They're used," Emilia said. "But they're in really good condition. The stereo is German. Or maybe Swedish."

Emilia set the sleek stereo on the corner table in the studio. Mercedes watched openmouthed, clutching the expensive laptop case.

The stereo played CDs as well as digital tunes. Emilia tuned it to a radio station and Shakira pulsed out of the small but high quality speakers and the studio filled with music.

"Where did you get this?" Mercedes asked. "Did you buy it, Emilia? You have to take it back. It's too expensive."

"It's on loan," Emilia said. She turned the selection knob, looking for a station playing a Maná song.

"On loan?"

"Emilia." Mercedes was stern. "Are you going to get in trouble for this?"

Emilia gave up trying to find a Maná song and settled for Enrique Iglesias. "I doubt the people who lost it are going to come looking for it here," she said with a rueful grin.

Mercedes turned off the stereo. "Emilia."

"Confiscated goods," Emilia said dismissively. "Like my car."

"If you think it's all right." Mercedes looked longingly at the stereo.

"Let's go see if this laptop works," Emilia said.

They headed into Mercedes's office. The laptop came to life immediately. Mercedes put on the kettle for a celebratory cup of tea.

"How's Kurt?" Mercedes asked when they were settled on her sofa with mugs of tea.

"I was there this morning," Emilia said. "The doctor doesn't know why he won't wake up."

"Oh, no," Mercedes said.

"I'm so scared," Emilia said.

The dam broke and she began to cry.

CHAPTER 21

"I told you before not to get in touch again," Alan Denton said.

"Nice to see you again, Señor Denton," Emilia replied. The Pinkerton agent's execrable Spanish and extreme self-importance immediately set her teeth on edge.

Denton looked around the cafeteria of the Hospital Santa Lucia. "At least I applaud you for coming up with a unique place for a conversation. I don't expect to be recognized here."

"Would you like a cup of coffee?" Emilia asked, with a nod toward the self-service line. Her own cup was on the table in front of her. The cafeteria coffee was fairly horrible but as long as it was loaded with caffeine she didn't care.

Unable to deal with the loneliness of the penthouse apartment, she'd spent the night with Mercedes. The two friends barely got any sleep. Emilia had returned to the hospital early and sat by Kurt's bedside for half an hour, listening to the steady rhythm of the machines bleating out the status of his heart and lungs.

"No, thank you." Denton's lip curled as he eyed the gaggle of people filling paper cups from the coffee urn.

"We'll get right to it." Emilia pushed the Missing Persons report to him. "The late Marco Sandino Varela. Like I told you on the phone, I'm interested in anything else Pinkerton might have turned up. We both know the whole story doesn't always make it into the official Missing Persons report."

Denton folded his arms. "I'm sure the police were given everything they needed, Detective Cruz."

"But maybe Pinkerton needs what I have." Emilia took a sip of the vile coffee to hide her impatience. "You can close out the case for Pinkerton so your company won't look completely stupid for never contacting law enforcement in the city where he went missing. Namely right here in Acapulco."

Denton's eyes narrowed. "And why would you be so concerned with Pinkerton's reputation? Looking for a job, Detective?"

Emilia shrugged. "I'm not looking and I don't care about reputations. I care about giving Marco's mother some answers."

"Always the humanitarian, Detective."

"I don't think you're as much of a *pendejo* as you pretend to be, Señor Denton," Emilia said and prodded the report closer to him.

"I don't think we can do business today, Detective." Denton pushed his chair back.

Emilia held up a hand. "Marco walked out of that school," she said. "Bribed the guard to open the gate after curfew."

After a long pause, Denton scooted the chair back to the table.

"A girl in a sporty blue car with white stripes picked him up," Emilia finished.

"Marco's car?"

"A girl was driving it," Emilia said.

Denton rolled his eyes. "But was it Marco's car?"

"Are you saying he had a car?"

"Yes." Denton's face tightened with annoyance. "Marco drove it when he wasn't at school."

"A car." Emilia pulled the Missing Persons report back to her side of the table and skimmed it yet again. "There was nothing in here about him having a vehicle. No one at the school mentioned it."

"School doesn't allow students to have cars," Denton said. "Marco's parents kept it in a garage in Acapulco so he could have access to it whenever he wanted. Paid more to store the car than the rent on most apartments."

Emilia couldn't believe how sloppily the boy's disappearance had been handled. "Did anyone check to see if it's there now?"

"We did. It's gone." Denton eyed the other patrons in the cafeteria. A few people in scrubs. The rest were well dressed, likely family and friends of patients.

"*Madre de Dios*," Emilia swore. "The car's *placa* numbers and description should have been in the report. Did the parents report it missing or stolen?"

"Don't know," Denton said. "The car actually belongs to his father's political party. Not the family. There might be registration issues."

"A car missing in Acapulco yet no one called the Acapulco police." It was a rhetorical statement. Emilia heard the bitterness in her tone.

Denton raised his hands and let them fall on the table in a gesture of both humor and resignation.

"But now here we are," he said coolly. "Talking."

Emilia took a sip of lukewarm coffee, conscious that she was wound up and handling the conversation poorly. She mentally counted to five and looked out the long windows at the spectacular views. The hospital was a tall building. From the vantage point on the top floor, the cafeteria afforded patrons a near panoramic view of the mountains surrounding the bay.

"Point taken," Emilia said. "All right. Marco left the school. A month later he's arrested for murder and his parents want to know why. We're going on the theory that somewhere between the time he left Colegio San Bruno and his death, he was recruited by a Santa Muerte priest to carry out assassinations of El Machete gang members."

The smirk left Denton's face. "Santa Muerte? I didn't hear any of this."

"He killed two members of the El Machete gang," Emilia rolled on. "In each case he stayed at the crime scene long enough to erect a shrine to Santa Muerte and leave some scary prayers to intimidate the gang. In retaliation, El Machete is stringing up corpses marked with the number nine. You might have seen the news on that."

Denton stroked his chin. "Marco died after being arrested?"

"Yes."

"Very convenient."

Emilia's hand tightened around the paper cup of coffee. "What do you mean?"

"Police in Mexico have a reputation for brutality, in case you haven't noticed," Denton said. "The kid runs away, somehow is picked on a bogus charge of murder, you find out who his parents are and to keep from admitting the mistake, the kid conveniently dies."

Emilia felt her blood boil. "The autopsy says otherwise."

Denton gave a sardonic laugh. "Of course."

Emilia furiously stuffed the Missing Persons report into her bag. She'd had three conversations in her entire life with this man and each was more odious than the last.

"You think the police in Acapulco are that incompetent?" she asked, her voice shaking with anger. "Let's review. Pinkerton in Mexico City gets hired to find Marco on the assumption he's the victim of a kidnapping here in Acapulco. Pinkerton pokes around and turns up nothing. Doesn't press the school to talk to his friends. Eventually, the case is turned over to cops in Mexico City who do a lot of nothing, too. A Missing Persons is filed that doesn't even include his car. And still nobody thinks to talk to the cops in Acapulco. Instead, you're ready to blame us. This is the shoddiest investigation I've ever seen."

Denton looked at her with a combination of scorn and disbelief. "You really are the most naïve so-called public servant I've ever encountered, Detective Cruz. I'm amazed, truly, that you have survived this long."

"An excellent and well reasoned response," Emilia

snapped. She swung the strap of her bag over her shoulder and snatched up her coffee cup.

"You don't have any idea what's really going on, do you?" Denton asked, his voice larded with derision.

"I know a bad job when I see it," Emilia said, but something in his tone gave her pause. She put the coffee cup back on the table.

Denton leaned forward. "You think nobody was worried that this kid was kidnapped and missing?" he hissed. "But every time we dug, we came up against Sandino senior's corruption. The kid's father has sucked every peso out of his political party. Marco's car is just one example of how he spent money like water. Why do you think he went to Pinkerton in Mexico City? The cops in Mexico City instead of the police here?"

"Professional connections." As soon as the words passed Emilia's lips, she heard how stupid they were.

Judging from his look of utter contempt, so did Denton. "Sandino couldn't afford to have any law enforcement in the state of Guerrero look into his activities," he said. "Didn't matter that his kid was missing. Had to keep everybody at arm's length. I guess he convinced his wife they were doing the right thing, but I would have thought a sharp detective like you would have figured it out."

"Sandino helped get Carlota elected," Emilia said slowly.

She recalled the awkward conversation with Obregon in the gym. *Don't go after the parents*, he'd said.

"There you go," Denton said. "More at stake than a kid."

CHAPTER 22

"A sporty blue car with white stripes," Silvio said.

"That Marco's father paid for with party money," Emilia said in triumph. "Why they went to Mexico City to start the investigation and not here."

"Amazing he had enough left over to get Carlota elected."

"Don't laugh," Emilia said. "I'll bet a thousand to one that Marco gave the keys to his waitress girlfriend and she used it to pick him up at the school."

Silvio tilted his chair back. His left hand meandered across his flat stomach to absently rub at the stitches on his right side. "Leave out the father's political mess," he said. "We find the car or the girl who picked him up and the father has heartburn, that's his problem."

"Denton didn't have either the *placa* numbers or the garage where the car was kept," Emilia said.

"Doesn't matter. What are the chances the car is back there now?"

"None," Emilia said. "Denton says they checked."

It was late in the day. Macias and Sandor were at their desks, speaking in low tones. For the past few days they'd been huddled with the Organized Crime unit, in a futile attempt to dig up dirt on the Los Nueves gang. Ortega and Nuñez were there as well, still starched and pretty in their suits and ties. Castro hadn't been around much lately and when he was, he looked like a dog kicked to the curb. Gomez had always been the leader of that pack and with him reassigned to the holding cells night shift, Castro was at loose ends. Lieutenant Baez had announced he would be interviewing candidates from the uniformed ranks who'd scored well on the detective exam with the intention of bringing in three new detectives as soon as possible. The odd number made it clear he wasn't expecting Gomez to come back.

Silvio scratched his side again. "You think the girlfriend dumped Marco and kept the car?"

"Maybe she was the recruiter," Emilia suggested.

"A pretty girl who's a Santa Muerte priest?"

"No, member of the cult. Recruiter for the priest."

Ortega came over to Silvio's desk. "You're looking for a car, right? Blue with white stripes."

"You got anything on that?" Silvio asked.

"Try looking for a Mustang Cobra," Ortega said. "I saw one a couple of months ago. Bright blue with two white stripes down the hood."

"Thanks," Emilia said. "We'll check it out."

"Doing what I can," Ortega said to Silvio.

Emilia stared as Ortega walked back to his desk. "What's his problem?" she hissed. "Can't talk to women?"

Silvio frowned. "How many blue Mustang Cobras can there be in the state of Guerrero?"

"Knowing Sandino, it would be a new car, too." Emilia stabbed at her keyboard. "We can check out Ford dealerships if the registration database doesn't give us anything."

"Want to bet how many times the database will crash before we find out?" Silvio scooted back to his own keyboard.

"I thought you gave up gambling," Emilia said over their computer monitors.

Silvio guffawed then immediately clapped his hand over the ribs on his right side. "Don't make me laugh, Cruz," he said, wincing.

The system was excruciatingly slow, complicated by the clunky police intranet interface. But after an hour of dropped searches and database reboots, Silvio slammed down a hand hard enough to make Emilia's desk rattle.

"*Rayos*," he swore. "I can't fucking believe it."

"What did you find?" Emilia stood to peer over their back-to-back computer monitors.

"There's a fucking blue Mustang outside in the impound yard." Silvio shoved back his chair. "Picked up in Colonia Solidaridad four weeks ago."

The blue Mustang was parked in the section of the impound yard reserved for wrecks. While it still had four tires, all the mirrors were missing, the driver's door was gone, and the trunk had been jimmied open. The spare tire was gone. The screen set into the dashboard over the center console was smashed. No doubt someone wanted to remove the space-age looking dashboard instruments and surround-sound stereo but couldn't figure out how to extract them intact.

While Silvio investigated the trunk, Emilia slid into the driver's seat. The car was all but stripped but she still pulled down the visors and checked the glove compartment, as well as the two cup holder in the center console. The leather seats fit snugly against the console and the parking brake on the driver's side made for an even tighter fit on that side but she jammed her hand in as far as she could go and felt around.

She maneuvered herself over the console, sat in the passenger seat and did the same thing.

Her fingertips touched paper. Stiff paper.

"What are you doing?" Silvio loomed in the empty driver's door opening.

"Something is stuck down here." Emilia forced her hand further into the space and managed to catch the paper between her first two fingers. She slowly drew it out.

It was a photograph of Marco smiling broadly with his arm around a girl. From the angle, it was a selfie taken with his free hand. Marco had on board shorts and his upper body was trim. The girl wore a cropped tee shirt and black bikini bottoms. She was laughing as the breeze blew her short black hair. Everything about their body language said they were lovers.

A sandy beach and frothy ocean made for a playful background. A yellow surfboard was stuck in the sand some distance behind the girl.

"*Madre de Dios*, Franco." Emilia shoved the picture at

Silvio. "It's her."

He plucked the photo out of her hand and backed up as Emilia launched herself over the console and out of the car. "Where do I know her from?"

"I've been looking for her for a year," Emilia sputtered. "Her name is Lila. Lila Jimenez Lata. The girl missing from my old neighborhood."

Emilia glanced at her watch. If she hurried, she could see Kurt before visiting hours were over. Silvio was still in the squadroom, looking at the latest email with a case file citation. A murder in the state of Puebla with a Santa Muerte angle.

Ortega was ahead as Emilia headed down the hall to the rear door. He glanced around, saw her, and speeded up.

What was his problem? Never talked to her. Pretended she didn't exist. Emilia lengthened her stride.

Ortega whipped down the hall so fast his suit jacket flared out behind him. He shoved open the door. Emilia broke into a jog and got to the exit before he could close the door behind himself.

"Hey!" Emilia swerved in front of Ortega and held up a hand. "Thanks for the car tip, *chico*."

"Sure," he said distantly.

"Do you and I have a problem no one told me about?" Emilia demanded.

Ortega held up his hands. "Not on my account," he said. "Nuñez and I are here to work."

"Good for you," Emilia said. "But I'm a detective, too, and I'd like to know why you think you're too good to talk to me."

"Listen," Ortega said uncomfortably. "Gomez told us about your set-up."

Emilia threw back her head and folded her arms. Nothing associated with Gomez was going to be good. "Exactly what did he say?"

"I'm a married man," Ortega said. "I got two kids. I may not be the best husband in the world but I'm not the worst, either."

"Good for you." Emilia waited for more.

Ortega shifted from one foot to the other. "Nuñez just got married. She's a nice girl."

"Great," Emilia said. "You're both married. Congratulations. What does that have to do with Gomez? Or me?"

"We don't need to buy trouble, you know what I'm saying?"

"No, I don't know," Emilia said between gritted teeth. "Spell it out, Ortega."

The suited detective flushed, his face turning the same crimson as his tie. "Gomez said you're the gatekeeper to Baez," he said. "Anybody wants a good assignment or vacation time has got to, uh, accommodate you. The way you like it."

His words were thick with innuendo. Emilia felt her blood pressure soar through the top of her head. "And you believed him?" she exploded.

Ortega looked at his shoes, studiously avoiding Emilia's searching stare. "You're a good looking woman, Detective, and you're in Baez's office a lot," he said. "Gomez said—."

"Gomez played you," Emilia interrupted. "And Nuñez, too. He and I had a little run-in awhile ago and he didn't come out of it so good. If you want to talk to *el teniente*, go right ahead. I wouldn't have either of you naked on a bed of roses."

She stalked away, leaving Ortega with his jaw hanging open.

Every time she thought things in the squadroom had settled down, that she'd finally been accepted, somebody always proved her wrong.

CHAPTER 23

"Remember that meat cleaver I took off the butcher at the Mercado Oriente?" Emilia asked. "It's still in the kitchen. When you wake up, we should give it to Jacques."

Kurt's hair looked longer. A curl had strayed onto his forehead. Emilia smoothed it away.

Once again she was decked out in a long green surgical gown over her street clothes.

"We won't tell him where it came from," she said.

The only answer was the steady bleep of the machines.

"Do you remember the fire at the El Tigre restaurant? What happened at the market was like that." Emilia fell into storytelling mode and told him the story of the time they'd been at the fancy restaurant that caught fire. How Kurt had rescued the mayor even as the building threatened to collapse around their heads.

She didn't know why she chose to recount that event to the man in the bed with the air pump whooshing softly in the background. Maybe because she wanted to reach through the coma and remind Kurt of who he really was. The real Kurt was a soldier before he'd managed a hotel; a man who saw combat and hadn't flinched, who was strong in ways she was not.

Kurt always knew who he was and what he was capable of doing; a man who could handle a dozen problems at a time and think it easy. A man who'd taught her that courage didn't need to be paired with bluster and aggression the way most Mexican men defined it.

"You've got to fight this thing, Kurt," she said softly. "We're both strong. You can do it and I'll be right here until you do."

Emilia watched the green spikes of the heartbeat monitor. Yet again, the doctors had assured her that all of Kurt's vitals were fine. All the blood chemistry and nervous system tests had come back negative. He was in top physical shape, apart from the bruises sustained in the accident and even those were fading fast. The doctor had removed the stitches on his arm and torso.

There was no medical reason for the coma.

She sat next to his bed, her hand on his cheek, until the nurse came in.

CHAPTER 24

Fighting morning traffic on the way to Coyuca Lagoon, Silvio had laughed like an idiot when Emilia recounted her conversation with Ortega. Now sitting in the kitschy dining room at El Loro Rojo, however, the big detective's expression was completely without humor.

"No." Herman Schmidt was emphatic. "No, I never saw this girl."

The oil cloth on the table was still sticky. The ceramic frogs and suns on the wall still beamed down from their haphazard places on the wall. A roach scuttled along in the crack between the floor tiles and the wall.

The hostel was empty except for the German, his wife, Emilia, and Silvio.

Itzel Schmidt didn't serve coffee this time. In a knit shirt and skirt that clung to her thick midsection like peel on an orange, she sat with her arms folded and stared blankly at her husband. Her apron was long overdue for a wash.

"You said before that Marco had been around the hotel for a couple of days," Emilia said. "Using the facilities."

"I suppose," Herman said. His knee jiggled nervously, reminding Emilia of the Canadian boy they'd questioned at the same table.

"The girl would have been with him. They were probably very close."

"No." Herman slid the photo back to Emilia. "No, she was

never around here."

"Itzel." Emilia turned to the wife and held out the photo. "What about you? Did you ever see her?"

"I never seen her neither."

"Okay, then." Silvio stood up. "Thanks for your time."

Herman stood, too. His simple white cotton tunic and pants of a Mexican *campesino* were naturally wrinkled. "I'm sorry you came all the way for nothing."

"Longshot," Silvio said. "Had to ask." The two men shook hands. Herman ignored Emilia and didn't offer his hand.

Once in the car Silvio started the engine and got the air conditioning going.

"Did you believe them?" Emilia asked.

"Not one word," Silvio said.

"She was mad at him," Emilia said. "Blamed him for us coming and asking questions."

"She could have been pissed at him for anything," Silvio said.

Emilia looked into the side mirror. Herman and Itzel were on the veranda of the hostel staring at the car. Itzel was leaning away from her husband. "No," Emilia said. "She was mad at him because we were there. She's still mad."

Silvio glanced in the rearview mirror and put the car in reverse. "Let's double check their story."

They drove over the top of Coyuca Lagoon to Barra de Coyuca. In addition to the usual riot of colorful wares, like the Mercado Oriente in Acapulco, the market was packed with Day of the Dead merchandise; leering sugar skulls, cellophane twists of *tamarindo* candy and bags of square homemade marshmallows.

Ana recognized them both as Emilia and Silvio approached the counter but her eyes swung to Silvio. He acted like he didn't notice although Emilia was sure he did.

"Hello, Ana," Emilia said. "We're back to do more shopping."

Ana smiled broadly, revealing four brown teeth standing apart like sentries.

"We wondered if you ever saw this girl around the El Loro Rojo." Emilia put the picture of Marco and Lila on the counter.

"Sure," Ana said immediately. "That's Liliana and her boyfriend."

"Liliana?" Emilia pressed. "What's her full name?"

"Liliana Jimenez, I think," Ana said.

"That's really helpful, Ana." Emilia wanted to pump a fist in the air. Lila Jimenez Lata, straight from the *Las Perdidas* binder of missing women. "When did she work there?"

Ana sidled closer to Silvio. "For about four, five months, maybe? Last month she disappeared like all the rest."

"And the boyfriend?" Emilia queried. Silvio pulled out his phone and tapped and scrolled with great intensity.

"Marco," said Ana. "Marco something. "One of the crazy kayak boys with his boat and his paddle. He swarmed around that girl like a bee to a flower."

"At the El Loro Rojo?" Emilia pressed. "He was always

there?"

Silvio pointed to the phone as if he had an important call and walked out.

"Sure." Ana's eyes followed Silvio. When he passed out of sight she refocused on Emilia. "They were crazy about each other. In love, Liliana said all the time. But Itzel was upset because every weekend Marco stayed in Liliana's room with her."

"Liliana lived at the El Loro Rojo?" Emilia asked.

Ana showed the teeth again, happy to be talking about her employers. "Sure. In the room behind the kitchen. All the waitresses get room and board. Otherwise nobody would work there at night. No buses. Of course, Liliana's young man had a car."

"Did Itzel fire her?"

"Maybe," Ana said with a shrug. "But I think she ran away with the boy, like all the rest. That's why Itzel said no more."

How many lies had Herman and Itzel told them? And why?

Emilia roamed the stall and picked out a set of capiz shell wind chimes. Circular mother-of-pearl discs were linked to a round wooden hoop by fishing line.

Oddly enough, Ana's stall was missing the full array of Day of the Dead tourist mementos.

"No *muertos*?" Emilia asked, half jokingly as she found her wallet. "This close to the Day of the Dead? Seems like every store I've been in has some."

"No more *muertos*." Ana began to painstakingly wrap the chimes in newspaper. "Did you see the odd ones that Señor Herman had? Strange *muertos*."

"Strange?" Emilia stopped looking for the exact change. "What do you mean?"

"Black *muertos*," Ana said. "Dressed just like him. Someone sent them to him in a box. A gift, I suppose."

CHAPTER 25

All that remained of the Mini Super Mickey was a smoking cement shell.

Emilia and Silvio leaned against the hood of his sedan and watched the arson investigator talk to the crime scene techs while the firemen coiled spent hoses. The roof of the little convenience store had collapsed and debris was everywhere. The blackened walls sat in a giant puddle of chunky, sooty water.

Ash floated in the air. Emilia brushed some off the sleeve of her denim jacket and the knees of her khaki ankle pants. She'd picked the wrong day to wear sandals.

The street was blocked off and at least a dozen uniformed officers roamed around, asking questions. What seemed like the entire neighborhood hung over the barricades. Those watching were quiet, which to Emilia felt more ominous than a riot.

Two teams of techs were there; Rodriguez and Bayardo along with Suarez and a tech Emilia didn't recognize.

All four techs plus the arson investigator suited up, put on masks, stepped over the rubble, and cautiously went inside.

Silvio cleared his throat. "How's your friend Mercedes?"

"She's doing all right."

"How's Hollywood?" Silvio asked.

"The same," Emilia replied.

"Doctor say anything?"

"They're going to do more tests tomorrow. Nervous system function, something like that."

"What do they think they're going to find?"

"I don't know," Emilia said. She squinted at him. "Can we talk about something else? Like why somebody sent Herman Schmidt black *muertos*. He's not a member of El Machete."

Silvio pulled off his sunglasses to squint at the disaster in front of them. "Or how Baez let Gogo Garcia Figueroa walk right into this."

"We should have had surveillance on the place," Emilia said.

"Now he's dead and we don't know anything more than we did a week ago."

The techs came out of the remains of the Mini Super Mickey. One of them pulled off his mask. It was Rodriguez. Emilia peeled herself off the hood of the car to talk to him, Silvio right behind her.

"One female body," Rodriguez said. "Hefty but too badly burned. Looks like she was trapped by the cash register when the roof fell in. Arson guy says she likely died from smoke inhalation. Second body is male, teen or early 20's."

Gogo and his mother.

"That's it?" Silvio asked. "Any young kids? There was a kid who worked the parking lot."

"Just the two bodies," Rodriguez confirmed.

"How about Santa Muerte relics?" Emilia asked. "An altar? *Muertos* or candles?"

"What about a number nine?" Silvio added.

"If there was anything, it fried." Rodriguez turned to look at the cement hulk. "Gasoline was used as the accelerant. We're not going to find anything."

There was no point in staying.

"Let's go see if Macias and Sandor turned up anything," Silvio said. "Los Nueves might not have left their usual calling card, but I think we can blame this one on them."

The late afternoon sun sparkled, the breeze carried a salt tang, and the beer was cold. Emilia had never been out for a drink with three male colleagues before. A career milestone.

"We have one piece of good news," Sandor said. "Been working with Organized Crime. They think Adonis Rugama Moreno is El Machete's El Commandante."

"Never heard of him," Silvio said.

"Six degrees of separation from El Machete," Macias said. "In and out of the bull pen for petty stuff. Word on the street is that he tangled with some real bad dude and is now out to get him."

"What did they tangle over?" Emilia asked. "Territory? Meth sales?"

Macias grinned. "If Organized Crime believes their snitch, it was a girl."

Silvio gave a bark of laughter.

"He hasn't been seen lately," Macias went on. "But until

we find him laid out next to a Santa Muerte altar, Organized Crime says he's the one stringing victims up on billboards and marking them with the number 9."

"Well, that's something," Silvio said. "Other than that we've got a dead teenaged *sicario*, a missing girlfriend who might not know he's dead, and a father whose political fortunes are more important than his kid."

"Not to mention the owners of the El Loro Rojo," Emilia added. "Happy to lie through their teeth for no good reason."

They were at one of the little eateries along Avenida Teniente Azueta, just a stone's throw from the dock on the western side of the city that serviced local fishing boats. A community platter of fried everything sat in the middle of the table; French fries, fried shrimp, slices of fried yucca, popcorn-sized chunks of breaded and fried fish. All meant to be eaten hot and washed down with a cold beer.

Silvio unconsciously rubbed the right side of his ribs with one hand as he snagged a shrimp with the other. "You think El Machete delivered those black *muertos* to Herman Schmidt?"

"If we believe the woman in the Mercado Oriente," Emilia said. "Which makes Herman mixed up in this somehow. But aside from paying protection money to El Machete, I can't figure out how."

"Maybe that's enough to put the El Loro Rojo in the middle," Silvio said.

"Who are you talking about?" Macias asked.

"The owner of the hostel at Coyuca Lagoon," Silvio

provided.

Emilia sat back with her beer as Silvio described the incident at the Mercado Oriente and the conflicting stories they got about Marco and Lila at Coyuca Lagoon. He wrapped up with Ana's comment about black *muertos*.

Sandor chewed a fry. "I thought this new gang had cornered the market on scary *muertos*."

"Maybe two can play that game," Macias suggested.

The little restaurant catered to a mix of locals and tourists. They'd taken the big table on the front patio where they could watch the foot traffic. The menu was tacked to a post by the sidewalk. A big sign over Silvio's shoulder read *Bienvenidos Amigos Turistas!*

Emilia was fairly certain that the tourists would feel less welcome if they'd known the three men and one woman on the patio all carried automatic handguns under their jackets.

"The owner of the El Loro Rojo lied like a rug," Silvio finished. "The girl worked for him. Her boyfriend was there off and on for months. They had to have known who he was. Yet when they saw him after the murder, they say he's just some tourist only been there a day or so."

"The German's scared," Sandor suggested. "The *muertos* were a message to shut up."

Macias scooped up some fried shrimp. "Maybe they aren't the same *muertos*."

"A special order for black *muertos* wearing the same clothes that Schmidt wears." Emilia looked around the table. "Ordered by someone with a big knife tattoo while Schmidt lies through his teeth. How many of us really believe in coincidences like that?"

No one answered her. The breeze ruffled Macias's hair. Sandor sighed and grabbed another piece of fish.

"So now what?" Silvio swirled the last of his beer around the bottom of the bottle. "We follow the usual plan? Let the gangs fight it out?"

"I don't think we can," Emilia said.

"Worked pretty good the last hundred times," Silvio said.

"We'll never find out what really happened to Marco," Emilia said. "Plus, I think we have a bigger problem on our hands than local gangs here in Acapulco."

She moved the platter of food to one side and spread out the map on which she'd plotted the case file citations. "These are all the Santa Muerte-related murders in Mexico over the last three years that look like ours."

Macias gave a low whistle. "Shit," Sandor murmured at the same time.

Silvio had seen most of the emails but even he looked stunned at the sight of all the red ink on the map.

"Thirty-two murders in eleven different states," Emilia said. "From Oaxaca to Baja California. If the dates are any indication, they've been up and down the coast four times in three years."

"The entire Pacific coast," Sandor said. "What the fuck is going on?"

Emilia's finger roved over the map. "This gang travels all over. They don't try to hold territory. I think we're looking at the Mexican equivalent of a *norteamericano* serial killer."

"A wandering band of Santa Muerte *sicarios*," Silvio said. "*Rayos*, I'm too fucking old for this."

"Picking off meth merchants and recruiting school boys," Emilia said. "The map shows a pattern but not a motive."

"Selling meth?" Sandor opined. "On the move so they don't get caught?"

Macias took a long pull from his beer bottle. "Maybe it's some perverted sense of Santa Muerte justice?"

"Have you shown this to Baez?" Silvio asked.

Emilia met his stare. "Not yet," she said.

"Even so," Macias said. "What's Baez going to do about it?"

"Waste another opportunity," Sandor said.

Macias reached for a greasy handful of yucca. "Maybe we should find Adonis and tell El Machete to lie low."

"In that case, Carlota gets her wish. No more bodies on billboards," Emilia said and grabbed the last French fry. "But this gang will just cruise on to the next town."

"Every other gang holds territory," Silvio said. "They fight for a foothold. Control their streets. They mark their spot, like alpha dogs. Why not them? What makes this Santa Muerte crowd different?"

"Do you remember the tech who came out to Coyuca Lagoon when we found the first altar?" Emilia asked Silvio.

"Sure," Silvio said as he chewed a piece of fish. "Fucker ran off. Didn't do his job."

"Don't you think it's time we found out why?"

☼

Emilia yawned as she walked through the lobby on her way to the elevator. Behind the reservation counter, Luis raised a hand and Emilia tiredly returned the greeting. Christine's new assistant concierge was on duty and looked absorbed in his computer screen. Across the vast lobby, the white grand piano sounded like a complete orchestra, thanks to Serge, the new Russian pianist. The music was lovely and classical and nothing Emilia recognized.

Beyond the piano, the two-level Pasodoble Bar was full of guests laughing and talking against the dramatic backdrop of star-studded sky and restless dark ocean.

As she punched the button for the elevator Emilia's stomach rumbled. She'd only had a few French fries with her beer and she was starving. No doubt Jacques would serve her up a five-star dinner if she went to the restaurant, but there was no way she was going to put on a dress or even walk the short distance.

Bits of ash from the Mini Super Mickey swirled down the drain as Emilia washed her hair in a scalding hot shower. She threw on one of Kurt's shirts and a pair of workout capris and padded barefoot to the kitchen. Jacques had left several containers of food in the refrigerator, including a roasted chicken. Emilia loaded a plate with slices of chicken and a pile of roasted vegetables, grabbed a beer, and sank into the sofa in front of the television. A show with a laugh track provided light and company as she ate with her fingers.

Across the room, the door latch clicked softly as someone inserted a keycard.

Kurt. Kurt was home.

Emilia leaped up. The plate spilled off her lap. Food cascaded everywhere.

The door swung wide and Christine stepped in. The concierge looked trim and elegant in a navy mini dress and matching flat sandals. Her blonde hair was pulled back with a navy and white band.

An older woman came in with her, an overweight *gringa* clad in an unflattering orange knit tunic, a long denim skirt, and bulky brown sandals that looked like they had started life as work boots. Her gray hair was chopped into an irregular bob and tucked behind her ears. She held onto a big vinyl handbag with work-roughened hands.

Emilia knew immediately who she was.

"Oh, Emilia," Christine said silkily, looking at the mess on the rug. "I didn't know you were here."

"You should have called first, Christine," Emilia said. She switched on a lamp by the sofa and muted the television.

"I know, I'm so sorry," Christine purred. "Here, let me introduce you to Kurt's mother. She just flew in."

The concierge guided the older woman further into the room. "Mary Rucker, this is Emilia Cruz," she said, switching to English. "Kurt's friend."

Emilia held out her hand. "How nice to finally meet you," she said in the same language. "I hope you had a good trip all the way from the farm in New York."

Mary Rucker turned to Christine. "What did she say?" she asked loudly. "I can't understand her."

Emilia dropped her hand.

"Emilia speaks Spanish, you know," Christine said to Mary, the conversation still in English. "She says she's glad to meet you."

Mary Rucker looked Emilia up and down. "This is Kurt's girl? Well, I didn't expect much better, him taking up with a wetback and all."

"Did Kurt tell you I'm a police detective?" Emilia asked.

Mary Rucker waved a hand as if warding off a wasp. "Tell her to speak English," she said to Christine. "I can't make heads or tails out of what she's saying."

Christine turned to Emilia, eyes gleaming in triumph. "Mary came as soon as she could," she said, switching back to Spanish. "I'll take her to the hospital tomorrow to see him."

Emilia replied in the same language. "I presume you've made arrangements for her to sleep somewhere?"

"Of course," Christine said. "I'll show her the apartment before we go downstairs to dinner."

"You really should have called first, Christine," Emilia said. "This isn't a convenient time."

"I know, I know," Christine looked at the overturned plate. "I'm so sorry. But it seems a shame for Mary to have come all this way and she doesn't even get to see where her son lives. We'll just be a minute."

Emilia watched, rooted in place by fury and helplessness, as Christine guided Mary down the hall to the bedroom, where Emilia's clothes lay puddled on the floor along with a wet towel, then into the office. They came back to the living room and poked into the kitchen, both remarking on the open food containers, and toured the dining room where Emilia's shoulder bag and holstered gun were on the table.

"It was so sweet of you to let us come by, Emilia," Christine said. She ushered Mary to the front door. "We'll be going now. Dinner awaits."

Emilia squatted to collect the remains of her dinner, so angry she could hardly see what she was doing.

"When is that girl leaving?" Mary asked Christine loudly in English as the door closed behind them.

CHAPTER 26

The tech's full name was Diego Bayardo Lanzas. Silvio timed their arrival to be an hour after Bayardo's shift ended. The young tech looked scared as he opened the door to all four detectives.

The apartment he shared with his wife and mother-in-law was in a small building not too far from the beach at Playa Caletilla on the western side of the bay. The apartment was nicely furnished but not spacious. Emilia, Macias, and Sandor crowded together on the single sofa, which was the only seating in the room.

One wall was taken up by a wide screen television. On the opposite side, flowered curtains a window; a cheerful setting for a Day of the Dead *ofrenda* displayed on the wide sill. The middle of the altar was an artful arrangement of three silver cups often given as christening gifts, three child *muertos, and* several plastic baby rattles.

An altar to three dead children.

Mangoes, limes, and a cluster of finger bananas were a green counterpoint to clusters of fresh marigolds. White candles rose above the fruit. *Papel picado* streamers looped across the window above the altar.

Bayardo brought in another chair but Silvio stopped him, saying they wouldn't be there long. His wife Flavia, obviously pregnant, smiled nervously as she offered the visitors *aqua de jamaica* or a cola. No one accepted. She sat in the kitchen chair and Bayardo stood next to her.

"You've been working the same cases as all of us," Silvio said to Bayardo. "The billboard murders."

"Sure." Bayardo's face was tense. "Did I do something wrong?"

"We're working the Santa Muerte murders, too," Emilia said. "You wouldn't. So we figure you know something we don't."

Flavia put a protective hand on her pregnant belly. She would have been pretty without the pockmarked skin. The too-tight tee shirt, knit shorts, and plastic flip-flops didn't help.

Staring at his wife, Bayardo gave his head a tiny shake. "I don't need to explain myself to you," he said. "I talked to Rodriguez. He's my boss."

"There's a range war going on out there," Silvio said with heat. "An old woman and her son died yesterday, trapped inside a burning building because of this Santa Muerte cult."

"Not my fault," Bayardo said.

"Santa Muerte?" Flavia asked fearfully.

"Go in the kitchen," Bayardo told her.

Emilia slid onto her knees in front of Flavia before the young woman could rise from the chair. "He helped you, didn't he? You kept losing babies. Miscarriages. A Santa Muerte priest helped you."

"Go in the kitchen, Flavia," Bayardo commanded.

Emilia touched Flavia's hand. "Tell me about the Santa Muerte priest, Flavia."

"She doesn't have to say anything," Bayardo said.

"He's a good man," Flavia whispered. "They call him El Acólito."

The Acolyte.

"Tell me about El Acólito, Flavia," Emilia pressed. "Please. How do you know about him?"

"I kept losing babies." Flavia's eyes filled with tears. "They'd grow and then die inside me. The doctor said I was healthy. At the hospital, they didn't know why it kept happening."

She looked up at her husband, her eyes watery. Bayardo put his hand on her shoulder.

"My mother brought me to see El Acólito," Flavia said. "Last year. On the night of the Day of the Dead, when his power is strongest. He prayed to Santa Muerte for me. He prayed an intercession so that bad spirits would leave my body and my husband's seed would grow into a healthy baby. And it happened . . ." Her voice trailed off.

"I need to talk to El Acólito, Flavia," Emilia said. "How can I find him?"

"El Acólito only can be seen at special times."

"Like the Day of the Dead?" Macias interjected.

"So the day after tomorrow," Emilia said.

"Yes," Flavia said. "But you aren't believers. You don't need him to hear your prayers."

"It doesn't matter," Macias said. "We need to find him. El Acólito is doing some bad things."

Flavia pressed both hands to her stomach. "If I tell you,

he might take away the baby."

"We won't let El Acólito take away your baby, Flavia ," Silvio said in a surprisingly soft voice.

"I'm scared." Flavia started to weep. Bayardo looked ready to cry, too.

Silvio bent down to Flavia. "You need to help us find El Acólito."

"You cannot go," Bayardo said to Silvio. "His intercessions are for women only."

"Women?"

"Women carry purity within themselves, he says." Flavia sniffed. "That is why only women can come with their statues to be blessed and their petitions."

"Statues of Santa Muerte?" Emilia prompted.

"Yes, women bring big statues, little statues, all kinds of statues. Candles. Money. Offerings to Santa Muerte."

"Where?" Silvio barked.

Flavia began to cry again.

Bayardo sighed. "I took them to a big field beyond the highway to Ixtapa. There's a dirt road and some abandoned houses." He bent to his wife. "Tell them."

They waited while Flavia wound down, one hand on her belly and the other pressed to her eyes.

"We walked down the road," Flavia said at length. "For a long time. It was like a party, everyone carrying their statues and candles and singing. At midnight we found the tent. El Acólito came out and prayed to Santa Muerte for us and we sang. His disciples found the women with the most urgent petitions and invited them to pray with El Acólito himself."

"How did they know who had the most urgent problems?" Emilia asked.

"He told them." Flavia rubbed the swell of the child inside her. "He knew. He is El Acólito."

CHAPTER 27

"I can do this," Emilia said. "We've got an entire day to plan. A couple of hours tonight and we'll know if this is the Santa Muerte priest who recruited Marco Sandino Varela. We can arrest him tomorrow. Maybe the rest of Los Nueves, too."

She and Silvio were in *el teniente's* office. Lieutenant Baez tapped his pen on his desk. His deliberation was maddening. Emilia wanted to jump out of her chair and shout him into making a decision. The *right* decision.

She had to go to this intercession.

"Detective Silvio," Lieutenant Baez said finally. "What do you think?"

The big detective shifted uncomfortably. "There's something about this entire case, this range war, that doesn't add up," he said. "A key piece of the puzzle is missing."

"I agree," Lieutenant Baez said. "You've turned up some solid information like how Marco left school and the name of the girlfriend. But we have not identified motivation and the gap worries me."

"There's always something we don't know." Emilia waved a hand at the closed door and the squadroom on the other side. "That's why we have a ton of cold cases."

"I'd feel better about Cruz going into this alone," Silvio continued, ignoring Emilia. "If we knew what we were looking for."

"Could the range war extend to this meeting?" *el teniente* asked.

"It's an Intercession," Emilia corrected him. "Where women go to pray. For healing."

"El Machete could retaliate at this rally or intercession or whatever it is." Silvio threw Emilia a dark look. "We could be putting Cruz right into the middle of it. Let's not forget we think this Santa Muerte outfit burned down the store that was El Machete's main distribution point."

Lieutenant Baez tapped that *maldita* pen again. "You think El Machete could do something at the rally instead of another billboard murder?"

"Ratchet up the intimidation factor," Silvio offered.

"It's a spiritual event," Emilia said in exasperation. "Santa Muerte or not, he's not going to torch a bunch of his female followers."

Lieutenant Baez did that annoying pen tapping thing again.

Emilia jumped up and put both hands on the desk. "Please, *teniente*," she pleaded. "If we want to find out what happened to turn Marco Sandino Varela into a killer, this is our only shot."

The intercession could be her only shot, as well. Too many frightening things had happened since she first read those prayers from the altar. Emilia couldn't articulate what she believed to herself, let alone anyone in the squadroom, but she had to go.

Anguish and destruction to Your enemies and to all they

hold dear.

More tapping. Emilia loathed that pen.

"Have you ever done undercover work before?" Lieutenant Baez asked.

"No," Silvio said before Emilia could answer.

Emilia whirled on her partner. "You're forgetting the Agua Pacifica operation at the Maxitunel," she said.

"The case that got Rico Portillo killed," Silvio said.

"I saved your ass," Emilia flashed back, refusing to let him use Rico's death to keep her from solving this case.

Silvio raised his hands in mock surrender.

Emilia turned back to Lieutenant Baez. "All I have to do is carry a statue. Act like I believe whatever I hear."

Lieutenant Baez drew a deep breath. "If this El Acólito is who we think he is, he's the head of a violent gang beheading his enemies and marauding up and down the country. If he finds out there's a cop in his crowd and you're alone, you won't be coming back."

"He's not going to find out I'm a cop," Emilia argued. "Bayardo will guide us to the rendezvous point and from there I'll blend in with the crowd."

"No gun, no badge, no wire," Lieutenant Baez said. "If they get suspicious, you have to be clean."

"I know. Please, *teniente*. Please."

"Do we have any other leads to pursue?" Lieutenant Baez asked.

"That's the problem." Silvio spread his hands. "No."

"All right," Lieutenant Baez said. "But I want this

orchestrated so tightly that every scenario is accounted for. Timing, the rendezvous, the pickup. Everything."

"Well, it had to happen sooner or later," Silvio said.

"What are you talking about?" Emilia asked.

"Just now with Baez," Silvio said. He walked swiftly through the parking lot, forcing Emilia to trot to keep up. "You fucking manipulated him."

"I did no such thing. I convinced him that this was our best shot to figure out what happened to Marco and give the kid's parents some answers. Stop Carlota from calling him every other day."

"You knew I didn't want to do this," Silvio growled. "But you had to get your way."

"It's not like we have a Plan B," Emilia pointed out. "Even you admitted we have nothing else."

"I have a bad feeling," Silvio said doggedly.

Emilia stopped as realization dawned. "The El Acólito show isn't open to bad-tempered men," she said. "That means a woman has to do this job. Only a woman can do it. That's really the issue, isn't it?"

Silvio stopped, too, car keys in hand. "What are you talking about?"

"Don't deny it." Emilia shook a finger at her partner. "For as long as I've been in this squadroom, you've insisted that a woman can't do this job. It must have come as a nasty surprise that this time a woman was essential. I'm the only one in the entire squadroom who can do this. Your whole identity up in smoke."

"I've treated you fair," Silvio said. He slapped her finger away. "We're both smart enough to know something about this case smells bad. But Baez has the hots for you, so you all but promise him a blow job if he lets you do this. No wonder Ortega and Nuñez believed Gomez."

"*What?*" Emilia exclaimed.

"I'm surprised Baez still had his pants on when we walked out of his office," Silvio rolled on. "Or are you going back later?

Emilia felt blood pound in her ears and a red film dropped over her vision. Working with Silvio was like balancing on a runaway rollercoaster. The man who'd come to the hospital and fixed the door of Mercedes's dance studio was gone. In his place was an angry *pendejo* damaged by his wife's death and ready to be as randomly cruel to others as fate had been to him.

"That's one step too far, Franco," Emilia heard herself say.

"Did you really think he's going to gift you with the Senior Investigative Conference with no strings attached?" Silvio snarled. "Baez was just paying it forward and you pocketed the change."

"You need counseling." Emilia was so furious it was hard to squeeze out the words. "Full-time."

"Counseling isn't the answer to everything," Silvio

charged.

"We're done," Emilia said flatly. "When this case is over, I'm asking Baez for a new partner."

Silvio took a step back.

"When this is over, Cruz," he said. "You can go to hell."

Emilia picked up a change of clothes at the penthouse and swung by the hospital before going back to the police station.

As the elevators doors swished open on the trauma services floor, Christine was standing there with Mary Rucker.

Emilia stepped out of the elevator.

The other two women stepped in.

No one said a word.

She was Kurt's mother, Emilia told herself as she donned the long green scrub gown. No matter what, the woman deserved respect for that reason alone.

Christine, however, was another matter. At some point, Emilia would get even.

The doctor spoke to Emilia before she was admitted to the room, again remarking on Kurt's excellent health and obvious athleticism. The most recent CAT scan had shown no brain injury; no cranial fracture, fissures, or distress. In short, there was still no identifiable reason for the coma.

A specialist from Mexico City was on the way.

As before, the machines in Kurt's room beeped and

hummed. Emilia sat in the visitor's chair pulled up to the side of the bed. To avoid bedsores, the nursing staff had turned him slightly toward the chair.

Emilia watched him breathe. The cuts and bruises had all but disappeared. He had not lost muscle tone.

"You'd better wake up before Christine kicks me out of the hotel," Emilia said. "She hasn't said anything to my face but I know from the way she looks whenever we're together that she thinks I should leave." Emilia smoothed his hair. "Funny, I was worried about coming to live in the hotel and now I'm worried I'll have to go."

Kurt's chest rose and fell.

Emilia gripped his unresponsive hand. "I might not be here tomorrow," she said. "I have to work on a case tonight. Wish me luck."

The beep of the machines was the only response.

Wracked with urgency, Emilia leaned close to Kurt. She couldn't leave him like this to walk blithely into Santa Muerte territory.

"Wake up, Kurt," she ordered. "Just wake up, okay? Open your eyes. You don't even have to keep them open. Just blink at me once, okay?"

She searched his face for signs that he heard her. His skin was smooth as marble. The nurses must have shaved him.

"Blink," Emilia whispered. "Blink if you know I love you."

She stayed there, holding his hand, until her time was up.

CHAPTER 28

"You get in there, blend with the crowd," Silvio said. "You're just there to recon the priest."

"I know the plan," Emilia snapped. He'd been a jerk, micromanaging the simple operation while avoiding having to speak to her directly. Both of them had used Macias and Sandor as cut-outs. "It's not like I can do anything else."

"Macias and Sandor will be on the other side," Silvio said. "I'll wait here. Just follow the crowd back."

They were by the car parked in a clearing across from a thick banyan tree, its multiple rooms forming a thicket around the broad base. Cornfields stretched out on either side of the dirt road.

They'd reconnoitered earlier in the day. Bayardo had guided them to the clearing, saying that last year it had served as the rendezvous spot. Emilia had seen a few small farms. Now the shacks and barns and animal pens were shrouded in darkness.

More cars and trucks pulled in. Women hustled out with their Santa Muerte statues. Men got ready to smoke, play cards, and otherwise pass the time until their *mujeres* came back from the intercession.

Sparks flared as campfires were lit. A community feeling prevailed as the crowd grew.

Women passed Silvio's car in groups of three and four, each woman clutching a statue. Several had flashlights or children's glow sticks to light the way. Many held small offerings to attract El Acólito's attention; a cigar, a pack of cigarettes. One woman carried flowers wrapped in black gauze and an unmarked bottle that probably contained homemade *mezcal*.

"Good luck, Cruz," Macias said. Sandor gave her a grin.

"You couldn't have bought a lighter statue?" Emilia asked, resting it on her hip.

The yellow garbed Santa Muerte statue was as long as Emilia's arm, with a wooden scythe and black beads for eyes. The Skeleton Saint held a globe the size of a tennis ball. The robes were the ritual color for healing. Emilia had known what her cover story would be as soon as they brought the statue into the squadroom.

"Get going," Silvio said.

"*Pendejo*," Emilia muttered loud enough for him to hear as she walked away.

Bayardo's wife had given them good information. Emilia looked like the rest of the younger crowd in jeans, tee, cross trainers, and zippered hoodie. Older women wore their generation's uniform of knit skirts and tops or polyester dresses.

Along with the statue, Emilia carried a flashlight, a bottle of whiskey, and a candle with a Santa Muerte charm pressed into the wax. A blanket was folded over her arm. Handy, Emilia was told, to sit on as El Acólito performed the intercession.

She merged with a group of women as they passed

Silvio's car. More women followed. Emilia's flashlight picked out paths in the cornfields. There were low conversations, nervous giggles, and the distant hum of engines as other vehicles dropped off women and girls to start their trek to El Acólito. Emilia noticed a few older men walking with those she supposed were their wives and daughters. They continued for a distance then peeled off.

All of the women carried a statue of Santa Muerte. Some were even larger than Emilia's. The dark gold of wealth and the yellow of healing were the most popular. The rest were white or red. Emilia did not see any black statues.

Many of the walkers carried candles, the flames protected by a paper cup. As the procession swelled, Emilia saw more offerings to Santa Muerte; boxes of candy, small homemade pictures of La Santissima, bottles of liquor, small pieces of tooled leather or shell ornaments. Someone carried shell chimes like those she'd bought at the Coyuca Lagoon souvenir shop. The clear tones carried on the night breeze.

Women greeted Emilia and she smiled and murmured back. One woman held out her lit candle and Emilia touched the wick of hers to it. The new flame sizzled, flared high and strengthened. The woman saw the charm and said, "May La Santissima bless you," and Emilia said "Blessings to you," as if she was in church. It must have been the proper response because the woman smiled and pulled Emilia into her group. Her name was Lora. Her friends' names were lost in the chatter of the crowd. Emilia stayed with them, grateful to be hidden in plain sight.

Flickering candlelight and steady flashlight beams twinkled together in the dark. The procession flowed around the cornstalks like a river of bobbing lights. It was a party. Singing and laughter and high hopes. Everyone's prayers would be answered. Santa Muerte was watching over them. Protection, healing, love. It would all be theirs tonight.

Emilia gave a start as she was hit in the face by droplets of water. One of Lora's friends laughed and held up a spray bottle. "Holy water," Lora explained, blessed by El Acólito himself last year.

They were returning for a second year, seeking Santa Muerte's help for an aging father, a faithless husband, to give thanks for a child who had survived an illness.

"You seek healing?" Lora asked. Her statue was also robed in yellow.

"My mother is ill," Emilia said. "I need his help to heal her."

"El Acólito will take care of you and your mother," Lora said wisely.

"And you?"

Lora shifted her statue to the other hip. No doubt it was as heavy as the one Emilia carried. "I have the cancer," she said. "But Santa Muerte will cure me."

She spoke without any doubt.

"What can you tell me about El Acólito?" Emilia said.

Lora gave Emilia a reassuring look. "He will like you," she said. "You have the right gifts."

Emilia felt cheered by the crowd, as if she was at a party

where everyone was her friend and wanted good things for her. She'd felt it as soon as her candle wick had flared and burned. A glittering optimism, a lightening of the load, a sense that her problems had fallen away.

Padre Ricardo would recover from his heart attack. Ernesto would sharpen knives again; the scissors hadn't hit him in the eye, after all. Sophia would be fine, too, taken care of by Tía Lourdes and Tío Raul the same as when Emilia's father died. Mercedes had already put the robbery behind her, thanks to Silvio and his unexpected handiness.

Kurt would wake up.

A brisk trade went on as women traded items. Lora gave bread to another woman and received a stick of incense in return. Lora lit the incense from her candle and carefully blew the smoke against everyone's Santa Muerte statue. One woman didn't have a statue but she had a small picture of Santa Muerte painted on a rusted piece of metal no bigger than Emilia's palm. The tiny image was exquisite.

Emilia estimated they were two miles from the rendezvous point. At least 300 women continued through the night, their candles pinpoints of light. Broader beams of a flashlight swept the throng now and then. Overhead the night sky twinkled with diamonds and a silver crescent moon.

A cheer went up and Emilia saw the glow of lights in the distance. A rocket screamed into the night sky and burst overhead into a giant sparkler. Emilia heard herself cheering with the crowd.

Two more rockets blossomed overhead, creating a

canopy of twinkling, shivering sparks. The crowd broke like water parted by a stone and saw a stage lifted above the dirt and decorated with an archway of white flowers tall enough for a man to walk through. The flowers looked translucent. Other-worldly. Emilia gaped at the sight until she realized that Christmas lights were wrapped around the arch under the blooms.

Besides the flowers, twin statues of Santa Muerte dressed in white stood like guards. The defensive feeling was encouraged by pyramids of white rifles. From where Emilia stood she didn't know if they were real or wooden carvings made to resemble assault rifles painted white. Emilia looked at her newfound friends' faces to see what they thought of the display but all she heard was oohs and aahs. For most of them, this was a display of opulence, evidence of El Acólito's power and success and Santa Muerte's powers of protection.

Lora staked out a place on the ground and all the women spread their blankets and sat. The field around the platform filled with people, the candles massing together to give the place the look of a lighted stadium. The air was thick with a mix of incense, body odor, and marijuana.

The feeling of well-being passed through Emilia again. This was like being at a rock concert. Maybe the members of Maná would run through the floral archway and begin to sing.

A group near Emilia's blanket set up a small altar, with a red-robed Santa Muerte taking pride of place. Candles, a bottle of some homemade spirit, a black *barro* pottery jar and a big conch shell made up the offerings. Emilia doubted that El Acólito favored shells, judging from what had been on the altars she'd seen lately, but she didn't comment. Other altars held photos, handwritten notes, food, tobacco, tequila. Many women held pictures of children, *los angelitos* who had died. The intercession to Santa Muerte would not be the Catholic Church's prayer for the repose of the child's soul, but a call for the soul to come and connect with its family once more.

Recorded guitar music blared out, signaling a start to the event, and a cheer went up. A man stepped up on the stage, set a microphone on a stand, and waved his arms for attention.

He was disappointingly ordinary in a plaid shirt and jeans. The microphone crackled as he admonished the crowd to go home peacefully after the ritual, not drink or smoke, or cause trouble for the men who had sacrificed to allow their women to come. Emilia nearly snorted at that but the women around her listened intently.

The plaid shirt was replaced by a man in a long white robe. Next to Emilia, Lora clicked her teeth.

"El Acólito?" Emilia asked?

"No," Lora whispered back. "His priest.

"A real priest?" Emilia was surprised to hear that the man would be a real priest, after what Father Ricardo had told her.

"Father Jeronimo wears a white cassock," Lora said. "But he is only a priest to El Acólito who is the true acolyte of

Santa Muerte."

No one else seemed bothered by this bit of religious muddle, but Father Jeronimo's role was soon made clear. He was the warm-up act, preparing the audience for El Acólito's special blessings and for the dedication of their lives to Santa Muerte.

Emilia followed along, repeating the phrases Father Jeronimo bellowed emotionally into the microphone.

"Muerte Santísima, you are welcome into my house!"

"Muerte Querida of my heart, take me under your protection!"

"Glorious and powerful Muerte, cast Your divine protection over Your believers."

He was emotional, imploring Santa Muerte to hear their petitions on this holiest of all holy days, the Day of the Dead. Father Jeronimo shouted, implored, danced, shook his fist, and wept as the crowd responded.

He was a mesmerizing, charismatic figure. Emilia felt the emotional level of the crowd swell. All around her women sobbed, fainted, screamed, clutched at their hearts, and declared that they would be faithful to the teachings of El Acólito and to Santa Muerte. The effect was powerful and intoxicating. Emilia felt herself carried along, moved by the force of such a mass of devotion.

The performance lasted for 25 minutes, building and building. The air crackled with estrogen and electricity as Emilia held up her candle for the ultimate veneration of the white-robed statue of Santa Muerte. The field was blanketed with flickering light. Father Jeronimo held out his arms so that the power of Santa Muerte could flow through his body and reach to the ends of the earth. Just when Emilia's arm was aching and trembling, Father Jeronimo let out a scream of thanks and the field erupted in the climactic moment of collective celebration. Father Jeronimo whipped up the crowd again, the emotional high as addictive as a drug. Just when it seemed that he couldn't squeeze any more frenzy out of the audience, a man burst through the decorated archway and bounded onto the stage. Father Jeronimo fell onto his knees, his arms stretched before him in a posture of extreme veneration.

The women bolted to their feet and went wild.

"El Acólito," Lora shouted joyfully.

Emilia stretched to her tiptoes to see past the women in front of her and gulped air at the sight of the newcomer. He was a big man, as tall as Kurt, and heavily muscled with the sculpted look of a body builder. He was shirtless, clad in only loose white cotton trousers. They hung low on his hips and she was pretty sure he was naked beneath.

His torso was tattooed from shoulder to navel with multi-colored flowers, skulls and images of Santa Muerte. His face was hollowed under the cheekbones and around the eye sockets with makeup. His lips were striped with vertical lines to enforce the skull-like image. Swept back from his face, wavy hair brushed his shoulders.

"My daughters," El Acólito said and spread his arms wide. "Welcome!"

There was no need for the microphone. El Acólito owned the stage with a deep, resonant voice and expansive gestures that pulled the audience as if every woman was on a string attached to his fingers. Sensuality and power emanated from him with every word.

"My daughters," El Acólito exclaimed. "You have come for Santa Muerte's powers. To heal, to protect, to punish. But are you worthy? Have you sacrificed to show your deepest faith?"

He ran back and forth across the stage, pointing to a woman here, another one there. Asking if they were deserving of Santa Muerte's protection. He flung his arms wide, his abdomen and pectoral muscles flexing. He threw back his mane of hair and bellowed at the sky, bringing down the power of Santa Muerte to run through his veins and extend The White Lady's pure light over all of the faithful.

He was riveting and beautiful and fearful all at the same time.

El Acólito told the women that he was there to hear their petitions, that he would give them instructions to live good lives in keeping with the wishes of Santa Muerte. When every woman in the crowd was committed, fully committed in her heart, he would implore Santa Muerte to intercede for each one of them. The emotions of the crowd seesawed from adoration to fear and back again.

El Acólito raised his arms above his head and clenched both fists. His pectoral muscles jumped, causing Santa Muerte to ripple across his body. He would pray now alone to invoke the spirit of Santa Muerte and come out again when it flowed through him. Screams mixed with the cheering and Emilia saw several women faint. El Acólito disappeared through the archway.

The recorded music blared again and the crowd settled down. White robed men walked through the crowd, collecting the liquor, cigars, and other offerings in big baskets. They occasionally stopped to talk to selected women. One bent to Emilia. "Why do you need El Acólito's intercession?"

"My mother," Emilia said. She showed him her yellow statue. "My mother is ill."

"Stand up."

Emilia got to her feet while Lora and friends watched open-mouthed.

The white robed man looked her up and down. "You are ready to pray with El Acólito?" he asked.

"Yes." Emilia held out the bottle of whiskey.

"After the intercession, go to the back of the stage." He took the bottle and handed her a yellow plastic coin in return. "Show this and El Acólito will pray with you. Don't give it to anyone else. El Acólito asked me to give it to you alone. He knows your mother's illness can be cured."

He moved away.

"You were chosen!" Lora exclaimed.

El Acólito's adherents continued to move through the crowd, doling out coins. Emilia sat on her blanket again and showed the coin to the nearby women.

An audience with El Acólito himself would allow her to learn more about this mysterious man and his organization, although from the wording of the prayers she'd already pegged him as the force that had recruited Marco Sandino Varela. The words of every message found on the altars or in the boy's knapsack had been repeated during the ceremony.

The guitar music was replaced by a roar that started at the stage and spread to every spectator. El Acólito bounded through the arch again. His white-robed minions placed candles on the stage by his feet. With a dramatic flourish, El Acólito struck a match against the tattoo of Santa Muerte on his chest, and lit the candles.

His minions returned to place a heavy scarf like a Catholic priest's stole around his neck. As the ends draped down his bare chest, Emilia saw embroidered black images of Santa Muerte.

El Acólito held out his arms, passed his hands over the candle flames, and began to chant. The words were unintelligible but slowly rose in volume. His hands lowered until they hovered in the flames. Restless murmurings rose from the crowd along with sobs of anticipation.

Without warning, El Acólito threw his hands together and boomed out the prayers that Father Jeronimo had taught the crowd at the beginning of the ceremony. Hundreds of voices answered and Emilia found herself chanting along with everyone else. El Acólito implored Santa Muerte to come to them, to hold the faithful in her hand as proof of her holy protection.

An array of fireworks blasted up from the ground in back of the stage, soared into the sky, and burst into silver droplets. "The proof of her power," El Acólito shouted and flung out his arms held out like *Jesu Cristo* on the cross. Screams erupted across the field.

Fireworks continued. The crowd, mesmerized by El Acólito, reacted with noise and singing and pleas for him to touch them, pray with them. El Acólito did just that, walking off the stage and into the crowd where the women reacted as if he was *Cristo* himself, touching his pant legs, brushing their fingers against his. The fireworks continued and Emilia felt the earth shake as the big rockets fired.

Or was El Acólito making the ground move as he made his way through his worshippers?

Lora and the others who'd seen Emilia receive the yellow chip walked with her to the back of the stage. A handful of other women with plastic coins were there. The color of each coin coincided with the color of their Santa Muerte statue.

Dozens of candles were lit, revealing the shadowy outline of a low stone house. The makeshift stage was built around a side entrance. Drained by the spectacle, Emilia wondered if she had the energy to use this opportunity to find out what happened to Marco Sandino Varela.

The first woman brought inside emerged 10 minutes later,

tears of joy streaming down her face. "Santa Muerte has heard my prayers," she whispered and floated off to a knot of friends waiting for her.

Emilia was next. A robed man brought her inside. The walls were pale stucco but beyond that she could see almost nothing. She surrendered her coin and the man guided her down a hallway by the light of a candle and into a room simply furnished with a table and two chairs. The man told her to place her statue of Santa Muerte on the floor and sit. El Acólito would come soon to bless her statue and pray with her.

Emilia glanced at her watch. It was after 2:00 am. Silvio, Macias, and Sandor would be getting worried.

A battery-powered lantern glowed on the table, next to a stainless steel bowl of ice containing several plastic bottles of soda. Emilia read the label and couldn't resist a snicker. Apparently, Santa Muerte priests liked orange Fanta soda. After the other-worldly performance she'd just witnessed, orange soda was absurdly ordinary.

"Hello." It was El Acólito.

The makeup was gone, revealing a fatally handsome man. High cheekbones, a square jaw, the manly shadow of a beard. Wavy hair tumbled across his forehead. A white cotton shirt hid the tattoo.

"Hello," Emilia replied.

He sat in the opposite chair and held out a hand. Emilia placed her hand in his.

"Let us pray, sister," he said. He didn't close his eyes.

They were as brilliant as if he'd swallowed a lit candle. "Tell me why you have come."

The man's stage presence was undeniable but up close he was like cocaine. Strikingly beautiful and full of promise. He'd said less than a dozen words to her but Emilia felt as if they'd known each other forever.

"My mother," Emilia said. "She had a breakdown years ago and now she's like a child. Sometimes she doesn't know what she's talking about."

"This hurts you." El Acólito stared at her without blinking. His eyes were brown, like a muddy and stormy sea.

Emilia felt herself wanting his approval. "Yes," she said. "I want her to be normal. To understand what's happening around her."

"Does she live with you?"

"No."

El Acólito repeated the prayers from the intercession, but softly, pressing her hand as he spoke. Emilia closed her eyes and felt herself sway in rhythm with his words.

When the prayer ended he released her hand. "There," he said. "Your mother's health will be restored. Our prayers have the power to make it seem as if she was never ill."

He was so sure that for a moment Emilia believed him, too. She smiled. "Thank you."

"Have you come very far to see me?" he asked. He took two bottles from the dish of ice and handed one to Emilia.

"Acapulco," she said.

El Acólito opened his soda bottle, the seal breaking with

a soft *snick*. He drank down a big swallow, then passed the cool and damp bottle over his forehead.

"You must be tired," Emilia said.

He grinned as if she was an old friend. "I lose about five pounds with every performance," he confided. "Do I smell like sulfur from the fireworks?"

"A little," Emilia admitted and grinned back at him. "But it was spectacular." She twisted off the cap of the Fanta bottle, hearing the welcome sigh of escaping gas that proved the seal had not been tampered with. The orange soda soothed her throat, parched from hours of chanting in the dry night air.

"We owe it to the followers," El Acólito said. He leaned back and watched her. "I have to make it worth their while."

"Is that why you do it?" Emilia asked and drank more soda. She was glad she had the bottle to play with. As his eyes bored into her, Emilia wasn't sure she had the skill to extract information from him, let alone a discussion of Marco's fate. "What about your family?"

"My followers are more important."

"What about . . ." Emilia lost her train of thought.

El Acólito leaned across the table and stroked Emilia's cheek.

Her whole body felt heavy and her eyelids wouldn't stay open. Before her brain slugged to a complete halt, Emilia knew that under the orange Fanta label, there was a mark in the plastic bottle where a needle had injected a blue *reina* solution. A hot pin was probably used to melt the plastic and close the hole.

"But I liked you," she said stupidly.

Blackness closed in.

CHAPTER 29

Emilia opened her eyes. Bright light assailed her.

She squinted against the glare. Her head pounded. Her muscles were stiff and sore.

Her last memory was of El Acólito's smile as she drank the soda.

A few deep breaths helped. She was lying on a thin blanket. Metal springs poked through. Instead of her clothes, she had on a long white men's tee shirt. Her legs were bare. A fly settled on her calf. She tried to brush it away. Her right hand jerked and a chain rattled.

She was handcuffed to the squared edge of a metal cot.

"She's awake." The voice was female and young.

Emilia turned to see the speaker. A girl around 18 years old was sitting crossed legged on a cot several feet away. She was also wearing a white tee shirt and cuffed to a metal bed frame.

The girl would have been pretty if it hadn't been for the tear-stained cheeks and reddened eyes. "I'm Blanca," she said. "What's your name?"

"Emilia." As she scooted herself into a sitting position, Emilia discovered she wasn't wearing panties and there was a soreness in her pelvis she didn't want to acknowledge. She managed to sit cross-legged and pull down the shirt to cover herself.

"Don't worry about that," Blanca said. "We've all seen

each other's everything. They don't give us clothes very often."

Emilia looked around. Five other girls sat on cots, dressed in long white tee shirts. All were pretty and looked to be in their late teens or early 20's. Several had magazines. One clutched a bottle of nail polish and looked vaguely familiar.

The room was a sort of dormitory, with cots laid out in two rows of three on a dirt floor. Emilia's cot was in the middle of the first row with her feet pointed toward a corrugated metal door set into a ceiling track that took up half of the narrow end of the room.

Blanca's cot was closest to the stucco wall. If the girl could stand, she would be able to look out of the single window laced with raw iron rebar. There was no glass.

Across from the room, cement boxes created a dirty mosaic the length of the wall. Overhead, daylight showed between bowed and warped wooden slats.

Troughs, Emilia realized as she looked at the cement bins. Once upon a time the place had been a horse barn.

"Stinks in here, doesn't it?" Blanca asked. "They only give us a bucket to pass around."

"How long have you been here?" Emilia.

"We've been in this place for two days," Blanca said.

"How did you get here?"

"I was working in Iguala." Blanca's face crumpled. "My boss said he'd give me a ride, but first we had to see the Santa Muerte procession. He introduced me to El Acólito and the next thing I knew I was like this." She felt up her manacled fist.

Before Emilia could ask another question, the girl on the other side hissed wordlessly. Every girl grabbed the handcuff chain and silently slid down on her cot. Emilia did the same, rolling to face Blanca. The younger girl put her finger to her lips and closed her eyes.

The door began to roll open but stopped halfway.

"Not now. I have to go." The voice from the other side had the unmistakable German accent and timbre of Herman Schmidt. "I told you they left those *muertos* for me to find."

"They don't know who you are." The second voice was the rich baritone of El Acólito.

"I can't leave the place alone," Herman said. "They're going to burn me out, just like you did that store."

"My friend," El Acólito said. "You are under the protection of the White Lady."

"The police came," Herman said. "Twice. Itzel is scared."

"My mother needs to place her trust in Santa Muerte." A third voice joined the conversation.

"Ah, Pablito." El Acólito's voice was muffled as if he'd turned away from the door. "This is true but mothers deserve our respect."

The third voice, presumably that of Pablito, said something indistinct.

"Carlos and I will bring you back," El Acólito said, his voice clear again. "I will speak with her."

"Thank you, Acólito," Herman said.

"You're leaving me here?" Pablito asked.

"Miguel and Tito will be back soon," El Acólito said. "The bus is acting up. They had to stop in Acapulco to make repairs."

"We'll need it tomorrow morning for the delivery," Pablito said.

"Tomorrow?" This from Herman.

"Six packages up the coast," El Acólito said. "Prime female beef. Ten thousand dollars each. Don't worry, you'll get your cut."

They all laughed.

"When we get back, Pablito," El Acólito said. "You can pick one and take her in the truck."

"A farewell present," Pablito said.

The laughter of the three men faded, as did their footsteps.

An engine roared to life outside the window. Emilia heard the engine shift into gear and tires crunch on gravel. The sound was eventually lost in the distance.

Silvio's instincts had been right. The rest of the puzzle came together for her as Emilia lay chained to the cot.

They were human traffickers.

Waitresses at the El Loro Rojo came and went so quickly because Herman sold the girls to El Acólito. Los Nueves didn't hold territory because El Acólito and his friends were always on the move, hiding their trafficking business behind the drama and mystery of the Santa Muerte intercessions. They took women, killed gangs like El Machete that got in their way, and moved on. That's why Los Nueves didn't hold territory like other gangs.

Emilia dimly recalled the map she'd made. The red ink of Santa Muerte murders was the trail of El Acólito's trafficking network. Drugs were almost certainly involved, but their main moneymaking endeavor was selling women over the border to brothels in *El Norte*.

One by one, the girls cautiously sat up.

"Do you need to pee?" Blanca asked. "We can pass you the bucket."

"No," Emilia said. If anything she was dehydrated to the point of dizziness. "Is there any water?"

"I have some." Blanca used her left hand to reach between her mattress and cot springs. She pulled out half a bottle of water, causing a shower of rust to the dirt floor, and handed it to Emilia. "Don't drink all of it," she said. "It's my whole ration for the day."

A few sips and Emilia was able to think more clearly. "Do you know how the other girls got here?"

"Most are from the intercession in Iguala," she whispered back. "Like me."

"I went to find love." The girl on the cot on Emilia's other side smiled ruefully.

"That's Pilar," Blanca said.

"I had a red statue of Santa Muerte," Pilar said. She was a big girl with a high forehead, wide eyes, and a messy braid trailing down her back. "El Acólito picked me. I thought I would die from happiness."

Whispers rippled around the barn as different girls told their story. Each girl was single and from somewhere between Acapulco and Iguala. Emilia mentally marked her map with a trafficking corridor between the two cities.

Within the last ten days, every girl had either been chosen at a Santa Muerte intercession, accepted a ride from Herman Schmidt, or dated a man they only knew as Pablito. The girls spoke of being drugged and waking like Emilia; chained and violated. They all had been transported at least once while chained in a van. They didn't know where they were now.

As the stories were told, Emilia saw that the girl with the nail polish was not chained.

"Liliana's the favorite," Blanca whispered. "She's been here the longest."

The short dark hair, the slightly slanted eyes, the china doll mouth. "Lila," Emilia croaked. "You're Lila Jimenez Lata."

"How do you know me?" the girl asked.

"I've been looking for you," Emilia said. "Your grandmother asked me to find you."

"Berta?" The girl was shocked.

"Yes, Berta." Emilia had to twist her torso to maintain the conversation. "You were working at the El Loro Rojo, weren't you?"

"For that disgusting German groper," Lila said, rolling her eyes. "He said he'd introduce me to someone who'd help me get an acting job. That's why I ran away from Berta. She never let me do anything more exciting than dancing lessons. I want to be an actress."

"You met Marco at the restaurant, didn't you?"

Lila smiled tremulously. "He's going to get me out of here, you know. Acólito said if Marco did him a favor, he'd let me go."

"She doesn't want to go," Pilar murmured. "She's in love with El Acólito."

Emilia shook her head. "Marco isn't coming, Lila," she said. "Marco's dead."

"No, he's not," Lila said.

"Yes." Emilia couldn't believe she had to tell the girl the news like this; chained and half naked. "He had a heart problem no one knew about."

Lila's eyes filled. "How do you know?"

"I, uh." Emilia hesitated. She couldn't say she was a cop; there was no way of knowing if the girls could be trusted. "I know his mother," she said finally.

"He ran away from school for me," Lila sniffled.

"I know," Emilia said. "Where did he go?"

"He came to stay with me at the lagoon," the girl said. "He used to kayak there all the time before he had to go back to that horrible school."

"Did the Schmidts know he stayed with you?"

"Of course." Lila swiped at her eyes, weepy yet at the same time surprised that Emilia would have to ask. "Marco even paid Itzel rent."

Pilar hissed. Every girl instantly feigned sleep again.

The door squealed along the track. A young man looked around. Presumably this was Pablito. He was as short and thick as Itzel Schmidt, his girth accentuated by tight jeans and an even tighter black tee. His hair was a little too long and swept to the side in a poor imitation of El Acólito. He left the door open.

Emilia watched from under her lashes as Pablito patrolled the cots, an automatic handgun in his right hand and a cheap flip phone in the left. He halted between her cot and that of Blanca, stuffed the phone in the back pocket of his jeans, and bent to slide his free hand between Blanca's legs.

The bedsprings groaned as Emilia rolled off her cot. Still bending over Blanca, Pablito turned to see. Emilia grabbed the metal frame with both hands, forced herself up, and swung the cot as high and hard as she could.

The edge caught Pablito at chest level. He stumbled and went down on one knee. Emilia swung the frame again, her muscles screaming in agony as she labored to lift it high enough to ram it against his head.

Pablito dropped the gun and caught the frame with both hands. Emilia stayed on her feet and the unwieldy platform of webbed springs seesawed between them. A rusty prong dug into Emilia's arm and she cried out even as she drove forward, pinning Pablito against the wall.

There was a rattling noise behind Emilia. Blanca slammed Pablito in the knees with the edge of her cot. He bellowed and tripped and let go of Emilia's frame.

The sudden release spilled Emilia backwards. The cot bounced to the ground, taking first her handcuffed wrist and then the rest of her body with it. As Emilia fell, a racket erupted over her head. With a flash of white and long legs,

Pilar's cot crashed down on Pablito. Emilia struggled to her feet to see Pablito squirming out from under Pilar's bedsprings, the girl grunting with the effort to keep him down. Emilia wrestled her frame on top of Pilar's, flattening Pablito before he could crawl away. Crying loudly, Blanca shoved hers into the fray as well, hemming him in.

The end result was a tangle of bodies and bedsprings and a near empty water bottle rolling like a misplaced toy. Pablito was pinned to the dirt floor by a pyramid of rusty metal and the weight of three women still handcuffed to the cots.

"Where's the key to the cuffs, *pendejo*?" Emilia demanded breathlessly.

"Fuck you, cunt," Pablito roared. He tried to arch his back and throw them off.

Emilia shifted her weight to keep him pinned. "The key, *pendejo*," she shouted.

He continued to curse and struggle, heaving and rattling the metal springs. Blanca sobbed in fear.

"What do we do now?" Pilar whispered.

The bedsprings shifted as Pablito clawed at the floor in an effort to muscle away.

Emilia worked her free hand between the springs and stuck her thumb into his eye as far as it would go.

Pablito screamed. Blanca screamed. Pilar gasped. The other girls sat frozen on their cots.

Emilia plucked her bloody thumb out of his eye socket and wiped it on her bare thigh. Dry heaves shook her unexpectedly. Nothing came up.

Pablito passed out.

The barn was suddenly silent, except for the incongruous sound of birds on the other side of the window opening.

"Is he dead?" Blanca quavered.

"No," Emilia said. Both Blanca and Pilar stared at her as if she'd sprouted angel wings. "Don't move. He won't be out long."

Emilia shifted until she could see the back pocket of the unconscious man's jeans. Again she worked her left hand between the thicket of springs and carefully drew out the phone. She repeated the process, this time searching for the key to the handcuffs and came up empty.

The phone alone would have to save them.

Emilia flipped it open. One bar of service. One bar of battery.

She punched in Silvio's cell phone number. After four rings it went to voice mail, as she expected. He never answered calls from unknown numbers. "It's Emilia," she said after the tone. "Call me back. Fast."

She broke the connection. All of the girls still stared at her.

"Lila," Emilia called. "Get the gun. It's over by the window."

Rusty springs creaked as Lila got up. "I don't like guns," she said.

The big automatic was near the window. With any luck, they'd be able to shoot off the handcuffs and still have half a dozen rounds left.

The phone rang. Emilia hit the green button. "Franco?"

"Where are you?" Silvio demanded.

The rush of relief at hearing his voice was profound. "It's a human trafficking network," Emilia gabbled. "Women. Probably selling them to brothels in El Norte. Herman Schmidt is part of it."

"*Rayos*," Silvio swore.

"There's a bunch of us in a barn. I think this was a horse farm. No electricity or running water. Driving distance from Acapulco. I heard tires on gravel but no other traffic so we're not near a paved road. You'll have to trace the call and work from there."

"On it," Silvio said. "We'll find the cell tower routing the call. Just stay on the line."

"This phone doesn't have much juice left." Emilia heard how fast she was speaking. "El Acólito went to take Herman Schmidt back to Coyuca Lagoon. He'd been gone awhile. Maybe an hour. He could be back any time. They're supposed to be moving up the coast tomorrow morning to deliver these women to the next link in the trafficking chain."

"Are you all right? Is anyone hurt?"

"Bring a rape kit," Emilia said, willing herself to sound professional. "Bring six."

"Hang in there, Cruz," Silvio said. "Hollywood woke up last night."

The phone screen went black and Silvio's voice

evaporated.

Emilia felt terror close in. That fragile connection was a lifeline and now it was gone. The call might not have been long enough for the technical magic needed to trace the location.

Blanca gave a little scream as Pablito began cursing and squirming to get out from under the web of bedsprings and the weight of three women. Emilia looked around.

The gun was still on the floor by the window.

"Lila," Emilia called. "Get the gun."

This time, the girl crept to the gun and nudged it with her bare toe.

Emilia held out her free hand. "Lila. Give it to me."

Lila picked up the gun by its muzzle.

They all heard it at the same time; the whine of an engine forcing a vehicle over uneven terrain.

"Lila, hurry," Emilia urged.

The noise grew, like a stinging bee closing in.

Gun pinched between her fingers, Lila edged to the window. She reached through the steel bars and let go. There was a soft thud as the gun hit the ground outside.

"You bitch," Pilar bawled.

The vehicle ground to a stop. The engine died. Car doors opened and shut. Male voices laughed at an unheard joke.

Lila scrambled back onto her cot.

"Hey, Pablito!" El Acólito's voice boomed through the open door. "Where are you?"

Blanca hiccupped in fear. At the same time Pablito stirred

and gave a howl of pain.

"What the fuck?" El Acólito appeared in the wide doorway. Another man, presumably Carlos, was right behind him. Both carried handguns.

"What do we have here?" El Acólito asked. He strolled to the thicket of bedsprings, like the lead actor about to deliver the pivotal monologue and chuckled at the women perched on top. "A little uprising?"

"Acólito," Pablito gasped. The empty eye socket leaked blood and pus. "Please."

"She called the cops," Lila burst out, pointing to Emilia. "She took his phone and called the police."

El Acólito's smile faded.

"But I liked you," he said, in a telling parody of Emilia's voice. He made no move to free Pablito or take the phone out of Emilia's hand. "I guess this means we'll be leaving sooner than expected."

"What about the delivery?" Carlos asked.

"We don't have time." El Acólito leveled the gun at Emilia, the ugly muzzle no further away than the length of the cot. "Money and connections down the drain. I'd like to say you were worth it. But you were just one more bare ass."

"You're nothing but a con man," Emilia breathed.

El Acólito thumbed off the safety.

Emilia knew without a doubt that he was going to kill her. Shoot her like a dog as she sat trapped and chained. Fear closed her throat.

Negotiation would be useless. She had nothing to bargain

with; he'd already had her body and chose to sell it. There would be no appeal to his better self because there was no such thing. Begging would only be a waste of pride.

Blanca began to cry, hiccupping and sobbing at the same time. Pilar whimpered. Neither girl moved.

Emilia raised her chin and fixed a picture of Kurt in her mind. Strong and tanned, confident and lean, wet hair pushed back from his forehead, ocean-colored eyes sparkling. She was secure in his arms on the swimming dock as the sun came up and enveloped them in a new day.

El Acólito shot Pablito in the head.

The body jerked. Brains and blood splattered the wall, the floor, and all three women perched on the bedsprings.

Blanca screamed uncontrollably.

El Acólito tucked the gun into the waistband of his jeans at the small of his back, and walked out. Carlos dutifully followed. Two minutes later, the vehicle outside the window roared to life. Tire crunched on gravel again.

"No!" Lila launched herself off her cot and raced out the door.

"Lila!" Emilia yelled.

"Take me with you!" The girl's plaintive scream soared through the window as her footsteps pounded past. "Take me with you!"

Emilia heard the truck stop. Lila shouted again. A car door opened, then closed again. The engine revved. The sound of the vehicle faded, replaced by Blanca's exhausted sobbing and the twitter of birds.

They eventually got Blanca calmed down and the three cots disentangled. Encumbered as they were, it was impossible to move Pablito's body out of the barn so they dragged themselves and the protesting bedsprings into the shade of a tree. Emilia searched the ground below the window, but the gun was gone.

She'd been right about the property being an abandoned farm. The men had stayed in the main house a stone's throw away. The makeshift stage was gone but evidence of the construction could be seen in discarded bits of board and wilted flowers. Emilia and Pilar dragged their cots with them on a trip to the house to forage for food, water, and a way to cut off the handcuffs.

Moving was a nightmare. The sun heated the metal cot frames, sweat intensified Emilia's already severe dehydration, and gravel cut into bare feet. The house was dark. The rooms were empty. They found a pile of food wrappers and half a bottle of water which had rolled into a corner. No handcuff key or even a slender piece of wire to jigger the clasp. No electricity, generator, or phone. Or clothes.

Emilia took a sip of water and handed the bottle to Pilar. "I'm going to walk as far as I can," she said. "My friends are looking for us. If I can find a turnoff or a main road, they'll see me."

She followed the dirt track and the fresh tire marks, pulling the metal cot beside her like a reluctant dog. There was little shade and Emilia panted in the heat. The smears of blood on her skin and tee shirt stank of death.

The road blurred but she kept going, her thoughts narrowing to the next step, the next yank on the hot metal frame.

A wider dirt road intersected the track. The brown landscape rippled, playing games with the piercing blue sky and flaring sun.

Emilia knew she couldn't go any further, much less decide to go right or left. She sank into the dust, drew up her knees and pulled the tee shirt over her legs to give the sun the least amount of skin to fry. At least if she was going to die, it would not be where El Acólito had chosen.

Her right forearm arm was spotted with blood from the cut caused by the rusty springs during the fight with Pablito.

As she waited for a miracle, her arm throbbed and swelled. Emilia watched a red streak slowly creep up her arm; a line of infection inching towards her heart.

CHAPTER 30

"Hey, Em."

"Hey yourself," Emilia said.

Kurt put a big bouquet and some magazines on the table by her hospital bed. He leaned over to hug her. Emilia pulled him close and buried her face in his crisp cotton shirt, reveling in his scent of ocean and musky cologne. He carried no ill effects of the coma or the accident which precipitated it.

"How's the arm today?" Kurt asked when they broke apart.

"Better." Emilia held out her right arm. After four days, the infection was finally under control and her forearm was no longer the swollen hot mess it was when Silvio and the others found her. "I might be able to come home tomorrow."

"Jacques said he'll be by this afternoon," Kurt drew up a chair and sat down next to the bed. "Said he's packing a hamper. He's convinced hospital food in Mexico will kill you."

"It's not great," Emilia acknowledged. "Did he say if he'll bring risotto?"

Kurt laughed. "I'm fairly certain you can expect that and a lot more."

"I can't wait to get out of here. I just want to go home. Forget any of this ever happened."

They'd talked about everything. The blue *reinas*, the

assault she couldn't remember, her certain knowledge that she was going to die as El Acólito pointed his gun. Emilia was angry that she'd walked into a trap and frustrated that she couldn't remember. Telling him had been awkward at first. Later the words poured out in a wave of release and relief. Kurt listened with full attention, the way he did everything.

The only thing Emilia didn't share was the nagging worry that if her memory suddenly came back, her mind would shatter like her mother's.

There was a tap on the open door. Lieutenant Baez and Silvio stood in the doorway.

"Can we come in?" Lieutenant Baez asked. He wore his usual sharp suit and carried a big manila envelope.

"Hello," Emilia said.

Silvio introduced Lieutenant Baez to Kurt and held out a hand. "Good to see you up and about, Rucker."

"Freak accident," said Kurt. "I think once we get Emilia home, we'll want to stay away from hospitals for awhile."

"Good, good." Lieutenant Baez smiled at Emilia. "We've put you on personal leave for three weeks. More if you need it. Time to relax and take advantage of counseling."

"I'll make sure she does that," Kurt said.

"You'll be glad to know that both Herman and Itzel Schmidt have been arrested and charged with human trafficking," Lieutenant Baez said. "Organized Crime also arrested Adonis Rugama Moreno. El Machete's El Commandante. Apparently, the feud with El Acólito's group began when Schmidt picked up Rugama Moreno's girlfriend."

"That's all good, isn't it?" Kurt asked.

"Very good," Silvio said. "Acapulco is a lot safer without El Machete."

"We've got some additional information about the case." Lieutenant Baez cleared his throat. "Of a personal nature. Perhaps we should speak in private?"

"Kurt can stay," Emilia said.

"All right," Lieutenant Baez said.

Kurt sat on the edge of Emilia's bed. His hand found hers.

Silvio shut the door to the hospital room. Both men sat in the extra visitor chairs.

"We have the DNA results of your assailant," Lieutenant Baez began. He drew a paper from the envelope. "The DNA shows that he is a close relative of yours, Emilia. In fact, it would appear that he is your brother."

"I don't have a brother," Emilia said.

"The results are conclusive," Lieutenant Baez said. "If El Acólito was your assailant, he's also your brother."

"I don't have a brother," Emilia repeated but it was hard to speak against the humming in her head. Her chest felt heavy and it was hard to breathe.

"Em?" Kurt asked. "Are you all right?"

The humming in Emilia's head sorted itself into words.

His hair was curly, but yours was straight.

"Em." Kurt's voice cut through. "Drink this."

He handed her a glass of water and Emilia obediently

drank.

They all waited while she got herself under control and handed the empty glass back to Kurt.

"Was he in the DNA log?" Emilia asked. "Did it give you a name?"

"No," Silvio said. The big detective sat forward in his chair, hands clasped between his knees. "There's nothing on that DNA profile anywhere."

"Without what you did, we'd never know that this human trafficking organization exists," Lieutenant Baez said. "It's just a matter of time before he's caught. Faster if we had a name, of course, but we'll find him."

Silvio stared at her with his usual grim expression, no sympathy or understanding. Kurt's hand was right there but she didn't reach for it again.

"I can get a name," Emilia said.

CHAPTER 31

Two days later, Emilia greeted Tío Raul as he lifted the hood on an old Oldsmobile. She climbed the stairs to the apartment over the garage. It was no longer the familiar place she'd grown up, full of family and noise, but the safe haven for a lie that got bigger with every step she took.

"Emilia!" Lourdes gave her a happy kiss and pulled her into the kitchen. "You haven't been around much lately. Your mother and I were worried. Ernesto is much better, you know. So is Padre Ricardo. Your mother and I were at the rectory yesterday and he asked about you."

"That's good," Emilia said distractedly.

"Sit, sit," Lourdes admonished her. "I have fresh *conchas* from the *pastelería*. We'll have some with tea. You look too thin. Isn't that man of yours letting you eat?"

"I don't want any tea," Emilia said.

Lourdes frowned and stopped in the middle of filling a kettle from the big jug of bottled water on the counter. "Emilia, what's wrong?"

"I have a brother," Emilia said abruptly. "A brother no one ever spoke about."

Lourdes put the kettle on the counter.

Emilia waited.

Lourdes sank into a chair at the kitchen table. "How did you find out?" she asked at length.

"I'm a detective," Emilia said. "It's my job to find things

out."

Lourdes covered her face with her hands.

"What happened to him?" Emilia sat facing her aunt.

"Ah." Lourdes dropped her hands. Her eyes were teary. "I can't talk about this, Emilia."

"I need to know." Emilia's voice was flat. "I think it's better that I hear it from you rather than my mother."

Lourdes wiped her eyes with the hem of her apron. "It was a long time ago, Emilia."

"It matters right now, *tía*," Emilia said.

"Raul and I decided long ago that we wouldn't tell you," Lourdes protested weakly. "Tell anybody. There was nothing we could do. She was rich and . . . and we had nothing."

"Who was rich?"

Lourdes touched the hem of her apron to her eyes again. "When your father died, Sophia became a child again, as if her mind had to run and hide. The widow of your father's employer was much stronger. She didn't break the way Sophia did."

Emilia focused on breathing normally.

"The woman said that Sophia owed her a child," Lourdes continued softly. "They didn't have any and she was still young. The woman blamed your father for the accident. Said she was owed the son she never had. When she kicked Sophia out of the chauffeur's house, she took your brother as her own."

"That's kidnapping," Emilia said.

Lourdes shook her head. "Sophia was afraid the woman would take you both. She was rich. Rich people take things."

"Nobody did anything?"

"Sophia was so broken." Lourdes lifted her hands in a gesture of resignation. "What sustained her was the thought that he'd have a good life. As the years went on Sophia made her peace with what had happened. She never talked about it again. She had you and that was enough."

"He's older than me?" Emilia asked. "Or younger?"

"Older by just 12 months," Lourdes said. "His name was Ernesto, too."

"Ernesto Cruz Encinos," Emilia said.

Lourdes smiled. "Ernesto and Emilia. He called you Baby."

Emilia closed her eyes against pain that bit hard enough to draw blood. She shook it off. "What was the family's name?" she pressed. "The name of the widow?"

Lourdes shook her head. "I don't know, Emilia. I only remember that the man was a doctor. I don't even remember what kind." She reached across the table and clasped Emilia's hand. "You can't tell your mother that you know. It would kill her."

"I can't promise," Emilia said.

"Emilia," Lourdes spoke with urgency. "You have to remember what your father's death did to your mother. Her mind cracked."

"I have to know," Emilia said bitterly.

"We gave you a good home," Lourdes said. "Your brother

got a good home, too. What happened was almost 30 years ago. What difference does it make now?"

Emilia shook off her aunt's restraining hand and got to her feet. "It matters to me," she said.

☼

She knew the date of his death and that he'd been a doctor.

Emilia sat in the basement of the *Jornada de Acapulco* newspaper offices and inserted the panel of microfilm into the machine. The internet had made microfiche obsolete but the newspaper had only digitized the last 5 years. The rest was only available as bits of slowly fading celluloid, subject to humidity and lack of interest.

"We get so few visitors," the librarian had said as she searched the archive. The mousy and bespectacled woman finally found a box of film marked with the date of that long-ago October.

It was expensive to place an obituary. Emilia knew she'd never see one for her father. Like so many other things, obituaries were reserved for the wealthy. If her father's employer had been rich enough for a chauffeur, they were rich enough for an obituary.

Emilia began with the anniversary of the day her mother and stepfather had come to dinner in the penthouse, scanning the grainy newspaper images for death notices or the report of a fatal accident car. The news was full of articles about long-dead politicians, the construction of tall buildings that were part of today's cityscape, and a teacher's strike.

Emilia slid the film to the next day.

The obituary was published on the sixth day. Doctor Raphael Hidalgo Ramos, a gastroenterologist, died in an automobile accident. He left behind a wife, Karina Escobar de la Vega, his parents, two sisters, and a brother.

There was no mention of the death of his chauffeur.

The sun had set while Emilia was in the newspaper office. By the time she got to the police station, the day shift for uniformed cops was long over.

It was the first time she'd been back since convincing Lieutenant Baez to go to El Acólito's intercession. The place felt empty and unwelcoming as she pushed open the rear door by the holding cells.

"Hey, Cruz." It was Gomez, back in uniform and lounging behind the tall holding cell desk. There were three men in the cells, all asleep on the benches. Gomez draped himself over the counter and puckered his lips at her. "Hear you finally got a hard one," he said. "We both know it should have been me."

Her gun was out of its holster and pointed at him before Emilia had a conscious thought.

The grin faded from Gomez's face. He straightened and backed away from the counter, his hands in the air. "I was only kidding, Cruz," he said, as if they were sharing a joke. "Lost your virginity and your sense of humor at the same time, eh?"

Emilia flung herself against the counter and jammed the gun into the soft flesh under his chin, white hot anger consuming any coherent thought.

Gomez's eyes bugged out.

Emilia smelled fear and nicotine on his breath as he tried to pull back. She flicked off the safety and forced the gun deeper into his throat. "Don't run away, Gomez," she said softly. "The next time you want to be funny, I want you to remember the look in my eyes."

"Cruz," he whimpered.

Valdez came out of the men's bathroom and froze. He stared at the tension-filled tableau at the holding desk.

"Fuck you." Emilia abruptly snapped the safety back on and stalked down the hall to the squadroom. Maybe Gomez would draw his own weapon and put her in his sights. Maybe Valdez would watch him shoot her in the back.

She didn't care.

The squadroom was empty. Emilia turned on the lights and fired up her computer. She stared at the double murder board as the machine chugged to life.

Pictures of Herman Schmidt and Itzel's son Pablito were on display. A map of Mexico's western states hung to the side, with red tacks showing the locations of the murders memorialized with Santa Muerte relics or altars.

El Acólito's trail of death.

When her computer screen brightened, Emilia navigated to the *cédula* database. Karina Escobar de la Vega, age 56, lived at an address in the upscale Las Brisas neighborhood in the hills above the eastern side of Acapulco Bay. The address was no more than 15 minutes from the Palacio Réal.

A little more digging revealed that Karina was married to Hector Gamboa Proctor, president of the Grupo Cardenas Investment Bank. They owned three cars.

Emilia could not find any evidence of children.

She searched for Ernesto Cruz Encinos, born the year before her, and came up emptyhanded. Emilia tried several name variations, on the assumption that Karina had changed the child's surname to her own or even to that of her second husband. A shrew who'd steal another woman's child and raise him into a murdering rapist monster would hardly think twice about changing his name.

Thousands of names came up. But she had no idea if any of them was El Acólito.

The former curly-haired Ernesto Cruz Encinos, aged three.

Gomez was gone when she left the station. Valdez pretended not to see her as Emilia passed the holding cell desk on her way out.

CHAPTER 32

The house in Las Brisas was a blinding white collection of blocks, all stucco angles and tinted glass, surrounded by a white iron fence topped with square finials that matched the architecture. It was so early that the sun was still staining the sky pink. The glow softened the house's sharp modern lines.

Emilia pulled up next to a matching cubist guard shack.

The guard popped out and immediately said she was in the wrong place. He wore a simple black uniform with a private security company logo on the sleeve and cap.

Emilia held up her badge. "I need to speak to Señora Karina Escobar de la Vega," she announced. "This concerns a police investigation."

"La señora is not available now," the guard said with practiced ease.

Emilia got out of the Suburban, crowding the guard back into his shack. "I suggest you call the house and let la señora know the police are here to talk to her about Ernesto Cruz Encinos." She waved her own phone at him. "If she is still unavailable, I will have a few police cars come and blockade the house until such time as she is available."

The guard picked up an old fashioned handset. He kept an eye on Emilia as he made the call and repeated the name of Ernesto Cruz Encinos. A moment later he pressed a button and told her to park on the circular drive. The gate swung open with an electric whine.

A maid in a gray dress and white apron opened the front door. Emilia followed her through a foyer with a floating glass and mahogany stairway to a large sunny room at the rear of the house. The walls were pale aqua, as if to gently mimic the huge turquoise swimming pool beyond floor-to-ceiling French doors. The pool curved like a crescent moon, with white umbrellas and potted palms shading a circular patio tucked into the concave side. A gardener pruned the plants on the pool deck while a pump bubbled the water.

Inside the room, tall fig trees in glazed pots transformed the corners, while two white sofas faced each other in the center of the room and Chinese rugs anchored groupings of chairs upholstered in pale shades of lavender and peach. A grand piano punctuated a side wall beneath a collection of watercolors in slender gold frames. The room was huge, yet the soft colors and clever furniture placement created a sense of intimacy.

Emilia drifted through the space. There were several framed photographs on a table by a sofa. She snatched them up one by one, looking for the face of El Acólito. The photos were of places she didn't recognize.

She crossed the room to the piano; sure she'd never seen such a grand instrument in a private residence. A mirrored tray of glass paperweights sat on top. Reflected colors swirled inside each clear glass orb. The paperweights represented the height of luxury. Each simple item of beauty probably cost more than Emilia made in a year.

Footsteps sounded on the tile. Emilia turned to see a trim

woman stride swiftly into the room with the buoyancy of someone in good physical condition. Her shoulder-length auburn hair was pulled into a low ponytail and her subtle makeup made her look at least ten years younger. Her white shirt and dark jeans were simple yet of obvious high quality.

"I'm Karina Escobar de la Vega," she said without offering her hand. "How may I help you?"

"I'm Detective Emilia Cruz Encinos." Emilia held up her badge. "I need to ask you some questions about your son."

The woman slowly lowered herself into one of the plush lavender chairs, never taking her eyes off Emilia. "You're Sophia and Ernesto's daughter, aren't you? Sophia's little girl."

"Yes."

"*Madre de Dios, Madre de Dios*," Karina murmured. "I never . . . I'm just so surprised . . . I'm so sorry." She straightened in the chair. "Please, please sit down."

Emilia sat next to her. A gilt table separated the two chairs. "I need to ask you some questions about your son," she repeated.

"My son." Karina inhaled, her eyes on the ceiling, before giving Emilia a sad smile. "I always expected this day would come, you know. That you or your mother would come looking for him."

It wasn't the reaction Emilia had expected. "When was the last time you saw him?" she asked, conscious of the other woman's distress.

"The last time we saw Rafa was more than five years

ago," Karina said. "Christmas time. We quarreled. He left. I called a few weeks later, hoping he had gotten over his anger. He said we were no longer welcome in his life and never to contact him again. A year later a detective we hired said he'd become an evangelical preacher."

"Rafa?" Emilia queried. "Is that his name now?"

"Raphael Gamboa Escobar," Karina said. "We always called him Rafa."

"You changed his name," Emilia said accusingly.

Karina lifted her hands in supplication. "Of course. He was my son and he needed to carry on the name of this family."

"Ernesto Cruz Encinos was—is—my brother," Emilia said. "How did he come to be your son named Raphael Gamboa Escobar?"

Karina's mouth tugged downward. "You need me to tell you?"

"I'd like to hear your version," Emilia said.

"It's not a happy story." Karina clasped her hands together.

Emilia waited.

"My first husband Raphael was a good man, a doctor," Karina said finally. "Your father Ernesto was our chauffeur, but he was very smart. Quite an extraordinary man, really. They became quite close. Even died together."

"I know this part," Emilia said coldly.

Karina pressed a fingertip to the corner of her eye. "Raphael was buried a few days after the accident. Ernesto was buried the day after. I should have gone to Ernesto's funeral. Should have stood next to poor Sophia, but I couldn't face another coffin. For a week I did nothing but clutch at Raphael's suits and weep."

Emilia sat without moving, waiting to hear the admission that she'd kicked out a widow and stolen a child.

On the other side of the French doors, the gardener went on manicuring the plants. Some of them were citrus trees, Emilia realized, which had probably supplied the silver bowl of *mandarinos* sitting on the gilt table. They made the room smell like oranges.

"A few days after Ernesto's funeral," Karina went on. "Sophia came to the door. She had both of you by the hand and I could tell she'd made you walk up the hill from the chauffeur's quarters to the main house. You and Rafa were both so little and the hill must have seemed so big."

"He had curly hair and mine was straight," Emilia said.

Karina smiled. "That's right."

"So what happened?"

"Sophia looked terrible," Karina said. "Uncombed hair, eyes red and swollen. You children were dirty. Rafa was sobbing. You were quiet. I remember you had a doll with you. You carried it by one arm, dragging it along."

Emilia's stomach tightened. This wasn't the right version of the story.

"Sophia said she was moving to her brother-in-law's house," Karina said. "There was only room for one child. She wanted me to take one of you."

The room swam for a long moment before Emilia caught her breath, inhaling the bitter taste of orange rind. "She asked you to take one of her children?"

"She told me to pick one of you."

Emilia shook her head. "No, that's not true."

Karina sat forward. "Don't you think I've replayed this scene in my head a million times? Wondered if I'd misunderstood? Or what would have happened if I'd said something different, made a different decision?"

"My mother didn't tell you to take one of her children," Emilia said stubbornly.

"Sophia said that if I didn't take one of you," Karina insisted. "She'd leave you both in the market for a stranger to find."

Even as she wanted to jump up and accuse the woman of lying, Emilia knew it was the truth.

The room was light and bright but there was no oxygen in it.

Lourdes had unwittingly told Emilia a lie, one that protected what was left of Sophia's fragile sanity and, in a strange way, the Cruz family honor. But it was a lie all the same.

Emilia found her voice. "So you chose him."

"He was hysterical," Karina said simply. "How could I take the quiet child and leave her with the screaming one? She was nearly hysterical herself. I picked up Rafa and he sobbed into my neck. Sophia pulled you back down the hill and an hour later you were both gone."

"And you never tried to give him back?"

Karina shook her head. "No, I was appalled at what Sophia had done and Rafa needed stability. He knew something was wrong. Even at that age he was extraordinarily perceptive." She gave a shaky smile. "I remember it like yesterday. He was a beautiful child. You both were. But that day, he wouldn't stop screaming. I finally took him into the kitchen and gave him a popsicle. He quieted down. For the next 20 years, every time he was upset or angry or wanted to chase another dream, I gave him a treat."

"Like chocolate *pastel de tres leches*?" Emilia asked.

"Yes," Karina said. "I've made that for years. How did you know?"

Emilia shrugged and looked around the room. "Is this where he grew up?"

"Yes." Karina waved vaguely in the direction of the foyer. "We moved here when I remarried. Rafa was about five. We gave him the east wing of the house as his boy cave. If anything, my husband spoiled him worse than I did. When Rafa wanted to become an actor instead of going to college, we bought him an apartment in Mexico City. My husband introduced him to friends there, got him some auditions. Rafa made a few commercials and landed a part in a *telenovela*. Did you ever see *Rosa Quintana*? Rafa was the boyfriend. He used the stage name Rafa Gamboa. Said Escobar had too many drug cartel associations."

Emilia nearly laughed at the irony but her chest was too

tight for laughter. Her mother and Tía Lourdes had watched *Rosa Quintana* regularly when it was on a few years ago. She wondered if they knew that the actor Rafa Gamboa was Sophia's discarded son.

"And after the show ended?" Emilia asked.

"Rafa was impatient to be famous. He auditioned for movie roles. If he was cast, he insulted the director. If he wasn't cast, he made a scene. Even threatened one when his part got written out. He got a reputation for being hard to work with. We gave him an allowance, so it wasn't like he was desperate for money. He was desperate for attention."

"Do you think this had anything to do with his mother giving him away?" Emilia heard her choice of words. *His* mother. Not *my* mother.

"You can't begin to know," Karina said softly. "I've lain in bed so many nights wondering the same thing. He was so young when it happened. Did he understand? No matter what I gave him, it wasn't enough. I was the wrong mother."

They sat in silence. One the other side of the French doors, the gardener took his clippers and hose and moved out of sight.

"How is Sophia?" Karina asked.

Emilia was at a sudden loss for words. "She remarried, too," she finally said.

"Good." Karina smiled. "I was always torn, you know. Wanting to know how you and Sophia were doing but afraid she'd try to take Rafa back if I reached out. I hope she's well. Happy."

Emilia put one of her business cards on the gilt table next to the bowl of mandarin oranges. "This is my cell phone number," she said, standing up. "If Rafa makes contact, or you remember something that could help me find him, please call me."

Karina also got to her feet. She was only a few years older than Sophia but had the grace and maturity the other woman lacked. "You said you're a police detective," Karina said, as if just recalling that fact. "Are you looking for Rafa for personal or professional reasons?"

"Both," Emilia said.

Karina hugged herself, as if bracing for a hurt she saw coming. "What's he done?"

"Murder," Emilia said. "Rape. Human trafficking."

Karina blinked furiously but a tear rolled down her cheek. She didn't wipe it away. "I'm not surprised. *Por Dios*, but I'm not."

They walked together to the expansive foyer. The maid appeared but Karina shook her head and the girl disappeared again. "I'm glad you came," Karina said. "I always wondered what happened to you and now I know you grew up into a beautiful woman."

Emilia hesitated. "If I'd been the one crying that day," she heard herself say. "Would you have picked me?"

"Yes," Karina said. "I suppose I would have."

As Emilia got into the Suburban she wondered what her life might have been like. The best schools, college, two loving parents, a house full of luxury and safety and wealth.

Who might she be today but for the simple fact that she hadn't cried?

She drove back to the Palacio Réal. The penthouse was empty; Kurt was in his office. Emilia sat in the living room. Eventually she texted Silvio.

Raphael Gamboa Escobar, aka actor Rafa Gamboa.

That done, she muted the phone, put on her bathing suit, and rode the elevator down to the main floor. She walked through the lobby to the beach and kept going along the shoreline past the edge of the hotel's property. Eventually the sand became rocky and gray. She stopped.

Pelicans and seagulls chased across the midday sky while small black vultures poked their red heads between the rocks looking for dead fish washed in with the morning tide. This remote slice of Puerto Marques was only accessible by foot from the Palacio Réal and few ever ventured this far from the hotel's luxury. The water lapped at the sand more aggressively here and dangerous whirlpools hid in the deep. Signs warned would-be swimmers.

Emilia spread her towel in the shade of some scrub pine, sat down, and hugged her knees.

She stayed like that, staring at the hungry birds and the foamy ocean and seeing nothing, until the sun dipped toward the horizon and she knew that the lie would end with her.

CHAPTER 33

"How are you doing?" Silvio asked. His voice on the other end of the connection was dampened by street sounds.

"Okay," Emilia said. She leaned against the wall enclosing the balcony outside the penthouse bedroom. Far below, hotel guests picked at a breakfast buffet set up in the Pasodoblc Bar or braved the morning tide as it licked at the hotel's private beach.

"I left you three voicemail messages yesterday," Silvio said.

"I'm on personal leave, remember," Emilia countered.

"We found Gamboa's *cédula*," Silvio said. "An old address in Mexico City. No cell phone listing. No criminal record. Lieutenant Baez is putting together a package and sending it out on the wire. The *federales* and every police department in the country will have it by tomorrow."

Emilia didn't respond. There was sympathy in his voice and it made her nervous.

"We're talking to Sandino senior and his wife this afternoon," Silvio continued after a moment. "The mayor is coming with them. We can brief what happened, but it's your story to tell. I thought you'd want to be there."

"Yes," Emilia said. "I would."

He told her what time to come. For a moment Silvio seemed like he had something else to say. Emilia wondered if he was going to bring up that last argument and ask if she still wanted to split up their partnership.

The hesitation got awkward.

Emilia cut the connection, saying she had an errand to run before coming to the police station.

Ernesto was in the courtyard at the grinding wheel when Emilia pulled up to the house. His cheek was slightly puckered by the accident and his jaw wobbled but the scar wouldn't be too bad. Emilia raised a hand in greeting, trying to ignore the way her heart pounded.

Sophia was in the kitchen in the midst of a baking project. Half a dozen egg shells were on the counter and she was beating the whites in a bowl with a fork. She wiped her hands on her flowered apron, which she wore over a clashing floral dress. "Emilia," she exclaimed. "What a nice surprise."

Emilia held up a hand to ward off her mother's intended hug and watched the familiar vague smile settle on Sophia's face. "Mama, we have something important to talk about."

Sophia laughed and picked up her fork and bowl again. "The world is full of important things, *niña*."

"I went to see a lady yesterday," Emilia said. "Someone you knew a long time ago."

"Really? That's nice." Sophia's right arm worked like a piston to beat the eggs. "Let me finish this and I'll make us some tea."

"Mama, I met la señora," Emilia said, watching her

mother. "The woman who used to make the chocolate *pastel de tres leches*."

Sophia's movements slowed. "Who?"

"Karina Escobar de la Vega," Emilia said. "The doctor's wife."

"No, I never knew her." Sophia began beating the egg whites again, her face tight with concentration.

Emilia pulled the bowl out of her mother's hand and threw it across the room. The clay smashed against the edge of the kitchen table and the soupy egg mixture puddled on the floor. "The woman you gave your son to, Mama!" she yelled. "Ernesto, your three year old son. The son named after his father."

"Look what you've done." Sophia scampered across the kitchen to the table. The comparison between her child-like mother in the tiny kitchen and the trim woman in the airy mansion in Las Brisas hurt so much that Emilia sank into a chair, her chest on fire.

She watched as Sophia collected up the pieces of crockery, laughing a little as frothy goo dripped from the shards. "Don't worry, Emilia," her mother said gaily. "I'll get a new bowl."

"Mama." The word came out as a hoarse whisper. "Mama, listen to me."

Sophia threw the pottery into the trash and wiped her hands on her apron. "Are you sick, Emilia? Shall I make you some tea?"

It took a supreme effort for Emilia to stay calm. Anger

and shame ran through her veins in equal measure. She was looking for answers from a woman whose mind might never be able to provide them.

"Mama, I know that I have a brother," she said. "Lourdes and Raul know, too. You gave him away when he was three and no one ever spoke of him again. I want to know why."

"Yes, I'll make some tea," Sophia said as if Emilia had put in a request. She busied herself filling the teakettle with bottled water, finding mugs and teabags, and fiddling with a match to light the stove.

Emilia pressed a hand to her forehead, closed her eyes, and willed herself to calm down.

The kettle whistled. Sophia filled the mugs with steaming water and dunked the same teabag into both. Emilia raised her head as Sophia put a mug in front of her.

Her mother sat and sipped her tea. Emilia didn't touch hers.

"You've never suffered, Emilia," Sophia said in a conversational tone. "You don't know what it's like when bad things happen."

"I'm a cop, Mama," Emilia said slowly. Her mother's voice was different. Assured. "I know about bad things."

"That's a job," Sophia said dismissively. "I'm talking about life. When suffering becomes your life, you make decisions. They aren't wrong or right decisions. They are just what you do to get by."

Emilia caught her breath. For once her mother was speaking to her as an adult. "There was no need to do what you did, Mama," she said. "Lourdes and Raul would have found room for another child. You could have gotten a job, helped find a bigger apartment."

Sophia narrowed her eyes. "La señora took him. I had no choice."

"No, Mama," Emilia said. "That's what you've told yourself for years but we both know it isn't true. You wanted to get rid of one of your children and she picked him. Do you know why? Because he was crying. She wanted to help you, so she took the child who was crying and left you with the one who wasn't. Me."

"Yes, that's right," Sophia snapped. "She picked your brother. Now you know. Do you feel left out?"

"No, I'm mad because you've been faking it my whole life." The realization hit Emilia like a freight train. "Everyone had to protect you from anything too hard so you could wallow in denial. Live out a fairy tale of pretending that you never gave away your child."

"Shut up!" Sophia shouted.

"You lied to me, Mama," Emilia exclaimed. "Everyone lied so you wouldn't ever have to face what you'd done. Poor Sophia. Leave her alone. Just let her exist beautifully because her husband died so tragically."

Emilia's voice rose until she was shouting, too, but she couldn't stop her words any more than she could stop that train by standing in front of it. "You've been so clever. Convinced us all with your big act. Pretending to have the mind of a child so you could erase the past. Sent your daughter out to sell candy on the street because you were too broken to work. Do you know how often I was frightened, Mama? How many times I had to fight? You used me, Mama. You used me so you could go on living your lie."

"How dare you speak to me like that," Sophia exclaimed.

The defiant look in Sophia's eyes and the steady anger in her voice said it all. The veil was lifted. Just like her son, the mother fooled everyone.

"Why, Mama?" Emilia asked furiously. "Was it to atone for giving him away? A way to punish yourself? Or simply so you'd never have to get a job and do real work? Always be the center of attention, too."

"Get out," Sophia yelled.

"Answer my question, Mama!" Emilia jumped to her feet. "All these years! Why did you do it?"

Sophia hurled her mug across the table. Emilia dodged. Tea sprayed. The mug shattered against the wall like an exploding bomb.

The front door banged open. Ernesto trotted into the house, his leather grinder's apron glinting with steel shavings.

"I heard shouting," he said. His jaw wobbled to one side. "Is everything all right?"

"Emilia broke a mug," Sophia said cheerfully. "It was an accident."

She gave him a vaguely happy smile, the kind she'd worn a thousand times before.

Emilia felt the blood pound in her head. For the first time

in her life she recognized the well-rehearsed expression for what it was.

A ticket to ease and kindness and having others provide for her.

A mask of guile and manipulation.

"Emilia has to go back to school now," Sophia said. She prattled on about the eggplant she'd found in the market that morning as her husband patiently picked up bits of china.

Emilia left the house. Her hands shook so badly she could barely get the car keys out of the pocket of her jeans.

CHAPTER 34

Puentes was behind the holding cell desk when Emilia came into the station. She shot him with her thumb and forefinger, the same as always. He gave her a nod but didn't return the gesture.

All the detectives were at their desks in the squadroom. Everyone said something to Emilia, even Castro, but there was tension in the air. The double murder board was gone, replaced by new pictures of more recent murders.

Emilia had just pulled out the *Las Perdidas* binder when the parade came in. The mayor's security detail, then Carlota herself, followed by Marco Sandino Varela's parents. Lieutenant Baez came out of his office, shook hands, and offered seats at the conference table. Emilia and Silvio joined them. The rest of the detectives disappeared, the security team took up positions at the door to the squadroom, and Carlota looked at Lieutenant Baez expectantly.

The mayor was as glamorous as always in a tight-fitting gray dress and slingback suede heels, her hair twisted into a French knot to show off diamond cluster earrings. In comparison, Doctora Varela had lost weight and her simple navy suit hung on her now bony frame. The physician wore no makeup and the skin on the back of both hands was red.

"The last time we met," Lieutenant Baez began, speaking to Sandino and Doctora Varela. "We opened an investigation into the whereabouts of your son Marco between the time he left school and his arrest at Coyuca Lagoon in hopes that it would lead us to understand his actions."

"I ordered an investigation," Carlota corrected him.

Lt Baez dipped his head in acknowledgment. "And we have a report for you, thanks to Detective Cruz."

He gave Emilia a *go ahead* nod. She took a breath before swiveling the *Las Perdidas* binder so that the parents could see the photo of Lila Jimenez Lata. "Did your son ever mention this girl to you? She called herself Liliana, although her real name is Lila Jimenez Lata."

"No." Doctora Varela shook her head as she absently pawed the top of one hand with the other.

"Marco met her at Coyuca Lagoon." Emilia left the binder where it was on the table. "She worked as a waitress at a hostel called El Loro Rojo and boarded there. Apparently, your son frequented the place when he went kayaking and swimming in the lagoon. They began a serious relationship. He gave her the keys to his car, told her where it was parked. The night he disappeared from school, it was because he ran away to be with her. He bribed the guard at the gate and Lila picked him up outside the school gates."

"The school called it a kidnapping," Sandino said indignantly.

"School administrators were unaware that the students paid the guard for many services," Silvio interjected. "Opening the gate at off hours was just one of them."

"What we found out," Emilia picked up the story again, marveling at how detached and professional she sounded. "Is that the owner of the El Loro Rojo and his stepson were part of a human trafficking network run by a Santa Muerte cult leader. He scooped up Lila but Marco was able to follow. According to eyewitnesses, the leader of the ring promised that Marco could ransom Lila by murdering the cult leader's enemies and leaving Santa Muerte altars at each scene."

Doctora Varela began to sob, narrow shoulders heaving, chafed hands covering her face. Her husband slumped, his suit jacket folding like an accordion. His mouth opened and closed, but no sound came out.

"This girl." Carlota waved an imperious hand at the binder as if raw grief wasn't on display. "Where is she now?"

"To our knowledge, she is still with the cult leader," Emilia said. "Voluntarily."

"We have made several arrests," Lieutenant Baez added. "The cult's main procurer in the Acapulco area and rival gang members. Also thanks to Detective Cruz, four women were rescued from the human traffickers and reunited with their families."

Sandino asked a question. Doctora Varela wound down. The conversation continued but Emilia's part was done. It had been strange to describe everything as a dispassionate police report. As if the experience with El Acólito had happened to someone else.

Eventually there was nothing else to discuss. Carlota said they would go now. Sandino walked like a man after a public flogging; head low, shoulders hunched, feet barely lifting from the floor. Emilia doubted he'd be much of an asset to the mayor come the next election. His wife trailed behind with arms folded, an expensive purse dangling from the crook of an elbow and her face contorted with the effort to hold in tears.

They were each alone in their grief.

Carlota flapped a hand at her security detail. The men closed ranks around the sad couple and escorted them out of the squadroom. One of Carlota's guards stayed by the door to wait for her.

"Is there something else, señora?" Lieutenant Baez politely asked Carlota.

The mayor lifted her chin. "I wished to acknowledge Detective Cruz's police work," she said. "I was informed that this was an extremely . . ." She paused, searching for a word. "Hazardous undertaking. Yes, hazardous."

"Yes, it was," Lieutenant Baez said.

"You will resume your duties?" Carlota asked Emilia.

"Detective Cruz will spend some time on leave," Lieutenant Baez said before Emilia could reply.

The mayor gave a thin-lipped smile. "Very well," she said. "Someone from my office will contact you, Baez. We'll put out a press statement about shutting down this human trafficking ring."

Partially shutting it down, Emilia wanted to say. But there was no point.

Carlota snapped her fingers at the security guard and he followed her out.

"Can I speak to you in my office, Detective Cruz?"

Lieutenant Baez asked.

Emilia tucked the *Las Perdidas* binder under her arm and followed him into the office. He indicated that she should sit down.

He sat behind the desk. "I hear you came into the office the other day, despite being on leave," he said. Lieutenant Baez's tone was as calm and measured as always but there was something wrong. Emilia could see it in the tension tightening his shoulders and the lines around his mouth.

"I needed access to the *cédula* database," she said.

"Detective Silvio could have done that."

"I suppose so." Emilia waited.

Baez fiddled with the same damn pen. "It would appear that you had an altercation with Officer Gomez that night."

"Gomez?" Emilia had all but forgotten the incident. It seemed so unimportant in light of everything else that had happened. "He joked about wishing he'd been my rapist. I didn't think it was funny."

"I understand." Lieutenant Baez gave a heavy sigh. "But you drew your weapon on another officer. There were witnesses and the incident was recorded on the closed circuit feed. Officer Gomez has filed a complaint and there will be an inquiry."

Emilia laughed. "You're kidding."

"No." There was no levity in Lieutenant Baez's expression and Emilia realized he was serious. "As of right now you've been placed on paid administrative leave vice personal leave."

Emilia knew there was a significant difference between the two. "Does this mean I can't go to the Senior Investigative Conference?"

"I'm sorry." Lieutenant Baez paused. "I have to ask you to turn in your weapon."

"I'm suspended?" Emilia heard her voice crack.

"Administrative leave." Lieutenant Baez looked at her sadly. "Keep your badge but I need your weapon, Detective."

Emilia slowly drew her gun from its shoulder holster and laid it on his desk.

Lieutenant Baez ejected the round from the chamber and pulled out the magazine. He swept the weapon and the rounds into a desk drawer. "I'll make a note of your cooperation for my successor," he said. "I've given my notice and will be leaving Acapulco next week."

"You resigned?" Still stunned, Emilia swept her gaze around the office, noticing for the first time the pile of boxes in the corner.

The man's lips pinched into a rueful smile. "I'm not the right fit for this job," he said. "I'm going back to my previous position in Mexico City."

"No," Emilia protested. "You can't leave." She wanted to shout like a spoiled child that he couldn't go, that he'd been decent, that he'd been the only one in her whole police career who hadn't called her by just her last name.

"I wasn't prepared for the intensity of the cases here in Acapulco," Lieutenant Baez admitted. "My decisions reflected that. I blame myself for what happened to you. Even to the poor Garcia Figueroa boy and his mother. This place needs someone like Detective Silvio. I've recommended that he replace me."

Emilia was dumbfounded. Baez was running away. Running back to his safe job catching accountants while back in Acapulco cops pulled headless bodies out of tents and cut down the mutilated from billboards.

Lieutenant Baez held out a business card. "If you're ever in Mexico City, I'd like to buy you dinner."

Silvio caught up with her as Emilia rushed out the rear door and into the bright light of the parking lot. The *Las Perdidas* binder was still under her arm and she'd had the presence of mind to snatch her shoulder bag off the back of her chair before blundering out of the squadroom.

"Cruz." Silvio grabbed her arm. "I heard about the administrative leave."

"Gomez filed a complaint," Emilia said furiously. Anger rushed in like fire filling a gas can. "Of all people, Gomez files a complaint against me. Nearly raped me in a toilet stall and has the gall to file a complaint when I tell him to shut the fuck up?"

"With a gun in his face? What were you thinking?" Silvio propelled her away from the door and into relative privacy around the corner of the building. "He's been out to get you since you sent him to the hospital. You handed revenge to the asshole without him having to lift a finger. Valdez saw the whole thing, said he was sure you were going to blow Gomez's head off. It was on camera, too."

"I should have blown his head off." Emilia jerked her arm away, the bag swinging against her hip. "It's what he deserves."

"You understand he'll get himself back into the squadroom over this, don't you?" Silvio said. "Baez managed to get him out, which was a miracle. But now he'll get his detective badge back. The union will see to that."

Emilia shrugged. Her shoulder holster felt ridiculously light. "Doesn't matter. My career is over."

"Listen to me," Silvio said. "The good news is that everybody from Salazar on down and across western Mexico knows they owe you. If you hadn't gone in, it could have been years before El Acólito and the Los Nueves trafficking ring were identified. Just lie low for a couple of weeks. What Gomez said to you is on the tape, too. It'll blow over and when it does, they'll give you a medal."

"For getting raped?" Emilia asked bitterly.

"For being a good cop," Silvio said.

"El Acólito didn't kill me," Emilia said. "I'll always wonder if he knew I was his sister. Maybe he'll tell me before I kill him."

"Cruz." Silvio lowered his voice. "You've got to get past what happened."

"Sure," Emilia said. "Just as soon as I find my brother and

kill him."

"You can't live on revenge," Silvio said. "Trust me. I know. It eats you up."

Emilia shrugged. "I don't care."

"Call the counselor," Silvio urged. "Talk it out."

"Counseling." Emilia gave a mirthless laugh. "You're telling me to go to counseling?"

Silvio stared at her, sadness in his eyes. "I'll go with you," he said.

Beyond his wide shoulder, Emilia studied the cars in their tidy rows. Sunshine glinted off chrome and made even the dullest paint job sparkle.

It had cost Silvio a lot of male pride to make that promise. Emilia wanted to reassure him that she'd get help. Tell him that she wasn't broken by what had happened.

But she couldn't.

Bring anguish and destruction to Your enemies and to all they hold dear.

"Good luck with the lieutenant job," Emilia said.

CHAPTER 35

She packed a suitcase and left Kurt a note.

It was late in the evening when he showed up at the rectory. From the little bedroom, Emilia heard him speaking to Padre Ricardo, inquiring after the priest's health following the heart attack and politely refusing a cup of tea.

And then he was in the doorway, filling it with yellow hair and starched clothes and that indefinable self-confidence that had always drawn Emilia to him like a magnet.

"What's going on, Em?" he asked quietly. "Why are we here and not at home?"

"I need some time alone," Emilia said.

"How long?"

"I don't know."

There was a narrow bed, a dresser, and a crucifix. Kurt's presence shrank the space until there was barely room to breathe. Emilia sat on the bed, her back to him. Any ability to think was gone.

Kurt came close enough for her to feel the warmth of his body against her shoulders. "What are you looking for, Em?" he asked.

"I don't know," Emilia said. "I don't even know who I'm supposed to be."

"I know who you are," Kurt said."

"No, you don't. I'm not who either of us thought I was.

Certainly not somebody who deserves to live in a grand hotel with someone like you."

"Em, you're upset." Kurt touched her arm. "Come home. We'll sit on the balcony and talk until the sun comes up. We'll work this out."

"Go away, Kurt," Emilia whispered. "Please."

Silence settled over the room like a darkening cloud.

"If that's what you want," he said finally.

"I'll call," Emilia lied.

He didn't move. She heard him breathe.

"Blink if you know I love you," Kurt said.

The softly spoken words went through Emilia like a knife.

His footsteps moved away. Voices filtered down the hall as Kurt spoke again to Padre Ricardo. A door opened.

He left.

Emilia swiped at her eyes. They were dry.

El Fin

Discover Emilia's next case in 43 MISSING.

You're invited

You're invited to stay up to date with Emilia and the team in the Mystery Ahead newsletter. Get behind-the-scenes details and must-read recommendations every other Sunday.

Subscribe and receive the Detective Emilia Cruz Starter Library with 2 novellas and the Who's Who guide to the series.

Go to carmenamato.net/starter-library.

There are extra goodies ahead, too.
- A favorite recipe from a meal featured in the book,
- Glossary of Spanish words, and
- An excerpt from the next Detective Emilia Cruz novel.

Easy Chocolate Pastel de Tres Leches

For the cake

1 box devil's food or dark chocolate cake mix

1 cup water

1/3 cup vegetable oil

3 eggs

1 cup whipping cream

1/2 cup whole milk

1 can (14 oz) sweetened condensed milk

1/3 cup Kahlua liquor

For the topping

1 cup whipping cream

¼ tsp cream of tartar

1/2 teaspoon vanilla

1/2 cup toasted slivered almonds

1 cup flaked coconut, toasted (optional)

1 tbsp cocoa powder (optional)

1 Tbsp. Kahlua (optional)

Heat oven to 350°F (325°F for dark or nonstick pan). Grease or spray bottom only of 13x9-inch pan.

In large bowl, beat cake mix, water, oil and eggs with

electric mixer on low speed 30 seconds, then on medium speed 2 minutes. Pour into pan.

Bake 30 to 38 minutes or until toothpick inserted in center comes out clean. Let stand 5 minutes. In large bowl, mix 1 cup whipping cream, whole milk, condensed milk and Kahlua. Pierce cake every 1/2 inch with toothpick. Evenly spread mixture over top of cake. Cover and refrigerate at least 3 hours or overnight until fully chilled and mixture has been absorbed into cake.

Chill a metal or china bowl in the freezer. When very cold, use to beat 1 cup whipping cream, cream of tartar, and vanilla on high speed until stiff. Frost cake with whipped cream mixture. Dust with cocoa or drizzle with Kahlua if feeling daring. Sprinkle with coconut and nuts.

Cut into squares and serve.

Glossary of Spanish Terms

Commonly used words in the Detective Emilia Cruz series

Abarrotes: snacks

Agua de jamaica: cold tea made with dried hibiscus

Amigo: friend, buddy

Barrio: neighborhood

Cabrón: slang meaning dumbass

Campesino: subsistence farmers, country dwellers

Casita: little house

Cédula: identity card

Chica: girl

Comida: the main meal of the day, usually eaten in early afternoon

Conchas: sweet rolls topped with sugar and shaped like a conch shell

Dios mio: my god, an exclamation

El Norte: the United States

Guayabera: men's button-down shirt with a straight hem and multiple pockets

Halcone: word meaning falcon, used to mean a person acting as a lookout

Hombres: men

Jefe: chief, person in charge

Jitomate: tomato

Libro: book

Loco: crazy

Lotéria: lottery

Madre de Dios: Mother of God, used as exclamation

Maldita: damn, damned

Mercado: market

Mujeres: women

Muertos: papier maché skeleton figures used to decorate Day of the Dead altars

Narcomanta: banner bearing a message from a gang or cartel

Norteamericano: North American

Ofrenda: altar

Palapa: traditional Mexican shelter roofed with palm leaves or branches

Papel picado: streamers of tissue paper cut into silhouette designs

Pastelería: pastry shop

Pendejo: asshole, jerk

Permiso: excuse me

Placas: license plates

Prima: female cousin

Privada: enclosed subdivision and/or the gate to the property

Prohibido el paso: "Keep out" warning

Queso fresco: soft cheese common in Mexican recipes

Rayos: exclamation, similar to "oh hell"

Reina: queen

Salsa verde: tart green salsa usually made with tomatillos

Sicario: cartel henchman or assassin
Talavera: hand painted pottery from Puebla
Taqueria: taco restaurant
Tiendita: little store
Tío/Tía: uncle/Aunt

Excerpt from 43 MISSING, the next

Detective Emilia Cruz novel

Ready, Emilia Cruz Encinos told herself. *Absolutely ready.*

Her fingers beat a nervous tattoo on the steering wheel as she waited for the heavy steel gate to roll aside. With a final groan of metal-on-metal, it locked into the open position. Emilia took her foot off the brake and the heavy Suburban lumbered past the high concrete wall surrounding the police station in central Acapulco.

The uniform assigned to the guard shack trotted to the driver's window, forcing Emilia to stop and roll down her window. "Hey, Detective Cruz," he said. "Haven't seen you around lately. Been on vacation?"

"Sure," Emilia lied. "What's new?"

"Lieutenant Silvio's kicking ass and taking names," the uniform said, eyeing her with interest.

"Like nobody expected that," Emilia heard herself say. His face was familiar but she didn't know him well.

The uniformed officer gave an awkward laugh, slapped the Suburban's white paint, and went back to his post.

It was very early and the parking lot behind the squat stucco building was mostly empty. Emilia tucked the Suburban into a space, killed the engine, and gulped air. Her heart was racing, which was ridiculous. She was a detective who knew how to do hard things, going back to work.

In more than 12 years, she'd only taken two breaks, both after being injured in the line of duty.

The first time she'd been shot.

This time was . . . worse.

Her eyes flicked to the rearview mirror. The uniform was watching her from the guard shack. With exaggerated gestures for his benefit, Emilia remade her ponytail, as if her hair was responsible for the delay in getting out of the car. Giving her hands something to do helped focus her breathing.

Emilia finally grabbed her shoulder bag from the passenger seat, and got out of the vehicle. In black jeans, loafers, denim jacket buttoned over her empty shoulder holster, and her detective badge on its lanyard around her neck, she could pretend it was just another day.

Because she was ready.

Emilia forced a tough strut into her walk as she crossed the parking lot and yanked open the rear door into the station.

Puentes, a young uniformed officer, was behind the holding cell desk. He gave a start when he saw her.

She shot him with her thumb and forefinger, the same as always.

"Detective Cruz," Puentes said haltingly.

I'm not going to shoot you. Emilia smiled, although her face felt brittle and her heart still thumped uncomfortably fast. "How are you doing?" she asked.

"Good, good." Puentes took a step away from the counter,

putting more distance between them. "You?"

"Glad to be back." Emilia felt his eyes follow her down the hall to the detectives squadroom. Puentes had seen her pull a gun on another cop. Emilia had been a fool to react to the garbage coming out of Detective Gomez's mouth, but the fear on that *pendejo's* face had been worth the mess that followed.

She pushed open the door and relaxed a fraction when she saw that the squadroom was empty.

The big space had been updated by the previous chief of detectives, Lieutenant Baez, but it looked even better than Emilia remembered. More organized. The walls were plastered with pictures and evidence cards from current investigations, but everything was aligned instead of the usual jumble of tacks and scribbles. The dozen metal desks each boasted two monitors. In the far corner, chairs upholstered in gray tweed ringed a sleek conference table. On the other side of the room, near the copier, a matching dark wood hutch held the coffee maker, a tray of clean mugs, and a built-in mini refrigerator.

Madre de Dios. New computers? A refrigerator?

"Cruz." Her former partner, Franco Silvio, filled the doorway to the lieutenant's office. "Grab a cup of coffee. We can talk before the rest of the crew reports in."

"Morning meeting still at 9:00 am?" Emilia asked breezily, like it was an ordinary Monday.

"Same as before," Silvio said.

Emilia dropped her shoulder bag on her desk and got

herself a cup of fresh coffee. Silvio must have just made it, knowing she was coming in early.

A good sign.

She followed him into the office, past the placard on the door reading *Lieutenant Franco Silvio*. He closed the door and pointed to the pair of gray tweed chairs for visitors. As Emilia sat, he went behind the wide desk, coffee cup in hand.

Silvio's new responsibilities fit him well; he'd traded in his white tee shirt for a button-down, but still wore jeans and a shoulder holster and gun. The wiry crew cut, surly expression, and heavyweight boxer's physique remained unchanged.

"How are you doing?" he asked.

"Great, just great," Emilia caroled. "How's it feel to finally be the grand *jefe*?"

Everyone had known Silvio was long overdue for promotion even before she become his partner. His storied past, as well as a campaign to derail his career by the head of the police union, had kept him on the street until his talents won out.

"Finally getting some respect around here," Silvio joked but his expression wasn't light. "Been a little worried about you, Cruz."

"I'm ready to hit the ground running," Emilia said. She unbuttoned her jacket so he could see the empty shoulder holster. "Do you have my weapon?"

"Later." Silvio slid a folder towards her. "Here's your next assignment."

The desk was that of a busy man, with stacks of case files and random pads and printouts. The walls of the small office were newly painted and a framed poster announcing a championship match hung on the wall over a filing cabinet. Emilia recognized it from the room in Silvio's house where he kept his boxing memorabilia. That fight had been his last on the professional circuit in Mexico.

There were no other decorations. No picture of Isabel, his late wife.

Emilia put down her mug on the desk, next to a brass lamp casting a soft glow over the piles of papers. "The El Acólito case, right?"

"Nope," Silvio said smugly. "The national task force."

"Task force?" Emilia exclaimed. "Is the El Acólito investigation a national task force and nobody told me?"

Silvio shoved the file folder closer to her. "No, it's the Amistad 43 case in Michoacán." he said. "The one and only national task force."

Emilia blinked at him. "Seriously?"

"Any detective would give their right arm to get this kind of career shot," Silvio went on. "Not to mention an all expenses paid trip to Mexico City."

"I can't go to Mexico City," Emilia said, still not quite taking in his words. The Amistad 43 task force was a big deal. The media in Mexico had been talking about it for weeks.

"You have a week to get yourself together," Silvio said.

Emilia flapped a hand at the door to the squadroom. "No,

I'm working the El Acólito case right here."

"You're not fit for duty," Silvio said bluntly. "No armed assignment."

"Six weeks administrative leave," Emilia countered. "I did everything I was supposed to do."

"You never talked to the police counselor about what happened," Silvio said.

"I've done nothing but talk my head off about it," Emilia said, but her voice sounded uncertain in her own ears.

"I got nothing official, Cruz," Silvio said. "No doctor sign-off. Nothing."

"Nobody made you go to counseling after Isabel died." Emilia went into attack mode. Taking orders from her former partner was going to be bad enough, but at least Silvio should understand what she had to do. After, all, when his wife was murdered, he'd gone after the killer.

"Lieutenant Baez didn't make it mandatory," Silvio said.

"I covered for you," Emilia pointed out. "When Baez asked if you had anger issues, I said no, Franco's just being his normal *pendejo* self, he'll be fine."

"I didn't ask you to."

"But I did," Emilia said. "You owe me, Franco."

Silvio calmly folded his arms, heavy muscles straining the rolled sleeves of his shirt. "You have to be cleared by the police counselor before you can come back to the squadroom."

Emilia pressed a hand to her head. A vein throbbed with anger under her finger. He didn't use it much, but she knew

Silvio had a heart buried under the stone face and mountain of muscle.

"Franco," she said, forcing herself to sound calm. "I'm here to find El Acólito. He's been running around free for six weeks. Who knows how many more people he's killed, raped, or sold. All I want to do is find him. There's no need to play games."

"I busted my ass to get you on the national task force," Silvio said, unmoved by her reassuring tone. "You need something that gets you away from Acapulco and time to get past what happened. The *federales* are on the El Acólito case. They're handling it."

"If I go, and I'm not saying I will," Emilia said. "Will I have access to the El Acólito files? Can I be working with the *federales?* If not, you know they'll fuck it up somehow. They always do. Giving up our jurisdiction—."

"Stop right there, Cruz," Silvio interrupted. "The bottom line is that the El Acólito investigation isn't your turf. Never going to be. I won't have you involved again."

So much for wheedling. Emilia's temper exploded. "Who are you to tell me—."

"I'm the fucking chief of detectives for the city of Acapulco." Silvio slammed his hand down on the desk, making the two mugs rattle. "It's my responsibility to make the assignments around here. Take it in, Cruz, that's the way things are now."

Emilia clenched her fists. "That's not fair, Franco, and you know it. I deserve—."

"How's Hollywood handling things?" Silvio interrupted. "This task force is as much of a favor to him as it is to you. You're probably turning his hair gray."

Silvio's nickname for hotel manager Kurt Rucker often irritated Emilia but this time it stopped her in her tracks. "I . . . I haven't seen him in a couple of weeks," she admitted.

"Hollywood's been travelling?"

"I moved out."

"You moved out of the Palacio Réal?"

"Yes." Emilia had traded the penthouse apartment she shared with Kurt on the top floor of the Palacio Réal for a monk's cell in the rectory of San Pedro de los Pinos. It was much easier to hide from her life in a church than in Acapulco's most luxurious hotel.

Silvio spun his chair, tapped his keyboard, and swiveled the screen to show Emilia a spreadsheet. "You didn't register a change of address."

"I'm . . . it's a temporary place," Emilia mumbled. She couldn't stay in the rectory forever. "I'll do it when I'm settled."

"What about your car?" Silvio demanded.

"My car?" After everything that had happened, the clunky old Suburban's fate was the last thing Emilia was worried about.

"You're responsible for an official vehicle." He thrust a thick finger at the screen. "We're supposed to know where it is at all times."

Emilia snorted. "Aren't you the petty bureaucrat all of a

sudden."

"Okay, Cruz," Silvio said, tamping down his obvious annoyance. "We'll sort it out later. The important thing is this task force assignment. You could be the cop that solves the riddle."

"You're sure that's what this is?" Emilia narrowed her eyes at him in suspicion. "The Amistad 43?"

"Yes."

Emilia opened the folder, curious in spite of herself. Like everyone else in Mexico, she'd seen the news reports about the task force. It was a last-ditch effort to investigate the disappearance of 43 students from a rural teaching college from the village of Amistad in the state of Michoacán. The students had gone to Lindavista, a nearby city of about 80,000, to commandeer buses for a trip to a protest rally in Mexico City. But they'd been intercepted by local police, rounded up, and turned over to a drug gang.

The students were never seen again.

Get 43 MISSING on Amazon or your favorite bookseller.

ABOUT THE AUTHOR

Carmen Amato turns lessons from a 30-year career with the Central Intelligence Agency into crime fiction loaded with danger and deception.

Starting with *Cliff Diver*, her award-winning Detective Emilia Cruz mystery series pits the first female police detective in Acapulco against Mexico's drug cartels, government corruption, and social inequality.

The series was awarded the Poison Cup for Outstanding Series from CrimeMasters of America in both 2019 and 2020 and has been optioned for television.

Her Galliano Club historical thriller series was inspired by her grandfather who was a deputy sheriff during Prohibition.

Originally from upstate New York, Carmen was educated there as well as in Virginia and Paris, France, while experiences in Mexico and Central America ignited her writing career.

Every other Sunday, Carmen shares her top secret(s) in the Mystery Ahead newsletter.

Subscribe at carmenamato.net.